The scratching came from the rear of the house. The sound was as grating as a fingernail moving slowly down a blackboard.

"That's no house cat," Dee said softly.

"Certainly not any house cat I'd want to meet," Carl agreed.

Dingo had whirled around, fangs bared, the hair on his back standing up like a wire brush.

Purr. Scratch.

"Dee," Carl said. "When I give you the word, hit the rear floodlights."

Carl walked to the fireplace and picked up a heavy poker. By the rear entrance, he softly unlocked the door and put his hand on the knob.

"Now!" Carl said. The backyard filled with light as Carl jerked open the door.

The stench that assaulted his nostrils very nearly overpowered him. But it was the shock at confronting . . . whatever the hell it was . . . standing on the back porch that momentarily stunned him.

CAT'S EYE
WILLIAM W. JOHNSTONE

Pinnacle Books
Kensington Publishing Corp.
http://www.pinnaclebooks.com

This novel is a work of fiction. Names, characters, places, and incidents are either the product of the author's imagination or are used fictitiously, and any resemblance to actual persons, living or dead, events, or locales is entirely coincidental.

PINNACLE BOOKS are published by

Kensington Publishing Corp.
850 Third Avenue
New York, NY 10022

Pinnacle and the P logo Reg. U.S. Pat. & TM Off.

First Printing: December, 1989
10 9 8 7 6 5 4 3

Printed in the United States of America

Dedicated to Martin Roberts

Book One

On a starred night Prince Lucifer uprose,
Tired of his dark dominion swung the fiend.
— *George Meredith*

Chapter 1

The lightning woke him.

He sat up in bed and rubbed the sleep from his disbelieving eyes.

Strangest storm he had ever witnessed. Lightning, but no thunder. Fierce lightning that lit up the skies and lashed at the earth with hard, sulfurous bolts. Maybe the thunder was hidden behind the terrible barrage of lightning striking the earth, Carl thought. Yeah, that had to be it, 'cause the lightning was pounding the earth like incoming artillery rounds, coming in without a break between the shatteringly bright flashes.

There had to be thunder. Right?

Sure. The thunder was there. Had to be. The sounds of lightning slamming the ground were covering the thunder, that's all. Something was damn sure causing the windows in the house to rattle.

Then the lightning struck so close it crackled the young man's hair as the electricity danced over his flesh.

The lightning ceased as abruptly as it began. But that last hard thrust had knocked out the lights. Carl looked at his radio on the night stand. Where the digital numbers had been there was nothing but black.

Just like the room.

Black. Silent.

Then a very soft and odd sound reached the young man. A throaty sound. He couldn't place it. He listened. The sound stopped. Probably the wind, and nothing more.

He grinned in the darkness. Quoth the Raven.

Carl stopped grinning and tensed as the loud scratching began in the room next to his bedroom. Cold goose bumps suddenly began spreading all over his flesh as he remembered. . . . No! He fought that memory away. And stay away, damnit! he shouted in his mind.

He'd just moved into this house. That room was empty. There was nothing in that room. Absolutely nothing.

The scratching continued. Harder this time. A frantic sound to it.

Carl tossed back the covers and swung his feet to the floor.

He almost cried out as his bare feet touched the floor.

The hardwood floor was like ice.

The bedroom suddenly turned cold. Very cold. Carl sat on the edge of the bed—forgetting momentarily the cold floor beneath his feet—and stared in astonishment as his breath frosted the air when he exhaled.

In *June?*

That strange sound—the first strange sound—began as soon as the scratching stopped.

It was louder now, and Carl knew what it was. He wished he didn't.

It was a slow, steady, ominous purring, the low vibratory sound causing Carl to grind his teeth together.

Steady now, boy, he told himself. Just calm down.

10

All that is over and done with. Several years back.

But the memory of that time had not and would never completely leave his mind.

The purring stopped. No more scratching was heard. The room temperature became normal. The floor was no longer ice cold. The electricity came back on, the digital hands on the clock radio blinking on — blink, blink, blink. He would have to reset the damn thing.

Blink. Purr. Scratch.

It started again.

Carl picked up his watch from the nightstand. Five o'clock. He had a pre-arranged meeting with a client at ten, and it was a good hour-and-a-half or two-hour drive, so it was about time to get up anyway.

Blink. Purr. Scratch.

He jammed his feet into his house slippers and stalked into the hall, throwing open the door to the empty room and clicking on the lights.

The room was empty. No cats or rats or mice or squirrels or any other little furry critters.

He stepped further into the room, his eyes wandering over the baseboards, searching for scratch marks. There were none that he could see.

The door slammed closed behind him.

The lights went out, plunging the room into darkness.

Purr. Scratch.

Daphne ("For God's sake call me Dee") Conners opened her eyes as her radio clicked on, filling the darkness with music. She lay in bed for a few moments with her eyes closed, enjoying that time between sleep and being fully awake. She vaguely recalled being awakened just before dawn by a

11

strangely silent lightning storm. Or had she dreamed it?

Then she remembered that her father had set up a meeting for her that morning. At ten A.M. Here at her A-frame in the Blue Ridge Mountains. Her father worried too much, she thought, pushing back the covers and slipping from the warmth of the bed. She was very capable of taking care of herself. Besides, all writers get crank calls and ugly, nasty letters. Sometimes fans became obsessed with their favorite authors and said and did things they didn't mean. But they really didn't want to hurt anybody.

Or at least that's what she kept telling herself. Over and over. What had been happening was so damned weird she wasn't even sure it was happening. Maybe what she needed was a long rest.

But the very idea of her father hiring a private detective to watch her for a few weeks! He'd probably be some seedy sort with little beady eyes and bad breath, she thought as she walked to the bathroom to shower.

Dee was that rarity in the writing business. At the very young age of twenty-three she had two best-sellers in the historical romance field behind her, and had just signed a very lucrative contract for five more novels.

Dee was headstrong, extremely independent, basically a loner, and very pretty. Not beautiful, but more than cute; "pretty" summed it up. She had grown impatient with college — the University, of course; unthinkable to go anywhere else — and dropped out her sophomore year. Her mother had cried and her father had stomped around and blustered and hollered . . . none of it to any avail. Dee had started writing full-time.

She certainly didn't have to work. At anything. She

was independently wealthy, having come into her inheritance from her grandfather at age eighteen. But she wanted to write, and by God, nothing was going to keep her from that. She wanted to write about Virginia—warts and all. And Virginia had just as many warts as any other state.

Her first book brought that out. Painfully so. She was immediately dropped from membership in several clubs she belonged to in and around Charlottesville. Which was fine with Dee, since she never attended any of the functions anyway. The stuffy, snooty, insufferable bitches bored the hell out of her. And their yuppie husbands were even worse; they reminded her of lapdogs.

Hell with them all.

She thought briefly of that strange, silent lightning storm she'd witnessed just before dawn. Odd, she thought, as she fixed toast and a poached egg for breakfast. With a fresh cup of coffee at hand, she went into her office and turned on the computer. She could get a couple of hours' work done before Sam Spade showed up.

Then the phone rang.

Carl leaned against the hall wall, sweat pouring from his body and his chest heaving. He had been forced to kick the door open. Now his foot hurt. The damn knob just would not turn. And that scratching and purring had seemed to intensify in the closed and pitch-black room.

He had panicked. And that was not like Carl. He was too much like his dad to lose control the way he'd done.

He pushed away from the wall and looked at the shattered door. The lights had clicked back on as he had bolted into the hall.

He forced himself to calm down. He walked into the bedroom, made up his bed, and laid out the clothes he would wear that day. His boss had told him he would probably be staying over—maybe for a week, or longer—and to pack accordingly. He packed while the coffee was brewing, then showered and dressed. There had been no more purring or scratching.

He put his suitcase and garment bag in the car and went back into the house, turning off the coffee machine and checking to see that all the lights were off. He stepped out onto the front porch, hearing the door lock as he closed it.

He also heard something else.

Purr. Scratch.

"Hell with you," Carl muttered, and stepped off the porch, putting his back to the strangeness.

Or so he thought.

It was her mother.

Dee had braced herself for another obscene call. Relief flooded her when her mother's voice sprang into her ear. They chatted for a time.

No, the private detective had not yet arrived.

Yes, the guest cottage was ready.

She would be just fine.

She was sure he would be a very nice man.

Thank you.

Goodbye, Mother.

Pushing her slight irritation aside, Dee returned to her computer and lost herself in work. Two hours passed quickly and she was satisfied with her work. She had found the hook and the manuscript was coming along nicely.

She looked at the clock. Nine-thirty. She didn't want

to start another chapter only to be interrupted by Charlie Chan, so she shut the computer down and walked out onto the porch of the A-frame and sat down.

She caught a glimpse of something moving at the edge of the timberline just as a very foul odor reached her. The movement was probably made by a deer, but that odor was something else. It wasn't from a skunk, she knew that. The smell was . . . filthy, obscene. The word evil came into her mind.

A breeze sprang up and the odor was gone.

Dee settled back into her chair to wait for the private eye.

"She sure likes seclusion," Carl said to himself as he guided the car up the grade, deep timber on both sides of the road.

But it sure was beautiful country.

He had left the Interstate just before reaching the Blue Ridge Mountains and cut south on a state road. Following the directions given him, he turned onto a county road and drove deeper in the mountains. He knew only the name of the person he was to meet with. Nothing else about her.

Daphne, for Christ's sake!

Probably seventy years of age and an old maid, he had speculated. Looks under the bed every night for spooks and things that go bump in the night . . . secretly hoping to find a man under there.

Carl Garrett had wanted to be a cop all his life; to be just like his father, Dan Garrett, who had been the sheriff of Ruger County. But his life had been shattered by his father's death. And Carl had yet to pick up all the shattered pieces. He had dropped out of college at the end of his junior year, where his major had been law enforcement, and gone to work for a private investigations firm in Richmond, with offices all over America and in a dozen foreign countries. The firm specialized in criminal investigations. Carl found he had a flair for the work and moved up rapidly within the firm. He had done a little bodyguard work—escorting, as they called it—but not much. The firm had only taken this new job, according to his boss, because Mister Conners was one of the richest men in the world and hadn't even blinked at the fee, inflated by the boss because he didn't like his men acting as babysitters and had hoped to discourage Conners.

"I should have known better," he had told Carl over the phone.

Conners had handed the boss a signed check and told him to assign his best man to it and fill in the numbers.

Carl got the nod.

He turned into the driveway and headed up to the A-frame structure built on the flats. The house and about an acre of land was surrounded by a six-foot-high chain-link fence. He smiled when he spotted the young woman sitting on the long front porch. If that was Daphne Conners, he had a feeling he was going to like this job. As he got out of the car and drew nearer, getting a better look at her, he was sure of it.

"Miss Conners?"

"Yes. You're the private eye?"

Carl laughed. "I guess some people still call us that. I'm Carl Garrett."

"You don't look like a keyhole-peeker."

"We don't do much of that, Miss Conners. Ninety-five percent of our work is in the criminal field."

"But money talks, right? Especially my father's money."

"I wouldn't know about that, Miss Conners. I'm a field investigator, not the head of the firm."

"Stop calling me Miss Conners." She narrowed her eyes and cocked her head to one side. "How do I know you're not the man who's been . . . bothering me?"

Carl removed his credentials from a back pocket and laid them on the porch floor, then backed away. His I.D., with photo, showed him to be a bonded and licensed private investigator in the state of Virginia. In addition there was his VHP gun permit. Also included, thanks to his dead father's connections in certain government agencies, was a Federal gun permit, allowing him to carry a concealed weapon in any state in the Union.

"Very impressive." Dee brushed back a lock of light brown hair as she waved him on up to the porch and pointed toward a chair. Handing the leather case back to him, she said, "You sure are young to have all those credentials. Nothing from INTERPOL?"

Carl caught the twinkle in her pale blue eyes. "Oh, I'm working on that, Miss . . . ah, Daphne."

She grimaced. "For God's sake, call me Dee. Coffee?"

"That would be nice."

"Sugar and cream?"

"Just sugar. One."

"Sit still, I'll get it." She smiled at him. "Enjoy the view."

He did, as she walked into the house, but it wasn't of the Blue Ridge Mountains. About five-five, he guessed; very nicely put together. And he accurately pegged her as a person who would speak her mind whenever she got damn ready to do so.

He wondered why her father had insisted she have a bodyguard. Not that she didn't have a lovely body to guard, mind you.

17

In the three and a half years that he'd worked for the agency, Carl had acted as escort for perhaps half a dozen or so very rich people. And he had come to the conclusion that with most of them, their elevators didn't go all the way to the top.

A foul odor drifted past his nose, and he grimaced. "Jesus!" he said. "That cesspool sure needs some work."

Carl did not see the figure standing at the edge of the woods, looking at him through eyes of reddened rage.

Chapter 2

The coffee was very good, and unlike any that Carl had ever drunk. He guessed that she ground her own beans and they were very expensive.

"The name Garrett is somehow familiar to me," she said, looking at him.

"My father was sheriff of Ruger County. He was killed several years ago."

"Ahhh! Yes. I don't think anybody ever got the full story of that . . . incident. Yeah, I was a junior at the university when that happened."

"So was I."

"No kidding! What house?"

Carl grinned. "None. I never went in much for that fraternity stuff. What sorority were you in?"

She returned his grin and her face was suddenly pixyish. "None. Much to the mortification of my mother. One of Virginia's first families and all that," she said, acquiring a pretty good English accent, "don't you know?"

"Oh, quite!" He managed a passable cockney accent.

"I dropped out," she told him.

"So did I."

They shared a laugh on the porch and both of them

leaned back in the chairs, enjoying the coffee and each other's company and the quiet of the mountains.

"I hate to bring up business," Carl said, breaking the silence. "But I am on your father's payroll—in a manner of speaking."

"He can afford it."

"I imagine."

She took a sip of coffee. "Do you have a gun with you?"

"I have a pistol, a rifle, and a shotgun in the car."

"Ever shot anybody?"

"On the job or in self-defense as a civilian?"

More to this young man than meets the eye, she thought. "Either."

"Yes, I have."

One, or more? she thought. "Did they, uh . . . ?"

"Die? Yes. One was a rapist who jumped bond and the bonding company hired us to get him. I had him cornered in an old shack down on the Virginia-North Carolina line. He came at me with a knife."

She silently absorbed that for a moment and decided she would not pursue that line of questioning any further. Instead she blurted out, "I've been receiving obscene phone calls now for about three weeks. I've come home, here, and found that someone has been in the house, rummaging through my things. They've taken . . . very personal items. Bras, panties, that sort of thing."

"Your father was right to hire us. You're dealing with a nut. What did the police say?"

"Well, living out here, it's the sheriff's department. They were very nice and cooperative. They believed me at first."

"At first?"

"They did something at the phone company's main switcher, or whatever they call it. Whenever my number rang, they could do some sort of electronic search and find out where the call came from. And I was taping everything here. I'd get a call, but nothing would show up at the terminal headquarters. And when I'd play them the tape, I heard everything very clearly, but believe it or not, the police couldn't hear anything. They finally wrote me off as a kook."

"Are you a kook?"

"No. I'm a best-selling author of historical romances. That isn't to say there aren't some kooky writers. But I'm not one of them. I write under the name of Daphne LaCrosse."

"Daphne LaCrosse! My sister and my mother read your books! They're big fans of yours!"

A smile danced around her lips. "I'm glad to hear it."

"But getting back to business, I would like to hear one of these taped calls after you've told me everything."

"All right." She slanted her eyes over his long, lanky frame and mop of what she guessed would always be slightly unruly brown hair. An attractive young man. More rugged-looking than strictly handsome. Certainly not one of those blow-dried, buttoned-down types that she detested. And he wasn't a jock, either. Those turned her off completely. Carl Garrett looked like he could take care of himself, and would back up from very little—if anything.

It was her nature to make up her mind quickly about people, and she decided that she liked this long, lanky young private investigator.

"I've also been followed—many times over the past month. By kids, would you believe, always kids. Well . . . seventeen, eighteen years old, I'd guess. But no, no one has tried to hurt me or make any kind of physical contact. And I also get the feeling that I'm being watched, from the woods. I'll admit to you what I have not and will not admit to my parents: I'm scared."

"With good reason. Do you like animals?"

"What?" The quick shift took her by surprise. "Oh. Yes. Very much. Why?"

"You need a dog. A trained guard dog. They're expensive, but well worth the money. I know a man who trains them. I can have one up here this afternoon if you're agreeable."

"If you think it's necessary. Of course. Yes. I think I'd like that."

"Use your phone?"

"Certainly. Come on," she said, rising from the deck chair, "I'll show you where it is."

The interior of the A-frame was impressive. Expensive chrome lighting and lamps and leather furniture. Tasteful paintings lined the walls. And the A-frame was much larger than Carl would have guessed from the outside. One very large bedroom upstairs created the ceiling for the modern kitchen in the rear. The den was massive, the fireplace huge.

"My office," she said, pointing to a closed door.

Carl spotted the phone and made his call. The dog would be there by early afternoon. Carl gave the man directions and hung up.

"Where do I bunk?" Carl asked.

Dee hesitated, then said, "The guest cottage is ready. But I think I'd feel better if you were closer. Use that bedroom there." She pointed to the second closed door on the lower level and smiled impishly. "Providing I can trust you, that is."

"I was a Boy Scout," Carl said with a straight face.

She rolled her eyes, and smiled.

* * *

Carl knew instantly that he didn't like the deputy. He had spent his entire life around law enforcement and could pick a hotdog out of a crowd — an officer who lived and breathed law enforcement, who was only too ready to bust anybody for anything at anytime, who made the kind of comments designed to provoke resistance in the hope that force would become necessary.

"Never did have much use for private detectives," Deputy Harrison said.

"I never had much use for hotdogs," Carl replied calmly.

Both young men were about the same age. Harrison was heavier and several inches shorter, and his mouth was stuffed full of chewing tobacco.

The deputy flushed and looked hard at Carl. "If you carryin' a weapon, you gonna be in a lot of trouble, boy."

Carl handed him his Federal gun permit. Most cops, both urban and rural, never saw a Federal gun permit, for the simple reason that they were very difficult to obtain.

Harrison shifted his cud and returned the permit. "First time I seen one of them," he admitted.

Carl handed him his VHP gun permit. Harrison glanced at it and a little more of the bluster went out of him. "I get the picture," he said. He looked at Carl. "You Sheriff Garrett's son?"

"Yes."

"Sheriff Rodale and him didn't get along."

"So my father said, several times." Rodale, Carl knew, had to be dragged screaming and kicking into the twentieth century. His style of law enforcement went out about the same time as the gunfight at the O.K. Corral. Virginia Highway Patrol rated Reeves County as having the worst record of law enforcement

23

in the entire state. And, off the record, Sheriff Rodale was rated as being the worst sheriff in the entire United States.

"Phew!" Harrison said, as that foul odor drifted under his nose. "Y'all better get that septic tank looked at."

"It isn't the tank. I checked it just before you drove up. I don't know what it is or where it's coming from."

Harrison had appeared while Carl was just about to get a pistol from his car. News of a stranger in the county had spread very fast. Carl knew, from reading intelligence reports about Reeves County and Sheriff Rodale, that the sheriff was on the take from a dozen different places and had a spy network of assorted good ol' boys and rednecks that would rival the CIA. The state of Virginia had tried for years to put the man in prison, but Rodale had sidestepped each move with the grace of a ballet dancer slipping on owl shit.

"That woman in yonder is a nut!" Harrison said, looking at the house.

"I don't think so."

"Then you ain't as smart as you think you are."

A dozen rejoinders sprang into Carl's mind. He checked them and smiled at Harrison. "I'm smart enough to know that being hassled is against the law. And that Edgar Conners is plenty irritated with the sheriff's department in this county."

Those were evidently the magic words. Harrison forced a very thin smile and said, "See you around, boy."

" 'Fraid so."

Carl watched the patrol car leave and knew he had made an enemy. But he detested Harrison and all his breed. Harrison was the kind of man who threw away everything in the newspaper except the sports page. He could tell you the third-string quarterback of his favorite team, but didn't have the foggiest idea what continent Peru was on. On the back bumper of his pickup truck, with chromed roll-bar and fourteen lights and at least three antennas, there would be several bumper stickers: I WILL GIVE UP MY GUN WHEN THEY PRY IT FROM MY COLD DEAD FINGERS. COON HUNTERS ARE GREAT LOVERS. ANYONE WHO DON'T LIKE FOOTBALL SUCKS.

Harrison would kill a deer out of season in a heartbeat and tell you that was his right, but would give an out-of-towner a ticket for going three miles over the speed limit.

"I can't stand that man," Dee called from the front porch.

Carl turned. "I can understand why."

A slight rustling sound came from the nearby woods. Carl frowned.

"How much of this land do you or your father own, Dee?"

"About ten thousand acres. The reason so many people around here don't like my father is because he won't permit hunting on any of his property. It's all fenced and posted, but some still slip in and hunt. The house has been shot at more than once, and before I put the fence up, the tires on my car were cut several times."

"You think it was connected to what's been happening to you recently?"

"No."

Carl had changed into jeans and hiking boots and he now slipped into a shoulder holster rig and checked his 9-mm Beretta. Every other round was killer ammo, bullets that exploded upon striking soft tissue.

"Why are you putting that on?" Dee asked.

"Because I've got a very strong feeling someone's out there. I'm going to check out the woods. You get back

25

into the house. Please," he added.

Carl left the fenced-in area, carefully closing and securing the gate, and walked into the deep timber. Immediately a strange sensation hit him. He could not quite identify it.

Then it came to him, bringing with it old memories of those terrible days just before his father died fighting the evil that had sprung up in Ruger County several years back.

Carl remembered the terror that had spread like wind-whipped wildfire through the town and the surrounding area. He vividly recalled the hideous metamorphosis that had changed humans into drooling subhumans who stalked the countryside, seeking human flesh. And the ordinary house cats that had attacked their owners in a frenzy of blood lust.

Carl leaned against a tree and struggled to put all that out of his mind. Right now he needed to concentrate only on the job at hand.

A twig snapping within the forest alerted him to danger.

The foul odor that he had smelled several times that day now enveloped him. It was so putrid he had to fight back nausea.

What in the hell was out there, lurking—rotting was probably more like it—in the shadows of the forest? It was his job to find out. He was being paid to protect Miss Daphne ("For God's sake call me Dee") Conners, a.k.a. Daphne LaCrosse, famous writer. So get on with it, he told himself.

The young man moved deeper into the timber, avoiding the areas where the sun managed to weakly penetrate the timber.

Something dark flitted through the timber. Carl caught only a glimpse of it.

It did not seem human, but then neither was it like

26

any animal he had ever seen.

What the hell *was* it?

Carl headed in the direction the fast-moving and elusive shape had taken. The foul odor became stronger. Another shape pranced through the timber. Again Carl could only catch a glimpse of it.

Pranced?

Yes. That's what it did. An arrogant strut, almost as if he—it, whatever—was deliberately mocking Carl. But this figure had a more human shape to it.

He heard faint singing.

Singing? In the middle of a forest?

Carl paused, listening. Not singing. It was . . . chanting, male and female voices together.

Carl walked on, deeper into the forest. He guessed he had walked about a quarter of a mile from the A-frame, and still he did not seem to be getting any closer to the chanting.

Hell, now it was behind him!

He turned around. The chanting now seemed to be coming from near the house. He hesitated, then decided to return to the house; Dee Conners's welfare was his first concern.

But, as if in a dream, he could find no landmarks. The woods seemed to have changed, becoming more swamplike than forest. Nothing looked familiar. Carl stopped and took several deep breaths, calming himself. He looked up, trying to locate the sun. He could not see it. And he was tired, as if he'd been walking for miles.

Now the chanting seemed to be coming from his left. He struggled to ignore it as he walked straight ahead. The hypnotic chanting must be muddling his brain.

Now a single, very sweet female voice was singing to him—a siren's song that was like what he imagined

Ulysses had heard.

He walked on, forcing everything except the house out of his mind. He caught a glimpse of the A-frame, but it was wavy and unclear, fading in and out of his vision.

He struggled on, a dozen explanations for what might be causing this leaping into his mind. Maybe some sort of gas seeping from the earth that was toxic, perhaps mind-altering.

The siren's song ended abruptly as he approached the clearing. His head cleared. As he stepped out of the timber he was having difficulty remembering just what had gone on back in the timber.

"Shapes." He forced the word from his mouth. "Shapes and singing and chanting. And the forest seemed to change before my eyes."

He knelt down, pulling a small notepad from his back pocket, and quickly jotted down all he could remember.

Dee ran out of the house. "My God, where have you been, Carl? I was about to call the police. For all the good that would have done me."

He looked up, stood up. "What do you mean where have I been? I went into the woods for a few minutes."

"A few minutes? What went on in there?"

"A lot of strange, weird stuff, I can tell you that. Dee, I don't think it's safe for you to remain out here." He looked up at the sky. The sun was dipping low on the horizon. Carl lifted his arm and glanced at his watch. "Jesus Christ!" he muttered.

Dee walked to the gate, pushed it open, and came to his side, looking at him with worried eyes. "You've been gone for five hours, Carl!"

Chapter 3

He realized that he was hungry, and very, very thirsty. He drank two big glasses of water before his thirst was eased. Suddenly he yelled and dropped the glass to the floor.

Dee ran through the house in time to see him tear off his boot and jerk the maggotlike worm from the flesh of his ankle. Goddamn thing had bitten like he imagined a piranha would bite!

Gritting his teeth against the burning pain in his ankle, and fighting revulsion over the slimy, squirming worm trapped between his thumb and forefinger, he told Dee, "Get me a jar with a lid on it. Hurry."

Carl dropped the worm into the jar and screwed the lid on tight. He found a knife and punched a very small hole in the top of the lid. He assumed the thing needed air to survive. He wasn't sure about that. But he damn sure recognized the maggotlike worm. From several years back.

Dee poured rubbing alcohol over his wound, a sensation which brightened Carl's afternoon considerably. Sure.

Through the momentary haze the burning alcohol caused, Carl fought to retain some hold on sanity. The worms he had seen, and thought destroyed, in Ruger

County years past were still here, living in those woods. That explained the terrible stink. The Old Ones were once more surfacing, bubbling and struggling to reach the top of the earth. And with them would come terror and death and domination from forces on the dark side of light.

Satan.

But to whom could he tell his story? Who would believe him? Father Denier had died with Carl's dad as they both gave up their lives to destroy Anya, the child of the Devil, and her damnable cat, Pet. But she had left a legacy of evil behind her. No one knew how many of her converts still walked the Virginia countryside, patiently waiting for the call to come forward.

Dee's voice jarred him back to reality. "I should have known when I saw that weird lightning this morning that this was going to be a really strange day."

Carl spun around. *"What!"*

"There was this sort of silent storm. Lots of lightning but no thunder, if you can imagine. Then again, I was the only one to see it. I called a couple of my friends this morning to see what they thought about it. They said they hadn't noticed any storm."

"I saw it," Carl told her, then held up his hand. "We'll talk about it later. Did Mister Jackson bring the dog?"

"He's out back. Half husky and half German shepherd. He sure is big enough. Mister Jackson said his name is Dingo."

"Let's walk out together so he'll know that I'm with you and we're friends."

"He doesn't look all that dangerous. Just big."

"He's dangerous. Believe me. That's the only kind of dogs Mister Jackson breeds and trains."

Dingo looked to be about a hundred pounds. There were no husky markings on him except for the way he held his tail as Carl approached. His color was a light tan. His head was massive and his jaws about like a grizzly bear. He had one blue eye and one brown eye. Always a lover of animals, Carl won him over easily.

"You object to animals in the house, Dee?"

"Oh, no. I lost my chow last year and still haven't gotten over the loss. I had him for twelve years. I love animals."

Carl noticed that Dingo occasionally glanced at the deep woods. Every time he did, the hair on the dog's back bristled.

"He knows something's wrong in there."

"Like what?" She stared at the woods.

Carl shook his head. "I . . . I'm not sure. Come on. Let's go into the house. I'll tell you what I can remember."

Carl relived the memories of Ruger County that night. He dreamed the horror again and again. The mangled and half-eaten bodies, the terrible transformations of people he'd known who became drooling beasts. The morning his father died so that the nightmare could end.

But it hadn't ended.

Carl woke up bathed in sweat.

The singing was once more drifting sweetly and seductively from the dark timber, floating like heady and hypnotic perfume through the open window.

Carl slipped from bed and dressed, stepping out into the dark den. Dingo was lying at the foot of the stairs. But he was not asleep. The animal was tense and very alert.

"What is that sound?" Dee called from the top of the stairs.

"What I told you about. Don't listen to it."

"How do you not listen to it?" She walked down the stairs. Dingo rose and stayed by her side.

"Think about something else. Concentrate on your big toe—anything. What time is it?"

"Four o'clock."

"Keep the lights out." He looked at Dingo. "Guard," he told him.

The animal looked at him as if to say, "What the hell do you think I'm doing, fool!"

"Sorry," Carl muttered to the dog. "You know your job better than I do, I guess."

"I don't need any lights to make coffee. I'll make some toast too."

Dee turned toward the kitchen and Carl moved toward the front door. They both stopped as the chanting and singing ceased and a heavy purring began.

Dingo growled.

Scratch!

The scratching came from the rear of the house, and it grated on those inside like a fingernail moving slowly down a blackboard.

"That's no house cat," Dee said softly.

"Certainly not any house cat that I'd want to meet," Carl agreed.

Dingo had whirled around, fangs bared, the hair on his back standing up like a wire brush.

Purr. Scratch.

Every fiber within the dog wanted to go outside to confront whatever was out there. But Jackson had trained him well. He would attack only if his mistress commanded it or if she was in immediate danger . . . from something the animal could see.

Carl had carefully inspected all around the house. He had noticed the security lights mounted on both the front and rear of the A-frame. He moved toward the rear of the house.

"Dee, when I give you the word hit the rear flood-lights."

Carl hesitated, then walked to the fireplace and picked up a heavy poker. By the rear entrance, he softly unlocked the door and put his hand on the knob.

"Now!" Carl said. The backyard filled with light as Carl jerked open the door.

The stench that assaulted his nostrils very nearly overpowered him. But the shock at confronting . . . whatever the hell it was . . . standing on the back porch momentarily numbed the young man.

With a wild shriek, the man—Carl could only guess it was a man—leaped from the porch just as Dee screamed. That was enough for Dingo. With a snarl of rage the big dog almost knocked Carl down as he tore out the back door, with one thought on his mind: to rip out just as big a piece of the intruder as he could.

But the man scaled the high chain-link fence with the grace of a deer and was gone into the night, outside the perimeter of light.

Dingo drew up short of the fence and let it be known in no uncertain terms that he now had the trespasser's scent and would be waiting for a return bout.

Dee had recovered from her fright enough to function and was spraying the kitchen with deodorant. The spray slowly overrode the stench.

Carl called to Dingo and the animal reluctantly returned to the house, still clearly irritated that the foul-smelling intruder had gotten away.

"What was that thing?" she asked, her voice trembly.

"I don't know," Carl admitted.

And in truth, he didn't. The figure he had seen on the porch was not anything like those hideous creatures that had roamed Ruger County. But he was certain it was what he had seen prancing through the woods the previous afternoon.

He could not see the face; that had been shrouded by a hood. But the hands were human. He had seen the hands; they were not animal paws, not hooked and gnarled.

"He . . . it . . . went over that tall fence like a deer," Dee said, breaking into his thoughts.

"Yeah. And so fast that Dingo couldn't catch it." So was it human or animal? he silently asked himself. "I'll say it again, Dee. It isn't safe here for you."

"It's some sort of a trick, Carl. Many of the people in this county resent me and dislike me. I just don't believe in the supernatural."

He had not told her about the events in Ruger, for many reasons. Chief among them was the fact that the government had warned them all: If any of them ever went public with it, the consequences could be dire — and besides, who would believe them?

Carl had never told anyone about the events that led up to the death of his father. But he felt it was time to break that silence . . . at least with Dee.

"Let's make some coffee, Dee. It's time for us to have a talk."

She sat in silence, mentally trying to absorb and sort out all that Carl had told her. The coffeepot was empty and the sun was trying to push aside the darkness by the time he'd finished.

"Your mother?" she finally asked.

"Moved to Florida. She tried to stay in Valentine, but she just couldn't. Too many memories, both good and bad."

"Your sister?"

"Dink, that's her nickname, went with her. She's attending the University of Florida."

"Your friend, Mike?"

"Believe it or not, Mike did graduate and moved up into the Northwest. He has his own construction business and is doing well."

"You witnessed your father's . . . death?"

"No. I was with Mother. Captain Taylor told me about it. He said it was the bravest and most unselfish thing he'd ever seen another man do."

"The priest?"

"Father Denier. He died with my dad. I wish he was here. I don't know if I can go through this again."

"Do you have a choice?"

Carl looked long at her, as the sun's rays began to touch the land, driving away, temporarily at least, the evil that darkness always brings—creeping insidiously and relentlessly on silent feet through the purple shadows. "What do you mean, Dee?"

"You listened to the tapes last night."

"So?"

"You heard what the others couldn't hear."

That he had. The filth that had poured out of the speaker was unequaled in intensity and verbal degradation. "Yes. So I did."

"We both saw the silent storm the other morning. No one else did."

He had to admit that was true.

"You're obviously in this as much as I am."

"Dee, you may think this is off the subject, but I'm not so sure of that. You surely must have known how many residents of this county feel about your father."

"Sure. Probably a good twenty-five percent hate him. If he can buy a piece of property and turn it into

35

a nature trail or safe haven for birds and deer and all sorts of animals, he will. He owns property all over the United States that he's turned control of over to environmental groups or wildlife groups. And he always does it right in the middle of so-called prime hunting land, or where the rednecks come to ride their three-wheelers or four-wheelers, not caring what they destroy or pollute with those stinking damn machines."

Carl grinned at her as the rhetoric became heated. "You don't have to convince me, Miss Daphne. I'm with you in the treatment of the land and the wild critters who live in it."

"I'm sorry. It's one of my pet peeves. Why did you ask that, Carl?"

"Did you come in here and build this A-frame—and I can see that it's not over two or three years old—just for spite?"

She grinned back at him. "You *damn* right I did! I told you about all this acreage my father owns. Dad has tried to turn all this over to some conservation group; turn it into an animal refuge, with hiking trails and so forth. Make it for *all* people to enjoy. But every time some group agrees to take it, they get really hassled. A few of the cops ticket them every time they get behind the wheel of a car. Tires are cut, windshields smashed out. And more than one person has been verbally intimidated, and a few have been brutally beaten. No group wants to take it and put the lives of its members in danger. Carl, I'm a Virginian, I love this state. I'm very wealthy, Carl. I could live in the south of France if I so chose. But I chose to live here. Right here in Reeves County. And I'm not picking on this state. I know from personal experience, working with environmental groups since I was fourteen years old, that you can go into parts of *any* state, any county in the United States, and find cruddy and crappy people. But I live here, Carl, and nobody is going to run me off this land."

Carl sensed that part of that last sentence was a clear message to him: that she didn't want to hear any more talk about it not being safe and that it would be best if she packed up and left.

"Some things are coming back to me now. Over the last couple of years, haven't there been several people lost around here and nothing ever found of them?"

"Oh, yes. And the state police suspect that a lot more than just a few have vanished around here. More than a dozen families of transients have pinpointed this area as the last place their relatives were spotted—never to be seen again."

"We didn't get them all." Carl spoke the words very softly. "They just moved northwest about fifty miles—into the timber—and waited for another signal that the Old Ones were ready to surface."

Dee rubbed her arms as if she was cold. She probably was—from fear. "And you think these . . . Old Ones are surfacing?"

"Looks like it. And I doubt that Sheriff Rodale is aware of the horror. That fat pig—no pun intended—hasn't got the imagination to understand what's about to bust wide open all around him."

"I'm . . . not really sure that I do myself. I mean, I heard all your words, and could feel some of the horror—it came through in your voice. But I'm not sure I really understand."

"All those people who were in Ruger County, from the CDC . . ." Carl was talking more to himself than to Dee. "I don't know how to get in touch with them. I have only that worm on which to base my story. No solid proof of any killings. Captain Taylor is retired. I don't have any idea where he went."

"How about those men from the government?"

"I don't know. I never knew their real names. They all go by phony names."

They were silent for a time, enjoying the coolness of the early morning. It would be warming up considerably in a few hours.

"There is something else you have to consider, Dee."

She waited for the other shoe to drop, with a feeling she wasn't going to like what she heard.

"If you decide to stay here, we may be all alone in this fight."

Chapter 4

Dingo came out onto the porch and sat between their chairs, reminding them that they were not entirely alone.

Dee laid a hand on the dog's big head. "Whatever that thing was standing on the back porch this morning, Dingo certainly wasn't afraid of it."

The dog looked around at the sound of his name, and then swung his head back toward the woods at the side of the house.

"No. He wasn't. That thing was almost human, Dee. I saw its hands. But it possessed superhuman athletic abilities."

"*Almost* human?" She glanced at him. "Are you convinced this is not just some sort of elaborate hoax?" Dee still clung to a faint hope.

"I'm convinced. But convincing others is going to take some doing considering the skimpy evidence."

"Do you want to meet with my father, Carl? I can assure you he has the money to hire a private army."

"Suppose he orders you to pack up and leave this area."

"I'll tell him to stick it in his ear!"

She probably would too, Carl thought, a grin crossing his lips. "If it's all right with you, let's wait a couple

39

of days."

"Suits me."

Carl stayed close to the house all that morning. Nothing out of the way happened. No singing or chanting, no more unwanted intruders, no sightings of dark-robed beings, and no more foul smells. But the feeling they were being watched did not go away. Dingo did not appear to be alarmed or unduly alert. He circled the yard about once every half hour, then returned to a spot, usually the same one, on the front porch.

Carl approached Dee with an idea he'd been mulling over. "How do you feel about spending some money, Dee?"

"Whatever you think is necessary, do it."

"It's going to be expensive," he cautioned.

She smiled at him. "What do you consider expensive?"

"Off the top of my head, I'd say between five and ten thousand dollars."

She put a hand on his arm and proceeded to tell him just what Daphne Conners was worth.

She had named a figure that was so high Carl could not even fully grasp the enormity of it. He had then asked Dee what she did with the money she earned from book sales. Without blinking she'd said, "I give it all to various charities."

Her income from the interest alone on her inheritance amounted to something like eighty-five hundred dollars a week. Most of it she put back into interest-bearing accounts or relatively safe stocks and bonds. And that didn't take into account the monies she received from her stock in the family's dozens of factories and businesses scattered all around the Free

World.

Carl just couldn't comprehend that much money.

Dee was not blasé about her wealth. It was just that she had been born into money and was not impressed with it, since she had not had to lift one finger to earn it.

Carl spent about thirty minutes on the phone, lining up a company to do the work he had in mind.

"It's going to be very noisy around here for a few days," he told Dee. "This outfit has security at night for its equipment, so the house will be guarded. We'll leave Dingo here — the automatic food-and-water-dispenser Jackson brought will insure he has plenty to eat and drink; he's used to those things — and we'll pull out and prowl the county. When we get back, the work will have been completed."

"For all that's going to be done, it seems like a low figure."

"They're getting the timber," Carl told her. "That's why it's low."

The workmen and the trucks began arriving just after dawn the next morning. Carl showed the foreman what he wanted done.

"Piece of cake," the hard-hatted man said. "Four days, max."

Carl and Dee pulled out in Dee's Jaguar. "I've been through all the defensive driving schools," she told him. "How to avoid terrorists and kidnappers and all that. This car is armor-plated and the glass is bulletproof."

"It isn't cop-proof, though," Carl said, twisting in the seat and looking back just as a sheriff's unit pulled in behind them and cut on its flashing lights.

Dee glanced in the rearview mirror. "Harrison," she

said, her voice dripping disgust.

"Naturally. Well, go ahead and pull over," Carl told her. "There isn't any point in making matters worse by refusing to stop."

Harrison made a big deal out of the stop by getting on his outside speaker and telling Dee to step out of the car and keep her hands in sight.

"That asshole!" Carl said, having had a gutful of Deputy Harrison. He pointed to the modular phone. "That thing work?"

"Sure."

"How do I use it?"

She quickly showed him.

"Thanks. Now go on and see what Stupid wants. I got a call to make."

Carl made his call and adjusted the rearview mirror so he could see what was going on in the sheriff's car behind him. After a few moments, Dee got out, slammed the door, and stalked back to the Jag.

Harrison pulled out and waved cheerfully as he drove past.

Dee opened her mouth and let loose a stream of cuss words that would have sobered up a career wino in less time than he could chug-a-lug a half pint of sweet lucy.

Carl let her wind down. When she paused for breath, he said, "I don't see any tickets. He's just a hotdog cop. They just like to hassle people."

She cut her hot eyes at him. "Carl, I could have bought a publishing company in order to get published. My father could probably buy *ten* of them! But I have never believed in using my wealth as a lever against people. Harry Harrison has just changed my mind. That is the last time that man is ever going to hassle me. And that's a promise."

Carl didn't tell her that he had just hung up from

42

calling his home office, and that right that moment, the boss was on the horn to Mister Edgar Conners at his corporate headquarters in Richmond. It would be interesting to see what the next few days brought.

"You want me to drive?" he asked.

"Please. I am so damned mad I don't know what I might do."

Carl headed south, out of Reeves County. He had given up his plans of touring the county, getting a feel of it. At least for awhile. He had some serious thinking to do.

"Sit down," the mayor of Butler, Virginia, county seat of Reeves County, said to Sheriff Rodale. "Shut your big fat mouth. And keep it shut."

"You cain't talk to me like that!" Rodale hollered.

"I just did, you fat pig," Mayor Purdy told him.

Rodale sat down heavily in his chair. Wilber Purdy was about the only man in the county who could get away with talking to him in such a manner. For the simple reason that Purdy was the richest man in the county. Purdy owned the bank, the biggest store, and more land than anyone else, and had a lot of political clout.

"Who twisted your tail this afternoon?" Rodale finally asked.

"Shut up! Let me tell you something, Rodale. There are people in this world you can hassle, and people that you'd damn well better let alone—"

"Hell, I know that!"

"And I told you to shut up! I just got off the phone not ten minutes ago, from talking with several attorneys who represent Mister Edgar Conners. Mister Conners is not very happy with the law enforcement in Reeves County. Now Sheriff Rodale, you are aware

43

of Conners Broadcasting, are you not?"

"Yeah," Rodale said, getting the drift of where all this was going. "He owns newspapers, radio and TV stations, bunches of factories, and mining stuff—big man on Wall Street. I ain't stupid, Wilber. I may talk that way, but that's 'cause the people like it."

"Whether you are stupid or not is a matter of opinion. You have done some extremely stupid things in the years I have known you. And that is a lifetime."

"Yeah!" Rodale grinned as he leaned back in his chair. "You recollect the time you and me—"

"Shut up!" Purdy yelled at him. "I did not come here to speak of childhood reminiscences. Rodale, I want a muzzle and a short leash put on Harry Harrison. . . ." He paused as a very foul odor drifted under the closed office door and past his nose. He grimaced in disgust. "What in God's name is that smell?"

"I don't know. I first smelled it plain about two weeks ago. Old Lady Barstow up on the ridges complained about it about the same time. Now she's up and disappeared. Since yesterday."

"Disappeared? Where'd she go?"

"How the hell do I know? She's just gone. I got people workin' on it, but they ain't turned up nothin' yet."

The smell, and it seemed to be coming from the cell-block area of the jail, vanished. Purdy turned his attention back to the sheriff. "No more hassling of the Conners woman, Rodale. None. Period. You understand me?"

The sheriff got his back up and his red neck turned even redder. "Damnit, Wilber! We let up on that rich bitch and she's gonna turn ten thousand acres of the best huntin' land in the state into some sort of sissified preserve so's city folks and fags can come in and oohhh and aahhh over a bunch of goddamn butterflies."

"I don't care, Rodale. And you'd better know this, too: That young private investigator her father hired to come in here and protect her is the late Sheriff Dan Garrett's son. And he doesn't work for some sleazy operation. The Richland Agency is worldwide and highly respected. And for your information, he's the young man who killed that rapist down on the line a couple of years back. And the same young man who, when some thugs jumped him in a Richmond parking lot last year, put both of them in the hospital with broken arms, caved-in ribs, and one of them with a skull fracture. With his bare hands, Rodale. Advise young Harrison to stand clear. No more hassling. Is that understood?"

The sheriff spread his hands wide and sighed. "All right, Wilbur. All right. Message received. The queers and the sissies and the butterflies have won, I reckon." A sadistic glint came into his eyes. "But I sure never knowed you to back down and knuckle under just 'cause of one man 'fore this day."

Purdy stared at the man until Rodale cut his eyes away with a curse. "I think it's time for you to consider retiring, Rodale. As a matter of fact, were I you, I would begin putting my house in order. You just can't accept the fact that this is the twentieth century. Now I know for a fact that you are well-fixed. This will be your last term in office, Rodale. Your last chance to turn things around and retire with a good name. I'd do that if I were you."

Wilber Purdy walked to the door. "And get that broken sewer line fixed. It's disgusting." He stepped out into the hall and closed the door behind him.

Rodale looked at the closed door and resigned himself to his fate. The sheriff knew that without Purdy's support, there was no chance of his being reelected.

45

Purdy was the real power in the county.

Well, hell! he thought. I been in office damn near twenty-five years. Maybe it is time to hang it up and go fishin'.

"Or go count butterflies with the sissies and the fags," he muttered, then shuddered at the thought.

Carl checked them into a motel in Lynchburg, adjoining rooms. He stretched out on the bed and began adding up what he would need in order to combat the evil that was about to rip Reeves County apart. It really wasn't a very long list. Mostly what he needed was the arch angel Michael to come down from God's side with his mighty sword.

Carl put wishful thinking aside and got pen and paper and began listing known facts and suppositions.

Was he certain that this was the same type of evil that had struck Ruger County several years back?

No, he wasn't. Only time would prove or disprove that. But time was something that could not be allowed to march on while he sat back and did nothing.

He had to have allies; where to find them?

Carl knew better than to approach most ministers with his unsupported theories. They would listen politely and then show him the door, probably with a suggestion that he seek professional psychiatric help.

He jotted down that he would come back to the problem of allies.

How many of the godless would he be facing?

No way of knowing until they began to make their move.

Could he persuade Dee to leave?

No.

He put aside pen and paper, knowing that he was simply delaying the inevitable, stalling because he did

46

not want to return to Reeves County. The evil had killed his father and several of his friends, had changed decent human beings into monsters.

He looked up at the ceiling. "Why me?" he questioned.

He received no answer. He hadn't been expecting one.

The young man lay back on the bed, his mind busy.

One thing he could do was try to convince Dee to clear off all ten thousand acres. But that was a short-range solution. Once those . . . things—Carl really wasn't sure what they were or what to call them—in the woods realized what was happening, they would strike, putting the timbermen in danger.

He rose from the bed, walked to the drape-covered windows, and found the cord, opening the drapes. Night was settling over the land.

The darkness slowly circled the country, spreading its deepening purple shroud over the land. In Reeves County, in the timbered acreage that surrounded the A-frame home of Dee Conners, strange shapes were gathering, human and subhuman alike. They formed a tight circle around a pool of mist and began chanting, faces to the sky. The night seemed to be made of pitch, so dark that movements did not shadow. They chanted ancient words from a language that had been long dead until now. The circle moved to the left, then to the right, in toward the misty pool, out again. Voices called out for assistance, casting vocal pleas to dark gods.

And the dark gods replied, lancing the sky with vicious streaks of lightning, to be seen by only a selected few. In the small clearing, around the misty pool, the human and subhuman danced and pranced

47

in joy as the silent voices from the darkened sky spat forth the reply they had been waiting for these past four years.

The Old Ones were near the surface, coming closer and closer. Soon they would break through. Pet and Anya, the twins, were once more walking on the earth, altered somewhat, thanks to Sheriff Dan Garrett and Father Denier, but nevertheless among the living—so to speak.

The human and subhuman turned their faces toward the wicked lightning and hissed and howled and chanted their pleasure.

It would be very soon.

Soon.

It made no difference that the workmen were cutting back the forest, away from the house in the woods. They were not cutting back far enough to bother those who gathered around the misty pool of light. Even if the men did try to cut further . . . well, accidents had been known to happen. Subtle accidents. Like those hunters who wandered too deeply into timber only to emerge with their minds forever altered. They looked exactly the same. But they were not.

In Lynchburg, on a bed in a darkened room, Carl Garrett tried to talk to God. He did his best to make some sense out of why he, like his father, had been chosen to fight the good fight against overwhelming odds.

If God replied, it was in a manner that Carl could not comprehend.

Yet.

Chapter 5

For the most part, it was a silent trip from Lynchburg to Richmond. Dee was determined that Carl meet her father.

"You're the boss, Dee. I go where you go."

The home—more a mansion—was in the most exclusive section of the city.

Carl found himself liking both Edgar and Louise Conners. Louise put on a few more airs than Carl was comfortable with, but Edgar was as easy to be around as any man Carl had ever seen. While mother and daughter sat in the house and talked, Carl and Edgar went for a walk.

"I think my lawyers got things all straightened out in Reeves County, Carl."

"There are things going on in Reeves County that your lawyers have no control over, Mister Conners. Not unless they have a direct line to God."

Conners pointed to chairs by the pool and both men sat down. "You want to explain that, Carl?"

Carl was silent for a moment, wondering how in the hell to explain anything this bizarre. Finally he said, "You believe in the Hereafter, Mister Conners?"

"I sure do."

"Heaven and Hell?"

"Yes."

"You believe that . . . well, old gods from long-forgotten ancient religions could resurface?"

"Ummm," Conners said, scratching his chin and giving that some thought. "For the sake of getting some sense out of you, let's say that I do."

"Mister Conners, with all your money, with all your power, and with all your connections, did you ever try to find out what really went on in Ruger County a few years back, or did you just accept what was printed in the papers and spoken about on the air?"

"I hit a stone wall, boy. I was told, damned bluntly, that if I wanted to continue receiving government work for my factories that take government contracts, I had best stop asking questions."

"You want to know what happened?"

Conners thought about that for a moment. He lifted a telephone on the table and requested coffee out by the pool. He cut his eyes to Carl. "This have anything to do with my daughter?"

"Yes."

"Very well. Wait until the coffee is served and then tell me what you know about what happened in Ruger, and what you need to deal with whatever is happening in Reeves."

"I need a miracle, sir."

"Oh, come on, son! Your boss told me you were one of the best men he had. You're awfully somber about this. What's the matter? You and Dee not getting along? She speaks very highly of you."

"We're getting along fine, sir. But it's not safe for her there."

"She isn't going to leave, Carl. That's her home. And come what may, she'll stick it out. Chow-Chow is buried there."

"Who?"

"Her dog. Some . . . damn trashy people poisoned the dog last year. You find out who did that, and there's a ten-thousand-dollar bonus in it for you."

"The law won't do anything about it, Mister Conners. It's a misdemeanor at best."

"The law, boy," Conners said in a very cold voice, "won't have a goddamn thing to do with it."

"Yes, sir." Carl's reply was softly offered.

The coffee served, and sugared and creamed and stirred, Carl said, "As close as I can figure it, from what my dad said and some others later informed me, it started just about the time Christ was born. Twins were born into this ancient religion. Two females, one in human form, the other a cat."

Ed Conners spilled coffee down the front of his shirt. He wiped at the stain with a napkin and fixed a thoroughly jaundiced set of eyes on Carl. "Are you fucking joking with me?"

"I'm fucking serious as death. Sir."

Conners refilled his cup. "Go on."

"Then the pair were entombed alive. Hundreds of years later, archeologists disturbed the burial site and unknowingly set them free. My thesis was to be on this, sir. I did a lot of research, both before and after my father died in hopes of killing the pair. I don't know whether he succeeded or not."

"Are you trying to tell me . . ." The words choked on the man's tongue. He could not force the words out of his mouth.

"That Pet and Anya are in Reeves County? I don't know."

"Pet and Anya?"

"The cat and the girl. They are one and the same. They're both shapechangers."

"You . . . want to explain that, son?"

"Each can become the other. That is when they are

51

vulnerable. Any other time, they are impossible to kill. Their cycle used to be to resurface every twenty-five years. But since another Source, or Force, has been found in Reeves County, the Old Ones are breaking free of their entombment. Believe me when I say that when they surface—"

"Wait a minute! Just hold on. Who entombed these . . . what'd you call them? The Old Ones?"

"God, I suppose."

"*God!*" Conners almost yelled the word. "When?"

"Mister Conners, I don't know. Thousands of years ago, I guess. They are almost too hideous to look upon. They're monsters. Anya called them the Master's Disciples. My dad and Father Denier sacrificed themselves, after enticing Anya and Pet onto a steel grid, allowing themselves to be electrocuted along with the horror."

"That's when the government put a lid on what happened."

"Yes, sir. If you'll wait right here, I want to get something from the car to show you."

Carl was back in a few minutes, with the jar containing the maggotlike worm. Conners took one look and shuddered.

"What is that damn thing?"

"Part of that which was entombed with the Old Ones. Enough of them can eat your leg off in minutes." He lowered his sock and showed the man his ankle, and what just one of the thumb-sized creatures of Hell could do. The wound was healing nicely, but the scar would be there forever.

It took Ed several moments to fully recover, and during those moments the enormity and the awfulness of what the young man had told him and showed him sank in. He pointed to the savage worm. "Are these things susceptible to any type of poison."

"I have absolutely no idea."

"I'd like to take this to my lab—it's located just outside of town. Let a few of my lab people do some work with it. See what they can come up with."

"I'm glad to be rid of it."

Conners lifted the phone and punched out a number, talking for a few minutes. He replaced the receiver in the cradle and looked at Carl. "Someone will be out here in a minute to get this. . . ." He cut his eyes to the snapping, maggotlike worm in the peanut-butter jar. "Whatever the hell it is. Your immediate plans, Carl?"

"With your permission, I'll stay here for a couple of days. I have a shopping list of things that I couldn't obtain, but you probably can with no trouble." He handed the man a folded sheet of paper.

Ed looked at the first item and his eyes widened. "You want a flamethrower?"

"Yes, sir. And as many full containers as you can get me."

"Do you know how to use these things?"

"No, sir. But I can learn."

"I'll show you. I handled one in the Marine Corps." He sighed and shook his head. "Boy, I'm going to ask you just one time, and I'll not bring it up again: Are you putting me on with this tale of yours?"

"No, sir. But I want you to convince Dee to stay here with you and your wife."

He shook his head. "I can try. But I can tell you the outcome before I even begin. She'll tell me to stick it in my ear."

Carl smiled. "That what she told me she'd do."

"Believe it. Of all my children, that girl has more of me in her than any of the others."

Ed loaned Carl a pickup truck from his local factory and Carl began loading the equipment as it came in. Ed pointed out that nearly everything loaded in the bed was highly illegal.

"If I get stopped and searched by a trooper, I'll just tell them I was delivering a load for you," Carl said with a grin.

"Oh, wonderful!"

"Have you told Mrs. Conners any of what's going on in Reeves?"

"No. I started to do that several times, but each time I shut my mouth before I stuck my foot in it. You do realize how farfetched your story is."

"Oh, yes. And don't think the other side doesn't know it too."

Ed leaned up against a fender of the truck. "Does the, ah, I mean, well, does the *Devil* show up for this . . . affair? Jesus, I feel like an idiot asking that!"

"I hope not," Carl told him. "It's written that no mortal can gaze upon the features of the Dark One and live."

Ed rubbed his temples with his fingertips and sighed heavily. He muttered something inaudible under his breath.

"Have you convinced Dee to stay here?" Carl asked.

"Are you kidding! I mentioned it twice. The first time she said no very sweetly. The second time around she turned the cream I had put on my cereal into buttermilk. Carl, I'm sending men into Reeves County. Their cover story will be that they're in there scouting for a plant site."

"I hope they're both tough and smart," Carl said, a note of reservation in his voice.

"They are." The older man smiled. "You remember when that nut in Iran seized American holdings and held some Conners Industries people hostage—that

54

was just before the embassy takeover?"

"Yes, sir."

"These are the same men who went in and got my people out."

Carl followed Dee back up to the Blue Ridge Mountains. With the load he was carrying—and Dee still didn't know what was under the tarp—he stayed well within the speed limit and followed all the rules. Any Virginia trooper who looked under that tarp would probably have a mild heart attack; and that would be just before he had Carl spread-eagled on the pavement with the muzzle of a pistol stuck in Carl's ear.

As they passed through Butler, Deputy Harrison passed them traveling the other way. He did not even look at them. Carl smiled, thinking: Amazing what power just one man can have.

He and Dee were both amazed at the amount of work that the crew had done in four days. The timberline had been pushed back more than five hundred feet in all directions and every scrap of brush had been cleared.

"There is no way they could have done all that in four days," Carl said in astonishment.

"Here's why," Dee said, holding up a note she'd found on the gate. "It's from the foreman. Dad sent a crew up to lend a hand." Her eyes touched his. "You want to tell me what's in the truck?"

But petting Dingo and calming him down came first. The big dog was jumping around like a young pony, so happy he was going around and around in circles.

"I never thought another dog would replace Chow-Chow," Dee said. "But I was wrong."

Dee had found a friend and protector, and Dingo had found a home.

Then Carl threw back the tarp, and when Dee's eyes finally sorted out all the cargo, her mouth dropped open.

There were cases of .223 ammo, boxes of various types of grenades, and other cases and crates that held—well, she didn't know what they held.

"Are you planning on starting a war?" she asked, finally finding her voice.

"Yes." Carl spoke the word grimly. "My own special brand of Jihad."

"That's a Holy War."

"Yes. It is. And one other thing you'd better understand, Dee—"

"I don't want to hear any further comments about me going away," she said interrupting.

"I wasn't going to say that. I was going to say that this is one Holy War we'd damn well better win. We either win it, or we die—very unpleasantly." His words were offered in a very cold manner.

Looking at the tall young man with the serious eyes, Dee finally got the last ten percent of doubt knocked out of her. She knew this was not going to be some sort of happy adventure where the good guys always win and the bad guys fall by the wayside like bowling pins and the hero sweeps the heroine up into his arms and they sail off into the sunset to live happily ever after.

"If you're trying to scare me, Carl . . . you just succeeded."

"I hope so, Dee. After the . . . horror was over, I went to a lot of funerals over in Ruger County. Some of the caskets were empty."

"Why?"

"Because either the dead were eaten, or we couldn't

find all the pieces."

Dee had helped him unload the equipment—in silence. His words had touched her and affected her as he had hoped they would. They stacked the equipment in the huge den; actually about sixty percent of the entire lower floor was the den.

"Sit down, Dee," Carl told her. "It's classroom time."

She sat down, hands in her lap, and looked at him.

"Can you shoot any type of firearm?"

"Because of our wealth, with the constant threat of kidnapping or being killed by some nut who resents the rich, Daddy made all of us learn weaponry. I am competent with a pistol, rifle, and shotgun."

"You have weapons in this house?"

"I have a shotgun in the closet and a handgun in my nightstand."

"Loaded?"

"Of course not!"

"Then they're not worth a damn for anything except throwing at your assailant. You might as well be armed with a fly-swatter."

"I could bluff them with the guns!" She said indignantly, sticking out her chin.

"You don't bluff with a gun, Dee. Either you're going to use it, or you're not. Don't ever pick up a gun in any bad situation unless you're mentally prepared to use it. You try to bluff someone with a gun, and odds are you're gong to wind up badly hurt or dead. My father preached that to us all our lives. There are no little kids in this house, so there is no point, conditions being what they are—and about to get worse—why your weapons shouldn't be ready to use. Go get them and let's see what you can do with them."

She was a surprisingly good shot with the pistol, a

57

Colt Diamondback .38-caliber with a four-inch barrel. The shotgun was a Browning pump, twelve-gauge. Carl loaded the pistol with hollow-nose ammunition and the shotgun with buckshot.

"If they get into the house," Carl told her, "grab that shotgun first." Then he added, "It makes a big mess, but that buckshot will sure stop somebody."

Back in the house, Dee clicked on the radio, set to a local station. They both paused as the announcer read the local news.

"The body of lifelong resident, Mrs. Ermma Barstow, was discovered about noon today by boys out hiking. Local law-enforcement personnel are being very quiet about the condition of the body, but the boys reportedly said it looked like she had been attacked by a bear. They further stated that parts of the old woman were scattered over a wide area and that she had been eaten. To compound the mystery, the boys also said there was a very foul odor lingering in the woods near Mrs. Barstow's body, and that the odor did not come from the mangled remains. We'll bring you further news of this tragedy as we receive it."

Carl walked to the window and looked out at that part of the woods where he had wandered for several hours. He glanced back at Dee. "It's begun."

Chapter 6

Sheriff Rodale had looked at the ripped and scattered remains of Mrs. Barstow and had almost thrown up. He had seen all kinds of sights over the long years behind a badge, but he could truthfully say that he had never seen anything quite like this.

Deputy Hotdog Harrison had upchucked his lunch. The chief deputy, Jim Hunt, who really ran the sheriff's office, and who despised Sheriff Rodale with as much intensity as a mongoose hates a cobra, knelt down beside the torso of the woman.

Rodale walked up and squatted down like a fat frog. "What'd you think, Jim?"

Jim looked around him; the other deputies were busy securing the area, marking off the locations of various body parts, and taking pictures of the scene.

"We don't want this made public, Ned. Not just yet."

"What made public?"

"Her heart's been torn out."

Rodale looked, swallowed hard. "Why would a bear tear out the heart?"

"No bear done this," the chief deputy said. "Those are human teeth marks."

"Great God Almighty!" Rodale said in a hoarse whisper. "You mean a human bein' ate on the poor old woman?"

"Yes. And not a very large human. More like a child. And look here," he said, pointing with the tip of a pencil. "Those are paw prints of a cat. And right there"—he pointed to the ravaged piece of the body—"is where the cat ate."

"What are these little black specks all around the body and on the body and everywhere else?" Rodale said, pointing a finger.

"I don't know. They look like flecks of something that's been burned. And here is something else that puzzles me. Those are some sort of footprints leading away from the body and into the woods. But this left print doesn't have a big toe, and the right print is minus a couple of other toes. The paw prints are deformed. I never seen anything like it."

The lawman in Rodale surfaced, overriding the man's normal laziness and indifference. "Damn rough country to go barefoot. Boys!" he called to his deputies. "Not a word about this to anybody. Any statements got to come from Jim here. Anybody who talks is fired that day and I'll run his ass out of the county."

"Newspeople from Lynchburg and Charlottesville is gonna be all over this place in a few hours," Jim noted. "I'll get the coroner to do an autopsy and then have him seal the casket."

"What you think, Jim?" In all matters concerning law enforcement, Rodale always deferred to his chief deputy.

"Satanism, I reckon. I always knowed it would someday come to Reeves. It was just a matter of time. It's everywhere else."

Jim Hunt slaughtered the English language, but it was not due to ignorance. He was a very well-read man and highly intelligent. He was a hillbilly and proud of it. He was comfortable with his colloquial-

60

isms, and anybody who didn't like it could go sit on a candlestick as far as he was concerned.

But unlike Rodale, Jim was not on the take from anybody and never had been. He was a God-fearing Baptist, and not only enforced the law, but obeyed it.

Both the laws of God and the laws of man.

He had stayed on with Sheriff Ned Rodale through the worst of times for the simple reason that he knew if he left, Reeves County would have no law enforcement. It galled him that Rodale was such a spiritually weak, immoral man. But, Jim reckoned, everybody had a cross to bear, and Rodale was his.

Jim, alone with the torso now—Rodale had waddled off, chewing antacid tablets and belching—again looked at what was really puzzling: The footprints and paw prints turned bloody about twenty feet from the torso; not coming toward it, but going away from it. He would have normally checked that off as both human and animal wading through the blood around the torso, but he didn't believe that to be the case this time. There just wasn't that much blood in or around the parts. And it looked to Jim like it had been lapped up.

And something else: The prints seemed to be more firmly placed as they left the scene. Around the torso, the prints seemed to be staggered and wavy—no, that wasn't the right choice of words. Shaky instead of wavy. As if the pair of them were weak before they attacked the body, and then gained strength after—he swallowed hard—dining.

Jim got an evidence bag and tweezers and small brush from his kit and began gathering up the strange black flecks from on and all around the body. He would send them to the lab and see what the lab boys could come up with.

Calvin Bartlett, the county coroner, arrived at the

scene, looked at the scattered body parts, and knelt down beside Jim. "No bear did this, Jim."

"I know."

"What does Rodale think?"

"Rodale doesn't think. After twenty-five years in law enforcement, I doubt he could lift a print. Man can judge the quality of the sheriff by his deputies. Take a look at Harry Harrison and add it up."

Calvin smiled. "Word is that Wilber Purdy told Rodale to hang it up. This would be his last term in office."

"So I heard."

"And that you're going to be the next sheriff of Reeves County."

"I ain't heard that."

"Would you take the nomination if offered?"

"Don't know." He pointed to the torso. "Heart's been tore out."

"Have you found it?"

"No. I reckon it was eat by whoever done this."

"Devil-worshippers?"

"That's what I told Ned. Now maybe he'll go on back to the office so's I can get on with the investigation and find out something."

"You don't believe it was devil-worshippers?"

"I don't know what I believe, Calvin. Only thing I do know for sure about this mess is that I ain't never seen nothin' like this here in my whole life."

"What is that you have in the evidence bag?"

Jim held it up for the man to see. "I don't know what it is. Something burned, I think. Here, you take it and see what you think it is."

The coroner went to work and Jim eased that prickly sensation tingling the back of his neck by slowly turning his head and putting woods-wise eyes to the dark timber. Somebody, or some *thing*, was out there, watching the proceedings.

Jim deliberately turned his head. The sensation only intensified. "Evil," he muttered. "It's evil."

"That was my father," Dee said, replacing the receiver. "That . . . horrible-looking worm you gave him died this afternoon. And not from testing."

"That's not good, Dee. I told your father that I remembered Doctor Goodson, up in Ruger County, saying that they had a life span of about twenty-four hours. This means the species has toughened, with a life span of about a week."

"And that's bad, right?"

"How'd you like to see about ten thousand of those things crawling toward you?"

She shuddered.

"Right. I also told your father that nothing except fire or crushing them would stop them. But he wanted his people to try."

"And now we . . . do what?"

"Wait for them to come to us. I'm not going back into those woods unless it's absolutely essential."

"The reason you had Daddy get the flamethrowers . . . the worms, right?"

Carl smiled, and it was not a pretty smile. "That's one of the reasons, Dee. Fire will stop just about anything that walks."

"You said electricity killed the girl and the cat, right?"

Carl sighed. "Presumably, Dee. But when you're dealing with the supernatural . . ." He shrugged his shoulders.

The two forms materialized into human shapes.

63

Sort of. They were charred black. When they walked, tiny flakes of destroyed flesh sloughed off their bodies and fell to the ground. It was very difficult to tell exactly what they were. They appeared to be sightless; they were certainly hairless.

In earthly shape, both were horribly deformed. They lurched and staggered as they walked. Since the lips, along with the hair and the eyes and most of the flesh, had been burned away by the millions of volts of electricity that surged through their bodies while they were in earthly form, the teeth of the girl and the fangs of the cat were forever visible and glistening wetly.

It had taken the girl, Anya, and her other self, the cat, Pet, several years to gain the strength to once more test their powers in earthly form. The ancient gods, the Old Ones, had died on that voltage-charged grid in Ruger County. That tremendous surge had mutilated bodies, ruined flesh, and caused months of anguish for Anya and Pet.

But it had not destroyed them. Nor had it destroyed their hate.

Their limitless hate had only intensified as the months festered by and they agonized among the for-ever-damned in the dead and rotting darkness of the netherworld.

Now they were back. And they knew that the son of the man who had devastated their original plans and who had come very close to destroying them was near. The young man had made his silly and ridiculously human preparations for war. No matter. He would not succeed. Reeves County had been carefully and qui-etly and insidiously nurtured for this moment of tri-umph.

For the past three years the forces emanating from the dark side of life had been cultivating those who dared enter the woods under whose ground lay another pocket of old gods, lying in wait for the moment when they too would be called forth.

And that moment was very near.

Anya and Pet stopped, detecting the nearness of human life.

The flesh of that stupid and Bible-spouting old woman had been nourishing, but it was not nearly enough. In their weakened form, Pet and Anya needed flesh and blood daily to maintain them.

They sensed that much-needed nourishment was very close by.

They waited. Two charred and grotesque creatures from a world that had survived everything God and His people on earth could hurl at them over the eons.

A poacher slipped through the woods, his rifle at the ready, his eyes searching for a deer to kill. He stepped into a small clearing, and the pair leaped, Pet's teeth ripping into the throat of the man. His scream turned into a bubbling gurgle as his blood gushed forth, to be eagerly lapped up by Pet and Anya.

Anya's charred hands tore at the chest of the man. The girl, subhumanly strong, ripped open the chest cavity and tore out the still-beating heart.

She shared the life-sustaining organ with Pet. Then they dined on the liver and the kidneys before shredding long strips of flesh, stuffing them greedily into their mouths.

Blood began leaking from the open lesions on the charred bodies as the twin horrors gained new strength while dining on the flesh and sucking the blood from the dead poacher. They cracked bones and sucked marrow from them.

All around them, the forest had grown silent, as animals lay very still in their burrows and dens and nests, sensing that danger was near.

In a feeding frenzy, Anya and Pet, now covered with blood, scattered bits and pieces of the man as they chomped and tore and cracked and sucked. Then, with new strength filling them, they moved on through the timber and over the ridges.

At the hospital in Butler, Doctor Calvin Bartlett pulled back from the microscope, his eyes wide in shock and disbelief.

The tissue taken from the mangled carcass of the woman was thriving with life cells! But unlike any that Calvin had ever seen.

How could that be?

Surely his eyes were playing tricks on him.

He put fresh samples on the slide and fixed the glass in place, checking again.

He straightened up, shaking his head in disbelief.

Behind him, on the metal table where the various parts of the Barstow woman were scattered, a hand began to move, the fingers wriggling as new life reached them.

Bartlett sensed motion behind him and turned, his heart rate picking up. Nothing. He silently berated himself for behaving in a most unprofessional manner and returned to the microscope, hoping that he would not again view the impossible.

But there it was.

He straightened up, hearing a very odd sound. It sounded like . . . purring.

Scratch. Purr.

"What the hell?" Bartlett muttered, looking all around him.

But the lab was empty, except for the ravaged body of the woman and the slightly rattled doctor.

He returned to his work, not seeing that the eyes in the severed head had opened and were staring at his back, that the lips had curved in a macabre grin.

Scratch. Purr.

"Now damnit!" Bartlett said.

He walked to the door and jerked it open. Nothing. He looked up and down the corridor. It was empty. Then the doctor took a deep breath of air and instantly regretted it.

"Phew!" Calvin said, the stench filling his nose. "Time to call the plumber!"

He shut the door.

Scratch. Purr.

The sound was coming from the other side of the room.

"Sick and tired of this," the doctor muttered, as he walked past the table, heading for the opposite side of the room. "Wow!" he yelled, jumping about two feet in the air as something gave him a sharp goose right in the crack of his ass.

"All right," Calvin said, rubbing his butt. "Who's in here playing games?"

Scratch. Purr.

Now the sound was once more coming from behind the door leading to the hall.

Calvin was thirty-eight years old and had been practicing medicine in Reeves County since he'd gotten out of school. He was slow to anger and not a person that was easily spooked.

But he was spooked.

He fought back his alarm. Then something moved on the table filled with body parts.

But that was impossible.

He came very close to screaming as his eyes settled on a severed hand.

The hand had closed into a fist, with the middle

67

finger extended.

Old Lady Barstow was giving him the bird.

Chapter 7

"That's obscene," Jim Hunt said, staring at the rigid digit from Mrs. Barstow's right hand. "Did you try to fix it right?"

Calvin gave him a look that would frost glass. "I most certainly did not! Not after she goosed me."

Jim sighed and shoved his cowboy hat back on his head. Jim's frame was just about as spare as his small talk, but his leanness was all muscle and gristle and bone. "Now Cal . . . that there hand didn't goose you, boy. And as far as that finger bein' stuck up like that . . . well, that's just the rigors settin' in, that's all."

"Right," Cal said dryly.

Jim turned around and almost jumped out of his boots.

Old Lady Barstow's eyes were wide open and staring straight at him. One eyelid dropped in a macabre wink.

Cal smiled thinly. "That reflex is not unknown in death, Jim," he said, needling the man.

"Gave me a start, that's all," the chief deputy mumbled.

"Right."

Jim sat down. "What about this livin'-tissue business, Cal?"

69

"It's not just tissue. I can't explain the cells. They aren't human. Or animal, for that matter. There is no discoloration in the mucous membranes of the mouth, lips, or nail beds. There is no lack of corneal reflex. Her eyes move. Now Jim, she doesn't have any blood in her body, or darn little of it, so that explains the absence of cyanosis. I think," he added.

"What do you mean you think?"

"I've never seen anything like this. I don't know what to make of it. Look at her right hand, Jim."

Jim looked. The middle finger was waggling first at Jim, and then at Cal.

"That old woman was one of them Holy Rollers, Cal. Spoke in tongues and such as that. I'd wager she never made no obscene gesture in her life."

"What are you getting at, Jim?"

Jim dismissed it with a wave of his hand. "What I'm thinkin' is too silly to talk about. What about that black stuff I give you?"

"Burned flesh."

"Say what?"

"Burned dead skin."

"That don't make no sense. There wasn't no fire nowheres close to where we found the body."

"That's what it is."

Jim sighed and looked over at the head. Ermma Barstow gave him another wink.

Jim shook his head, pointed a finger, and said, "She starts talkin', Cal, that door over yonder is mine!"

"One thing about you," Dee pointed out. "You have to be the most patient man I have ever seen."

Carl drained his coffee mug. "When it starts, Dee, there won't be much time for resting." He looked off to the south.

"What's the matter?"

"Vultures gathering over there. And a lot of them. Something large dead in the woods."

"Like another dead body?"

"I'd bet on it."

"You want some more coffee?"

"I think not. I'd suggest a nap. Tonight might be sort of busy."

"I guess that's one way of describing it," Dee replied, her eyes on the circling vultures, about three quarters of a mile from the A-frame, moving closer to the earth.

The jailer at the Reeves County Jail wrinkled his nose as that foul odor once more drifted to him. He couldn't figure out the source, but it seemed to be coming from that row of cells where they put the really bad ones. Only one prisoner was housed there now. Josh Taft. The jailer hoped the smell choked Josh to death. Even by Sheriff Rodale's standards, Josh was a total no-good. Child-molester, wife-beater, rapist, thief . . . the list was as long as your arm.

This time he was in jail waiting trial for rape, and the judge had already said he was going to put Josh away for the rest of his life as an habitual offender. Even the scalawags in the county all agreed that it was about time.

"Hey, lard-ass!" Josh yelled at the jailer, his voice bouncing off the steel and concrete of the cell block. "You gonna do something about this smell? This ain't constitutional making me sit here and smell this shit! I'll call my lawyer about this."

"Shut up, Taft," the jailer yelled. "We're workin' on it."

"Well, you ain't workin' fast enough, John. I'll sue

71

the county for violatin' my rights."

"Screw your rights, you baby-raper," John muttered, walking to the radio room to answer a call from a county unit. He keyed the mike. "Go ahead, R-10."

"R-2 there?"

"Ten-fifty. He's still over at the lab."

"Buzzards circling over here on the Conners property. 'Bout a mile north from the woman's house. I'll be out of the unit to check on it."

"That's ten-four, R-10."

John logged the call, then picked up a can of room deodorant and sprayed the air. It helped, but that awful smell still lingered.

Mike Randall left his unit and climbed the fence, heading toward the circling buzzards. He felt pretty sure it was a dead deer or hog, maybe, but after seeing what was left of Ermma Barstow, he felt he had to check it out.

The deputy snapped loose the thumb-break leather that covered the hammer of his .357. He had no idea what he might be walking into.

The first thing he noticed was a rifle, a .270 it looked like, wrapped around the trunk of a small tree. It was horseshoed around the tree.

No mortal man could do that. Had to have been a bear, and a damn big one.

Mike jerked his .357 from leather as his nose began picking up the unmistakable and very distinctive odor of death.

Then his eyes found the scattered bits and pieces of the man.

He swallowed hard as bile filled his throat, and he began backing out of the woods. "Steady, boy," he said, calming himself. "Just stay cool and keep your head."

His eyes lifted and found the head of the man, jammed on a broken limb, the eyes wide and staring in silent horror.

Mike lost his cool and took off running, back toward his unit. He ran about a hundred yards, losing his hat but regaining his composure. He didn't want to sound chickenshit when he called in.

Calvin answered the call, listened grim-faced, and then hung up. "Mike Randall found another one, Jim. On the Conners property. Just north of the house."

Jim had moved to the table containing the head and various other body parts. He was leaning against the edge of the steel table.

"Yowee!" he hollered, jumping into the air as cold, bony fingers groped at his crotch. He slapped the hand away, bouncing it off the tiled floor.

"Hi, big boy," the head of Ermma croaked out hoarsely. "Why don't you come up and see me sometime? A hard man is good to find."

Cal put all the body parts in a cooler and locked and sealed it. Jim refused to touch any of the various pieces, especially the head, which did not utter another word nor give any sign that it ever had spoken.

Dee woke Carl, who had fallen asleep on the couch. "Sheriff's department car just pulled up out front, Carl."

Carl sat up and stuck the 9-mm back into the leather of his shoulder holster and went out to meet Mike Randall.

Mike, with all the other deputies, had already been briefed by the chief deputy on the tall young man who was staying at the Conners house. He looked with

73

open envy first at Garrett's Beretta model 92 hanging in leather in the shoulder holster—the model 92 could bang fifteen times before having to change clips. Then Mike looked at Dee, standing by the young man's side. Envy deepened.

"Sheriff Rodale wanted me to stop by here and tell y'all we got some sort of nut wanderin' in the woods around here. We found another body."

"Over where the vultures were circling?" Carl asked.

"Yeah." He cut his eyes to Dingo. "That's a mean-lookin' dog."

"He won't bother you as long as one of us is here," Mike said, assuring him.

"Would you like to come in and have some coffee, deputy?" Dee asked. Mike was one of the nicer people on the Reeves County S.O.

"That would be nice, ma'am. Thank you. It sure has been a long day. Let me radio in my twenty and I'll be right with you."

"He dates a real nice girl," Dee told Carl, as the deputy called in his location. "Judy Radisson. She's been out here several times. She heads the local writers group. Maybe we could have them out for a cookout."

"Suits me. You're the boss."

She smiled. "All business, aren't you, Carl?"

He locked glances with her. "I'm susceptible to a little playtime every now and then."

"Then I'll invite them here for tomorrow night."

"I cook a mean steak."

"I'll hold you to that."

Mike stopped dead in his tracks when he spotted the boxes of .223 ammo stacked in the den, along with the other crates.

"Y'all gonna start a war?"

"The war has already started, Mike," Carl said. "I

74

just like to be prepared."

Dee stepped in before Mike could jump on that statement. "What do you take in your coffee, Mike?"

"Uh . . . cream and sugar. What do you mean the war has started, Carl?"

"Was the second body much like the first one, Mike?"

Mike thought about that for a few seconds. If he opened his mouth about the case—cases now—the chief deputy would jump all over his ass.

"It's all right," Carl said. "I understand that you can't talk about it. So I'll tell you: arms and legs and feet and hands and entrails scattered all over the place; the body ripped apart by someone with enormous strength. The heart is missing. The kidneys and liver eaten. Most of the blood drained from the body and the bones cracked open, the marrow sucked from them. I've seen it before."

"I think . . . that you need to talk to the chief deputy, Carl. You seem to know a lot about this." Mike sat down on one of the couches, setting the coffee mug on the coffee table.

"I'll be happy to talk to him. Dee has told me that he's a good, solid, steady man. Not at all like Sheriff Rodale."

"I can't say anything about Rodale. But you got Jim Hunt pegged right." Then the young deputy put it all together. "Is this the way it started in Ruger County?"

"More or less."

"I never got the straight of what happened over there. I don't guess anybody did. Miss Conners, don't judge the whole department by the actions of Harrison and a few of the others. Jim Hunt is gradually getting rid of people like them. Law enforcement is getting better around here. I'm gonna take a chance, Carl. You best not talk to Sheriff Rodale. Whatever you got

75

to say, it better be said to Jim Hunt."

"All right. You going back up to the crime scene?"

"Right."

"Would you tell this Jim Hunt I'd like to speak to him?"

"Be glad to. What's in all these boxes?"

"Oh, just a few supplies I felt we might need."

"Sure," the deputy said, his tone indicating that he didn't believe a word of it.

"Boxes of .223 ammo, huh?" Jim asked.

"Yes, sir. And a lot of other stuff all crated up. I think he knows something that we ought to know."

"If he's anything like his daddy, he's a good, decent young man. What was your impression, Mike?"

The young deputy didn't hesitate. "I'd hate to mess with him, Chief. He's a real soft-spoken sort of guy. So tall and lanky that unless you take a good long second look, you'd guess his weight twenty-five, thirty pounds lighter than it really is. And he's got a mean look in his eyes. I think he'd be hard to handle you get him stirred up."

"Just like his daddy. Let's go."

Mike honked the horn to let them know they were outside and to please do something with that cockeyed dog with the head like a bear. Dee came out, petted Dingo, and opened the gate. Dingo took his time smelling Jim, which did nothing to calm the man. The dog finally stepped back and sat down right in the middle of the walkway, looking at the chief deputy.

"I guess we walk around him," Mike said.

"I knew that without askin'," Jim replied, stepping off onto the grass.

Dingo beat them to the porch and plopped down in front of the door. Dee manhandled him and dragged him away, then waved the men in.

Mike had never been in the service, but Jim had. He noticed some of the boxes stacked around the room. Grenades.

Dee had made a fresh pot of coffee and she served them just as the sun was sinking, casting long shadows around the Blue Ridge Mountains.

Jim noticed that with the coming of darkness, Carl's eyes occasionally shifted to the windows. He wondered who the young man was expecting—*what* might be more like it. He crossed his legs, remembering Ermma's bony fingers at his privates.

"I told Doctor Cal Bartlett to come on down here," Jim said. "He ought to be here in about five minutes. I hope you don't mind, Miss Conners."

"Not at all, Chief Deputy Hunt."

"Please call me Jim, ma'am."

"Only if you'll quit calling me ma'am and Miss Conners," she said with a smile. "Call me Dee."

"I'll do that, ma' . . . Dee. Cal is the county coroner," Jim explained to Carl.

"Then I'll wait until he gets here," Carl said, his voice soft. "No point is saying things twice."

"I ain't familiar with that type of grenade." Jim pointed to several boxes stacked in a corner. "Except they're all illegal as heck in civilian hands."

"Those are Fire-Frag grenades, Chief. Probably the most lethal grenades ever manufactured. Once you pull the pin, you're holding a pint-sized Claymore."

"You figure you'll have to use them things, Carl?"

"Yes."

Man ain't too long on words, Jim concluded. And he agreed with Mike's earlier assessment of Carl Garrett. Carl was very worldly to be so young. It showed in his eyes and mannerisms. But what the hell was he doing with all these explosives . . . and whatever was in all those other boxes and crates? If Rodale was to get wind of all this stuff he'd have him chunk the young man in jail.

What the hell was goin' on in Reeves County?

A car pulled up outside. Jim looked up, spotting the car through the glass of the storm door. "That's Cal."

Dee walked to the door and told Dingo to stay in the house. "I'll let him in."

Introductions made and coffee poured, the doctor looked at Carl. "Mike says you described the condition of both bodies without ever seeing them. I'd be interested in knowing just how you did that."

"I saw the same thing in Ruger County, about four years ago."

Scratch. Purr.

Dingo raised his head and looked toward the back. He did not growl.

Cal jerked at the noise, almost spilling some of the coffee.

"Relax," Carl told them all. "There is nothing out there that you can see. Yet," he added.

Dingo rose to his paws and walked to the back door, the hair on his back bristling. Still, he did not growl.

"We'll get back to them strange sounds in a minute," Jim said. "Carl, just what did you see in Ruger County?"

Carl spoke the word without emotion. But it chilled the three men to the bone.

"Hell."

Chapter 8

After a few questions directed toward Jim and the doctor, Carl began speaking. He spoke for fifteen minutes, nonstop. He was not interrupted at any time. Mike, Jim, and Calvin sat with a mixture of shock and disbelief on their faces.

Carl ended with: "My father didn't die in vain; he destroyed the Old Ones and temporarily put Pet and Anya out of business. But they're back."

"Who's back?" Jim blurted.

"The girl and her sister. Anya and Pet. That would account for the pieces of charred flesh you found around the bodies."

"I think you're crazy!" Cal told him. "The entire tale is insane—impossible."

"So is a talking head and a severed hand shooting you the bird and grabbing a feel of Jim's privates."

Jim blushed.

"I've reached the conclusion that neither of us heard that head talk," Cal said smugly.

"Oh?"

"Yes. We were both under a great deal of stress and our imaginations simply ran rampant for a moment."

"I'm sure that explains it. And the bizarre actions of that severed hand?"

"The hand fell off the table. It was not a deliberate movement."

"The waggling middle finger?"

The doctor sighed. "It can all be explained."

"Yes. I just did."

Darkness now walked around the house, shooing away the last vestiges of light.

"Not to satisfy my mind, you didn't," Cal said, challenging him.

Scratch. Purr.

"I suppose the wind—which isn't blowing—is causing that noise," Carl said with a smile.

None of the three men said anything.

"There is another thing you have to worry about," Carl said. "The press. I'm surprised they aren't in here now. One more mangled body and they'll be swarming all over this county."

"We aren't going to release the name of the latest . . . victim," Cal said. "He was a bachelor who lived along the ridges. I'm not sure he even had any relatives."

"That'll work for awhile. But the killing has just begun. Killing is only a part of what you'll be up against. Just a scratch from one of these creatures can cause a horrible metamorphosis in humans. Believe me, I saw it with my own eyes in Ruger County. So did my mother and sister, Captain Taylor of the Highway Patrol, Doctors Bennett and Goodson, and a lot of other people. You may call me a liar, but all of us can't be lying. Think about it." Before they could respond, Carl added, "And if you're so sure I'm fabricating all this, Doctor Bartlett, come out tomorrow morning and take a stroll in those woods over there." He pointed.

Cal said nothing.

"Can you explain the cells you viewed under a

microscope?" Carl asked, challenging him. "You'll find the same cells in the bits and pieces of the man killed today. Burn those body parts, Doctor. Destroy them before they destroy you."

"That is ridiculous!" Cal snapped. "Nonsense. I've got a call in to a forensic lab in Richmond. A friend of mine will be coming in early tomorrow. He'll get to the bottom of this very quickly, I assure you of that."

Carl spread his hands. "I tried," he said softly. "You're just going to have to see for yourself."

Jim stood up. "We'll not speak of this outside this house, gentlemen. Word gets out about . . . spooks and hants and hobgobblins and the supernatural, we'll have a panic on our hands. Worse than that, we'll have all sorts of nuts and kooks and so forth coming into the county. I don't want that. First order of business is to catch whoever is killing these folks."

"Oh, don't worry about doing that, Chief," Carl said without getting up. "They'll find you. Bet on that."

"Superstitious nonsense!" Cal said, and walked out on the porch, Jim right behind him.

"We'll see you and Judy tomorrow night, Mike," Dee said.

"We'll be here." The young deputy walked out to join the chief and the doctor. He closed the door behind him.

By his car, Jim said to Mike, "I want everything you can get me on Carl Garrett and what happened over there in Ruger County."

"You're not buying any of that crap, are you?" Cal asked.

"I don't know—yet. But you're not going to tell me that head didn't talk and that hand didn't grab at my dork and that middle finger didn't wave at both of us."

Mike stood by silently. He'd only heard about the head that talked and the hand that grabbed at Jim's

81

dick a few minutes before, in the house. As far as he was concerned, he believed Carl Garrett.

And he had a hunch the chief deputy did too.

"Jim, I don't know what to believe; except I most adamantly do *not* believe all that voodoo-monster business Garrett was trying to hand us."

"That's too bad, Cal."

"Oh?"

"Yeah. 'Cause I just made up my mind. I believe him."

Mike sighed with relief.

As soon as Cal unlocked the door to his lab, he stopped and Jim ran right into him.

"What's the matter?" the chief deputy asked.

"Something's wrong."

"Well, turn on the darn lights and let's see what it is."

Cal fumbled for the switch and flooded the lab with brightness.

Both men stared in silent disbelief.

The door to the slide-out cooler that had contained the various pieces of Ermma Barstow was shattered open. The head and hands were gone.

"How?" Cal managed to say.

Jim pointed to a security window set high off the floor, near the ceiling. The glass was smashed. "That's how."

"But why would somebody want to break in here and just steal body parts?"

"Nobody broke in, Cal. If that was the case, the way that window is shattered, there would be busted glass on the floor."

"What are you telling me, Jim?"

"Look at the door to the cooler. See the way the

door is U'd. That means it was broken out of, not into."

Cal started stuttering.

Jim patted him on the shoulder. "You wasn't busted into, Cal. You was broken out of."

"They didn't believe you?" Dee said.

"Mike did, and so did the chief deputy, if I read him right."

"And what will tonight bring?"

Carl cut his eyes from her to the window. "Terror."

The domestic animals in and around the town of Butler were the first to sense that something was very wrong. Dogs and cats that usually roamed for an hour or so before returning to the porches and doghouses and yards of their owners remained at home. And as is so common among pet owners, who generally take their pets for granted, the men and women and kids did not notice any difference in their animals.

The evening meal over, the families began settling down in front of TV sets, unaware of the evil that lurked and slithered and moved on silent paws just outside the squares of light the windows cast feebly upon the night.

But the dogs and cats noticed. Dogs and cats who normally hated and fought each other now lay together on porches, under porches, in doghouses, and in bushes around their owners' homes. And they were silent. No barking, no growling or hissing. They lay together in silent but very attentive wait.

The chief of police of Butler, Max Bancroft, stepped out onto his front porch for a breath of fresh air. He dearly loved boiled cabbage and cornbread, but it sure stunk up the house. He almost tripped over his dog, Beau, who was lying close to the front door.

"What's the matter, boy?" Max spoke gently to the animal. "You getting too old for the nightly chase?"

The setter looked up at him.

Max then noticed the animal's food bowl. The food was untouched.

"Off your feed too, huh, Beau?" He took a deep breath and grimaced as a foul odor filled his nostrils. "Jesus Christ! Ten times worse out here than in the house."

A scream of agony cut the stillness of the night.

Max jerked in surprise and stepped back into the house, getting his pistol from the holster that always hung on a peg just inside the door.

"What was that awful sound?" his wife, Doreen, asked, coming out of the kitchen.

"Sounded like a scream. I'll check it out." He held the door open. "You come inside, Beau. Stay in here. I'll be back in a few minutes, Doreen."

He stepped off the proch and began walking up the sidewalk, toward where he believed the scream had originated. Neighbors had gathered on porches and in the front yards.

"Just stay close to home," Max told his friends and neighbors. "If I need help, I'll give a holler. I don't want a bunch of people out here; I might shoot the wrong person."

"What's this I hear about another body being found up on the ridges, Max?"

"Yeah. It's true. We got a nut on the loose. That scream come from the Geason house, didn't it?"

"Sounded like it."

"Stay put. I might want you to call in and get a unit over here."

"I'll do 'er, Max. I'll stay right here in the yard and

84

listen for you."

Max Bancroft was not above fixing a ticket for a friend, or taking a fifth of whiskey as a gift. He knew that Sheriff Rodale was a jerk and law enforcement in Reeves County was a joke, but it wasn't a joke in Butler. Not to Max. Max was a pretty good cop. His town force was small, but they were nearly all good people. With the exception of Benny Carter. Benny was pretty much a jerk, with more muscle than brains, and liked to bounce people around. The only reason he still wore a badge was that the people he hammered on were white trash and troublemakers who usually deserved it. But Max knew that someday Benny would bust up the wrong person and there'd be hell to pay. He would have fired him years ago, 'cept he felt sorry for Benny's wife and kids. Max didn't think Benny could do anything else other than wear a badge. And that was a pretty sorry reflection on the profession.

But someday Benny would go too far with the wrong person.

Max stopped in front of the Geason house. Some kind of funny noise seemed to be coming from inside. He listened. The damn night was hot, and very oppressive; hard to breathe.

Max couldn't figure out if the noise was coming from a human or an animal.

Something crashed inside the house. Maybe Ralph Geason was beating up on his wife, but that wasn't very likely. Ralph was such a mousy kind of guy. Could be that Alice was whippin' Ralph's ass. That was more like it.

They were some kind of related to a family over in Ruger County. Had a young woman visiting them. Linda something or the other. Good-lookin' young woman, but sort of strange-acting. Beau didn't like

85

her at all. Growled every time she walked past the house. And that wasn't like Beau. The setter usually liked everybody and everybody liked him. Even the cat didn't like the visiting young woman. Arched her back and hissed and spat whenever Linda came into sight. A fellow could add all that up and it come out to be strange.

A crash followed by a moan drifted out to Max. "Call the station, Bob!" Max yelled. "Tell them to get a unit over here right now!"

Max hesitated for a couple of seconds, then said to hell with it and plunged alone into the unknown.

Mayor Purdy stepped out of his house to stand for a moment on the front porch; let that wonderful meal his Meg had cooked digest. They had colored help around the house during the day, but Meg insisted — despite their wealth — on preparing the evening meal herself. And now that the kids were all grown up and moved away, she insisted that they dine together.

Then that awful smell he'd experienced down at the jail wafted to his nostrils.

"Phew!" He fanned the air with a hand, thinking that it couldn't be just coming from the sheriff's department. No one could stay in the building long enough to get anything done . . . not that much got done anyway, he thought.

Something flitting through the shadows by the shrubbery turned his head. Wilber squinted his eyes. "What the hell was that?" he muttered.

The tall, thick running hedge had been planted behind a six-foot brick and wrought-iron fence; brick built up two feet off the ground and the wrought-iron fence extending four feet above that. The individual bars were four inches apart. Take a mighty skinny fellow to slip through that.

But Wilber had a moment of fear thinking that what he'd see was not human. What made it stick so in his mind was the additional thought that it wasn't animal either.

But it had to be one or the other. Didn't it?

Scratch. Purr.

The sounds turned Wilber around and around on the porch, looking in all directions. Their two house cats had taken off like a shot, diving under a low wicker table, and from all indications, they weren't about to come out anytime soon.

That fleeting, flickering shadow slipped in and out of what light shone out from inside the house.

"Meg!" Wilber called. "Bring me my shotgun, will you, honey. And a handful of shells too."

Wilber always kept the shotgun loaded up, but without a round in the chamber. He chambered a round and shoved another into the tube. That brought him up to five three-inch magnum rounds. Double-ought buckshot. "Go on back inside, Mother," he told his wife. "And get ready to turn on all the outside floods when I holler."

"What is it, Will?"

"I don't know, dear. Go on. Sing out when you're ready."

Wilber Purdy stepped off the porch and into the foul-smelling darkness.

On the other side of town, Sheriff Rodale pushed back his chair from the supper table and belched loudly, causing his long-suffering wife to cringe as she stood by the dishwasher in the kitchen.

"Fine eats there, Betty May!" he hollered. Then he lifted his leg and farted.

The dog got up from the dining room floor, a pained expression on its face, and left the room.

In the kitchen, Betty shuddered. Why, she asked herself — had to be a million times, at least — had she ever married that slob?

She'd known for years of his womanizing. He always had him a high-yellow gal stashed someplace in the county. She and Ned hadn't shared the same bed in more than ten years. He was a womanizer, he was totally obnoxious when he drank — which was every night — and he was a thief. Only God knew how much he'd stolen over the years and carefully hidden away in airtight jars in a dozen locations around the county.

And he was a slob. A redneck, white-trash slob. Had the manners of a hungry hog come slop-time. And he also beat Betty periodically. To keep her in line.

That was the main reason she hadn't left him. If she did, he had warned repeatedly, he would kill her.

And she believed him, for she knew there was a lot of blood on her husband's hands. Back in the early days, his enemies, real and imagined, had had a nasty habit of just disappearing, never to be seen again. All that had stopped a long time back, but the memories were still long and strong, and the hill people in the county pretty much did what Ned Rodale said. That was where his base was — through a combination of fear and the fact that he was one of them. The townspeople always voted against him.

Her husband had kept records over the long years. He knew who was behind in payments to whom; and he was always there with a little money to, as he put it, "hep out." He knew who was runnin' around on whom, and certainly was not above blackmail to get himself a piece of prime pussy every now and then.

Ned Rodale knew where the working stills were,

and got his share, either in votes or money; ditto with what gambling and whoring went on in the county.

Wilber Purdy really wasn't much better than Ned Rodale; he just had more finesse about him. The two had run around together as boys: the rich kid and the sharecropper's kid. Ned would always fight Wilber's battles for him, and a common bond was formed.

But Wilber had, she knew, seen the writing on the wall. If the county was to progress, Rodale had to go.

But that was all right. Ned didn't have any hard feelings toward his lifelong friend. He was realist enough to know that he couldn't change no more than a dog could stop pissin' on tires or chasin' cats.

Scratch. Purr.

Ned looked up, facing the dining room window, and began screaming.

The bodyless head of Old Lady Barstow was up against the window, her long red tongue licking the glass and her hands hovering just under and on each side of the head, the fingernails scratching at the glass. The eyes were wild.

Ned Rodale's bowels relaxed, filling his underwear, and the man passed out, tumbling to the floor.

Chapter 9

Max kicked the front door open and went in low, ducking to his left as soon as he was inside and flattening against the wall, down on one knee, his pistol in his right hand.

Place had a funky smell to it. He'd crawled up in a recently vacated bear's den one time as a kid. The smell was something like that. A wild, gamy odor.

He could hear hysterical sobbing coming from somewhere in the house.

"Alice? Is that you, Alice?"

Scratch. Purr.

Max couldn't figure that out at all. The scratching was too heavy for a house cat and the purring was more like it was coming from a big leopard.

Then the scratching and throaty purring stopped.

"Max?"

"Yeah, Alice. It's me. Where's Ralph? Where's the damn light switch?"

He fumbled around and found the switch, filling the room with light.

"Jesus Christ!" Max said, looking around him at the wreckage. The room looked like a tornado had hit it. Couch and chairs overturned, drapes pulled down, telephone lying in pieces in one corner.

A city unit squalled up, lights flashing.

Alice and Linda staggered into the room, both of them trying to piece together their torn clothing. "He went crazy, Max," Alice sobbed. "I stepped out to visit across the street, and when I came back he had beaten Linda almost unconscious and was raping her."

"Who?"

"Ralph!"

"Ralph?"

"Yes. Then he attacked me. He took me like . . . an animal. You know. It was filthy and degrading and he hurt me. He ran out the back when I tore the gag loose and started screaming."

"Check the back," Max told the city patrolman.

Max stood alone in the littered living room of the house while the women went off to change clothing. Every fragment of cop's intuition within him screamed that this was all wrong. Ralph Geason was probably the most honorable man Max had ever known, the type that holds a community together. Good husband, wonderful father; the type of man you could always count on to lead some charitable drive and the one who would work the hardest.

Ralph Geason went off his nut and did something like this?

Max just could not accept it. The chief had been a cop all his life—except for two years in the Army, where they had made him a cook—and knew that in the law-enforcement business anything was possible.

But this . . . situation just didn't set right with him. Linda had refused to meet his eyes; and he would have sworn there was a smirk on her lips. And what in God's name was that funky smell?

Something was all out of whack here.

Wilber Purdy was tracking the furtive movements of whatever it was on his property, staying between the hedge and the fence. He hadn't called for the floodlights because he did not want *it* to see *him*.

Then whatever it was growled.

That brought Wilbur up short. He'd caught six or eight glimpses of the thing and he knew it sure as hell was no dog.

"Come on out of there!" Wilber called. "Step out this minute or I'll blow your ass off!"

The sound that sprang from out of the darkness cut through to Wilber's heart, chilling him. It was like nothing that the mayor had ever heard before. It started as a high, shrill scream and ended in a roaring growl that backed Wilber up a couple of steps.

He lifted the shotgun and fired.

Jim and Calvin had managed to get Sheriff Rodale to his feet and into the bathroom so he could clean himself up. He smelled like an overflowing cesspool. The man was babbling and was clearly scared half out of his wits.

"Thank you for coming so quickly, Jim," Betty said, a weary look on her face.

"It's all right, Betty. We was just leavin' the doctor's lab when the call came in. Exactly what happened—do you know?"

"What happened?" Rodale hollered, as he waddled out of the bathroom, a robe belted around him. "I'll tell you what happened. I seen Ermma Barstow's head lookin' at me through that there winder!" He pointed. "Eyes all wild-lookin', and long red tongue just a-lickin' at the glass and her fingernails scratchin' at the winder. Hell, Jim, you can still see where she was lickin'!"

"For a fact," Jim said. "Can you get a sample of the saliva, Cal?"

"I'll get my bag."

"What the hell is goin' on in this county, Jim?" Rodale squalled.

"You best go lay down, Ned," Jim told him. "You don't look so hot. Color is all wrong."

"It's a damn miracle I didn't keel over dead!"

I should be so lucky, Betty May thought. "I've got some tranquilizers that will help you rest."

"I ain't no hippie dopehead, woman!"

"Take one, Ned," Jim urged. "They'll help you rest. I've took 'em from time to time. They ain't gonna hurt you."

"If you say so, Jim. Okay. You a good man, Jim. Damn good man." He waddled off up the hall.

Jim went outside to assist Calvin. "Don't say it, Jim," the doctor urged. "It would be much appreciated if you didn't say I told you so."

"The only thing I'm going to say is that we're over our heads in this thing. I got to get some help in here."

"For a fact," the doctor agreed. "And quickly."

The thing screamed just once and then roared. That horrible smell seemed like it was coming out of the creature's mouth. That was followed by a wrenching, tearing sound and Wilber could see the . . . God in Heaven, whatever it was . . . race across the vacant lot next to his property, leaving a slick-looking trail behind it.

"Call the law!" Wilber hollered to his wife. "Call the law! Never a goddamn cop around when you need one," he mumbled. "And turn on the floodlights!"

Wilber walked to the hedge and really started shaking as the floodlights highlighted the scene before him.

Whatever had been lurking there had torn the wrought-iron fencing out of the brick and mortar, bending the iron like taffy candy.

Wilber's legs started shaking so badly he had to lean up against a tree before he fell down. He could hear the sirens of the cop cars as they raced toward his property.

"What the hell is going on in this county?" Purdy muttered.

"Ralph stole his neighbor's car and took off," the city cop informed Max. "I've alerted the sheriff's department and the highway patrol. But if he gets into the timber, we'll play hell ever finding him."

"You call Jim Hunt?"

"He's on his way. There was some trouble over at the sheriff's house. And we got the other two units responding to trouble at the mayor's house. Shots have been fired."

"Anybody hurt?"

"I don't think so. It was a prowler."

"Where's Carter?"

"Gone to the mayor's house."

"Get on over there and watch that nitwit. You know the mayor is just looking for a reason to can him. I'll wrap it up here."

"This is damn sure one weird night, Chief."

"Yeah. And something tells me it's a long way from being over."

Edgar Conners's men were in a motel room, monitoring the events over a scanner.

"It's coming unglued," one said. "But damned if I can figure out what's causing it."

"It's gonna be a replay of what happened over in Ruger County," another said.

"But who knows for sure what did happen over there?" a third man said.

"I hit a stone wall, chief," Mike reported to Jim.

Mike had caught up with the chief deputy at the Geason house.

"Nothing from the VHP?"

"Captain Taylor filed his report the day the power lines exploded over there in Ruger. The FBI ordered most of it sealed and locked up, in the interest of national security. The trooper I talked to was in the office the day Taylor pulled the pin. He said Taylor was asked what happened over there in Valentine. He said he never would forget Taylor's words. The captain said, 'God won. I think.' "

The words caused a shiver to slowly work its way up and down Jim's spine. "We need to get in touch with Taylor."

"That'd be a good trick, Chief. Taylor was attacked and killed by a large animal, or animals—species unknown—at his fishing camp on the Shenandoah approximately four days ago. The body was just discovered this morning."

Jim put his hand on Mike's shoulder. "All right, Mike. You're not going to get much sleep tonight. When you're finished, take twenty-four hours off. I want you on that computer at the office. You can do things with it that nobody else can." Jim paused for a moment.

"You want me to do some hacking, Chief?"

"In a word, yes. Can you do it?"

Mike smiled. "Not on the one at the office. But I can with my own at the house."

Mike's major at college had been criminology and computer science. He could make a computer do everything except the boogie-woogie, and he was working on that.

"I want all the names you can get me of everybody who had anything to do with whatever it was that happened over in Ruger County. Then I want to know if they're still alive. I won't ask you to try to get into FBI files." He smiled. "But VHP is another story."

Mike smiled and nodded his understanding. "I got a few buddies," he said, and left it at that.

When Mike had gone home to start his lonely vigil behind his complex equipment, Jim walked over to Max.

"Can you figure this one out, Max?"

"It stinks, Jim. And I'm not saying that just because I knew and liked Ralph Geason. I just don't trust that damn woman that's been visiting the Geasons. And I'll tell you something else that's odd. My dog and cat don't like her either."

Jim smiled. "We can't get a warrant based on that. Where's she from, Max?"

"Ruger County."

Jim and Max checked in over at the mayor's house. They almost lost their supper when they looked at and smelled the green slime that had splattered the bricks when Wilber shot the intruder. The smell was identical to what Jim had smelled at both murder scenes and at the jail. And nothing human could have done that to the fence. He doubted even a great ape could have done that . . . and they damn sure didn't have any great apes around there. At least none that was all covered with hair and walked hunched over.

Max waggled a finger at Benny Carter. The big

man lumbered over. "Not a word about this, Benny. You are officially deaf, dumb, and blind. You understand what I'm saying?"

"Yes, sir, Chief."

"You don't know nothin' about nothin', Benny. You don't say nothin' to any kind of reporter."

"Yes, sir, Chief."

"Fine, Benny."

"Chief?"

"Yes, Benny?"

"What could have done this?"

"I don't know, Benny. But from now on, you answer unknown-intruder calls damn careful, you understand?"

"Yes, sir. I shore do understand that! Uh, Chief . . . the mayor said he wanted to talk to you just as soon as you showed up."

"All right. You coming, Jim?"

"No. I got to make a little run. Max, call Cal over to his clinic and tell him I said to get a sample of this green . . . stuff on the bricks. But to be damn careful handling it."

"I'll do better than that, Jim. Benny, go over to Doctor Barlett's clinic and tell him what's happened here. Give him a lift over here if he'd like."

"Yes, sir."

Jim drove straight to the A-frame of Dee Conners. He was not surprised when the sweep of his headlights highlighted Carl sitting on the front porch, an M-16 across his knees.

Carl let the chief deputy in and walked with him up to the porch, explaining, "Dee is taking a shower, getting ready for bed. I went to sleep for a couple of hours right after you people left. I'll stay up during the night."

Jim explained what had happened in town, leaving

nothing out. He ended with: "And the young woman visiting the Geason house is from Ruger County. Linda something-or-another." He describer her.

"I know her. She was my sister's best friend until after the incident. Then she never had anything else to do with Carrie. Linda changed dramatically. Became very withdrawn. Refused all offers of professional help."

"And your conclusion is?"

"I would watch her very carefully. I doubt that her being here is coincidental." He shook his head and sighed, the sigh audible in the stillness of the night. "Captain Taylor dead. I liked the captain. He was a fine, brave man."

"Boy, assuming the worst is about to happen here in the county, what do these . . . creatures hope to gain by all this?"

"According to what reports I was allowed to read after the incident in Ruger, the government's powers-that-be, mostly atheistic scientists, concluded that the surfacing is inbred. It's just something the creatures do by nature. The scientists felt the . . . beings were some sort of throwback to a much earlier time. The missing link, or something like that. They completely discounted any involvement by Satan."

"And your opinion of that?"

"Total bullshit. I felt Satan's presence. I heard Father Denier talking to Satan and felt the reply of the Prince of Darkness."

A mountain-bred, near-hard-shell, rock-solid Baptist, Jim Hunt could not suppress his shudder.

"Be very wary of any stinking pools of liquid that you or any of your men might find, Jim. That's where the Old Ones, the ancient gods will surface. And they'll jerk a person into those pools and eat them."

"The government, our government, suppressed all

this information?" Jim's words were softly spoken.

"They didn't have a choice in the matter. Can you even imagine the panic it would have caused—nationwide. Everybody with a gun, all over the United States, maybe the world, would have been shooting at anything that moved at night. I don't have to like what the government did, but I see why they did it."

Jim looked around him, at the silent vastness of the timber surrounding the A-frame. "I got to tell you, boy: You got more guts than I have, stayin' out here."

"I'm not afraid of these creatures. I faced them once before. I've made my peace with God and know that He will help me when and how He can."

"How do you mean?"

"You come across as a God-fearing man, Jim. You know that God rules the Heavens and Satan rules the earth. God gave us the faith to sustain us."

"God, guns, and guts."

"That's about the size of it."

Dee came out onto the porch, greeted Jim, and sat down. She smelled of soap. "More trouble?"

Briefly, Jim brought her up to date.

Laughter drifted faintly to them, coming from the dark timber around the house. The laughter was taunting and the evil contained therein was as black with sin as the night was dark.

"I just had me a thought," Jim said, after the laughter had died away. "If we don't contain this ourselves, and do it quietly—keepin' the press out of it—the government just might cordon off this area and then we'd really be in the pickle barrel."

"Yes," Carl agreed. "We're already fairly well isolated here. The mountains to the west, only a handful of very small and widely spaced towns in the county, and Charlottesville some twenty-five miles to the east. It's pretty rugged territory."

Jim stood up and walked to the steps. With his back to Carl and Dee, facing the darkness, he asked, "Will bullets stop these things?"

"Temporarily," Carl said. "It'll knock them down and keep them down, giving me the time to get some fire on them."

Jim turned around. "And just how do you propose to do that?"

"With a flamethrower I have in the house."

The chief deputy arched one eyebrow. "You can't be everywhere at once, boy."

"I realize that. But there is one thing we've got going for us that the other side is deathly afraid of."

"I'd be right proud if you'd tell me what that thing is."

"God."

Chapter 10

The night trudged slowly toward the dawning. Carl stayed on the front porch, with Dingo by his side. He occasionally dozed, knowing the dog would awaken him if anything attempted to cross the newly cleared ground and try to breech the chain-link fence.

Nothing did.

At dawn, Carl gave up his vigil and went to his bedroom to catch a few hours of real sleep.

At eight o'clock, the doctor from the lab in Richmond arrived at Calvin Bartlett's office. A bleary-eyed Cal greeted him.

"You look like shit, Cal," Doctor Robert Jenkins bluntly told him.

"Thanks a lot, Bob. I feel like crap too. I did manage to get a few hours' sleep, though. I slept here on the couch. Just got up and started a fresh pot of coffee in my office—come on. Believe me, you're going to need more than coffee before this day is over."

"What the hell have you got going here in Reeves County, Cal?"

Cal turned in the hall to face the man. "You want the truth?"

"Of course?"

"I don't know. I'm hoping you can tell me. Before it's too late."

"Sounds ominous."

"It's more than that, friend."

"Oh?"

"It's evil."

Carl woke up at ten, showered, shaved, and went into the kitchen to fix something to eat. Dee had beat him to it. While he was showering she had started the bacon, and was breaking the eggs and dropping them into a skillet when Carl walked in.

"The chanting and singing began just after dawn," she told him.

"If I heard it, I didn't pay any attention to it. Have you heard any news?"

"Nothing was on the local station about any of the . . . events of last night. The police must have really put a lid on it."

He smiled at her and nodded his head in agreement. "I don't expect that radio station to remain in operation much longer."

She looked up from the eggs. "Why?"

"Even though Valentine was and is off the beaten path, it still isn't as isolated as Butler. If the plan is to cut us off, the radio station would have to go." He paused, meeting her eyes. "Well, maybe not. What wattage is it?"

"I . . . really don't know. You can't hardly get it ten miles out of town."

"Probably two hundred and fifty watts. This time, I think the plan was thought out; Ruger County was an accident. Two men working in a mountain disturbed Anya and Pet, long before they were to have

102

awakened. This time, they've been awake and with several years to plan. And hate," he added.

"You think they know you're here, Carl?"

"Oh, yes. I'm sure of that. Killing me would be quite a victory for them. The son of the man who almost destroyed them."

"And they might not cut off the radio station after all?"

"I'm sure Anya has people in town who support the evil. Even though those people might not realize it consciously. They might decide to use the radio station. Tell me, you listen to it daily, right?"

"Well, yes. Or at least I used to, until about two, no, three months ago. Now I just tune in for the news."

Carl's smile was both sad and knowing. "Let me guess, Dee. They changed their format."

"Why . . . yes. That's right. They use to play a mixture of soft rock and pop and some country music crossovers. Now they've gone to heavy metal and really hard rock. Groups I've never heard of; I can't even understand the words. Nearly all the advertisers have pulled away. A lot of kids love the music—if that's what you want to call it—but more kids don't than do; they've told me so. But no adult I know of listens to it. With no sponsors, I don't see how they're making it."

"Oh, they've got a sponsor, Dee. And they only need that one."

"Who is it? I never hear any commercials."

"Satan."

Bob Jenkins pushed back from the lab table. Slide samples of tissue, skin, and saliva taken from the window of Rodale's house and the green slime that was taken from the fence littered the work table.

Bob said, "This green . . . crap, I believe, serves the same function for the whatever-the-hell-it-was as human blood for us. This saliva is highly infectious. These cells—my God, Cal, I don't know what they are . . . except that they're extremely infectious. Thank God they're not airborne. I mean, look." He waved his hand. "They've been exposed to air for hours. They're not dying—they're multiplying! I've poured every disinfectant and drain opener and full-strength floor cleaner in this place on them. They thrive on it! I doused a pattern of cells with a dozen of the strongest antibiotics known to humankind. They still live and reproduce, faster than anything I have ever witnessed in my life. They just keep splitting and splitting and splitting, each split producing a dozen, fifty, a hundred new cells—they come in clusters. It's, it's . . . both horrifying and fascinating. And deadly, Cal—very deadly."

"Fire."

"I beg your pardon?"

"Fire will kill them."

"Well . . . yes. Of course. But what are you driving at, Cal? If somebody becomes infected with this . . . name it, it's unknown . . . are you going to burn them at the stake?"

"It might come to that, Bob."

Doctor Robert Jenkins stared open-mouthed at his friend, shocked into silence by such a totally unprofessional statement.

Dee made sure Dingo had done his business before locking him in the house. He had plenty of food and water and if for some reason the house caught on fire, he could exit through one of the open windows. But that was about the only condition that would force him to leave when he had been told to guard and stay.

With Dee driving, Carl and Dee rode into town. Carl clicked on the radio. Dee punched the button that would switch it over to the local station and Carl listened for fifteen minutes before turning the volume down.

"Can you understand that crap?" Dee asked.

"Not much of it. And by the way, I haven't heard any familiar groups. But I know what they're singing about. I've infiltrated some satanistic cells while getting kids back to their parents. We do a lot of what is known as coven-busting. Then we take the kids to deprogrammers. Sometimes it works and we can get them back to reality. Many times — most times — it doesn't."

"I don't know much about cults or covens." She pointed to the radio. "What are they singing about?"

"Self-mutilation, assault, suicide, drugs, murder, sex; anti-establishment and anti-social rebellion against parents, society, education, and law and order. Some of the music tries to promote the ideals of absolute freedom, irresponsibility, and violence — and unfortunately, in many cases succeeds." Carl smiled faintly. "I don't mean to sound preachy, Dee, but since I'm still fairly young, the Richland Agency has used me quite often to infiltrate covens. I've become a reluctant expert on certain more aggressive types of music, and the satanic cults that have sprung up all over the nation."

"It certainly sounds like you have. But surely there aren't that many of them."

"The last statistics we have are from 1987. They show approximately one hundred and forty-five *thousand* covens in all fifty states. That's up from ten thousand covens in 1946; I believe that was the first year any really definite study was done."

"One hundred and forty-five *thousand* covens!" Dee said, shock evident in her tone.

"Yes. Boggles the mind, doesn't it?"

"Is anything being done about it?"

"Damn little, I'm afraid. And that only serves to point out the callousness that judges and law-enforcement people hold toward the treatment of animals. When the police do make an effort to arrest cult members for torturing and sacrificing animals, the judges slap them with a small fine and turn them loose. The music can't be stopped because it comes under the protection of the First Amendment — freedom of speech. The cults themselves are protected under the same amendment — freedom of religion. Talk about a macabre joke, that's it."

"If I'm correctly reading between the lines, Carl, what you're saying is that there could be a large cult, coven, right here in Reeves County which is planning to, or which is already assisting the horror we're facing."

"That is correct."

Mike was clearly exhausted as he sat down wearily in the chief deputy's office. "I got it, Chief. But boy, if I'm ever caught, I'm lookin' at a long prison term."

"That information will be destroyed just as soon as me and a few other people get a chance to review it. What do you have, Mike?"

"The crew chief and the men who worked with him in diverting the power that day over in Ruger County are all dead. One committed suicide, one was killed in a car accident, one fell from the bucket of a cherry picker, and another had a heart attack.

106

Of the government people involved, I can't find any who are still alive. Virginia state police strongly suspect Linda Crowley—she adopted the last name of Aleister Crowley, who was a leading advocate of satanism back around the turn of the century—is now the leader of a satanic cult based in Ruger County. And get this: a cult with cells all over the state. There is a lot more, but those are the high points. Or low points, depending on how you want to look at it."

Mike laid the computer printouts on Jim's desk.

"Thank you, Mike. Take the next twenty-four off. I understand you and Judy are goin' out to Miss Conners's house this evenin'."

"Yes, sir. Carl's cooking steaks."

"You're going to be awful close to the source out yonder. You be careful, boy."

Jim sat for a half hour, digesting the material on the printouts. It left him with a sour taste in his mouth and a dirty feeling generally. He locked the papers up in his office safe and walked outside just in time to see Carl and Dee drive past the building. The young man, as usual, appeared unconcerned. Dee looked worried. They did not see Jim and drove on past.

Jim got in his county unit and drove over to Doctor Bartlett's office.

He was introduced to Robert Jenkins and, over coffee, briefed the men on what Mike had told him.

Jenkins, already shaken by what he had seen that day, just about came unglued at Jim's words.

"Are you telling me that *Satan*, the *Devil*, is behind all this?" he asked, his voice shrill.

"That's what I'm tellin' you, Doc," Jim calmly replied.

Jenkins's mouth dropped open and he slumped

107

back in his chair.

"I just thought of something," Cal said. "Jim, have you noticed many of the kids around town have started wearing Nazi paraphernalia? Doesn't that fit in with some satanic cults?"

"I got to admit that I stopped payin' attention to what kids wear a long time ago. No, I hadn't noticed. But you're right about it fittin' in. And here's something else: accordin' to what we come up with" — he had not mentioned Mike's name, or his computer hacking, and had no intention of doing so — "Carl Garrett is some sort of expert about cults and covens and so forth."

"Who is Carl Garrett?" Jenkins had found his voice.

Jim brought the man up to date on Carl.

"I thought that tragedy over in Ruger County was caused by some sort of explosion," Jenkins said. "Some sort of government mishap."

"It was a government fuck-up was what it was," Jim told him, startling Cal because Jim almost never used hard profanity. "And then they just turned around and walked away from it, all the while knowin' that some of those people over yonder had changed sides — whether it was willingly or unwillingly don't make no difference. Fact is, they walked off and left them to fend for themselves. Maybe they had a reason; I don't know. I do know — least the way I feel right now — I don't want no government people in on what's happenin' here."

"How would you keep them out if they decided to come in?" Cal asked.

"Well, you couldn't —"

The phone rang, interrupting Jim. Cal picked it up and spoke briefly. He turned to the chief deputy.

"Carl Garrett and Miss Conners are on the way

over here. I gave them the okay."

"Fine with me." He pointed to the littered worktable. "What's all that stuff?"

"Why don't we wait until this Garrett person gets here," Bob suggested. "Then we won't have to duplicate our efforts." The doctor cut his eyes to the shattered drawer of the cooler across the big room. He sighed and shook his head. "I wish one of you would tell me this is all a great big practical joke."

"Don't nobody wish we could do that anymore than me," Jim told him. "After you brief us on what you've found about that green crap and the other stuff, I want to call a meeting of a few of the town's leaders—so to speak. Max, Mayor Purdy, the other doctors—and, I guess, Sheriff Rodale. I've finally got it through my head that we're up agin the supernatural here." Jenkins stirred at that but offered no rebuttal. "As for the preachers in this town, I don't know whether to include them or not. I do know I don't want none of them Holy Rollers in here. They'd get to jibber-jabberin', and talkin' in tongues, and we never would get nothin' done. And them snake-handlers up on the ridges can damn well stay up there." He sighed. "As far as my preacher goes . . . well, he's a good man and I like him. But he ain't gonna buy none of this here. That just ain't the way we're supposed to think. But I can't deny what I've seen and heard with my own eyes and ears." He shook his head and said sorrowfully, "First time in my whole en-tar life I ever wished a Catholic priest would show up."

"It doesn't make any difference what faith you are," Carl said from the doorway. "Father Denier told me that. One just has to believe that Satan lives and walks the earth." Carl pointed to the numerous slides and cultures on the worktable. "They're growing, aren't they?"

"Yes," Jenkins told him. "How did you know that?"

"Fire is the only thing that will kill them. Once a human being is infected, there is no cure. You can't kill the Devil. But fire will stop his minions and the filth they spread. Think about it."

Jim was the first to speak. "They come from the Pits."

"That's right. Now gather your community leaders. Here is as good a spot as any, I suppose."

"How . . . did you know I was going to do that?" Jim asked, suspicion in his voice.

"Just a guess, Jim."

But the hard-shell Baptist in Jim surfaced, and for a moment he looked at Carl as if the young man had suddenly grown horns and a tail.

Cal was the first to laugh at the man's expression and the laughter spread, snapping the tension like a dry forest twig under a work boot. Cal coughed, cleared his throat, and wiped his eyes. "Jim, the expression on your face was priceless."

Red-faced, the chief deputy had to join in the laughter. When his laughter had changed to a chuckle, he shook his head and said, "I tell y'all something. I growed up over yonder on the ridges. Went to one of them little country hellfire-and-brimstone-spoutin' Baptist churches. Lay preachers, mostly. Makes a man some suspicious. Old habits die hard, I reckon."

"Everybody enjoy the laughter," Carl said, dampening the mood. "Because in just a few days, I assure you, there will be precious little to laugh about."

Chapter 11

"Hell's bells!" Sheriff Rodale jumped up, flapped his arms, and hollered, even before Jim was half finished. "Call the damn FBI! Git the governor on the phone and call out the National Guard!"

"Oh, sit down!" Mayor Purdy told him. "You're actin' like a fool!"

Rodale sat.

Doctor Perry stood up. "Jim, do you expect us to believe all this nonsense you've been spouting? I for one don't believe a word of it."

Carl cut his eyes and looked at the man. "Believe it, Doctor."

"Nonsense!" Perry puffed.

"You'll believe it after you've seen those slides," Cal said, more than a slight edge to his voice. "Providing you know the difference between DNA and RNA, that is."

"Not to mention ATP and AMP," Jenkins added, taking a dislike to the young Perry.

Most of those in the room did not have any idea what the doctors were talking about. That did not prevent them from picking up on the sarcasm in the voices.

Cal then proceeded to tell the additional doctors

111

about the strange cells they had found.

Perry waved that off with a curt slash of his hand. "So what?" he challenged. "Certainly I don't have to remind you *experts* about certain human cancerous cervical cells that have been living in laboratories around the world for almost forty years."

"That's under sterile lab conditions," Bob told the man, while the others listened and wondered what the hell was going on. "Those cells are fed and the culture mediums closely monitored and changed. When they become too crowded with rapidly dividing cells, the populations are divided and placed in new containers." He pointed to the worktable. "Look over there, doctor. Those cells have been exposed to air for hours. They're thriving and growing and multiplying. You can't compare cells living under sterile lab conditions with what is happening here. There is absolutely no comparison."

With a sneer on his lips, Perry walked to the table and stuck a slide in place and studied the cell life under a microscope. After a moment, he raised his head, a very confused look on his face.

"Holy shit!"

"Not terribly professional," Jenkins said. "But at least it's concise."

Doctor Nelson Loring walked to the table and took a look. His face drained of color. He turned to face the group and said, "These are neither animal nor human."

"No kidding," Jenkins said.

Scratch. Purr.

"What the hell was that?" Perry asked, his voice loud in the suddenly silent room.

"A reminder from the other side of life that we are not alone," Carl told him.

"And what does that mean?" Nelson asked.

112

"It means that the Devil is walkin' amongst us," Jim said. "Or them that serve him."

"I don't believe that," Perry announced. "That's all superstitious nonsense."

A foul odor filled the room, the stench that of burning sulfur. A wind sprang from out of the stench, blowing papers around the room and knocking off several coffee cups, shattering them on the floor.

Hollow laughter echoed around the room.

Ned Rodale dropped to his knees, his hands clutched before him, and started praying while Jim looked at him, disgust in his eyes and on his face. "The many-headed beast is upon us!" Ned hollered. "Oh, Lordy! We're doomed to the fiery pits."

"Idiot!" Wilber Purdy muttered.

A rock was thrown through the window. It bounced off a wall and came to rest on the floor. Max grabbed a stool and stood on it, enabling him to look out one of the high-set security windows. Kids," he said. "Val Malone and Nick Jamison. Half a dozen others down there on the corner. They're getting in their cars, pulling out."

"Go arrest them heathen, Jim!" Rodale yelled, jumping to his feet.

"On what charge? Didn't none of us see them throw the rock. Settle down, Ned."

Scratch. Purr.

Rodale ran to the door and jerked it open, looking frantically up and down the corridor. There was nothing to be seen.

"Come out and fight like a man, goddamn you!" the sheriff squalled. "Show yourself, you cowardly bastards!"

Laughter greeted the words. But this time the laughter was heavy and dark-tinged.

113

Rodale was shaking so much it appeared he might fall down.

The phone rang. Cal picked it up and listened for a moment. He slowly replaced the receiver. "Very obscene message," he told the group. "From a girl. Teenager, I would say. She was, ah, very explicit as to what was going to happen to all of us."

"Did you recognize the voice?" Max asked.

Cal shook his head. "No. There was some rather violent type of music in the background."

The mayor said, "Other than the common usage, what do the letters AC/DC mean. I found that chalked on the sidewalk in front of my house this morning."

"Anti-Christ, Devil-Child," Carl told him. "There are several dozen symbols that satanists use. ZOSO refers to the three-headed dog that guards the gates to Hell. The letter S means Satan/stoner. FFF is Anti-Christ, as is 666." Carl now had their full attention, and with several, the looks were frightened. "NATAS is Satan reversed. 6, 9, and 13 are common occult numbers. Horns and tail added to any letter denotes Satan worship. A lightning bolt means heaven-to-hell strength. There are petagrams and hexagram circles. A circle within a circle means infinity-containment, control of evil, power. A star and a quarter moon is Lucifer/morning star. The swastika is very common among Satan worshippers."

"What the hell do we do?" Max asked. "Round up all the kids in town?"

"It isn't just the kids," Carl told him. "There are just as many adults involved as kids. Although kids are the most violent. Members of covens come from all walks of life. . . ."

"You tell them, fuck-head!" a voice boomed from an invisible source.

Rodale was now not the only one in the room who was very badly frightened.

Carl forced himself to ignore the voice and to show no fear. "All social and economic levels, and all ethnic groups . . ."

"Blah, blah, blah!" the voice boomed. Heavy and ominous and dripping with evil.

"The philosophy of satanists is this: A person lives only for today and should indulge in all life's good feelings. Satanism condones any type of sexual activity which properly satisfies the individual desires, be it heterosexual, homosexual, or bisexual."

"Get lots of pussy and ass!" the voice cracked like thunder. "Kill and torture and fuck. Kill and torture and fuck!" Wild laughter followed, the sound so loud it rattled cups and glassware in the room.

Then, as abruptly as it began, the voice stopped, leaving the room in silence.

"You will find within the cults and covens of the satanic worshippers"—Carl didn't let up or change his tone—"the criminal psychopath or sociopath. They are unable to experience guilt or remorse, they cannot form lasting relationships, they tend to seek high levels of thrills and excitement. . . ."

Outside, a car drove by, the radio playing a wild, almost unintelligible music, the speakers pushed to the max, the violent sounds slamming through the broken windows of the room.

"These people are very impulsive with a lack of conscience. Their behavior is very aggressive and dangerous, but they can show a great deal of superficial charm and intelligence. They are unreliable, irresponsible, pathological liars. Their behavior is anti-social with a lack of values. They torture and kill dumb animals and their cruelty is limitless. Their sexual behavior is casual and excessive. They have, for the most part, no life plan, except perhaps to fail at everything. Anyone who joins these groups is a born loser."

"What is your solution . . . your theory of how to combat this . . . evil?" Nelson asked.

The group was not prepared for the answer that Carl gave them.

"Kill them."

The blunt and harshly put statement from someone so young as Carl had been just about as nerve-rattling to the others as the horror they all now knew they faced.

Carl and Dee had left shortly after Carl's speech. Rodale had gone home. He had told Jim to take over. He'd see him at the office tomorrow. Maybe. He didn't know for sure. Felt real bad. Shore did.

"Rodale's coming apart at the seams," Max observed.

No one, not one among the group, had yet brought up the mysterious voice.

"You may have to shoulder the load, Jim," Wilber Purdy told him. "I mean, I know you've been doing that for years, but this time you may have to do it all."

Jim nodded. He'd already, reluctantly, reached that conclusion. "Let's talk about that damn voice, people. Somebody say something."

"The room was bugged and somebody had a speaker hidden?" Doctor Perry said hopefully.

The looks he received made him feel even more foolish than the remark.

"There is this to consider," Jim said, looking at Max. "Our departments may be infiltrated by satanists."

116

"I hadn't thought of that," the chief of police replied. "So much has been thrown at me, us, in the past hour or so, tell you the truth, I haven't really known what to think."

Jim glanced at the man from Richmond. "Did you plan to stay for a day or so, Doctor Jenkins?"

"Yes. I came prepared to stay for several days. Cal was rather evasive as to just what he was working on, so I packed accordingly. Look, people, let's get something worked out. No mention has been made about calling in the state police. Are they going to be notified?"

"And tell them what?" Jim said. "That the devil is trying to take over the town? Durned if I'll be the one to do it . . . at least not for awhile. They'd come in, all right, and stick us all in the booby house."

The chief of police said, "Jim, I'm going to vote that you take charge in this matter. You give the orders and I'll follow them."

Jim had been dreading those words, but he knew they would be coming. "I didn't know anything like that was comin' to a vote."

All the men in the room raised their hands in agreement with Max.

Jim nodded his head. "All right. I'll agree to run the law-enforcement end of it. But I think we'd all better look to Carl Garrett for the rest of it."

The group agreed to that.

"We have to decide on how much we tell our people," Max said.

"And how much do we tell the townspeople?" the mayor asked.

Jim was thoughtful for a few moments. "We sound out our law-enforcement people one by one and just play it by ear as to how much we tell them. Personally, I haven't seen any signs of personality changes

117

in my bunch. Harry Harrison would be the weak link, I'm thinkin'. He's been a bully all his life, and most bullies are cowards at heart. I'll have to watch him. Max, I'd suggest that you keep an eye on Benny Carter. As to the townspeople and them out in the county . . . I don't know what to say about that. But I'd bet that nine out of ten wouldn't believe us even if we was to level with them."

"Let's give it a couple of days," Wilber said. "It could be that we're all overreacting. I don't think so, but let's cling to that faint hope."

"What do you think about that last remark of Carl's?" Cal asked.

Jim sighed. "He said to carry a bible with us. If we go down, we can at least go out of this world holding on to the word of God. I think it's a good idea."

Snickering filled the large room, the sarcastic giggling grating on the already overstretched nerves of the group.

"The word of God," the heavy voice boomed. "Oh, my, yes. You most certainly must carry a bible. And this is how much that worthless gaggle of words will help you."

A long, loud, obscene fart erupted, fouling the air.

Chapter 12

To anyone not knowing what was taking place behind the scenes, the small town on the edge of the Blue Ridge Mountains would appear normal. School was out for the summer and smaller children were evident at play on the sidewalks and the lawns. The public swimming pool was filled to capacity with laughing and splashing kids, most of them preteens. There was a conspicuous absence of older teens. A lot of them were busy doing other things . . . like sleeping and waiting for the night.

Anya and Pet had gorged themselves on the flesh of a bum they'd found walking along a county road. The flesh was not as tasty as that of a professed Christian, but it would suffice for the time being.

Anya and Pet would rest for a couple of days and then try to call out the Old Ones. Matters were rocking along quite well without their help; besides, they needed the rest to gain more strength. The more converts to their cause, the stronger they would become. That was the way. They would never be as before — that was impossible. Dan Garrett and that damnable priest, Denier, had seen to that. But Pet and Anya had survived. It had been long years of agony, but they had climbed out of the searing pain to once more walk on the surface of the earth.

This time, they would not fail. They had been assured of that. By the Master.

In homes around the county, ear-weary mothers were standing on the frayed edges of patience as the violent, anti-social music pounded the terrible messages out at ear-shattering levels. Val Malone's mother could not take it another second. She jerked at the door to her daughter's bedroom.

It was locked.

She beat her fists on the door. "Val! Turn that damn music down!"

Inside the darkened room, Val cut her eyes to the door and turned the music up as loud as the speakers could take without shattering.

"Val!" her mother screamed, her words just audible over the roar. "Open this door!"

"Fuck you, bitch!" the seventeen-year-old muttered, as the room reverberated with the squallings of the singer.

"You wait until your father gets home!" the mother yelled. "Then we'll see how you behave."

"Fuck him too," the girl mouthed, then grinned, a nasty, evil curving of the lips. "Which is exactly what I intend to do."

She'd been working on her father for several months, deliberately letting him see her with very little clothes on; parading through the den, when he was alone in the house with her, wearing a sheer nightie with nothing on under it. She'd seen the way he'd looked at her and didn't think she'd misread it. Yeah. The old man was just about ready.

And just as soon as he stuck it in, he would be

120

one with them.

Forever.

"You little bitch!" her mother screamed, losing what remained of her patience.

Val laughed at her. Nick would see to her, just about the time Val was seeing to her father. Nick had a thing about Val's mother; he thought she was good-looking and would be a tremendous lay. Val didn't think so herself, but it would be fun to watch, no doubt about that. When the time came.

Soon.

Val's mother finally lost all vestiges of patience. Like many parents, she felt she and her husband had done their very best in raising their kids—which they had. Neither she nor her husband could understand what had gone wrong with Val. Her older brother had turned out exceptionally well. Now in college, he had never given them any more than the average teenage problems.

But Val was another story. The crowd of boys and girls she ran with all came from good homes; solid middle-class roots, raised with good standards. Yet all of them were rebellious. Of late, all of them had been behaving very strangely, from open rebellion to sitting in their darkened bedrooms listening to that awful music.

Liza Malone didn't know what to do. She was up against a stone wall and her head was bruised from beating it against solid teenage resistance. She walked out to the garage, got a hammer, and returned to the closed and locked bedroom door. She began beating on the door with all her strength, cracking the wood in several places.

The music stopped, plunging the house into a strange sort of silence. Liza stopped her frantic ham-

121

mering, dropping the hammer to the floor. The door swung open and daughter faced mother.

"Have you lost your damn mind?" the teenager asked, a savage tone to the question.

Liza slapped her.

Mother and daughter went at it. Val leaped at her mother, hissing like an enraged cat, her hands hooked into clawlike weapons, slashing at her mother, cursing her as she fought. Liza grabbed her daughter and threw her to the carpeted hall floor, losing her balance as she did. Mother and daughter rolled on the floor, yelling and clawing and slapping and hissing. Liza finally pinned her daughter, sitting on her, balled one hand into a fist, and gave the kid five on the side of the jaw. Val's eyes rolled back and she lay still, not quite unconscious, but hovering on the brink.

Liza's face was bruised and scratched from Val's long fingernails. She stood up, panting from her sudden exertions. She picked up the hammer and knocked the pins out of the hinges, then manhandled the door out into the hall, throwing it on the floor. Entering the dark and dank-smelling bedroom of her daughter, the mother began smashing the stereo equipment, the speakers, and every record she could find. She paused, catching her breath, then reached out and tore the heavy drapes from a window, flooding the room with light. It was then she noticed the strange drawings and diagrams thumbtacked to the walls of the room. Nazi swastikas, petagrams and hexagrams, lightning bolts and 666's were on every wall.

"You goddamn bitch!" Val screamed, charging into the room, running into her mother and knocking her down. Liza kicked out, one shoe catching Val on the knee, bringing the teenager down. Mother and daughter rolled on the littered floor, cursing and hitting each other. Val's hands closed around the hammer and she drew back and threw it at her mother's head with every ounce of strength she had in her. Liza ducked and the hammer crashed through the window and bounced off the side of the car that had just pulled into the drive, putting a dent in the door.

Tom Malone jumped out of the car and ran into the house. He could hear the cussing and hollering clear out in the front yard. He ran up the hall, jumping over the door and wondering what in the hell it was doing in the hall, and stood in open-mouthed shock in the doorway, looking at his wife and daughter slugging away at each other on the bedroom floor.

Tom grabbed his daughter and tossed her into the hall. Val hit the hall wall so hard it knocked the breath out of her. She sank to the carpet, stunned.

Liza got to her feet, her eyes wild-looking and her fists balled. "I'll kill that kid!" she panted.

"That's your daughter!" her husband yelled. "What the hell happened here? Have the both of you lost your goddamn minds?"

"Get out of my way!" Liza warned him.

But Tom was not listening. His eyes had just found all the drawings and symbols lining the walls of his daughter's bedroom. "Jesus God!" he breathed. "That's devil worship!" He cut his eyes to his wife. "Why haven't you told me about this, Liza?"

"Because I'm not allowed in this room, Tom! Don't you ever listen to me? I've been telling you for months that something was terribly wrong with Val. But you just don't listen to me. You're the one who

123

told her she could lock her door. You're the one who told me to stay out of her room and respect her privacy. How dare you blame *me* for *this?*"

Tom held up a hand. "All right, all right, honey. I'm sorry, and you're right: I haven't been listening." He turned toward the hall. Val was on her hands and knees, cursing them both as she tried to get to her feet.

Tom got her to her feet.

He grabbed her by her long, black hair and jerked her to her feet. Val screamed from the pain and tried to knee her father in the nuts. But Tom had grown up in the coal mines of West Virginia, brawling with older and bigger men since his early teens. He blocked the knee and backhanded the girl, misting her eyes and momentarily blurring her lopsided and evil world.

Then he gave her another pop to regain her attention. He cut his eyes to his wife. "Call Father Vincent. Tell Chuck to get the hell over here — right now."

Liza used the phone in her daughter's room — a private line, of course — to call the Episcopal priest.

Val tried to walk away from her father. He closed one big hand around her arm and jerked her back. "No. Huh-uh, kid. You stay put. We have a lot of talking to do."

"I ain't got a goddamn thing to say to you or that queer priest," she popped back at him.

She got popped. And once again, her world turned misty.

Through the mist, she heard her father say, "You silly, stupid brat. Don't you think I haven't been aware of what you've been doing — or attempting to do? Parading around me with practically nothing on;

giving me what you perceive as come-on little glances. I came home early to talk to your mother about your behavior. I don't know what's going on here, but I damn sure intend to see it stopped."

"Nick'll kill you!" she hissed at him.

"Nick will shit if he eats regular. And that's about all that punk is going to do. Nick is barred from this house. You are forbidden to associate with Nick—ever. You are grounded. UFN, baby."

"What the hell does that mean?"

"Until Further Notice."

He spun her around and marched her up the hall to the den and forcibly sat her down in a chair. Tom pointed a finger at her. "Every time you try to get up, I'm going to slap you back down, kid. And if you doubt it, try me."

She didn't doubt him for a second. Tom Malone was an easygoing sort of guy, a successful insurance agent, well liked by nearly everybody. He had gone through college on a boxing scholarship and served with honors with the 75th Rangers in Vietnam. His hands were big, flat-knuckled, and scarred. Everybody knew Tom was a man with no back up in him; mess with Tom Malone and Tom would hurt you and do it quickly.

"I'll stay here," she said.

"Fine. You have anything you want to say to me before Chuck gets here?"

"Not a damn thing!"

"Suit yourself, kid."

"I intend to do just that."

Liza washed her face, brushed her hair, and changed clothes, then joined her husband and daughter in the den.

"I started a pot of coffee," Tom told her.

"I'll put out the cups." She looked at Val. "I don't suppose you'd like to help."

"You got that right."

The Episcopal church was one of the smaller churches in the town—this was predominately Baptist country—but the church congregation was slowly growing. Father Charles Vincent was directly responsible for that. Chuck Vincent favored jeans and cowboy boots, enjoyed a couple of drinks before dinner, and pitched a mean game of horseshoes. But he had been worried about the lack of young people attending church. Not just his church, any church.

And the reason for that lack of attendance was baffling to him.

On his way to the Malone house, he was flagged down by Dee Conners, who was a friend of his wife. "I'm having a cookout this evening, Chuck," Dee told him, after introducing Carl. Sitting in the cars, the men nodded at one another. "Just a few of us, nothing elaborate. I'd love for you and Carol to come out, please, if you're not busy."

"I'd like that, Dee. We sure will." Chuck was curious about the young man with Dee. He sure was a hard-looking fellow.

Dee and Carl were abruptly pushed out of his mind when he saw the faces of Liza and Val. Both of them scratched and bruised. And strained.

Tom looked at Val. "You keep your butt where it is."

"I said I would, didn't I? Don't sweat it."

"I'll stay with her to make sure she does stay," Liza said.

The look the mother received from her daughter

was one of pure hate, and it was not lost on Chuck. He kept his thoughts to himself.

The priest whistled softly as Tom showed him Val's room.

"Tell me it doesn't mean what I think it means," Tom said, a hopeful note in his voice.

" 'Fraid I can't do that, buddy," Chuck said. "What hit this place, a mini-cyclone?"

"Yes. In the form of Liza." He told him all he knew about the mother-daughter showdown.

Again, the priest softly whistled as the story unfolded, his eyes taking in all the symbols in praise of the Dark One.

Tom ended with: "And talk around town is there's some sort of cult or coven expert in here. He's staying out at the Conners place. The town is buzzing about the unexplained deaths the last few days."

"I just met that young man. I'm going out there tonight for a cookout. I gather you want me to talk with Val?"

"If you think it would do any good, yes."

"It won't hurt. Come on."

The Episcopal priest didn't pussyfoot around with a lot of Biblical beatitudes. Liza almost spilled coffee down the front of her blouse when Chuck asked, "Val, how come you want to worship an asshole like Satan?"

And Val didn't hesitate with her reply. " 'Cause he's where it's at, man."

"Like sex and drugs and liquor and stuff like that, huh?"

"You got it, man."

"What does he promise you after death?"

"Life."

"Isn't that what God and His Son also promise?"

127

"Bullshit life. Our god is the real creator—the Gnostic Demiurge."

"The what?" her father blurted out.

She looked him square in the eyes. "The Demiurge is the God behind the creator God, an emanation of the transcendent God." She spoke as if speaking from rote. "Santanas is the messenger, bringing us the knowledge that there was a God behind the God who created the cosmos." She smiled. "And if you don't like that, daddy-dear . . . go fuck yourself."

Tom started to get out of his chair. Chuck waved him back. "Settle down. Violence is what they thrive on."

"You're pretty cool for an old dude, Chuckie-baby," Val told him.

The priest was all of forty.

"Thank you, Val. I do try to stay abreast of things."

"Now you're being sarcastic."

"Yes. I am. You're an intelligent young lady. Surely you can see why I would be offended by anyone worshipping my enemy."

"Oh, no, man! You shouldn't feel that way. He's the best friend you ever had. Without him you'd be out of a job."

The priest chuckled. "You do have a point. What's happening in this town, Val?"

"The first year of Anno Satanas began on Walpurgis Night."

"May Eve, huh? I thought that occurred about twenty years ago."

She shrugged. "This is a whole new ball game, man. All that other stuff has been bagged."

"What damn language are you speaking, girl?" Tom asked.

"Screw you."

"That's what you had in mind, isn't it?" her father reminded her.

"So? That isn't wrong according to our beliefs. Wouldn't you like to . . ."

Then she proceeded to tell them all what she would like to do for her daddy, what her daddy could do for her, and if Mommy-dearest and Chuckie-baby wanted to join in . . . well, man, the more the merrier. And it was all spoken in the most profane manner the girl could think of. It was perverted and sickening.

Tom and Liza looked shocked, with pale faces and trembling hands. Chuck didn't bat an eye. He stood up and walked back to her bedroom, studying for several minutes the symbols on the wall. He disregarded most, concentrating on only a few. He wasn't certain he understood all that he saw, but he felt he now knew enough to understand what was going on.

The signs and symbols he concentrated on were a jumbled-up mixture of Egyptian-Ethiopian-Assyrian; and that was not strange because voodoo had existed thousands of years before Christ walked the earth. And voodoo had its roots all over Africa.

The voice of Tom ripped through the house. "Come back here, goddamn you!"

Chuck walked back to the den. Val was gone. Tom was standing in the open front door, his face red and his hands balled into fists.

"Let her go, Tom," the priest said. "Nothing you or I or anyone else could say would change how she feels. She has made her choice."

The father turned slowly. "Are you saying it's irreversible?"

"For now. Perhaps forever."

Tom lifted his big hands. "Well . . . I mean . . . what the hell do we do now?" He shouted the question.

"I think we should all attend a party tonight."

Chapter 13

"A party?" Tom yelled at the priest. "My kid is gang-banging half the young studs in town, doing drugs and God only knows what else, and to top it off she's worshipping the Devil . . . and you want us all to go off to some damn party!"

Chuck waited until the man had yelled and stomped around the den, venting some of his anger and frustration. "Settle down, Tom. I told you the small cookout is being held at Dee Conners's place. That's where this so-called expert is staying. I'd like to talk with him and I think you should too."

"We weren't invited to the party, Father Vincent," Liza pointed out.

"That won't be any problem. I'll take care of that; I'll just call Dee. I think it best if we take two cars. One or the other might have to leave early. Now then, let's have some more coffee and talk about Val."

"I split man," Val told the group. "Before Vincent could start working some of his hoodoo shit."

"I know what you mean," another girl said. "When my parents saw all the stuff in my room, they called the preacher. He prayed and all that crap. It was kinda spooky. But when he said it was just a teenage fad thing, I really had to work to keep from busting out laughing. You going back home, Val?"

"I don't think so. It's pretty close to time, the way I hear. What I'll do is, I'll go home with one of you guys and call my folks; tell them I got to think on things, get my head straight. Then I'll come home. By that time, we'll be making our move and it won't make any difference anyway."

"Praise the Dark One!" Nick said.

"Praise the Dark One!" the group said.

While the rest were chanting the dark and evil phrases, two teenagers slipped away and out of the house. A block from Nick's house, they stopped on the sidewalk.

"You're right, Janet," Gary said. "We've been had."

The girl nodded her head. "I thought it was just a joke at first. You know, a way to get back at our parents. But when they sacrificed that little puppy the other night, I about puked. I felt so sorry for that puppy I wanted to cry."

"We gotta do something."

"What we got to do is be real careful, Gary," she cautioned.

He knew what she meant. Coven members made lifetime commitments to the group, which included a strict vow of secrecy and silence. That vow was not unlike the La Cosa Nostra vow of the Mafia. Members of covens were not allowed to disassociate themselves from the group after having taken part in or witnessed any of their many and various criminal perversions. Any member breaking the code of secrecy placed his or her life, and the lives of his or her family, in serious jeopardy.

Both Gary and Janet had heard what had happened to Lanny and Dora. The kids had wanted to break away — did break away. But before they could get to the police, they were caught, tortured, raped, sodomized, and then killed, their bodies dismembered with a chain saw and disposed of.

"But we gotta do something," Gary persisted.

"I know, I know, Gary. But we got to be cool with it. We've got to think out each move real careful."

"Are we through with the group, Janet?"

"All the way, Gary."

"God, I feel so much better just hearing those words."

Seventeen-year-old female fingers found and clutched at seventeen-year-old male fingers, as their eyes met. "I love you, Gary."

"And I love you, Janet."

"You got any ideas?"

"Janet . . . I want with all my heart to just run. Get clear of this town before it happens. And it's not just mumbo-jumbo — it's going to happen. But I just can't turn my back on innocent people. We have to make some sort of stand."

She rubbed his arm. "You're so brave."

He shook his head. "No, honey. I'm just scared!"

While the doctors worked frantically at Cal's small lab, Jim Hunt and Max Bancroft slowly cruised the town in Jim's county unit.

"Over there's another one." Max pointed out the lightning bolt over the swastika.

"Yeah. I see it. How many devil symbols does that one make?"

" 'Bout a dozen in the past fifteen minutes."

And the lawmen had been very conscious of the

hot, hate-filled, and hostile looks they'd been receiving while they cruised. Not just from young people, but from people of all ages . . . men, women, and kids. Not from the majority of the townspeople, far from it, but from enough people to make them very edgy.

"How did it get so far without us picking up on it?" Max asked.

"The Devil's slick, Max. We've heard that so many times, from so many preachers, we tend to just let it slide. We say it can't happen to us, not in our community. I think we became uppity about our faith. I'll not do that again."

"Look over yonder, Jim," the chief of police said softly, pointing.

A long row of cats sat on a chain-link fence, watching silently as the sheriff's department car approached and drove slowly by. The tails of the cats swished back and forth, as if following the clicking of a metronome. Click. Swish. Click. Swish. The eyes of the cats, coldly unblinking, never left the car and the men in it.

"Another group about the same size across the street, Jim. Pull over, I got an idea."

The men got out of the car and approached the second group of cats in a silent face-off with the cats across the street. The cats allowed the men to pet them and scratch them behind their ears, purring softly in contentment.

"Just like people," Jim said. "Some good and some bad. We've found some allies, Max."

"Yeah. But how do we tell them apart?"

"Just like people, Max. I reckon we can't until the action starts."

The cat purred under his touch and licked his

hand with a rough tongue.

As the sun began dipping more and more toward surrender to the night, and the guests began gathering at Dee's A-frame, one inmate in the Reeves County jail decided it was time to make his move.

For the past two nights, Josh Taft had been hearing voices and having some real pissers of dreams. Finally, in order to get some sleep, he had agreed—in his dreams—to the demands stated in return for his freedom.

Of course, Josh knew it was all a bunch of crap, but when you're in jail and facing the rest of your life being locked down hard in the bucket, you'll agree to damn near anything.

Sitting on the edge of his bunk, the evening meal over, Josh heard the voice tell him, "Now, Josh. It's all ready. Do it now."

Josh felt kind of stupid following the directions of a voice that he knew wasn't real. But he knew all those years in prison that faced him were damn sure real. And he also knew he wasn't the type of man that could survive behind the walls of gray-rock college—somebody would kill him.

So what the hell? He'd do what the voice had earlier told him to do. When he failed, and he knew he was going to fail, all it would get him was a good ass-whipin' from some of the guards.

He looked down at his hands. The voice had told him that when Josh was ready, just go to the door and stand. Then do whatever he felt had to be done. "Sure," Josh muttered. "Right."

"Are you doubting me?" the voice whispered.

Josh looked around him. His cell was empty—as

135

usual. The whole damn cell block was empty 'cept for him. So where the hell was this voice coming from? He didn't know it, yet, but he had already answered part of that question.

"Why me and not the others?" Josh asked, his voice barely audible. Hell, he didn't want the other prisoners to think he was nuts.

His lawyer said that defense wouldn't work anymore. He'd done it too many times; he'd pleaded not guilty by reason of insanity too many times in the past.

The voice giggled. "They are with you and waiting. You are their leader. So to speak."

Josh stood up. "Well," he muttered. "Sooner we get this over with the sooner I can forget all about it and get some sleep."

"Oh ye of little faith," the voice taunted. "If you will forgive a bit of plagiarism."

Josh didn't know what that meant, so he merely shrugged his heavy shoulders and walked to the door. The doors in the cell blocks opened with a key, or the jailer could push a main button that would open all of them. Individual cells could also be opened by button if the jailer so chose. It was all done electrically.

Josh heard a click. He knew what that click meant. The door was open. The thought that he was being set up entered his mind.

"Nay, nay," the voice said. "But I won't do your killing for you. There are still jailers and deputies you have to deal with."

"You let me worry about that."

"Oh, I shall, I shall!"

Josh hadn't heard any other clicks, but since he was the only prisoner housed on the so-called "bad side," the faint clicks probably would not penetrate the thick concrete and steel-reinforced walls.

Josh stepped out into the hall.

Somewhere in the jail he could hear laughter and the sound infuriated him, filling him with a sort of rage he had never before experienced. Josh felt ten feet tall and strong as a bear.

"Oh, you are," the voice told him. "Go on. The others are waiting for you to lead them."

Josh took a couple of steps and mentally went over the list of other prisoners. He liked it. They were good boys, most of them, rough and rowdy from up in the ridges. Ten at last count. Good ol' boys who didn't give a damn for law and order, and they was all lookin' at anywheres from five to twenty-five years. He figured they'd all come with him.

Josh reached the main cell block door and he heard the lock click open. He paused for a moment. If that voice had really told the truth about who it belonged to, by stepping through that cell door he had just lost his soul.

But did that really mean a damn to him?

Didn't take him long to come up with the answer to that: No.

He put his hand on the steel door. "How about the cameras?"

"They won't see you, Josh. Trust me."

Josh didn't figure he had a whole hell of a lot of choice in the matter. He looked out through the thick, reinforced glass. The big room called the run-around was empty.

Josh pushed the door open and stepped out about the same time as Carey Ellis pushed open the door from the other cell block. The men stood for a moment, grinning at each other. Carey was looking at twenty-five for second-degree murder.

Paul Grant came out next. Paul was a no-good from way back. Thief, child-molester, moonshiner (no telling how many people had gotten bad sick or just up and died from drinking his rotten 'shine — Paul made damn sure it was never sold in Reeves County), and two-bit car thief. Paul grinned.

A parade of human crud followed. Louis Easton, Mark Hay, Steve Larkin, Hal Richards, and guys Josh knew only as Fox, Levi, and Willis.

Josh motioned Carey over to him. "Go in the kitchen and get knives, meat cleavers, whatever." He grinned. "It's pig-slaughterin' time in Reeves County."

Carl was determined to make this evening as enjoyable as possible. He felt the good times in Reeves County, as in Ruger County, would soon be over. He sipped on a beer, waiting for Dee to signal him it was time to put the steaks on.

Carl had met and liked Tom Malone instantly. He looked and walked like a man who was sure of his ability to take care of himself, but without the cockiness and swagger of the bully. Tom and Father Vincent came out to the porch and sat down with Carl and Mike.

"I can't get a word out of Mike," the priest said with a smile. "Perhaps you can tell me what's going on in this town, Carl."

"Several murders to be sure."

Chuck laughed. "You're as close-mouthed as the deputy there. Just before I came out here, one of my congregation called and wanted to know about a secret meeting that was held over at Doctor Bartlett's lab today. Would you know anything about that,

Carl?"

A sweet, sad, and very inviting song drifted to the men from out of the dark woods. It was sung by someone with a lovely soprano voice in perfect pitch, blending in with the long shadows of the night. It touched all but one of the men on the porch.

"Don't listen to it," Carl warned. "And above all else, do not go into those woods."

With those words, the lovely song faded into a low and ugly menacing growl.

"What the hell?" Tom said.

"You said it," Carl told him.

Father Chuck Vincent sighed.

Tom looked confused.

Deputy Mike Randall looked scared.

A foul odor drifted to the men on the front porch. It was the first time the Episcopal priest and the insurance agent had smelled the odor of evil. Both of them fanned the area around and under their noses.

"The Old Ones are not far from the surface," Carl told them. "That smell signals they are close. Among other things. It's the odor that lingered around Satan."

"Gods of the old Egyptian order of Seti," Chuck said.

Carl looked at him. "Yes."

"That would explain some of the symbols back in Val's room."

"Val who?" Carl asked.

Tom explained about the fight and what led up to it and his daughter's running away.

"You had best be prepared for the possibility of her never returning," Carl warned the man. "The odds are not good."

"The way my wife feels right now that would certainly not disappoint her. I really believe that if I hadn't showed up when I did, Liza would have killed her."

"Or your daughter would have killed your wife," Carl said. "Remember this, people: Satan-worshippers are dangerous. Their anti-social behavior prompts them to commit violent acts just for the hell of it. And they have a total lack of conscience. Killing one of us would bring about no more remorse in them than swatting a fly or stepping on a roach."

"I talked to Jim this afternoon, Carl," Mike said. "He said go ahead and level with everybody out here."

"Have you told Judy anything?"

"No. I thought I'd leave that up to you."

Carl looked first at Tom, then at the priest. "You people better go fix yourselves a stiff drink. You're going to need it."

Chapter 14

Josh stepped around a corner and buried the meat cleaver in the deputy's head. The deputy died without uttering a sound.

Working the heavy blade free of the skull bone, Josh lowered the body to the tile floor and quickly stripped the weapon from the man, leather and all. He belted the rig around his waist.

"Hey, Melton!" a voice called from the other side of the concrete block wall. "You gonna make a career out of gettin' that coffee."

Josh walked around the corner to the interrogation room and lopped the second man's head off with one vicious swing of the meat cleaver. The headless deputy toppled from his chair as his head bounced on the floor, leaving a bloody smear.

Levi stepped into the room. "I got the radio operator, Josh. Ain't nobody else in the jail." He grinned, holding up a set of keys. "The gun cabinet."

"Let's go!"

"What about the other prisoners?" Steve asked.

"Screw 'em."

Louis laughed. "I done that to most of them, a couple of times."

141

Janet and Gary knew they were the objects of a hunt. They lay on the floor of an empty building across from Nick's house and watched as the coven members gathered and then spread out, leaving in all directions.

Janet shook her head. "I don't know what to do," she said, her words almost a wail of frightened confusion.

"We got to level with our parents," Gary told her. "We got to make them understand what is happening and what's about to happen in Butler."

"They won't believe us. I've told my parents so many lies over the past couple of years, if I tell them good morning they look outside to see. And my dad's been acting funny, Gary. He's been giving me some really strange looks lately."

"You mean, like . . ."

"Yeah. I mean like that."

"But your dad is a deacon in the church!" He was silent for a few heartbeats. "Janet, you think that maybe . . ."

"Yeah. I think, Gary. I think that nobody is going to be able to stop it now. I think all that stuff that Nick used to talk about, that stuff that you and I thought was only a bunch of hooey, is turning out to be real. You remember that Nick said the weak people in the town would be the first ones to join . . . and they wouldn't even know they were doing it?"

"Yeah. I remember. Your dad?"

"My dad."

"Awesome!"

"At least that. And here is something else to think about. Your folks and my folks are as close as sardines."

"Yeah. So that lets out going to my house for sure. And for sure we can't stay here. Sooner or later Nick is going to check this place out."

"Guess what, assholes!" The voice came from behind the kids.

They turned to look at several coven members, standing in the hall of the empty house. They held baseball bats in their hands.

"Now what?" Gary asked, as he and Janet rose to their knees.

"You gonna die!"

The escaped prisoners had turned the jail into a slaughterhouse before leaving by the back way. Blood splattered the walls of several rooms as the prisoners released their rage on the surprised dispatcher, the jailer, one unlucky deputy who had wandered in for coffee, and several prisoners they thought had been snitches. The convicts were all now heavily armed with high-powered rifles, riot guns, and pistols, with enough ammunition to start a major war.

Keeping to the shadows, they ran across a road and into a clump of trees behind a long-abandoned gas station. Under normal circumstances, their only thought would have been to find a car and get the hell gone from this area.

But these were far from normal circumstances.

And they had, to a man, made promises.

And when one makes promises to the Dark One, those promises are kept.

"Let's boost a car and get the hell gone from here," Hal suggested.

"We can't," Josh told him.

"Why the hell not?"

Scratch. Purr.

"What the hell was that?" Willis asked, looking around him.

Josh didn't know for sure what it was, but he had a pretty good idea. And looking at Carey, Josh felt the other con did too.

"I'm gettin' out of here!" Hal said, standing up and turning to leave

Josh pulled the man back down. "Don't go actin' like a fool, man. Think about it. Them doors didn't just open by themselves back yonder in the jail. All the closed-circuit cameras didn't quit operatin' just 'cause we wanted them to."

"I think we all done fucked up," Louis said.

"It ain't gonna be long 'fore somebody calls in," Steve reminded the others. "When nobody answers, they gonna be cops all over that jail. We can't just sit here doin' nothin'."

Mark Hay rubbed his crotch. "I want a woman. I got to have me a woman. Them sissy-boys back in the jail is all right, but they ain't nothin' takes the place of pussy."

"I'll opt for that too," Fox said. "Bound to be some kid walkin' around town. The night's early. We'll grab her and gang-bang her."

"First thing we'll do is get the hell away from the jail," Josh told them. "We'll clear the town and then worry about some snatch." He looked at each con just as that strange scratching and purring sound once more drifted to them. "Any objections?"

"I thought it was just a joke," Levi said. His voice held a slight trembling. "That it was all a dream. But if it ain't?"

Josh laughed at them. "So what the hell difference

does it make, boys? There ain't a man among us who ain't killed while we was stealin' or rapin' or whatever. It's just that Carey got caught doin' it, that's all. So what's the big deal?"

"What do you mean, Josh?" Mark asked.

"We was Hell-bound anyways. That's why we was chosen by . . ." He refused to say the word. He sighed as he met the eyes of the others, squatting in the gloom of the thicket. "I reckon . . . the one who talked to us all felt he might as well get some use out of us 'fore we checked out."

"But I been saved!" Fox cried out softly.

"How many times?" Josh asked scornfully.

Fox thought for a moment. "Oh, six or seven, at least."

"You asshole!" Steve told him. "And what was you thinkin' about when you went under the water all them times?"

Fox grinned in the gloom. "Pussy!"

Carl had told of the events in Ruger County and of what had transpired since he arrived in Reeves County — all that he knew, that is.

Father Vincent was the first to speak. "Sheriff Rodale really saw the hands and face of that old woman?"

"Yes. Saliva taken from the window proves that she was there."

"That's impossible," Tom said. "Kids stole her head and hands and rigged up that . . . scene. That's what happened. It's just kids, that's all."

The song of the siren came once more from the dark woods around the home. And with it came that strong and foul evil odor.

"It's . . . beautiful," Liza said, breaking the momentary silence.

"It's also deadly," Carl told the older woman. "It has hidden messages within."

Liza met the younger man's eyes. Images of them locked in sweaty embrace suddenly filled her head. His lips were kissing her breasts, sucking the nipples, gently biting them. His hand was between her legs, fingers seeking, finding, entering, working in and out. She moved her hand downward, grasping his hot thickness.

Liza jumped from the chair and shook her head. "Damn!" she said.

"What's wrong, honey?" Tom asked.

"Don't listen to that singing," she warned him. "It's hypnotic."

"What were you thinking?"

She glanced briefly at Carl. He met her eyes and she quickly averted them. It had all been so damned real. "It's nothing. It's nothing." But did she really want it to be nothing? She remembered the young man's lips, roaming over her body. She fought the question and the scene away. "I believe Carl, Tom."

"Oh, come on, honey!" He stood up to face her. "We've got some badly screwed-up kids in this town, that's all. The Devil is not walking among us. For Heaven's sake, baby, get real, will you?"

The song of the Devil's soprano touched his mind. The priest's wife was naked, standing before him. She slowly knelt and took his hardness into her mouth. In his trance, Tom could not suppress a groan of satisfaction as she took him.

He shook himself like a big dog and gripped the porch railing with both hands. "God!" The word exploded from his mouth.

146

"What were you thinking, Tom?" Chuck asked.

Tom could not meet the man's eyes. "I'd be embarrassed to tell you, Father."

The soprano hit another note and it was as if some invisible hand twisted Tom's head to one side. He tried to fight the movement. He could not. He was bent almost double. He could not speak as he stood like a misshapen beast while sexual scenes filled his brain. He was making love to Carol Vincent. She moved under him, moaning and whispering the vilest of things in his ear.

Tom tried to speak. But only animal-like grunting sounds could push past his lips.

Carl stood up and walked into the house, returning in only a few seconds, a bible in his hand. He held it up, letting the faint light catch the outline of the cross on the front of the word of God.

The siren's song ended with a horrible scream. With a grunt of pain, Tom straightened up, his face mirroring his inner fright.

"You still doubt me, Tom?" Carl asked.

Tom shook his head, afraid to speak, afraid his voice would fail him. His neck hurt. He stood silent, trying to rub the soreness away.

When Tom finally found his voice, he looked at his wife. "I'll feel better if I say it. I was thinking . . . sexual things. But not with you, Liza."

"I was thinking the same thing, honey. And you were not my partner."

"What's happening, Carl?" Dee asked.

Mike sat with his mouth open, Judy by his side, holding his hand.

"Mind games, I guess. I know something about covens and cults, people. Not about the inner workings of Satan. That's Father Vincent's field."

The thick woods lay dark and very quiet around the house.

"That was a good move, Carl," the priest said. "You getting the bible. That proves to me everything you said was true. At least in my mind." He looked at Tom Malone, who was rubbing his sore neck. "Kids — some of them — are most certainly in on this, Tom, but I don't believe for a minute that they are the main players." He smiled sadly. "I am afraid that all my years of schooling did not really prepare me for anything like this." He opened his mouth to say something else, then minutely shook his head and remained silent.

"Someone coming up the road," Mike said, breaking the silence.

The car slowed, stopped, and Jim Hunt got out, walking slowly up the way. Dingo met him at the gate, sniffed once or twice, and let him enter. Jim stopped at the foot of the steps.

" 'Fraid you're back on duty, Mike. There's been a slaughter at the jail. The jailer and two deputies dead and four prisoners dead. All the bad ones on sides one and two are gone. They emptied the gun cabinet and took the sidearms from the deputies they killed."

Mike jumped to his feet. "How the hell did they get out?"

"We don't know that. No signs of a forced breakout. Seems like all the doors just opened." He looked at Carl. "These ol' boys that busted out are bad ones. Most of 'em we was housin' for the DOC due to overcrowdin' in the state prisons. Rapists, murderers, and the like. I'm sorry to interrupt your eatin', but I'd feel a lot better if Mike was to escort you town folks back to town. We got to get the state boys

148

in on this, so y'all better brace yourselves. Ain't no tellin' what's liable to happen now. They sure to find out about the tore-up and eat-on bodies, and they're gonna be askin' questions. And I don't know just how to answer them."

"Tell them truth, Jim," Carl said.

"The truth? What is the truth? That we got ghosts and hants and bodyless heads and hands a-floatin' around? Some sort of wild inhuman creatures with green slime for blood slippin' through the night? A ten-thousand-year-old girl and a cat, both of them burned to a crisp? Old gods about to surface from the bowels of the earth? That what you want me to tell them? Folks, was I tell them state boys that, you know what's gonna happen? I'll tell you. We gonna have this county filled up with people—all sorts of people—nuts and cranks and weirdos and press people from all over the nation. We can't have that. I ain't never lied to the state police before. But I'm afraid I might have to this go-around."

"I don't understand," Tom said. "Why not tell them about what's happening?"

"The more people who know, the more innocent people will get swept up in it," Carl said. "I understand what you're saying, Jim."

Jim nodded his head. "Mike, get these people back to town and get into gear."

A dark chuckle rose from the equally dark timber, the tainted laughter followed by the foul smell. The chuckle touched Chuck Vincent harder than the others, the ominous laughter almost like a slap across his face. His own face tightened.

"Bastard!" the priest whispered.

His wife gave him a strange look. "Who?"

"The Lord of Flies. The Prince of Darkness. Satan. Can't you feel his presence? My skin is crawling from the filth that surrounds him like maggots on dead flesh."

A terrible pain filled Chuck's head. He put both hands to his temples as a cry of anguish sprang from his mouth. The pain was so intense the priest slumped from the chair and fell to the front of the porch.

He experienced a sharp blow to his butt and felt himself being propelled down the steps, to land in a heap by the chief deputy's boots.

"Onward Christian Soldiers," a heavy voice rumbled as lightning suddenly licked the night sky, with no following thunder. "Providing you can get up off your ass, that is."

Dingo sprang to his feet, hair on his back standing up and teeth bared as loud purring filled the night. It sounded as though a hundred lions were crouched in the darkness, waiting to spring.

The pain in Chuck's head gradually faded and Jim helped the man to his feet. The purring ceased its reverberating through the night.

"A piece of cake," the voice rumbled. "This won't even be a contest."

Carl began speaking from memory. "The Lord is my shepherd; I shall not want. . . ."

Wild shrieking bruised the night, the wailing seeming to come from the very deepest pits of Hell.

"He maketh me lie down in green pastures: he leadeth me beside the still waters. . . ."

The night was filled with a loud roaring. Carl was suddenly spilled from his chair and thrown off the porch, landing heavily on the ground. He rolled to his knees and faced the dark forest. "You're afraid of us!" he yelled. "With all your monsters and spooks

150

and supernatural beings, you're still afraid of us. You're afraid that without your direct help, you won't win."

Something flitted at the very edge of the fenced area. The shadowy shape never quite defined.

"Don't look at it!" Chuck yelled. "Don't look at it!"

Carl closed his eyes and pointed a finger at the darkness. "You interfered in Ruger, and you lost. And you know why. You broke the rules."

"Broke the rules?" Jim muttered, his eyes averted from the evil that slithered and pranced and spun through the darkness just outside the chain-link fence. "Rules? What is this, a game?"

"And you're breaking the rules now!" Carl shouted.

The cloudy darkness filled with slow, heavy breathing, each breath filled with the smell of decaying bodies.

Then the evil was gone, although none saw it leave. Instead they sensed the departing.

"Was that . . ." Judy couldn't bring herself to say the word.

"Yes," Chuck told her. "It was."

Jim began speaking. The others quickly joined in. "Yea, though I walk through the valley of the shadow of death, I will fear no evil: for thou art with me; thy rod and thy staff they comfort me."

From inside the timber, the siren's song began.

Chapter 15

Gary and Janet didn't wait around to be beaten to death by the baseball-bat-wielding coven members. They sprang to their feet and rushed them, the move catching the devil-worshippers by surprise. Gary tore the bat from a young man and smashed him across the back with it, knocking him to the dusty floor.

"Run, Janet!" he yelled.

"No way," she said grimly, and picked up a board from the floor. She faced those she once thought to be her friends. "Come on, you crazy bastards," Janet taunted them.

The coven members jumped at the pair, Gary and Janet swinging bat and board at the same time.

Bat and board connected with flesh and the coven members began screaming in pain as the blood squirted from their bruised and torn bodies. They dropped their clubs as Janet and Gary beat them unconscious and then ran from the old house into the fading light.

The kids ran blindly at first, then, as they paused to catch their breath, Janet said, "We can't just run and run, Gary. We got to have a place to run to!"

"I'm sure open to suggestions," Gary panted. "Home is out. I don't know who our friends are, or even if we've got any. That doesn't leave us much, Janet."

"How about that guy that Nick was carryin' on about the other night? That guy from Richmond who's supposed to be some sort of coven-buster."

"Yeah. Okay. But he's staying out with Miss Conners. And that's miles from town. We don't have any wheels."

She grinned at him and patted her legs. "We got these. Come on!"

"You're sure you wouldn't rather go on into town?" Carl asked.

"I'm sure. I told you: This is my home and nobody or *thing* is going to run me out."

"Anything happens to you," Carl said, "and your dad will have my ass."

She knew better than that. For the first time in her life, her father had immediately liked a boy or man that Dee liked. He had told her so, and also told her that she would be a fool to let this one slip away. And much to her surprise, her mother liked Carl, not once asking whether his ancestors came over on the Mayflower with the rest of the malcontents from England.

"I still want a steak for dinner," she told him. "Are the coals still hot?"

"They should be." He laughed aloud.

"What's so damn funny, Carl? I'm *hungry!*"

"Yeah. So am I. And that's what's so damn funny. Dee, just moments ago I was tossed off the porch, and so was Father Vincent, who also got an

153

invisible kick in the butt. The Devil, Dee, Satan, was right out there." He pointed. "And we're sitting here discussing having dinner! Dee, don't think of this as a joke. It isn't. We could be dead in the next heartbeat —"

Scratch. Purr.

Dee jumped at the sound as Dingo growled. The night once more became quiet.

"That was a warning, wasn't it, Carl?"

"Yes," Carl told her, as dark shapes began materializing just a few hundred yards outside the fence. They did not make any attempt to approach the house. They stood in silence, staring.

"Who are they, Carl?"

"I don't know. But I intend to find out if a bullet will stop them." Carl walked into the house, and seconds later Dee once more jumped as rifle fire shattered the night. Carl was shooting from the rear of the house. Dee saw two of the dark shapes spin and fall to the ground. The others scattered, running toward the safety of the timber.

Carl walked through the house, carrying the rifle. He leaned the heavy bolt-action 7-mm magnum in a corner and picked up an M-16, walking out to the porch.

"Call Jim Hunt, Dee. Tell him we've had trouble here and to come on out. Tell him code three. He'll know what you mean."

Jim was out in fifteen minutes, followed by an unmarked car. The two men who got out of the car were introduced as Virginia Highway Patrol detectives, and they were not happy about Carl holding the M-16.

"Is that thing fully automatic, boy?" one asked.

"Sure is, *man*," Carl told him.

"He has a Federal firearms permit to transport and carry automatic weapons," Jim said, stepping in before anymore words could be exchanged. "I ran it, and it's valid." He looked at Carl. "Sorry about them taggin' along, Carl. They been assigned here."

"How lucky for us," Carl said, slightly sarcastic.

"All right!" the second VHP man, who had been introduced as Lieutenant Daly, shouted. "Now look, damnit. We've been lied to for the past hour and a half, and I'm tired of it. The mayor has lied to us, the sheriff has lied to us, the chief deputy has lied to us, and the chief of police has lied. Now Carl, I know who you are. I was friends with your daddy. I came in shortly after the . . . incident in Ruger County. Is this going to be a repeat performance? And goddamnit, tell me the truth."

Carl stared at the man, finally placing him. He had been out to their home in Valentine several times, and had been very helpful in arranging the funerals and other matters.

Carl looked at the other detective, who had been introduced as Sergeant Tolson. "What about him?"

"What about him?"

"What does he know about Ruger?"

"Nothing."

"What's going on?" Tolson asked. He jerked a thumb toward Carl. "I don't like this guy's attitude, Hugh."

The look that Daly gave the sergeant stated that not only did the lieutenant not like Tolson's attitude, he wasn't too terribly thrilled with Tolson himself at the moment. "Let's you and me talk, Carl."

"Suits me."

"I have coffee, gentlemen," Dee called from the porch.

"That sounds good," Jim said.

Tolson walked to the gate, took one look at Dingo, and said, "If that dog comes at me, I'll put a bullet in its head."

Carl turned, planted his feet, and gave Tolson a solid right to the side of the jaw. The punch knocked the trooper off his feet and landed him on the ground. When the man opened his eyes, he was staring directly into the muzzle of the M-16. He lifted his eyes to look at Carl. The muzzle and the eyes of the man holding the weapon held the same deadly message.

"I just don't like you, you son of a bitch!" Carl told him.

"I certainly got that impression," the trooper said. "I think we got off on the wrong foot." He suddenly grinned. "I don't know what's going on here, but if you'll take that M-16 out of my nose, we can start all over."

Carl lifted the M-16 and held out his hand. Tolson took it and got to his feet. Standing up, he eyeballed Carl as he rubbed his jaw. "You 'bout twenty-five pounds heavier than I first pegged you. I haven't been hit that hard in a long time. Truce?" He held out his hand.

Carl shook the hand. "Truce."

"Tolson, go on with Jim and get some coffee. I want to talk with Garrett."

"Yes, sir."

When they were alone in the night, standing outside the chainlink fence, Daly said, "What's going on, Carl?"

"A repeat performance of what happened in Ruger. Only this time it's bigger and much better organized. Do you really know what happened in

Ruger?"

"I know bits and pieces of it, Carl. People like to talk, you know that. But I don't know what to believe and what not to believe."

Carl very quickly brought him up to date, watching with some dark amusement as the man's expression changed a dozen times during the briefing.

"Why isn't this . . . chanting or singing going on now?" Tolson asked.

"They don't want you in here either."

"Thanks a lot. It's so nice to feel wanted."

"You know what I mean."

"I suppose. This Linda Crowley, she's one of . . . whatever these things are?"

"We believe so."

"Any trace of this Ralph Geason?"

"Not that I'm aware of. But when he does surface, he'll be changed."

Daly was silent for a moment. "I liked Captain Taylor. He was one of the finest men I ever knew. These . . . things killed him, didn't they?"

"Yes."

"For no other reason than revenge."

"Yes."

"You know what I have to do, Carl."

"Don't call any more people in, Lieutenant. I just told you what happened in Ruger."

"I've got to make a report, Carl."

"When?"

"Well . . . within the next couple of days for sure."

"Hold off as long as you can. Will you do that for me?"

The trooper scratched his jaw. Sighed. "Okay, Carl. Two days, max. Then I've got to pull some

157

people in here."

"As soon as you do that, the press will be all over us."

"That isn't necessarily true. I can request they not come in convoy-style and I can also request plain-clothes."

"Lieutenant, everything I do is not going to be legal," Carl reminded the state cop.

"Like what?"

"Like those two bodies out there." Carl pointed toward the darkness.

The trooper's eyes followed the pointing finger. He unwrapped a piece of gum and stuck it into his mouth, chewing for a moment. "I don't see a damn thing out there, Carl," he finally said. "I think either it was your imagination or you're a terrible shot. I'll tell Tolson about the so-called shooting . . . in a few days. Right now, I'm going to get some coffee and pleasure myself eyeballing Miss Conners. You and Jim can go stomp around out there while I keep Tolson occupied."

At first glance the bodies were human-appearing. But under the flashlights' glow Jim and Carl could make out features that definitely were not human. The heavy, protruding brow, the simian eyes and nose, the wide, leathery, apelike mouth. And the teeth: more like fangs.

"Jesus!" Jim said, summing it up.

"I never saw or heard of anything like this in Ruger, Jim. Something new has been added."

"I could have done without it. What the heck are these things?"

"Holy shit!" The voice came from behind them.

158

The men turned. Tolson stood there, his eyes bugged out and his mouth open. The trooper appeared to be in a mild form of shock.

Tolson shook his head and cleared his throat. "I got the feeling I was being stalled. When Hugh went to the john I came out to see what was going on. Me and Hugh play the good guy-bad guy routine so often with suspects—with me always the bad guy—I sometimes can't shake the character. So I was being stalled and you've leveled with Hugh. How about leveling with me?"

"Squat down here and look at these things," Jim told him. "Carl will bring you up to date."

Tolson squatted. His squat didn't last long. By the time Carl finished speaking, the trooper was sitting on the ground, staring unbelievingly at first Jim and then Carl. Several times he opened his mouth to speak and several times he closed it. Finally he got to his feet to stand over and point at the dead horrors.

"These things have to be taken in for autopsy."

"Burn them!" Carl said.

"No way, man. This is proof that all you've said is not a bunch of baloney. We've got to have proof or we're all going to be labeled nuts! You know damn well the press is going to get hold of this. Sooner or later they'll be in here."

"I got to agree with him, Carl," Jim said.

"Neither one of you understand," Carl said, pleading with the men. "These things"—he pointed—"will rise again."

"Rise again!" Tolson blurted out, just as Daly walked out to join them, Dee with him. "You mean like . . . zombies or something like that?"

"Yes."

159

"I agree with that too," Jim said. "What was left of Old Lady Barstow durn sure come out of that cooler."

Both troopers looked at the chief deputy with a mixture of horror and disbelief in their eyes.

From the forest that surrounded them, the enticing song of the siren began.

"Don't listen to it," Carl warned. "Sing, whistle, pray—do anything except listen to that song."

Tolson looked toward the dark woods. "That's my mother's voice," he said wistfully. "She died when I was just a boy, but I'll never forget how pretty she was." He took a step toward the timber. "I'm coming, Momma. Yes. I hear you."

Carl knee-tackled the man and brought him down.

"Momma!" Tolson yelled, as they rolled on the cool ground. "Help me, Momma!" He began fighting Carl with the strength of ten men. He threw Carl from him.

"Pile on!" Carl yelled, struggling to get to his feet. "Don't let him go into those woods."

Everybody, including Dee, jumped on the trooper and rode him to the ground.

Jim, Carl, and Dee pinned the man while Daly worked to get handcuffs on him.

As soon as he was cuffed, the siren's song stopped and the woods fell silent.

"Hugh?" Tolson spoke. "What the hell happened? How come you got iron on me?"

"You thought it was your mother calling you from the woods. It took all of us to stop you."

"I don't remember anything. It's all a blank."

Daly unlocked the cuffs and Tolson sat up on the ground.

Dee looked at the bodies, a green, stinking slime leaking from the bullet holes in them, and wrinkled her nose in disgust.

"I'm going to override you on this one, Carl," Daly said. "Jim, call your coroner and have him come out here and get these . . . whatever they are. Tolson, we say nothing about these bodies. I promised Carl two days. Let's give it to him."

"Suits me," the trooper replied, standing up and brushing the dust from his clothes. "We damn sure want to keep this from the press as long as possible." He looked toward the dark timber and shook his head. "I never really believed in the Devil before. God and Jesus and the Hereafter, yeah, but not Satan."

"And now?" Jim asked, his voice soft.

"You're lookin' at a man who has just seen the light — so to speak."

Dee started screaming as a cold hand closed around her bare ankle.

Chapter 16

Ralph Geason crouched in the shadows of a warehouse and tried to make some sense out of what he had become. He could not. His brain could no longer reason in a human fashion. He had memories of his last night as a functioning human being, but they were cloudy and rapidly fading in what was now his animal-like brain.

He could remember Linda entering the bathroom where he was showering. He could remember the shock at her pulling back the curtains and standing there naked. He could remember the savage smile on her lips and the wild look in her eyes.

The rest was just a jumbled-up mass of confusion in his brain.

He knew he was being hunted and he knew he must be careful. He knew that for some reason—as yet unknown to him—he must survive for a few more days. He had become what he was for a reason, a purpose. He didn't know what, he didn't even know what he was, only that he was to be a part of something that was to happen very soon.

And Ralph knew he was hungry. Not for cheeseburgers or fried chicken or pizza. He craved something else. His taste buds now desired a much more primitive meal. Blood and raw meat. He would make his kill and drag the carcass back to his lair and feast, then he would sleep.

His lair. He looked around him at the dusty old warehouse. This was his lair. His. But something was missing. He pondered on that for a time, as he crouched naked on the floor, low growls emanating from his throat. Yes. He knew what it was. A mate. Life was not complete without a mate

He would make his kill and then find a mate with which to share the food.

Ralph scooted across the floor on all fours. He looked out a cobwebbed and dusty window. The night appeared safe. He pushed at the wall, seeking an exit. The wall did not move. He growled in frustration.

He scooted along the wall until coming to a door. Ralph crouched on the floor, studying the door. He understood this—sort of. He managed the doorknob and slipped out into the night. He had two things, and only two things on his mind: food and a mate.

Carl beat at the arm with a surveyor's stake he'd grabbed up from the ground, left there by one of the timber cutters. Daly dropped to the ground and was prying the fingers from Dee's ankle. He finally had to start bending and breaking the fingers in an attempt to free her. Shouting his rage, Carl grabbed the stake like a spear and drove the sharpened end into the center of the creature's chest. The living dead screamed as the stake penetrated flesh and pierced the heart. With a roar, the creature lumbered to its feet and staggered off into the night, the stake protruding from its chest, leaving a smear of greenish yellow slime on the ground, marking its escape into the timber.

Daly and Tolson were busy putting handcuffs on the wrists and ankles of the second body which was so far still lifeless. Both troopers were badly shaken by what they had just witnessed.

"I'll call in for the coroner," Jim said. "I got to find out if any of the escaped prisoners have been rounded up."

Carl put his arms around Dee and held her until she stopped trembling and crying.

"Can you walk?" he asked.

She nodded, her head against his chest. "Yes. I think my ankle is going to be bruised, but nothing's broken. That thing scared the *hell* out of me, Carl!"

"Lean on me. Let's get back to the house."

"We'll stay out here with this . . . ugly bastard," Daly said, looking down at the hideousness that lay on the ground.

The creature had opened its eyes and was glaring hate at those standing around it.

The moonlight glistened off the slime trail left by the living dead that had staggered off into the woods.

Carl and Dee met Jim halfway back to the house.

"The press picked up on the jailbreak," he told them. "I figured they would. We had to teletype other departments and warn them. I guess we'd better get ready for a lot of nosy people. I hate like the dickens for this to happen, but it's done, so we best get set."

"Doctor Bartlett on the way out here?"

"Yeah. Carl? That thing had two bullet holes in it and you run a stake through its chest. It's still alive. How the hell do you kill them?"

"Fire. It's the only way."

"But even that's not one hundred percent sure, is it? I mean, you say this Anya and Pet have returned, right?"

"They're gods. I'm not sure that a god can be killed. But those things"—he turned, pointing toward the savage-looking creature on the ground—"are in the service of the gods. They're minions. They can be killed."

"And Ralph Geason?" the question was posed softly.

"He's one of them, now. I saw it in Ruger County. There is no hope for him or any like him."

"That's a lot of killing, Carl."

"There is no other way. Resign yourself to it, Jim. It's the only way."

She had been on her way back from the movies when a hard hand clamped over her mouth and strong arms jerked her into the dewy and dangerous darkness. The escaped cons grinned as they silently lined up, awaiting their perverted turn, having their brutal way with the struggling teenage girl, grunting and panting and hunching between her widespread and naked legs.

After she passed out from mind-numbing fear, harsh pain, and total degradation, the cons tossed her naked and bruised body to one side, then continued on, searching for a safe haven in the town . . . and another girl to rape.

Alice Watson slowly regained consciousness and rolled over on her stomach, · pressing her face against the cool grass and sobbing hysterically for a few moments. She fought for control and gathered up her torn clothing, covering herself as best she could, then stumbled out of the darkness and into the street, where she was almost run over by Deputy Mike Randall, who was responding to an unknown-disturbance call.

Mike hurriedly placed her in the back seat and took her to the clinic, where Doctor Perry had just arrived to look in on a patient. Doctors Bartlett and Jenkins were on their way to the Conners property, after receiving the call from Jim.

Grim-faced, Perry took the rape kit from Mike and went to work. He had not yet been briefed on the trouble out at Dee's.

And Ralph Geason was stalking his prey.

"Big doin's in town," the pulpwood hauler muttered, sitting down on a bench in the schoolyard. He hauled out a pint bottle of hooch and took a deep pull. "Gawdam cops ever'where." He had just seen a cop car speed by and had ducked for the cover of darkness, not wanting to be picked up and charged with public drunkenness.

Champ Stinson — so called because he once fought professionally — heard a slight noise behind him. He turned around. He could see nothing in the darkness. Champ took another pull from the bottle and grimaced as the cheap bourbon burned its way down his throat and into his belly.

A meat wagon from the hospital sped by and

Champ wondered what was going on.

A low hissing came from behind him.

Without turning around, Champ said, "Git outta here, you gawddam mutt!" Champ didn't like animals of any kind. If he found a dog on his property, he shot it. No matter if it was wearing a collar with vaccination tag, he still shot it. And he hated cats even more than he did dogs.

Scratch. Purr.

That turned him around on the bench. But the sight before his drunken and bleary eyes amused him rather than frightened him. "Boy, you better git you some clothes on, you nitwit!"

Ralph Geason hissed and growled, crouching naked in the gloom.

"I'll kick your ass!" Champ warned, as Ralph inched closer.

Ralph roared and tried to stand upright; his stance was that of a great ape.

Champ stood up, finally getting it through his head that this was no joke. He balled his hands into fists and raised them. "Come on, then, you silly bastard!"

Ralph hissed and roared and jumped, the leap knocking Champ sprawling. Ralph was all over him, clawed hands tearing at flesh. With a scream of rage and pain, Champ slugged Ralph on the jaw, knocking the man from him. Champ got to his feet, planted them as firmly as he could, and gave Ralph a shot to the jaw, knocking the man down and momentarily out.

Torn and bleeding, Champ staggered off into the night, trying to remember where he'd parked his truck. His head felt funny, and his jaws ached . . .

kinda like he all of a sudden had more teeth than there was room for. But that was silly. He lurched around, found his truck, and cranked up, heading for the house.

Gary and Janet stopped at the chain-link fence. Both of them were footsore and tired . . . but they'd made it to the Conners place without encountering any more coven members. They stood looking at the big dog on the other side of the fence, who was looking at them. There seemed to be a lot of activity a few hundred yards from the house, and behind them, they could see the lights of the ambulance as it sped up the road.

The attendants didn't give them a second look as they jerked the gurney out of the back of the ambulance and ran toward the lights in the clearing.

"Another body," Gary whispered. "See it on the ground?"

"Yes. Why are we whispering?"

A horrible roaring cut short Gary's reply. Both kids stood in silence, watching at what they thought was a dead man began thrashing about, fighting his bonds and screaming in a language unknown to them and to anybody else standing close to the scene.

The screaming, roaring, fighting man was secured to the gurney and wheeled back to the ambulance.

". . . him to my lab," the young people heard Doctor Bartlett say. "And stay there with him. Keep him strapped down tight and don't say a word about this to anybody. I'll be about ten minutes behind you."

168

The ambulance pulled out, heading back to town. The man was still screaming.

"Hello," Dee said, causing both the kids to very nearly jump out of their tennis shoes. "Sorry," Dee apologized. "I didn't mean to frighten you."

"That's all right," Janet said. "It's been a scary night. Miss Conners, could we talk to you and that coven-buster?"

"Who? Oh. You mean Carl. Why, sure." She hesitated, looked at the young people for a moment, then swung open the gate. "Come on up to the porch. Carl will be back in a few minutes."

Both Gary and Janet picked up on her hesitation. "It's good to be cautious, Miss Conners," Janet told her. "I guess you know what's going on in town, right?"

Dee glanced at the girl. "Perhaps." She waved them to chairs and they both sat down with a sigh. "You sound tired."

"We walked from town."

"But that's *miles!*" She had to smile as Janet took off one tennis shoe and began rubbing her foot.

"Yes, ma'am," Gary said. "But we didn't have much choice in the matter. We split from the coven and now Nick and the others are trying to kill us."

Was this a trick? Dee questioned silently. It could well be, but somehow she didn't think so. The kids were obviously near exhaustion and they looked scared. They'd jumped about a foot in the air when she'd first spoken to them by the fence.

"Will you swear warrants out against them?" Carl asked from the door. He had come in the back way after spotting the two strangers sitting on the porch with Dee and had heard Gary's last few words.

169

Dee stood up and introduced them, telling Carl all of what Gary had just told her.

"It wouldn't do any good to swear out warrants," Janet said. "They'd all just lie and stick together. But I think I know where the bodies of Lanny and Dora were buried." She put her hands to her face and began to cry. Gary put an arm around her shoulders.

Carl waited until she had dried her eyes and blown her nose before holding up a hand. He concluded that not only was she telling the truth, she was also scared half to death. He wondered about Lanny and Dora—whoever they were. "I want to get Jim Hunt in on this—and the two state cops. You two just sit tight and relax." He left the porch, heading for the clearing and the lights.

"Come on," Dee said to Janet. "I'll show you the bathroom and you can wash your face. You'll feel better."

By the time Janet returned to the porch, the cops had gathered and Dee was brewing a fresh pot of coffee.

"A question, girl," Jim said. "How big is the coven in Butler?"

"They never let us know for sure. I do know that my group"—she looked at Gary—"our group, had about forty people in it. I think there are three groups in town, and one out in the county. Only the coven leaders are allowed to meet each other. My group was the senior of the young people's group. The only time the younger members were allowed to join us was when a lot of sex was involved."

"An orgy?" Daly asked.

"They're never called that, but I guess that's what it was. Everybody just sticks it in anything that's available."

"Boys with boys and girls with girls?" Tolson asked, a disgusted look on his face.

"Sure. If that's the way you like it. There are no sexual hang-ups in covens. The rule is, if it feels good, do it."

"There are younger members?" Daly asked. "Younger than you two?"

"Oh, sure. I started when I was twelve. And there were some lots younger than me. Whole families take part. You got some real perverts in covens. Dirty-minded men who say that sex before eight is great."

"Or that sex before seven is heaven," Gary added. "It goes on all the time."

Jim spat on the ground. Daly softly cussed. Tolson looked as though he'd like to puke. "If you two will testify," Tolson said, "we have a case."

"I'll testify," Janet and Gary said as one.

"Jim, what do you know about this Lanny and Dora?" Carl said.

"They disappeared just about two years ago. Manhunt went on for a long time. Finally it just petered out. We had absolutely no leads at all. I mean, not a one."

"They tried to leave the coven," Janet said. "Did leave. But before they could get to the police, Nick and some of the others caught them. They were both tortured and raped and then sacrificed. Their hearts were cut out during a black mass. Then their bodies were cut up with a chain saw and buried way out in the county."

171

"Do you know where?" Jim asked.

"Pretty close," Gary took it. "We weren't at the black mass when it was done, but we've both heard kids talk. They were buried right next to that little creek that runs north to south on this side of the mountains. By Flat Ridge."

"I know the spot," Jim said. "I'm thinkin', boys, that we may just be able to bust this whole thing wide open before the crap hits the fan full force."

"I'm thinking the same," Daly said. He looked at the kids. "The DA, kids—what do you know about him?"

"He's part of it," Janet told him. "Don't trust him. There is a whole lot of adults in the coven. If I had to guess, I'd say two hundred and fifty adults and that many kids, all over the county. The way we hear it, Reeves County was gonna be the headquarters for the entire state. And the Old Ones are very nearly ready to come up from out of the earth."

"Have you ever seen one of these . . . Old Ones?" Tolson asked.

"No, sir. But Linda Crowley has. She's from Ruger County and is pretty much in charge of all the covens here."

"The girl I told you about," Carl said, looking at Jim.

"There is something else," Gary said. "Another reason we came out here. We know who's been making the obscene calls to you, Miss Conners. It was Nick and Linda Crowley and some adults. We were both there a couple of times when they did it."

"More charges," Daly said. "I can get some warrants from the state. I'll get a couple of dozen signed warrants and fill in the names as we go

172

along. I'll have to do some arm-twisting, but I can get it done."

Conversation stopped as Mike's unit slid to a stop and the young deputy ran to the fence. Dee grabbed Dingo and held him while Carl let the deputy in.

"Alice Watson's been raped, Jim. The escaped cons grabbed her and took turns. They used her bad. And she's changing real fast."

"Changing?" Daly asked. "What do you mean?"

"It's not Alice Watson anymore. I don't know what it is strapped on that bed, but she . . . it doesn't even look human anymore. And I stood right there and watched her change. She's . . . turned all scaly and ugly. She's just a monster."

"Can she speak?"

"Not anymore. Not in any language I ever heard before. And Doctor Perry is about to come unglued."

"Bartlett and Jenkins left about five minutes ago," Jim said, glancing at his watch. "Mike, get on your way to town. Bump Dispatch and have a unit head the doctors off and warn them what's goin' down so they'll be prepared for it. Daly, you get them warrants pronto. We want to hit these devil-worshippers just before dawn." He looked at Janet and Gary. "You two got to be put under protective custody."

"They can stay out here with us," Dee said. "They'll be as safe here as anywhere . . . providing they don't want to go home."

"Our parents are part of it," Janet said. "They'd turn us over to Nick as soon as we walked in the door."

From deep in the darkness of thousands of acres

173

of timber, the siren's song began.

Jim touched the butt of his .357. "I ever get that woman in gun sights, she ain't gonna sing no more."

Chapter 17

Upon awakening from unconsciousness, Ralph Geason snarled, growled, and ran toward the old two-story high school building. Somewhere in his mind he remembered its musty halls well, having graduated from that very building some years back. And he also recalled that young people liked to gather in the basement of the building to drink and, in more modern times, smoke dope. He headed for the basement of the building.

Champ Stinson sat in his overstuffed chair in his den and wondered how come it was he who felt so bad. His left hand had turned into an ugly clawed thing and his right hand was heading in that same direction. And the thoughts that were racing through his head had, at first, frightened him. Now he was becoming comfortable with them.

Being the type he was—or had been; called white trash in some parts of the country—the thoughts suited him perfectly. The thoughts—dream-visions of things that had been and would be again, very soon, and for a brief period of time—were dark in nature and very primitive and very bloody. In his soon-to-be-reality Champ was a mighty hunter, of both animals and men: the apex of blood-sport. A real macho man.

Champ stalked the land, killing for pleasure, killing anything that got in his way, and he took women where he found them, killing them after raping them. But no sooner had he killed them, they returned to life. Sort of. A dead-eyed, shuffling type of life. They followed him around, mumbling and making all sorts of strange hand signals that didn't make any sense to Champ.

Champ didn't like that part of his vision-dream, so he mentally shifted gears and moved on.

He was enjoying himself until his wife started squalling at him.

"Lazy, drunken, son of a bitch!" Her voice cut through his visions and brought him back as close as he would ever again come to reality.

Champ opened his eyes and stared at the woman he'd married twenty-five years back. Although why he'd married her escaped him at the moment. He opened his mouth and spoke to her.

Her expression changed to one of bewilderment, then of anger. "What the hell's the matter with you, you bum? Can't you speak English?"

Champ figured he was speaking English; sounded perfectly all right to him. He spoke to her again. But it only seemed to make her angrier.

Then she made the last great mistake of her normal life on earth. She stepped forward and slapped him.

Champ came out of the chair with a roar and belted her a good one, knocking the woman clear out the closed front door and sending her flying off the porch. She hit the ground screaming, scrambled to her feet, and tried to run off into the safety of the night.

Champ loped along behind her, running in much the same manner as an ape, but with a lot more speed and endurance, laughing and grunting as he ran. He soon tired of the game, caught up with her, and broke her neck with one swift movement. He squatted by the body for a few minutes, grunting and poking at the cooling carcass. The headlights of a car approaching turned his head. Through the mist that had settled in his brain, he recognized the car as belonging to one of his sons. All four of Champ's sons were at least two bricks shy of a full wheelbarrow load, but it was doubtful that this one, Keith, even understood the rudiments of operating a wheelbarrow.

The car slowed and then stopped. Keith stuck his head out the window. He was stoned to the eyes, as usual. If dope could be smoked, snorted, swallowed, shot up, or stuck up his ass, Keith would be more than happy to oblige. Consequently, since what brains he possessed had been fried for approximately fifteen years, any type of conversation with Keith was something less than an intellectual experience.

"Hi, there, Daddy!" Keith hollered.

Champ grunted.

"What's the matter with the old woman?"

Grunt.

"She looks dead to me."

Grunt.

"Is she dead?"

Grunt.

Since he had pulled up even with his father and mother, the headlights illuminating the road ahead of him, Keith could not clearly see his father's face or hands and the change that had taken place. "What the hell's the matter with you?" the son shouted at the father.

Grunt.

"What'd you do to Momma? She's got to make biscuits in the mornin'."

Grunt.

Keith started to get out of the car. Champ stood up menacingly. The son shut the door and rolled up the window. He knew only too well his father's vicious moods. The gruntings now held a very ominous note. Keith jammed the car into reverse and backed up, the headlights catching the awful metamorphosis in his father. Champ ran in an awkward-looking lope toward the car. Keith floored the pedal and spun the wheel, spraying his father with gravel and dust in his haste to depart the scene.

Champ stood in the road and shook his clawed hands and roared at the fading taillights of the car.

For the first time in his life, Keith wished a cop was around.

Champ slung the dead body of his wife over a shoulder and loped off into the now-friendly and all-enveloping darkness.

Bartlett and Jenkins stood and looked at what had once been the teenager Alice Watson. She resembled a very large lizard; everything about her had changed. Her skin was scaly; only a few tufts

178

of hair remained on her head. Her fingernails and toenails were now long and pointed, feet and hands now clawed and curled. She could not speak, and her roarings emitted a very foul odor.

Nelson Loring had joined the others, coming in with Doctor Perry. "What are we going to do with her?" Nelson asked.

Bartlett glanced at him, a weary expression on his face. "Hell, I don't know! I'm over my level of expertise here. My God, we all are." To Mike: "Where are the state police officers?"

"Gone to get warrants so we can round up as many of the coven members as possible."

"It's a start, I suppose." He looked at Jenkins. "You agree we have to sedate her and that . . . thing we brought in?"

"God, yes! But how are you going to punch a needle through that hide?"

"Let's try injectable Valium. If that doesn't work, we'll jack them down with Thorazine."

"And if that doesn't work?"

"Try prayer," the coroner said grimly.

"The traitors are hiding out at the Conners house," Nick was informed. "The state police have gone into Richmond to get warrants for our arrest."

Like drug dealers all over the nation, the coven members had better and far more sophisticated communications equipment than the police.

Nick waved that off. "They can't prove anything. It's our word against Gary and Janet. But let's be on the safe side. Go back home and take down any posters and symbols that show our devotion to the

179

Master. Hide the more obvious records and CDs. Most of our parents are in the older chapters, so let them in on what we're doing and what the police are trying to do . . . if they don't already know, and I suspect they do. When are the police going to raid us?"

"Just before dawn, according to the radio."

"We'll be ready."

"You want to bunk in the guest cottage or on the sofas in the house?" Dee asked.

"I'm so keyed up I don't think I could sleep," Janet replied. "And I'd rather stay as close to y'all as possible, if you don't mind."

"We don't mind," Dee said with a smile. "And we both understand how you feel."

"You might arrest a lot of people," Gary said. "But they'll be ready for you. The covens have people in the sheriff's department and the city police. We don't know who they are. And they also have real fancy communications equipment. They listen to everything the cops say."

"Just like dope dealers," Carl said.

Janet looked at him. "Who do you think is controlling all the drugs in this county?"

"That's something we forgot to tell Mister Hunt," Gary added. "We've — they've — gotten a lot of new members by getting them hooked on whatever and then holding it over them, or away from them, as the case may be, to bring them into the various covens."

"Adults and kids?" Dee asked.

"Sure."

180

"What's in those woods over there?" Gary asked, looking toward the dark timber.

"You don't know?"

"No. Only the top-level people are allowed to enter those woods. But both of us keep hearing that the time is very near for total domination."

"They plan to take over the town?" Dee asked.

"At first," Janet said. "But what they really want to do is get as many converts as possible, and then destroy the town and the county. That's the way it always works, so we've been told. Destruction is the ultimate goal. A total end to law and order, so anarchy can prevail, all over the world. Those are Linda Crowley's words, not mine."

"It fits," Carl said. "And that's just one of the reasons they never succeed. They get too eager and tip their hand."

"And the other reasons?" Dee asked.

"Their final goals don't make any sense — most of the time. And fortunately for us, this is one of them — I was worried about that. They seem to not know the meaning of being subtle. This very thing has happened in Louisiana, out in Nebraska, New York State, Canada, down in Georgia . . . and those are incidents that have occurred over the past eight or nine years. Always with the same results: A lot of people are dead and lives are forever changed. And a lot of selfish, greedy, malcontented loser-types are allowed to go on a rampage."

Janet stirred at the words that hit her hard. "Suppose, Mister Garrett, that I was your daughter, and you came in my room and found me with devil-worship material, listening to the type of music that is associated with devil worship . . . what would you

181

do?"

Carl met her eyes with the coldest stare she had ever seen in all her young years. And Janet knew then that unless something awful happened to Carl Garrett, those she once called friends would lose this fight. She sensed that Carl Garrett had more of the qualities of the Archangel Michael in him than anyone else she had ever before encountered.

"I would talk to you at first," Carl said. "I would really try to help you out of your self-imposed abyss. If I failed, I would call a minister or priest. If he or she failed, I would then very carefully and very coldly assess the situation, and most probably take you out on some lonely country road some night and put a bullet in your head for the good of humanity."

Chapter 18

Armed with warrants from the state, every law-enforcement officer Jim could count on hit a dozen homes just before dawn. By the time the under-manned teams struck the third home, Daly summed it up.

"We've been had. Somebody tipped them."

There were no posters on walls that praised Satan, no symbols denoting satanic worship; none of the violent music could be found. The cops found startled-appearing young people and adults who loudly demanded to know what in the world was going on.

Grim-faced, the cops took them to jail and booked them on a variety of charges, ranging from murder to cruelty to animals.

Bonds were set in a hurry and by eight o'clock, many of those arrested were free, and those remaining in the bucket sat in their cells and smiled, knowing they would not be far behind.

But the lid was kept on and only a few members of the press entered the county. It did not take Jim long to see that many of the town lawyers were heavily involved with one or the other covens.

Sheriff Rodale stayed home, said he was not feeling well. Jim could handle it.

"The Constitution guarantees an individual the right to worship," a local attorney told the chief deputy. Jim noticed the man was unshaven and had a strong body odor. "You can't arrest someone just because they choose to worship the Devil."

"We didn't," Jim patiently responded. "They were arrested for the charges named on the warrants."

"We don't believe that," another lawyer said. "Those arrested tell us that you're harassing them."

Jim resisted a mighty impulse to step close to the guy and give the man some knuckles in the mouth. With an almost visible effort, he calmed himself and said, "We are harassing no one. This crap is over." He turned his back to the lawyers and walked back into the office.

The local attorneys smiled.

While this was going on, Mike Randall was leading the team digging up the area along Flat Ridge.

"Found it!" a deputy called. "It's a leg bone; the foot's still attached."

"Don't touch a thing," Mike ordered. "I'll get Doctor Bartlett out here. You people start securing this area and then back off. We'll let experts from Forensic take it from here."

Jim smiled grimly when the dispatcher came into his office and handed him Mike's message. He punched out Bartlett's number.

"How's the guests?" he asked the doctor.

"We have them heavily sedated and secured. They're quiet. For now," he added. "But we pumped enough Thorazine in them to kill a normal human being."

"Mike and his bunch found where Lanny and Dora were buried. I'll pick you up in five minutes."

"I'll be ready."

"What press is in here is sure to tag along," Jim warned.

"Brief me on the way out and I'll handle them for you, Jim."

"I sure appreciate that, Cal. Them reporters and all the local lawyers are about to rub me raw."

"Get used to it, Jim. I think a couple of those reporters are going to be here for the duration."

"How'd Carl get so hard, Miss Dee?" Janet asked. "I never seen anybody that young that hard in all my life." She carefully buttered a piece of toast. "You think he meant what he told me last night?"

A late breakfast. Carl had stayed awake all night, on the porch, on guard. He had gone to his room at dawn to get some sleep. At least Dee assumed he had. She had not seen him since the night before, sitting on the porch.

"He meant it, Janet. Why? Part of it is probably because of what he witnessed over the Ruger County. Don't forget, he lost his father fighting Satan. And I'm sure he lost several friends too. And he's penetrated a lot of covens in only a few years. He's personally seen the evil. Hard? Yes, he's hard. And now that you're here with us, aren't you glad he is?"

She smiled and slipped Dingo a bit of toast. "Yes, ma'am. I sure am."

Dingo nudged her leg with his nose, telling her he'd like another snack, please.

"What's in all these boxes?" Gary asked, eyeball-ing the crates stacked around the den.

Dee lifted her eyes to his. "Just some things Carl needs for the fight."

Gary was wise enough not to pursue it.

Those in the A-frame had slept soundly the past night, with no interruption of sleep from the song of the dark timber or the mysterious scratching and purring. And Dee was curious about that, wonder-ing what it meant.

But not certain she really wanted to know.

Breakfast over and the dishes washed, Dee turned to Janet. "If you're certain about your parents, Janet, how about some friends you'd like to call and tell that you're all right? Gary . . . how about you?"

The two looked at each other. Janet nodded and Gary took the cue. "Of our age, Miss Dee, there are three couples I'd trust enough to call. They know what's going on in town—they're both pretty sure their parents are part of it—and they've re-sisted. I got to warn you that while we *were* friends, that was a couple of years ago. Since they began to suspect we were part of a coven, they've backed away from us. Nick ordered us to recruit them, but we kind of dragged our feet."

"They're really nice kids," Janet added. "That's why Nick wanted them in so bad, anyway he could get them. He, uh, had some pretty, well, disgusting things in mind for the girls . . . and for the boys."

"Are their parents involved with the covens?"

"Yes, ma'am," Gary said.

"When Carl wakes up, we'll talk to him about it. He may very well say to call; we need all the allies we can get."

186

"I think," Janet said, "that if Carl ever gets turned loose on these coven members, he's going to make Rambo look like a peacenik."

Anya and Pet knew what was going on, but they were powerless to do anything about it. They could make no major moves until the Old Ones surfaced. And there was nothing either of them could do to hasten their arrival.

Josh Taft and his followers had taken refuge in a farmhouse a few miles outside of Butler. They had hidden in the timber around the house and watched while highway patrolmen searched the place and cautioned the man and woman who lived there to be on the lookout and to keep a weapon close by. As soon as the highway cops had left, Josh and his men had moved in. They had killed the man and were now busy taking turns raping the woman. None of them were aware of what they had become and what their victims were to become.

Ralph Geason slept in the basement of the Butler High School, waiting for the night to bring the kids.

Champ Stinson feasted upon the stiffening carcass of his wife, then covered the remainder of the torn body with brush and leaves, moved off a distance, and laid down to sleep.

Linda Crowley sat in the den of the Geason home and smiled. There had been some setbacks to the plan, but all in all, it was looking pretty good. She sensed that in three or four days the Old Ones would surface; once that happened, nothing could stop them. They had all grown stronger and wiser

187

in the years since Ruger County, and the plan was perfect. Carl Garrett was not the man his father had been. They really had nothing to fear from him. He could be dealt with. Once the Old Ones surfaced, they would . . .

Her thoughts were interrupted by something cold being pressed against her head. She knew what it was: the muzzle of a gun.

"Does Carl always sleep this late?" Gary asked, glancing at his watch. "It's almost noon."

"I'd better go check on him," Dee said, rising. "I haven't heard a sound from his bedroom." She glanced out the side window. His car was gone.

She returned grim-faced, a piece of paper in her hand. "He left us a note. Listen. 'Dee, I don't think the warrants are going to accomplish a damn thing. I've got to get us a toehold on this situation. Be back around two. Carl.' "

"What does it mean, Miss Dee," Janet asked.

"It means he's gone hunting — by himself."

Jim put his crews back to work, digging up the grisly remains of the young people. They found a leg bone here, a foot there, a hand in another place, and then a skull. Jim had dug out the old files on the two kids and was reviewing the papers when Mike called out.

"What kind of ring was it Dora was wearing?"

Jim lifted the papers. "Fourteen-carat-gold friendship ring. The initials L.G. engraved inside. Dora wore braces on her teeth."

"Here's the ring," Mike called.

"Here's the skull," another deputy called. "Braces still on the teeth."

"Now all we have to do is prove Nick and the other coven members killed them," Tolson said. "And we really have nothing that will hold up in court."

"I know it," Jim replied. "They'll just lie for each other. Carl said it would be this way. He's out doing something; called me at the office early this morning. Before dawn. Said he was at least going to find out for sure who was in the covens and their plans."

"How?" Daly asked.

"Same question I asked He said I really didn't want to know. So I didn't ask."

"That boy is as hard as a concrete nail," Tolson said. "I believe he'd go to any lengths to crack these covens wide open."

"That's the impression I got," Daly agreed.

"I don't give a damn how he does it," Jim said, his tanned face hard. "I just want it done. These people are evil. They've murdered, raped, tortured, mutilated, and the Good Lord only knows what else. I don't care what Carl does to them, or how he does it. Just as long as he does it in time."

Linda asked, "Carl?"

"You got it, Linda."

"You going to kill me, Carl?"

"Not yet. I have plans for you, Linda. Get down on the floor, face down. And do it slowly."

On the floor, she felt the bite of the handcuffs as the steel clamped around her wrists and Carl locked them in place.

"They're too tight, Carl."

"Get used to the pain, Linda. I assure you, it's minor compared to what you'll soon be feeling."

She felt a twinge of fear. "You don't have the courage to do anything like that. You're too much like your pukey father."

"My father had the courage to die well," Carl reminded her. "Do you?"

She said nothing. But the hate shining from her eyes was like twin beams of Hellfire.

"We'll see, Linda. Now get up!" He jerked her to her feet and slipped a light sweater over her shoulders, hiding the handcuffed hands behind her back.

"We're going on the back way," Carl told her. "At the edge of the yard, by the oak, cut to your right, through the neighbor's yard, and then it's a short walk to my car. You got all that?"

"Yes. I think you've done this before, Carl. I think you are not a very nice person."

"What would you know about being nice? I do what is necessary to combat the evil that people like you try to bring into this world. Now move your ass, Linda!"

She moved. "Where are we going, Carl?"

"Out into the country, Linda. I think you know where."

She laughed as they walked out the back door. "You're a fool, Carl! You would dare to take me out there? You're playing right into our hands by doing so."

"That's right," Carl said cheerfully.

Linda looked at him curiously, thoughts racing through her mind as they walked. She had known

Carl all her life, and had never thought of him as a ball of fire when it came to intellectual ability. What if she had misjudged him? What if he turned out to be like his father? And why was he taking her right in the middle of ground considered sacred by those who worshipped the Dark One?

The muzzle of the 9-mm punched her in the back, cutting short her silent questions. "Move, bitch!"

"Phone's for you, Harry."

Deputy Harrison walked to a desk as far away from the central receiving area as he could get and punched the blinking button. His hands were trembling. He had been expecting this call, and he was not looking forward to getting it.

"Yeah?"

The District Attorney's voice filled his ear. "The Old Ones are ready, Harry. Tomorrow afternoon at the latest. It's time for you to do your part."

"It's not going to be easy," Harry whispered. "Jim's a tough old bird."

"That's your problem."

"I don't know if I can pull it off."

"How do you feel, Harry?"

Harry knew what he meant. He felt lousy. He needed a line or two—bad. Three or four lines would be even better.

"Your reward will be waiting for you, Harry. Enough to make you very, very happy. Just get the job done."

"Where will the stuff be?"

"It'll snow in the usual place, Harry." The line

went dead.

Harry sat very still for a moment. Then, with a sigh, he stood up, hitched at his gun belt, and walked out of the office.

He didn't know how he was going to do it, but he knew it had to be done. All over the town, others were receiving phone calls. Calls concerning the mayor, the ministers around the area, the chief of police, and other civic leaders. Harry and the others had twenty-four hours to carry out their orders. Phase one had just received the green light.

Harry licked his dry lips. He needed some dope bad. He maybe had enough for a couple of lines at his house. He'd do one now, just as soon as he could get to his stash, and save the other one to snort right before he did what he had been ordered to do. It always made him feel so much better. Made him feel like a brand-new man.

Just thinking about it made him feel better.

He drove straight to his house.

He never had liked Jim Hunt. Jim never would drink or run around and chase pussy with the rest of them. Mister Goody-Goody.

It would be a pleasure to kill him.

The Master would be pleased, and would reward Harry handsomely.

Then Harry had another thought. He knew that no one had been assigned to kill that outsider, Carl Garrett; he'd come in too quickly and unexpectedly. Killing Garrett would really be a feather in his cap. And would be as much fun as icing Jim Hunt—maybe more fun. Carl Garrett really thought he was hot stuff. Big-time private cop and all that crap. Yeah. Maybe he'd go after Garrett first. Why not? He had twenty-four hours. Maybe he'd kill him in front of that snooty Conners bitch, and then Harry could dip his wick into some really prime stuff.

Just the thought of that got him all excited. He pulled at his crotch. She'd be one of those who'd cry and beg and promise all sorts of stuff if he please wouldn't stick it to her.

Money! Yeah! Money. She had lots of money. She'd give him lots of money, and then Harry could split from this town and head for the city. Richmond wouldn't be big enough; he'd have to head for New York or L.A.

The more he thought about it, the better Harry liked it. Of course, he'd screw the Conners bitch anyway—after she gave him the money. Then he'd kill her.

He laughed out loud.

It was because of people like Harry Harrison that secret occult societies had such difficulty maintaining low profiles over a period of time.

One link in the chain was about to break.

Chapter 19

The cat sat on the dresser and watched the woman brush her hair. Her lover lay on the rumpled bed, naked, his legs spread wide, his eyes closed, resting after lovemaking. The woman continued to brush her hair with long, careful strokes.

The cat turned its head at silent movements outside the window. If a cat could smile, this one did. Viciously. Movements outside the other bedroom window turned its head again. Cats of all sizes and colors had gathered silently, clinging to the sill and the screen, their eyes shining with hate and fury, tails swishing back and forth.

The cat on the dresser blinked once, and the outside cats disappeared.

"Come on, baby." The man spoke from the bed. "One more time before your stupid husband gets home. Just look what I got for you."

She turned and smiled at what he had. He could recover faster than any man she had ever known — and that was quite a feat on his part considering the number of men she'd known.

Neither one could hear the silent footfall of

dozens of paws striking the carpeted floor of the den, moving to the hall, then toward the bedroom.

She stood up to move toward the bed just as her cat jumped from his perch on the dresser. The big tom landed on her head, dug into her neck and shoulder with his back claws, and went to work on her face with his front claws. Her screaming froze the man on the bed in open-mouthed shock for a moment. That moment was all it took for his naked body to be covered with yowling, biting, clawing cats. Several went to work on his face while the others began raking at his soft belly and lower groin. Other cats were working at the woman's ankles and calves, soon bringing her down to the floor.

The man was jerking and kicking and screaming and flailing his arms as the cats clawed out his eyes, tore off his ears, mangled his privates, and opened his stomach. The cats pulled out his intestines and ran around the room, the guts tailing behind them like thick gray rope.

The woman had managed to roll under the pretty canopied bed, squashing and crippling several cats during the frantic rolling. It bought her only a few minutes of safety.

Several cats began eating at her toes and the soles of her bare feet while others slipped under the bed and once more began mangling her face. The man was already unconscious. It was over for the woman in only a few minutes.

The horde of cats, their fur covered with blood, began exiting silently from the death house. A big female stopped at the front room window and shook her back paw, trying to free a claw from a long strand of small intestine. The gut fell free with a small plop and the cat was gone out through the torn screen.

The woman moaned once, then the house was still.

The last cat to leave was the woman's big tom. He pissed on the carpet in the den to mark his territory and then with a silent leap, was gone.

The telephone began ringing. It rang ten times and then fell as silent as a stalking cat.

Carl called Dee from a pay phone. "Stay in the house and keep the kids in with you. Turn on the stereo and turn it up loud. Have a party. Don't even think about coming out to the guest cottage."

"If you say so, Carl."

"I say so." He broke the connection and placed another call.

"What'd you think?" Jesse Broward, a reporter from a Richmond paper, asked Sonya Richards, a reporter from a Washington, D.C., paper.

Both of them were good reporters, both of them young, in their mid-twenties, and both of them on their way up fast in print journalism.

"You know Millie Smith, Jesse?"

"Not personally. But I've sure heard of her. Why?"

"She was found dead in her apartment this morning. Attacked and killed by some sort of animal or animals."

"You're kidding!"

"No."

"I'm sure sorry, but . . ." He stopped, cocked his head, and looked at her. "Millie Smith. Sure. She covered the incident over in Ruger County a few years back, right?"

"That's right. And that was a big cover-up too."

"The twit who did all her leg work . . . what was his name?"

"Kenny Allen. He was found dead this morning. Killed the same way. I find that very odd, Jesse."

"I find it eerie myself. But where's the connection between that and this?"

"I don't know if there is any connection. But something tells me there is. You going to stick around for awhile?"

"Yeah, I think so. The boss told me to stay with this one."

She laughed as another piece of the chain-sawed pair of teenagers was lifted out of the ground. It looked like an arm. Both reporters lifted their cameras and clicked a couple of times. "You think we can stand all the excitement of a week in Butler, Jesse?"

"Aren't you going to strip me naked and rape me before you torture me?" Linda taunted Carl as he tied her into a chair in the guest cottage.

"I wouldn't stick a sterilized fencepost in you, Linda."

She spat at him and tried to bite him. Carl backhanded her, rocking her head to one side. A small trickle of blood leaked from one corner of her mouth.

"You get your nuts off beating up women, Carl?"

Carl pulled the curtain back and looked out the window. Father Vincent was just pulling in. Carl stepped out of the cottage and waved him over. He cut his eyes. Dee and Janet and Gary were watching from the A-frame. Carl motioned them back. The curtain closed.

Carl stepped out to meet the Episcopal priest. He carried a small bag, much like a doctor's bag. Chuck had a worried look on his face.

"Carl, I've never done anything like this before. My word, man, we only touched on this in school. I'm not even sure I know *how!*"

"Oh, you know how, Father. I've worked with priests of the Episcopal faith before."

"All right, Carl—all right. I know how. But there is an . . . order, a chain of command we must go through. This is not something that one takes on himself."

"We don't have time, Chuck. All you can do is what a mule can do."

"I beg your pardon?"

"Try."

"You're a goddamn liar!" Bullfrog Stinson told his younger brother.

"I ain't neither!" Keith stood his ground. "I know what I saw and I seen Daddy a-lookin' like somethin' out of a monster movie. And Momma was dead!"

"Well, where the hell-far is she?" Bubba demanded.

"How do I know? I 'spect Daddy toted her off

into the woods."

"Shit!" Bubba sneered.

Of all the brothers, Sonny possessed the most sense. Which wasn't saying a whole lot, but fifty percent of something is better than a hundred percent of nothing. Which is what the other three boys possessed in the way of brains. "Have you called the law?" Sonny asked.

"Hale, no! I ain't got no truck with no lawman." Sonny moved toward the phone.

"Hit don't work," Bullfrog informed him. "The phone company cut it off a couple of months ago. After Daddy tore up the last phone whiles he was likkered up."

"All right," Sonny said. "Keith, you show us where you last seen Daddy. We'll track him. Maybe Momma was kidnapped. We better git some guns."

They went to their pickup trucks and fetched their rifles and single-action cowboy pistols and struck out, with Keith in the lead. It wasn't the most awe-inspiring patrol in the history of Reeves County, but it certainly came close to being the strangest.

Keith would occasionally stop to pick a wildflower and sniff at it. But since over the past fifteen years Keith had stuck all that cocaine up his nose, it was doubtful he could smell much. However, no one really knew why Keith did anything—including Keith.

Disgusted at his brother's antics, Sonny finally took the lead. It wasn't difficult to follow the trail left by Champ. Broken limbs and torn-up bushes clearly marked the way.

"Looks like a wild animal done come this way,"

Bubba observed.

"I tole you," Keith said.

Then the trail ended.

The brothers looked all around, but the trail had abruptly ceased to be.

"He backtracked," Sonny said, after kneeling down and studying the ground. "But he ain't carryin' no load. See the difference in the footprints."

"He dumped Momma!" Bullfrog said excitedly. "Momma!" he started hollering. "Oowee, Momma! Hit's your boys, Momma. Is you in there, Momma?"

"I done tole you and tole you that she'd daid, damnit," Keith said. "How the hale is she 'pposed to answer if'n she's daid?"

A moan sprang from the stillness of the timber along the ridges. Not quite human, but something less than animal.

"Something's out yonder," Bubba said, looking all around him.

Sonny looked at him. "No kidding," he said sarcastically. "Let's split up and search."

A roar cut the stillness.

"That's your ass!" Bullfrog said. "I vote we stay together."

"Yeah," Bubba agreed. "You 'member what the Grand Dragon said at the las' cross-burnin'. Them pro-found words about strength in numbers."

Keith turned and came face to face with what had been his father. It took a couple of seconds for his brain to fully register the awfulness before him. His father had slipped up on them as silent as a cat. If what Keith had seen the night before had been bad, it was ten times worse in the daylight.

200

Some sort of greenish yellow slime was hanging in stinking thin ropes from his father's mouth. The man's lower jaw was all swollen up and jutting out, like some sort of monster. The eyes were all wild and red-looking, and it looked like his daddy's beard had spread all over his body. Champ stuck out one clawed hand to grab his youngest son, and that was enough for Keith.

Keith let out a scream that shook the leaves and rattled any dead branches, and then took off in a dead run. After a very quick look at the cause of the scream, Bullfrog, Sonny, and Bubba vacated the area, right behind their brother.

Champ roared, but did not pursue. Sometime during the dark of night, he had understood that his was a higher purpose, and that his time for action had not yet arrived. But it would be very soon.

He turned around and looked at the bloody and mangled and eaten-on thing that had been following him for hours. He grunted and moved on, what was left of his wife lurching along behind him, the head on her broken neck lolling and flopping to one side. Huge chunks of flesh were missing from her legs . . . thanks to Champ's appetite hours before. She held her arms straight out in front of her, the fingers constantly moving like small snakes. The two of them vanished into the woods.

Harry carefully, with trembling fingers, laid out a line and rolled up a dollar bill, sticking one end of the small cylinder up one nostril. He snorted up the line and shuddered in delight. He felt like a new man; nothing could stop him now. He was a giant.

He checked his .357. Loaded up full. He loaded a snub-nosed .38 and stuck that in his back pocket. He'd have to be careful with Jim; the old boy was wily as a fox. Harry shook a few hits of speed into his shaky hand and swallowed them. Not as good as snow, but they'd help. He stepped out of his room. First to kill Jim Hunt, then Carl Garrett. Then he'd take his pleasure with Dee Conners and come away a rich man.

Harry had it all worked out in his mind.

The last of the coven members had been bonded out of the Reeves County jail. They'd left smiling smugly.

Ralph Geason squatted on the dusty floor of the high school basement and slowly ate a live rat. The naked, snakelike tail of the rodent hung out of his mouth, flapping wildly as Ralph crunched the head and broke the backbone of the rat, finally swallowing it nearly whole. He picked a few hairs out of his mouth and belched. He felt better, even though he was still hungry. He would appease his appetites with the coming of night and the arrival of the young people—he was sure of that. He touched his throbbing erection and grinned savagely.

The doctors at the now-crowded laboratory looked at the hideous things that were strapped to the tables. They did not have the vaguest idea what to do with them.

Sheriff Rodale sat in his living room and drank whiskey straight from the bottle. He thought he might be losing his mind. His wife would occasion-

202

ally look in on him and think how wonderful her life would be if he would just drop dead.

Mayor Purdy sat on his front porch and wondered what was going to become of his town.

Chief of Police Max Bancroft tried—without giving away what was really taking place in town—to convince his wife to go visit her sister for a week or two. She told him she wasn't leaving until or unless he leveled with her about what was happening in Reeves County.

Val Malone and Nick Jamison toked on a joint and listened as Nick's mother screwed several of the younger coven members on the floor of the den. For her age, Val thought, the woman could really move her ass.

And Josh Taft stood with his mouth hanging open, looking at the farmer he personally had killed only hours before.

The man was standing in the door, staring and grinning at Josh.

A scratching, purring sound seemed to fill the farmhouse. And with the strange sounds, a heavy sulfuric odor came to his nostrils, so powerful it was almost overwhelming.

Josh laughed out loud.

"What's so damn funny?" Carey demanded. "That smell's about to make me puke!"

"Get used to it," Josh told him. "We're all going to be smelling it for a long, long time."

"What'd you mean?" Fox asked. "What is it?"

"Home."

"Home! What'd you talkin' about, boy? My home's over in Cumberland County."

"Not anymore it isn't," Josh corrected.

203

"Oh, yeah?" Fox said belligerently. "Well, where is it, then?"

"Hell."

Chapter 20

As soon as the men stepped into the room, the timber around them opened up in song and chant. Carl took a cassette tape out of his pocket and stuck it in the small stereo unit next to the TV. He punched the play button and religious music filled the room.

Linda visibly winced at the sound of Christian faith. "That's the worst shit I ever heard in my life!" she screamed out.

Carl turned up the volume until the music drowned out the singing and chanting from the woods.

"You son of a bitch!" Linda shouted. "You'll die long and hard for this."

Carl ignored that. "Names of everyone in the covens, Linda."

"Fuck you!"

Carl opened Father Vincent's small leather bag and picked out a cross. He held it against the young woman's head. She screamed as the cross touched her. The odor of burning human skin sprang forth. The flesh on Linda's forehead bubbled under the power of God.

"Names, Linda."

She spouted names and dates and plans and then tried to bite his hand. Carl jerked back just in time.

The cross removed from her forehead, Linda fought the handcuffs until her wrists were raw and bloody. "I'll tell you no more!" she screamed.

"Pray, Father," Carl told the Episcopal priest.

Chuck began praying for strength, for guidance, for help in order to combat the evil that was over-taking Reeves County.

Linda's wailing all but drowned out the quiet prayers. She began screaming words at them, in a language that neither could understand. Her stomach and chest began heaving, as if something inside her was struggling to break free.

"My God!" Chuck said. "What's happening to her?"

A clawed scaly hand suddenly tore out of the woman's stomach as a wild wail of agony broke from her lips.

Blood and pus and corruption sprayed from Linda's mouth. Carl and the priest jumped back just in time to avoid the stinking spray.

Another clawed hand punched through the woman's stomach. Dripping blood, the hand opened and closed, flexing its newfound life.

"Get out of here!" Carl yelled, shoving the priest toward the open door. "Move, Chuck. Get out of here."

A roaring began from deep inside the mangled body of Linda Crowley, breaking out of her bloody and pus-covered lips. Dee and Janet and Gary had disobeyed instructions and were standing outside the open door, watching.

Carl shoved the priest out the door and fumbled in his pocket for a lighter. He sparked the lighter into flame and touched the fire to drapes. "Get a can of gasoline," he yelled to Chuck. "Move, man—hurry!"

Blood, red mixed with a strange greenish yellow, poured out of Linda's jerking and pain-filled body as a hideous head protruded from the woman's chest. Her ribs cracked and tore through flesh as the monster within her fought free of her body. The mouth opened and closed, the jaws snapping, exposing long fangs that could rip off an arm.

Carl was vaguely aware of a clicking sound just outside the open door. He cut his eyes for just a moment and saw Dee there, her face pale, bravely taking pictures of the horror birthing within the guest cottage.

With one last violent shriek of pain, Linda slumped forward in the chair as the devil within her leaped forward, exiting its earth mother's body.

Sticking the lighter in his pocket, Carl jerked the 9-mm from his belt and began firing at the creature, the slugs ripping into the birth-slick and scaly, slimy body, tearing great holes as they slammed out the back of the devil-child. The creature howled in pain and fell back, kicking and yowling on the floor. Carl backed out the open door, the 9-mm barking and jumping in his hand just as the priest ran up, carrying a large can of gasoline.

"Douse that thing!" Carl yelled. "Throw the gas on it, Chuck. Douse the carpet with gas."

With a prayer on his lips, Chuck began emptying the gas can into the cottage and onto the creature.

Carl lit some dry twigs and grass and tossed the flames into the cottage.

When the gasoline fumes ignited, the searing whooshing sound knocked all three of them to the ground as the roof lifted off the cottage and the windows were blown out.

A horrible screaming ripped the burning air as the creature's flesh began bubbling and it sought escape from the flames.

Carl ejected the empty clip from his 9-mm and slapped in a fresh one. The creature appeared in the doorway, a burning, shrieking child of Hell. Carl drove it back with gunfire.

Dee reloaded her 35-mm camera and continued to take pictures as the heat grew more intense, forcing them further back from the cottage, which was now completely engulfed in flames.

Gary had raced to the house; he returned with a rifle in his hands. "I'll take the back," he yelled to Carl. "Case it tries to get out that way."

"Right there!" Carl pointed out a spot. "Shoot from an angle so you won't hit us."

The boy took up position.

But the fire had taken its toll. The devil-child lay on the burning floor and bleated out what was left of its unnatural and evil-born life. The roof finally collapsed, ending the now-all-too-human whimpering that was beginning to grate on the nerves of those outside the inferno.

Carl stretched out garden hoses and they all wet down the area around the cottage, to contain any fire in case the flames tried to spread. After only a few minutes, there was nothing left except smoking embers and still-intense heat. The body of Linda could be seen clearly, kneeling strangely on her face and knees amid the rubble, the handcuffs still in place around her bony white wrists.

Father Chuck Vincent fell to his knees and began praying.

Carl began reloading clips from a box of shells he got from his car.

Gary and Janet stood side by side, awe and fright on their faces.

Carl took the camera from Dee. He looked at Chuck, who had risen to his feet. "Chuck, stay here until I get back, will you?"

"Of course," the priest replied, his voice shaky. "Where are you going?"

"To town. I want Daly to get this film developed as soon as possible." He pointed to the rubble that was once the guest cottage. "Watch this. I don't want anything rising out of it. I'll be back as soon as possible."

Janet pointed a shaky finger at the smoking ruins. "Who got her pregnant? And what if there are more of them—like me?" She looked at Carl.

"Why would you think such a thing?" Dee asked.

"I got to think it, 'cause it may be true. Does the Devil impregnate women, or was it done by a devil-worshipper—a coven member? And if that's the case, how many more like her are there?"

"Exorcise her," Carl said, looking at Chuck.

"Carl, I don't know if I can!" the priest protested. "I can counsel people on fidelity and the value of the family; I can help with depression and alcoholism and other earthly matters. Priests nowadays don't *exorcise* people. At least none that I know of."

"You said you knew the procedure."

"Well . . . yes. I do. But . . ."

"No buts, Father. Dee can help you, or if you'd rather wait until I get back, I'll help. I've seen it done several times before."

The priest nodded his head wearily. "All right, Carl. I'll try. I'll try to remember what I was taught. We'll do it when you get back."

"Fine."

"No!" Janet said. "I won't have that monster tearing my body apart. I saw what happened to Linda. I'll kill myself first. Just leave me alone. When you get back, take me to the clinic and let a doctor look at me. If I'm pregnant, I'll deal with it myself. That's it, Carl. I mean it."

Gary touched her arm. "Janet . . ."

She jerked away. "Leave me alone, Gary. I got to deal with this myself."

Carl held out his hand. "Come on, Janet. I'll take you in now." He looked at the others. "Hold the fort down, people." He walked away, Janet by his side.

"When this is over," Chuck said, "I'm going to write a long letter to my professors at the seminary. I'm going to tell them to get off their stuffy asses and start teaching about Satan. For he is very real."

Daly sent a plainclothes patrolman with the film to state police headquarters to be developed. Carl looked in on the creature he had shot and at what had been the teenage girl. Both were conscious, but just barely, the doctors having injected them with massive amounts of tranquilizers. Carl told them all of what Linda had said, and then Doctor Bartlett took Janet to be examined.

Jim pulled Carl to one side. "Trouble, Carl. Harry Harrison left the office about three hours ago and hasn't been heard from since. Mike tossed his house and came up with all sorts of devil-worship material and a lot of signs of heavy drug use."

"That doesn't surprise me; he's the type. And there have been studies about the type of people who are most easily led into covens. Harry's a Type A. He was probably using drugs before he got involved with the coven. Any idea what he might be up to?"

"One," the chief deputy said glumly. "To kill people."

"Any particular person in mind?"

"Yeah. *Me!* I've stayed on Harry's butt ever since he hung on a badge. But that would be just one of the reasons. Linda said the plan was to kill the town's leaders first, then destroy the town. Then they were going to take a few of the upper-level coven members and move out into the county, then on to other towns, right?"

"That's what she said. She was talking so fast it was difficult to grasp everything that came out of her mouth."

Jim nodded. "Then it stands to reason I'd be on that hit list. They would know that I'd taken over the runnin' of the department. And everybody with any sense knows Sheriff Rodale is about as competent as a pig tootin' on a bugle. His wife called about an hour ago. Rodale's passed out dead drunk in a chair. Max Bancroft would be on the list. The city P.D. would nearabout fall apart without Max. The mayor and the members of the city council and all the preachers would be on the list. The doctors

211

would surely be on the list. And a whole bunch of other civic and county leaders. It don't surprise me that Oscar MacGuire is part of this devil thing. That's why the DA was constantly at odds with this department; and until it's proved otherwise, I ain't gonna trust nobody from his office neither."

The phone rang and a nurse called out that it was for Jim. The chief deputy listened, his face hard. He hung up and shook his head, walking back to Carl. "A slut that lives on the edge of town and one of her lovers have been found dead. By the poor guy that married her. A unit is out there now. They was tore all to pieces by some sort of animals."

"Cats," Carl said. "I saw the same thing in Ruger. Caution your people that not all cats are involved in this thing. Probably a very low percentage of them are taking orders from Anya and Pet. There'll be cats fighting cats before this is over."

"Is it gonna be over, Carl?" Jim asked, a dubious note in his voice.

"It'll be over, Jim. But it's going to be a bloody bitch before the end comes."

"You want to ride out to the slut's house?"

Carl nodded his head, picking up on the disapproval in the chief deputy's voice. And he knew that Jim would certainly be on the hit list, for Jim was a straight and moral man, highly disapproving of anything that went against the laws of God. A traditionalist in an era of permissiveness.

"Let's go."

Carl sat in the back seat with Tolson, Daly in the front with Jim. They had just cleared the department's parking area when Jim's radio squawked.

"Go to alternate frequency, R-2."

Jim changed to the tach frequency and lifted his mike. "Go ahead."

"Mike reports those crazy Stinson boys flagged him down about ten minutes ago, Chief. Hollerin' and carryin' on about their daddy havin' changed into a monster-man and their momma being killed. Mike says that even Keith was makin' sense for a change."

Jim looked at the speaker as if he couldn't believe his ears. "God works in strange and mysterious ways," Jim muttered. "I ain't never knowed Keith Stinson when he made sense about anything." He keyed his mike. "Tell Mike to bring them in, John."

"Ten-four, Chief."

The husband was an emotional wreck and the bedroom looked like someone had used it to butcher hogs. Blood had splattered the walls and bits of flesh and guts covered the floor.

"That damn no-good Paul Nunnery," Jim said through tight lips. "He carried his brains in his dick. I always knowed he'd come to a bad end."

"Burn the bodies, Jim," Carl said.

But the chief deputy shook his head. "I can't do that, boy. The law says there's got to be an autopsy."

"Jim, toss the law books out the window. Toss every rule and regulation and moral code in the garbage pile. There is no place for them in this situation."

"What a terrible tragedy," the DA's voice boomed from the doorway. "These fine, decent people."

"With one exception," Jim muttered. "You can

213

shoot him."

"Who is that?"

"Oscar MacGuire, the DA."

"Now you're getting the picture, Jim."

"You know I can't do that, Carl. As much as I'd like to. I was only runnin' my mouth."

"I'll give you twenty-four hours, Jim. Then you'll change your mind."

"I pray God you're wrong."

"I'm not." Carl walked out of the house to stand on the front porch. A tomcat sat on the porch railing, looking at him through arrogant and mocking yellow eyes.

"You son of a bitch," Carl whispered.

The cat purred and scratched at the railing, then snarled and hissed, showing Carl its teeth.

Chapter 21

Anya and Pet rested deep in the woods, near a slime-covered stinking pool of a greenish-yellowish liquid that strongly resembled pus oozing from an infected wound. The pool bubbled and gurgled and spewed forth noxious odors. Both knew the time was very close for the Old Ones to surface. It was now down to a matter of hours. And then the march toward victory could begin.

Anya and Pet exchanged message-glances, communication without words. A new element had been added, but neither of them knew exactly what it was or what it meant, only that this added development was on the side of the opposition. Neither knew how strong it was, or how it might affect them, only that it was present . . . in some form or another.

They also knew that a child of theirs was dead, destroyed at the hands of that damnable Christian puke Carl Garrett.

He had to be killed. Those who had the courage to approach and face the twin horrors of Anya and Pet had told them plans were being formulated to do away with Carl Garrett.

But as Anya silently observed, the young Garrett had a lot of his father in him, and doing away with him might prove to be a very difficult task . . . if not an impossible one.

Was there a way to sidestep the young man? Anya didn't know, but she was giving that a lot of thought.

The bubbling pool emitted a long stinking fart. The Old Ones were inching closer, the long climb from their ancient entombment deep in the bowels of the earth was nearly over. Their freedom would be soon. Very soon.

"I thought you said Keith was makin' sense," Jim said, turning to Mike.

"Well, he was. Sort of," the young deputy replied. "He must have popped some pills on the way in. He's sure off his nut now."

Jim grabbed Keith and shook him. "Boy!" he shouted. "Will you put your brain in gear before you put your mouth in motion?"

"He's done changed into a monster!" Keith said, managing to string a few intelligible words together and get them out of his mouth in a manner that could be understood—which was no small feat for Keith Stinson.

"Who's changed into a monster?" Jim asked.

"Daddy!"

"Where is he?"

"Up yonder on the ridges."

"Damn, boy, we got hundreds of miles of ridges in this county—what ridges?"

But Keith had drifted over into marshmallow land

again. He picked a plastic flower from a pot in the office and sniffed at it.

Jim shook his head in disgust.

" 'Bout four or five miles from the home place, Mister Hunt," Bullfrog said. "And Keith ain't fibbin' 'bout this. I seen Daddy with my own eyes." He waved his hand at his brother. "We all seen him. He's changed into something awful."

Jim glanced out an office window. Not enough hours of daylight left to risk a search. No man among them wanted to be caught out on those lonely wooded ridges after dark, and that included Jim Hunt.

"You boys plannin' on goin' back home for the night?" Jim asked.

"Hale, no!" Bubba hollered. "They's hobgobblins and hoodoos and spirit-people and the like up yonder."

"Then go get a room at the motel and stay out of trouble," Jim told the quartet. He looked at Keith. The fool had stuck the plastic flower behind one ear and was grinning like an idiot. "Just . . . leave," Jim said. The chief deputy could not for the life of him understand why people would voluntarily choose to destroy themselves with drugs. That was one of life's many great mysteries to the man.

A deputy stilled the ringing telephone. "For you, Mister Garrett."

Doctor Bartlett said, "Janet is pregnant, Carl. The X-rays show a very fast-growing fetus. It . . . ah, doesn't appear to be human."

"Where is she now?"

"Here. I sedated her and she's sleeping."

"How did she take the news?"

217

"Stoically."

"Can you keep her sedated?"

"Yes."

"Can you abort the fetus?"

"Impossible. None of us here have ever seen a fetus like it. It is literally, and I use that in the strongest sense, a part of her. To abort would be to kill the mother."

"So would the birth, Doctor."

"So you told me."

"Well?"

"I don't know."

"I'll be over in a little while, Doctor. See you then."

The dispatcher hollered out of the radio room. "Harry's been spotted, Chief. He's highballin' it out toward the Conners house. In the county unit."

A deputy answered the ringing phone and listened for a moment. "Charles Jennings is dead, Chief. Somebody shot him leaving his office just about two minutes ago."

"Who is Charles Jennings?" Carl asked.

"One of the town council members. John, bump Max and tell him what's going down. Ask him to cease all patrolling and assign officers to protect as many people as possible. You have the list, get to it." He turned as Carl walked toward a phone. "Where are you going, Carl?"

"Back out to Dee's."

"You be careful. Harry's probably full of dope and unstable."

Carl nodded and punched out Dee's number. He told her to arm herself and stay inside. He hung up and walked out the door.

218

In his car, he made certain a round was chambered in his 9-mm before he cranked up and drove toward the A-frame. Jim had told him that Harry was a speed freak, and Carl knew that speed-heads were among the most dangerous to deal with, being irrational and unpredictable, with oftentimes violent mood swings.

Carl felt—wrongly, part of him hoped—that tonight was going to blow the lid off Reeves County. Every fiber in his being told him the old gods were going to surface very soon, and he remembered only too well what had happened in Ruger when they did.

He checked his rearview mirror. A county unit was right behind him. He could make out Mike's strained face in the mirror. Jim wanted Harry Harrison taken alive. Law and order right down to the wire. Carl smiled, but it was not a pleasant curving of the lips. Law and order was just about to go out the window in Reeves County.

"Is that him?" Sonya asked, as Jesse made an illegal U-turn and followed Mike's unit, which was following Carl.

"That's him, Sonya. The coven-buster himself. I've been trying to do a feature story on him for over a year, but Carl Garrett doesn't grant interviews and he's constantly changing his address. He's a hard man to keep up with."

"It all fits, Jesse. Everything is coming together." She consulted a small notepad. Linda Crowley is from Ruger County. She is suspected of being a coven leader in the statewide network of cells.

219

Right?"

Jesse nodded his head. "Right. I've been following this devil-worship angle for over a year. She's a bigwig in the operation."

"She was in the house when Ralph Geason is supposed to have raped her and assaulted his wife and then run off the other night, right?"

"Right."

"Carl Garrett was seen by a neighbor leaving the back of the Geason house today. He had a gun in his hand."

"Right."

"Some kind of big secret goings-on over at Doctor Calvin Bartlett's office; ambulances seen coming and going and the clinic has been emptied of patients and is under guard. Undercover state pigs are in town. People are being murdered all over the place." She chuckled. "It's big, Jesse. Real big. And you and me, we have the story all to ourselves."

"Share a byline?"

"You betcha, Jesse. This is our ticket up from coach to first class. From sandwiches to caviar. We're on our way, baby!"

"You better leave Carl Garrett alone, Sonya."

"Hell with that, Jesse. A pig is a pig, whether he's public or private. I hate cops!" She looked up as something stepped between the county unit and Jesse's car. "Look out!" she screamed, just as Mike's unit rounded a curve and was gone from sight.

Jesse saw it at the same time, but he was driving too fast and could not stop or swerve in time to avoid hitting it. The front end of the car impacted against the man with a sickening thud, throwing him up onto the hood. His face spiderwebbed the windshield when he struck. The man grabbed hold of the lip of the hood in front of the recessed wipers and held on, pressing his bloody face against the windshield.

The hood had fallen away from his head, exposing the protruding brow, the apelike eyes and nose and mouth . . . and the fangs when he howled.

"Jesus God!" Jesse cried. He floored the gas pedal and began swerving side to side on the road, trying to shake the hideous creature.

The creature began hammering on the already cracked windshield.

"Do you have a gun?" Jesse screamed the question.

"Are you out of your mind? I hate guns!"

A hairy, clawed fist drove through the windshield, fingers groping for either passenger.

Jesse began swerving from side to side, frantically spinning the wheel, trying to dislodge the hideousness from the hood. The small car hit a patch of gravel and went into a spin, then a long sideways slide, with the creature howling and Jesse and Sonya yelling and screaming.

The car left the road and smashed into a tree, the impact crushing the grill and mangling the dangling legs of the creature, trapping him between car and tree.

Jesse had a bump on the head but other than that, was unhurt. "You hurt, Sonya?"

"I . . . don't think so."

The creature hammered on the hood of the car with its fists, howling in pain.

The reporter in both of them surfaced, shoving aside any aches and pains from the accident. They

221

both grabbed cameras and managed to get the sprung doors pushed open. Outside, they took pictures of the creature, with his great fanged mouth and bloody simian face. Then the thought came to them at once: If there was one of those things, there was probably more . . . whatever it was.

"Let's get out of here, Jesse!"

They took off running up the road. Around them, on both sides of the road, the timber suddenly appeared much thicker and darker and ever so much more menacing.

Carl came to a sliding stop and left the car, the 9-mm in his hand, hammer back. Harry's county unit was nowhere in sight. But two other cars were. He did not recognize them. But Carl had that giveaway tingly feeling on the back of his neck that told him Harry was close.

He locked his car and ran to the porch, where Dee was waiting.

"No sign of Harry, Carl. How about Janet?"

"Pregnant."

"*Shit!* The baby?"

Mike's unit slipped to a stop.

"Not . . . normal. And no, it can't be aborted. Either way, it's going to kill Janet. Doctor Bartlett has her sedated. She's sleeping. Who do these other cars belong to?"

"The kids Gary and Janet told us about. Gary called them just after you left." Her eyes searched his face. "Who's going to tell Gary?"

"I will. But not now." He turned to face the young deputy. "You following me, Mike?"

"Jim's orders. He says he wants Harry alive."

Carl spat off the porch. "Not fucking likely, pal."

"If Harry shows up, I plan on arresting him," Mike said, sticking out his chin.

"If Harry shows up, he'll come in shooting," Carl replied. "So I suggest we get off the porch and stop offering ourselves as targets."

Inside the A-frame, Gary's eyes were worried and his face showed the strain. "Janet?"

"Doctor Bartlett has her sedated," Carl said, telling the truth. "He wanted to keep her at the clinic so he can run more tests in the morning," he added, not knowing if that was the truth or a lie. He didn't know how he was going to tell the boy about his girlfriend.

Carl was introduced to Lib and Peter, Jack and Becky, Susie and Tommy. "Your parents know you're out here?" he asked.

"Our parents don't care," Tommy told him. "They left home and work about noon today. They didn't say where they were going. It's all coming unglued, isn't it? I mean, the coven business?"

"It's coming to a head," Carl acknowledged, his eyes flicking to the window just as a sheriff's department car roared by, heading back to town, Harry Harrison behind the wheel.

"I'm gone," Mike said, moving to the door. "Jim said to get him."

He was out the door and off the porch before anyone could make any attempt to stop him.

"Car's coming real fast, Sonya," Jesse said. "I don't like the sound of it."

"Me neither."

They both hit the ditch by the side of the road. Harry roared by. The reporters started to get up just as the sound of Mike's fast-moving unit came to them, the engine screaming. They hit the ditch again and stayed there until both cars were out of sight and sound.

Jesse's car was well off the shoulder of the road, nearly hidden by the timber. Neither Harry nor Mike had seen the wrecked vehicle as they roared past.

The reporters climbed slowly to their feet and began walking as the silence of the timber once more fell around them. Rounding a curve, they saw the roofline of the A-frame.

Up to this point, neither had brought up the creature that had clung to the hood, howling and snarling. As the house came into view, both of them feeling that safety was finally within their sight, Sonya said, "What was that thing back there, Jesse?"

"I don't know. But I don't believe in ghosts and things that go bump in the night. It was some sort of crazy person, I guess."

Several silver-gray shapes flitted across the road several hundred yards ahead of them, in sight only for a few seconds before disappearing into the timber.

The reporters stopped in the center of the road. "Jesse, those looked like wolves!"

"We have red wolves in this area—a few of them. Those weren't red wolves. There are no timber wolves in the eastern United States. Those were German shepherds, probably, running in a pack."

"Biggest police dogs I ever saw!"

"They get pretty big. I sure am glad to see that house. This is the loneliest stretch of road I believe I was ever on."

"For a fact. Jesse? You feel sort of odd about asking for help from the man we've set out to get?"

"*You've* set out to get, Sonya. I've been doing some thinking about it. I got nothing against Carl Garrett. From what I've been able to find out about him, he's done a lot of good."

Before Sonya could reply to that, a strange sound reached them as they walked up the lonely road. A very faint singing that seemed to be coming from deep within the timber.

"It's beautiful," Sonya said. "And . . . something else too."

Jesse listened and slowed his step. "Haunting. That's what it is." A mist covered his mind, clouding reason. He turned, heading for the timber.

A low snarl stopped him, clearing away the mental clouding and widening his eyes.

A huge gray timber wolf stood at the edge of the timber, watching the pair through cold yellow eyes.

Sonya tugged at Jesse's shirtsleeve. "Come on, Jesse. What's the matter with you?"

"That singing . . ." Jesse shook his head. "It . . . seemed to pull me toward the woods."

The wolf, now joined by several others, paced the pair as they walked toward the now-visible A-frame. The wolves made no attempt to leave the timber; indeed, they seemed to be acting as guards, discouraging Jesse from entering the woods.

When the reporters reached the wide clearing, the wolves stayed in the timber, watching them as they walked up to the chain-link fence.

"That's the strangest thing I've ever seen," Sonya said, standing by the gate. "I wonder why they didn't attack us. Instead, they acted like they wanted us to stay out of the timber."

"That's the impression I got," Jesse agreed. Once my head cleared from all that strange singing. I think they were just big dogs." He looked back at the timberline. The wolves were gone.

Sonya and Jesse turned their attentions to Dingo, who stood in the center of the walkway, looking at them. The big dog was not snarling or growling, but his stance and expression warned them they had better not enter the fenced-in area.

"All in all," Jesse said. "This has been a damn weird day."

Sonya looked toward the west. The sun was nearly gone and shadows were pushing away the light. For some reason she did not as yet understand, she shuddered, goose bumps rising on her flesh. "And now it's night," she said. "And I'm scared."

Chapter 22

Harry cursed long and loud as he barreled toward town. Everything was getting all screwed up. It wasn't supposed to be like this. This was supposed to have been easy. Kill the Garrett punk, ape Dee Conners, grab some money, and then ice Jim Hunt and split.

Now he had Mike Randall hanging on his tail and nothing had been accomplished. Harry rounded a curve, slowed down and put the unit into a slow spin. When he stopped, he was facing Mike.

Grinning, Harry floored the pedal and headed straight for Mike in a game of chicken. Just at the last second, Mike spun the wheel and left the road, ending up in the ditch, stuck in the mud.

"I'm stuck!" Mike yelled into his mike. "About a half a mile north of the old drive-in theater. Harry is just outside of town and should be approaching the four-way on Elm. Everything's all right out at the Conners place."

"Ten-four, R-10. Stay put. Someone will be out to get you in a little while. You need a wrecker?"

"Yeah," Mike said disgustedly.

"Ten-four."

"R-2 to R-10."

"Go ahead, Chief."

"How'd you get stuck, Mike?"

Mike cussed for a few seconds. "Harry ran me off the road playing chicken."

Jim had all kinds of follow-up questions about that answer. He thought he'd save them for later. Matter of fact, he wasn't real sure he wanted to know.

Mike turned his head just as a shadow fell over the driver's side window. He was looking straight down the muzzle of what appeared to be a .44 magnum. He watched the cylinder slowly turn as the hammer was jacked back.

The pastor of the First Baptist Church of Butler, Chris Speed, had heard all the rumors about what was going on in his town. Had heard about that so-called coven-buster staying out at that female writer's house. Both of them probably living in sin. Disgusting. Chris changed clothes and walked to his car. He was going to drive over to Sheriff Rodale's house and confront the man, find out what was going on in Butler. Sheriff Rodale was one of the best tithers in the church. Was in church every Sunday morning. Very good man, that Ned Rodale. Chris never believed any of those rumors about the sheriff. Probably spread by people of low morals who were jealous of the sheriff's dedication to the Lord.

Chris walked to the garage and looked at the tires on his car. All flat. On closer inspection he found they had all been cut.

"Hooligans!" he said. "Heathens! Undisciplined

228

young savages." He marched into the house and called the sheriff's department.

"You might want to handle this one, Chief," the deputy said. "It's Preacher Speed. Someone cut all the tires on his car."

"What the hell does he want us to do about it?" Jim griped. Jim did not like Chris Speed, thinking him to be a pompous windbag and a fool to boot.

"Wants us to come get him and take him over to Sheriff Rodale's house. You know how he thinks Rodale hung the moon and stars."

Jim smiled, remembering that Ned was sloppy, passed-out drunk. "You tell the preacher I'll be right over to do that little thing." He chuckled. "Yes, sir. Anything for the pastor. You heard from Mike?"

"Not a peep."

"Keep trying. You call Busby at the Ford place?"

"Doing it right now, Chief."

Mike hit the floorboards just as the .44 mag roared, the slug passing through the car's windows. He was out the passenger side and rolling in the ditch, coming up with his .357 in his hand, hammer back.

Mister Snelling, a man who owned a small neighborhood grocery not too far from where the unit was stuck in the mud, stepped around the car and grinned at Mike.

"You asshole!" Snelling said, jacking the hammer back and leveling the big .44 mag at Mike's head.

Mike shot him, the hollow-nose slug taking the grocer in the center of the chest, shattering the heart. The grocer dropped like a stone, the mag falling from his dead fingers and going off when it hit the ground. The slug knocked a hole in one of the front tires of the unit.

"Shit!" Mike hollered, just as the shakes grabbed him. This was his first time to fire his pistol at anything other than a paper target or a tin can.

He got to his feet and into the unit, grabbing up the mike and calling in.

"What do you mean, Mister Garrett?" Sony asked. "Why are we not going anywhere?"

"It isn't safe after dark. Especially not now. I think the lid is going to blow off the town tonight."

"The . . . lid?" Jesse asked.

"You two drink?" Dee asked.

"Oh, yes."

"Help yourselves," Carl said, pointing to the wet bar. "Then sit down. I've got a story to tell you. I was hoping it would be over before you people learned of it, but you're here and apparently you've encountered at least one of the creatures from the woods. You'd better know what you're up against."

Josh Taft and the other escaped cons sat in the farmhouse and looked at the man and woman, who sat on the floor, looking at them.

The man's throat was cut from ear to ear, but he was alive . . . and grinning at the pack of murderers and rapists and thieves and other assorted dregs of society. The woman was changing slowly, turning into a horrible-looking hag. She sat and cackled at the expression on the faces of the cons.

"I'm haulin' my ass!" Paul Grant announced. "I

230

don't know what's really goin' on around this whacky place, but I ain't gonna be a part of it no more."

Josh looked at the wicked lightning that abruptly began lashing the sky. Somehow he suddenly knew there was to be no following thunder; he knew the lightning was a message or a signal. He wasn't sure about which.

"Sit down, Paul," he said quietly. "I don't know exactly who would do it, or how, but you'd never make it out of this county alive."

"I'm damn sure gonna try, Josh!"

"Then you're a fool, Paul. Think about it, man. When we was all being whispered to back in the bucket. You gave yourself to the voice's demands, didn't you? Said you'd do anything to get out didn't you?"

"Yeah. So what?"

Josh chuckled without humor. "That was the voice of Satan, Paul."

Ralph Geason squirmed on the dusty floor, glad to see the night fast approaching. Soon the young people would be arriving. Hot, tight young cunts to mate with and fresh meat and blood to appease his stomach hunger.

He squirmed and growled in anticipation.

"There he is, Pastor," Jim said, pointing to Sheriff Rodale, who was sprawled on the couch, a whiskey bottle perched precariously on his big bare belly. "You wanted to talk to one of your flock, so talk."

"Hi, Preacher!" Ned hollered, his words slurry.

231

"How's your dick hangin', man? Say, how about you and me goin' out and runnin' the ridges, maybe chasin' up some pussy?"

Book TWO

Lead me, Zeus, and you, Fate, wherever you have assigned me. I shall follow without hesitation; but even if I am disobedient and do not wish to, I shall follow no less surely.
— *Cleanthes*

Chapter 23

Carl sat by the window and watched the lightning dance across the sky. He waited for the question he knew was coming.

"Why is there no thunder?" Lib asked, after viewing a wicking burst of lightning.

"Because the lightning is not natural," Carl told her, without taking his eyes from the sky. "It isn't nature's doings."

"Who . . . what is causing it?" Sonya asked.

"You had it right the first time. Who. Satan."

"Bullshit!" Jesse said. "I don't believe in that crap."

"You will," Dee told him. "And I don't think it's going to take very long."

Carl turned to face the people in the den. He had no intention of arguing the point with Jesse or Sonya. They would both change their minds—if they lived long enough to do so. "You said you saw wolves? Gray wolves?"

"We don't know for sure. Maybe they were big German shepherds running in a pack," Sonya told him. "If they were wolves, I believe they would have attacked us."

"There have been few documented incidents of healthy, full-grown wolves—unprovoked—ever attacking a human being," Dee told her, the conservationist and animal-rights activist in her surfacing. Carl smiled as she talked. "Man is the only animal who kills for sport. If those were gray wolves, I think it's wonderful that they've come back. I hope they stay."

"For God's sake, why?" Sonya asked.

Before Dee could reply, and before an argument started, that awful odor drifted to them. It was the worst Carl had ever smelled.

"Phew!" Sonya said. "What is that smell?"

The singing began, mixing with wild-sounding chanting.

"What kind of game are you playing, Carl?" Sonya asked him. "Whatever it is, it isn't funny."

Dingo stood up, teeth bared and the hair standing up on his back. He growled deep in his chest.

"Hit the floodlights, Dee!" Carl said, jumping to his feet. "We're in trouble! The Old Ones have surfaced."

What had been Alice Watson broke the leather restraining straps on her wrists, ankles, and across her chest and sat up on the bed. Doctor Bartlett's full-time nurse heard the noise and ran toward the room.

She jerked open the door, and stood inches from what appeared to be a huge Galapagos lizard that had learned to walk upright. It hissed at her, the foulness of its breath nauseating.

The nurse opened her mouth to scream just as a heavy clawed hand ripped across her face, taking out one eye, a cheekbone, and all the flesh on one side of her face. The nurse fell back against the corridor wall, the blood squirting from her face and puddling on the floor. As the woman was slowly sinking to the floor, the big lizard swiped with its other claw, the blow splitting flesh and cracking the nurse's skull, sending brains splattering on the walls and the hall floor.

The second creature grunted from its strapped-down bed. The lizard ran to its side and tore away the leather straps. The manlike creature stepped out into the hall, spotted the dead nurse, and reached down, tearing off one arm. It walked up the corridor, munching on the arm as one might eat a chicken leg, the lizard that was once Alice Watson right behind it.

An EMT, already goosy with fright at being in the same building with the creatures, opened a door and stood for a few seconds, staring in horror. He found his voice. "They're loose!" he screamed, trying to close the door.

The manlike creature jammed a thick arm between door and jamb, preventing the closing. The EMT used all his strength to keep the creatures at bay and in the hall. Hissing and spitting, her breath foul enough to stop a stampeding buffalo, Alice threw herself against the door, tearing it from its hinges and knocking the EMT across the room and to the floor, dazed and bruised.

Doctors Bartlett, Loring, Perry, and Jenkins ran into the hall—luckily at the far end of the long corridor. Alice and the creature turned, spotting the doctors, and began running toward them, hissing and howling, the savage sounds loud in the long hallway.

The doctors ducked back into the lab just as the deputy stationed outside the clinic ran into the hall, pistol in hand. He emptied the .357 into the backs of the hideous creatures, knocking them spinning and spraying the walls with a stinking greenish-yellowish body fluid. He fumbled for his speed-loader and filled up the wheel. Before he could fire, Alice and the other creature staggered over the ruined body of the nurse and stumbled into a room, slamming the door behind them.

"They're in the room right across from you!" the deputy yelled to the doctors, just as the EMT stuck his head into the hall.

The sound of breaking glass told them all that the creatures had left the building.

"Call Jim Hunt," Bartlett yelled to the deputy. "And Max Bancroft. Tell them the . . . creatures are on the loose."

Jim had driven to the edge of town. He stood over the body of the grocer, Snelling, and shook his head. The light was fading fast and Jim dreaded the coming of night. Like Carl, the chief deputy sensed this night was to be the opening to the gates of Hell.

"It doesn't connect," Jim said. "Snelling was one of the finest men I ever knowed. Just like Ralph Geason. They couldn't have been tied up in no devil coven."

"Devil's coven!" Pastor Speed snorted. "All that talk is a bunch of nonsense." He had recovered from the sight of the drunken and foul-mouthed Rodale.

Jim looked at the bigmouth, unable to hide the contempt in his eyes. Before he could reply, his radio started squawking.

"Alice Watson and that thing the state police brought in escaped, Chief. They killed Bartlett's nurse and took off. They're on the loose."

"Son of a bitch!" Jim's temper erupted, bringing the seldom-used profanity to his lips.

Pastor Speed look on disapprovingly. "What's that about the Watson girl, Jim?"

Jim squared his shoulders and let the preacher have it. Bluntly. "The bunch of trash that busted out of the jail grabbed her and raped her. She started changing into some sort of a lizardlike monster shortly after they done it to her. She don't resemble nothin' human no more. We brought in a . . . creature from out in the Conners Woods. He's something out of Hell. We had 'em strapped down and sedated over to the clinic. Now they're gone, on the prowl, probably lookin' for something to kill and eat. Like what was done to Old Lady Barstow and that poacher out in the woods."

Speed laughed in the chief deputy's face. He patted him on the shoulder . . . a very condescending pat that infuriated Jim. "My dear man, don't be foolish. Your imagination is running rampant. There are no such things as werewolves and zombies and creatures from the pits and that sort of Hollywood claptrap. Get a grip on yourself, Deputy Hunt. You're behaving like a child." He stood in front of Jim, chuckling.

Jim eyeballed him for a moment, then balled his right hand into a fist and busted the man right in the mouth, knocking the preacher on his ass, in the middle of a mud puddle in the ditch by the side of the road. Chris Speed flopped like a big frog, sputtering and hollering and waving his arms.

"I been wantin' to do that for near on to five years," Jim said. "Damn, but that felt good."

"I'll sue you!" Speed hollered.

The A-frame was literally crawling with cats of all sizes and description. They were clinging to the screens and to the shingles on the roof; they covered both the front and back porches, yowling and snarling and spitting. The sounds of their claws scratching on the wood and the glass were nearly mind-numbing.

Sonya's tough big-city-reporter facade crumbled and fell. She started screaming as fear gripped her in a cold sweaty hand.

"Watch the windows," Carl said, as calmly as the situation would permit. "I don't think they'll be able to get through both the storm windows and inside windows. I don't believe they can get a good enough purchase to hurl themselves with enough force at the glass to break it." I hope, he silently added.

"There's thousands of them!" Becky screamed, standing on the ragged edge of hysteria.

"Hundreds, probably," Carl corrected, having to raise his voice to be heard over the nerve-stretching yowling of the cats.

Susie began screaming and pointing at the front door. Several cats' paws were sticking between the door and the bottom mat.

Carl walked over to the door and stomped on the paws. The cats outside yowled in pain and jerked their paws out of the tiny space.

The cats began hurling their bodies against the front and back doors of the A-frame, screaming in rage when they found the doors to be too strong to penetrate.

Dingo showed all the signs of wanting to get into the thick of it—hair on his back raised, teeth bared in a silent snarl—but he also seemed somewhat subdued, as if knowing he would be torn to bloody ribbons should he venture outside.

The yowling and high-pitched screaming of the cats continued, mingled with the scratching of hundreds of claws against shingles and wood. The outside window screens were soon torn into shreds, and the cats had no place from which to get a grip on the single-pane security storm windows. Those who had been clinging to the screens began circling the house, many of them digging under the house, to yowl and claw at the underside of the floor.

"There has to be a logical explanation for their behavior," Jesse said, raising his voice to be heard over the cats' wild sounds.

Carl chose not to reply. Dee looked at the reporter, dislike and contempt in her eyes. Reporters in general were not her favorite people.

And that feeling was well-deserved, she believed. In her opinion, reporters seldom gave the rich their due for all the good they did, concentrating instead on the life-styles of individuals.

The yowling and scratching suddenly, as if on some silent command, ceased.

The abrupt silence was, for a moment, almost as bad as the frantic sounds that had preceded it.

"Are they gone?" Lib whispered in a very trembly voice.

Carl looked outside. For a moment, he could see nothing. Then a long tail dropped from the edge of the roof, swishing back and forth. He lifted his eyes to the fence. The top rail was lined with cats, running all the way around the house. He walked to the back porch. The porch floor was a solid blur of silent, staring cats. The front porch floor was the same.

241

"Let's shoot them!" Peter said. "We have guns. Let's kill them."

"It isn't their fault," Carl said. "They're only doing what an ancient god is telling them to do. Kill the god, and the cats will return to their normal behavior."

"Ancient god?" Sonya asked.

"Anya. And her other self, the cat, Pet. Somebody make a fresh pot of coffee and let's all try to relax. I'll tell you all what I know."

The teenagers slipped into the basement of the high school. Three boys and two girls.

They all noticed the gamy odor, but thought it to be only a dead rat. They'd all been coming here for months, and the smell of dead rats was not uncommon.

It really didn't make any difference to them: In a few moments they'd all be so high a skunk could walk through spraying everything in sight and none of them would notice.

They lit a couple of candles, turned a small portable radio on, and uncorked and passed the bottles of wine around, then rolled up some grass and laid out several lines of coke, taking turns drinking and toking and snorting.

After awhile, one boy stood up and walked to a dark corner of the huge basement to take a leak. Those remaining thought they heard an odd sound, then passed it off as nothing more than the creaking of the old school building; it was over fifty years old.

The boy did not return.

"Hey, Billy," a girl called. "What's happening with you, man?"

242

Silence greeted her question. Then an odd ripping sound reached their ears. None of them had ever heard anything quite like it. That was followed by a smacking sound.

"Hey, Billy!" the girl called. "What'd you doin' over there, man?"

What was left of a partially eaten arm was tossed in their midst. The hand was closed into a white-knuckled fist, the last living gesture during the most hideous pain Billy had ever experienced in his short life.

Boys and girls screamed in shock and fright as something from out of the smoking pits of Hell leaped into the small circle sitting around the candles.

Ralph grabbed one boy's head between his clawed paws and twisted, breaking the neck. He backhanded the other boy, the powerful blow fracturing the skull and shattering the jaw. Teeth popped out of the boy's mouth, rolling and clicking like bloody hard candy on the dirty floor.

The girls were fear-frozen to the floor, both of them noticing the jutting penis dangling from the creature's lower belly.

Ralph looked at the two girls and made his choice: The chunkier one would be the perfect mate. The second one was too skinny.

He killed her.

Roseanne began screaming as he tore the clothing from her, positioned her on her knees, and took her with one brutal, hunching lunge.

Ralph slapped her on the side of the head to silence her screaming. Roseanne got the message and silently endured the animal-like coupling and the clawed hands on her bare shoulders that were scratching her flesh and bloodying her.

Soon her head was feeling funny, and she found she was losing the ability to reason. She could not remember who she was or where she was or what had happened to the people she was with.

The metamorphosis had begun.

Roseanne began her climax. She threw back her head and howled like the beast she had become.

When the mating was concluded, Ralph went to his lair in the darkness and brought back a dead rat, presenting it to Roseanne. She ate it and grunted her thanks as the tail dangled out of her mouth. With a clawed hand, she stuffed the tail into her mouth and chomped, grinning at her new mate.

Chapter 24

Pastor Speed had crawled out of the muddy ditch with as much dignity as he could muster and politely declined a deputy's invitation to drive him home. He would walk, thank you. He wanted nothing more to do with the sheriff's department at this particular juncture in his life.

His mouth was swollen and painful where Jim had slugged him, but that was minor compared to his bruised pride — his ass hurt too, where he'd fallen on it.

He stopped and turned at the sound of a car pulling up and over to the curb. He sighed when he saw it was Chuck Vincent. He wasn't all that thrilled with the priest. Chuck Vincent was about the most unministerlike religious person Chris had even seen. Stomping around in those silly cowboy boots and going dancing and taking a drink or two before dinner. Chuck Vincent was, in Pastor Speed's opinion, a disgrace to the ministry. He should be, in Pastor Speed's narrow opinion, disrobed, defrocked, or whatever it was those idol-worshipping Episcopalians did to get rid of a priest.

Chris Speed had never been in an Episcopalian church in his life, and had about as much knowledge of the faith as a hog has of calculus, but as he was fond of saying, "I have a right to an opinion."

"Chris!" Chuck called. "What in the world happened to you? You're all muddy."

Mind your own business, you heathen! Pastor Speed thought. With yet another sigh, he walked to the car. "I, uh, was visiting a sick person and slipped. I'm all right."

A sick person with a pretty good left hook, Chuck thought, hiding his smile. "Get in. I might need some help."

As they pulled away from the curb, Chris asked, "What kind of help?"

"Roseanne Nealy's mother called a few minutes ago. She had just received an anonymous telephone call from someone who told her that Roseanne had been seen going into the high school with a gang of young people. Shortly afterward, the caller said, there had been screaming coming from the basement. She asked if I'd check it out."

"Why didn't she call the police?"

"She tried. All the lines were busy at both the police and sheriff's department. It's . . . ah, been quite an unusual twenty-four hours, Chris."

"So I've been told," Chris said around and through his mushy mouth. "All nonsense, of course."

Chuck gave him a quick glance. He's been told, he thought. And rejected it all. The damn pompous fool. "It isn't nonsense, Chris. Not at all. The town is in the grips of Satan."

"Poppycock and balderdash! Satan is surely here, Chuck, but it's in the form of filthy books and movies and TV programs, terrible music, all that dirty dancing, lack of direction and discipline among the young people, no patriotism, and dope."

He has part of it right, Chuck silently agreed, turning into the high school parking lot and stopping, cutting the engine. But he's in for a real eye-opener. Should be interesting to see.

Chuck lifted his eyes to the rearview mirror as headlights flashed behind him. He watched as Tom Malone got out of his car, a shotgun in his hand.

Chuck reached under his seat and took out a snub-nosed .38.

"My heavens, man!" Chris hollered. "That's a *gun!*"

"Sure is," Chuck said, opening up a half box of shells and dumping them into the front pocket of his jeans.

"You're taking this much too far, young man," the pastor admonished the priest in what he felt was his sternest tone. With his busted and bruised mouth, he sounded like a cross between Daffy Duck and Foghorn Leghorn. "And Tom is carrying a shotgun!" he cried. "What in the world is happening in this town?"

"I'm probably not the only one who has tried to tell you, Chris. You just won't listen. You've never been able to see past your own pointy, opinionated nose. You damn well better wake up."

"You can't talk to me like that," Christ blustered. "You . . . hippie!"

Chuck laughed in his face and got out of the car to greet Tom.

"What brings you here, Tom?"

"A phone call. From a woman who refused to give her name. How about you?"

"Same thing. Kids in the building and screaming?"

"You got it."

"Why do you have that asshole riding around with you?" Tom pointed toward Pastor Speed.

"I heard that!" Chris hollered.

247

Chris Speed was not the most beloved man in Butler, Virginia.

"If you're coming with us," Tom told him, "you'd better drag your butt out the car."

Bitching about the lack of respect shown him by certain members of the community—and Episcopalians in general, who were, in Chris's opinion, ranked right down there beside Catholics, and Jews too—Pastor Speed joined the two men in the darkness of the school parking lot.

"This is a fools' mission," Chris said.

"Must be," Tom agreed. "You're here, aren't you?"

The cats had vanished as silently and swiftly as they had arrived.

After telling his story, leaving his audience to believe it or not—and from the looks on the faces of the journalists, they didn't, though it appeared the kids did—Carl had looked outside and then tentatively opened the front door.

The cats were gone. There was not a trace of them except for the odor that clung silently in the dark night air.

They gathered on the porch of the A-frame and looked out at what they all knew—and what most would now openly admit—was the deadly but silent night.

"Where did the cats *go?*" Becky asked in a hushed tone, standing close to her boyfriend.

"Most of them went back to being normal cats, probably," Carl told her, turning his head toward the dark of the surrounding timber, just as the long and wavering howl of a wolf cut the air.

Dee looked at him. "Why are you smiling, Carl?"

"I think we've been sent some new and powerful allies."

"The wolves?"

"Yes."

"Who sent them?" Lib asked.

"It's a comforting thought, at least to me, to think that God did."

"Get a firm grip on your stomach," the trooper said, handing the just-developed pictures to Jim. "One man in the lab tossed his cookies when these were developed. And you'd all better know this: The governor has been notified of what's going on here in Reeves County."

"What's he going to do?" Jim asked.

"I don't know. I don't think he's fully convinced that all this is really happening."

Jim opened the envelope and looked at the blown-up 8x10's. His stomach did a slow roll-over at the hideousness. Daly and Tolson both grimaced and paled at the sight. The blow-ups were passed around, all the deputies and city police and state cops taking a look at the gruesome sight of the birthing of a demon child.

Jim walked to a chair and sat down, putting his face in his hands. After a few seconds, he sighed heavily and looked around at his fellow officers. "Let's take first things first, people. Try to put some order into this mess. A list of priorities, if you will. Although I ain't sayin' the order I'm puttin' this in is the way it ought to be. It's just a startin' point off the top of my head.

"First of all, has anybody got any notion of where to start lookin' for that dopeheaded Harry Harrison?"

No one did.

"We got word to all the people we figure might be on a hit list, right?"

Everyone nodded. All the city and county leaders that could be thought of had been notified . . . although most did not believe what they were told.

"That's their problem then," Jim said shortly; he had never been one who suffered fools well. "I ain't got the people to send out and hold their damn hands. Now then, has anyone heard anything from the folks out at the Conners place?"

No one had.

"Then somebody get on the horn and find out something." He pointed to a deputy. "You get a pencil and a notepad. We got to start takin' down ideas and suggestions on how to deal with this problem. We can't just continue to run around like a bunch of idiots." And that brought to mind the Stinson brothers—especially Keith. "Tom, you call the motel; see if them fool Stinson boys is behaving themselves. If they're not, go down and get them and we'll stick them in the pokey. Rich, make us a fresh pot of coffee. It's gonna be a long night."

"They went in here," Tom said, pointing to a side door that led to the basement of the two-story building. "I've heard Val talk about how the kids get in."

"What do they do down there?" Pastor Speed asked.

"Smoke dope, snort coke, drink booze, and fuck," Chuck told him bluntly.

Pastor Speed had never heard that particular four-letter word ever uttered from the mouth of a man of the cloth. "Heavens, Chuck! Your language is positively shocking."

"Join the real world, Chris," the priest suggested. "Come down from your lofty position and get your hands dirty for a change."

Chris bit back a sharp retort; after all, the men did have guns.

Tom turned the doorknob and pushed open the door. The smell of death hit them all, including Chris. No minister stays in the profession long before learning the odor of death.

"There's been trouble," Chris said. "That much is for sure."

Darkness and a very unfriendly silence greeted his words.

"I'll go first," Chuck said, taking a flashlight offered him by Tom. He clicked it on, and the pointing beam of light was comforting. The priest stepped onto the landing and began his slow descent. The odor of death became stronger with each step, mixed in with a strong animal-like smell.

The beam of light picked up what was left of a human arm, the hand closed into a fist.

Chris began softly reciting the 23rd Psalm.

"My God," Tom whispered, as the beam of light touched on the dead body of a girl. Her head had been crushed, with the brains hanging out.

"That's not Roseanne," Chuck said, his voice whisper-low. "I don't know that girl."

Tom took a closer look. "I do. But I don't know her name."

"There's a maniac loose in town," Pastor Speed said. "That's what it is." But a very small voice deep within the man found his words hollow and told him so. Chris shook his head in the darkness as the beam of light touched on a dead boy, the skull and jaw caved in from a powerful blow. "It looks like he was struck

251

with a baseball bat."

But no weapon was in sight.

"Let's get out of here and call the police," Pastor Speed suggested. "There is nothing we can do." He turned and was the first one up the steps.

"Man can scoot right along when the spirit moves him," Chuck said quietly.

"You blame him?"

"Hell, no!" the priest said.

And in the darkness of the timber called the Conners Woods, Anya and Pet sat quietly and rejoiced as the bubbling, stinking pools of liquid filth began attempting to discharge their odious inhabitants. Putrid, noxious fumes drifted from the thick bloodlike pools.

The gurgling foulness bubbled and popped as the inner heat worked its way upward. Something was trying very hard to exit from the stinking liquid. A grotesque, horribly misshapen object that only vaguely resembled a human hand, with twisted and gnarled and clawed fingers, shoved out of the stinking shit-smelling hole.

In isolated sections of the town, in basements of some of the homes of coven members, cracks began appearing in the concrete floors. Odious wisps of sulfuric smoke wafted out of the cracks. The foul-smelling smoke drifted around each closed basement, gradually spreading out to cover the entire floor. The mist was followed by a thick stinking liquid as slowly oozing as cold syrup, the liquid pulsed with newly freed life. It breathed like a giant leech, swelling and thickening as it gained freedom.

Then the foulness paused and was still for a moment, resting from its long upward journey, where it had been confined by God for immeasurable years.

The pulsing began anew.

The thickness protruding from the crack in each basement floor spread and became larger and better defined. The odor became a sickening stench, a rotten evil from a long-forgotten grave. It was no longer a semi-dead and rotting fetidness. A very audible sigh came from the crack, the sigh fouling the close air with decaying breath.

Coven members sat on the steps leading to the basements and watched in respectful silence as the growing, pulsing pools of long-stagnant slime grew with fresh, living, and very evil rot.

They watched through eyes that glowed with wickedness. They watched, and waited.

Chapter 25

Jim ordered a deputy to take Pastor Speed home, and then went with Tom Malone and Father Vincent to the high school to view the carnage in the basement.

It wasn't nearly as hideous as the men had described it.

There were no bodies. Plenty of blood and brains splattering the dusty walls. But no bodies.

"They were here, damnit!" Tom said. "We all saw them, Jim."

Jim squatted down in the glare of tripod-mounted spotlights and nodded his head in agreement. "I believe you, boys. I got no reason not to."

"Then?" Tom waved his hand at the emptiness.

"They either was toted off. . . ." He paused. "Or they rose," the chief deputy said, not able to suppress his shudder at the words.

"The undead," Chuck said.

"The what?" Tom looked at him.

"The living dead," the priest told him in a soft voice. "Doomed to forever serve the Dark Master."

"Satan." Tom's one word was delivered in a very soft voice.

"Yes."

"God help us all," Jim said, standing up just as Mike walked slowly down the steps to the bloody, dusty basement floor.

"They had some trouble out at Miss Conners's place, Chief. But they're all right." He very briefly explained what had happened. "None of the cats got inside the house. Those two reporters who stayed around are out there. And some kids too. Tolson and Daly are on the way out there to talk to them."

"Any sign of Harry?"

"Not a sign, Chief. He just dropped out of sight, seems like."

"He's around. He ain't far. You can bet on that. He's gone off the deep end like a lot of people in this town."

"You still think he's after you, Chief?"

"Bet on it." He glanced up at the yawning darkness just outside the door to the floodlighted basement. Something from out of a book he'd once read came to his mind: Satan was the master of the night. He glanced at his watch and was startled to see how early it was. He'd have guessed it was nearabouts midnight.

A deputy stuck his head inside the doorway. "Chief? Gangs of people gathering down on Main Street. Kids and grownups alike."

"What are they doing?"

"Nothin'. Just standin' around. Must be seven or eight hundred of them. Bill says it's the damnest sight he's ever seen. Spooky was his word. Chief Bancroft says he's gonna need some help."

"Tell him we're on our way. And get in touch with Daly and Tolson. Tell them we're gonna need them back in town. They should be out at Miss Conners now. Bump Dispatch and tell him to call them."

"You go on with them, Carl," Dee told him, after receiving the call and giving the message to the state cops.

"Your dad hired me to protect you, Dee," Carl reminded her.

"I'll be all right. Dingo is here and I know how to use a gun. Besides, you said yourself you didn't think the cats would be back tonight."

"Thinking and knowing are two very different things. I'd better stay."

"We're going," Sonya said. "We've got stories to write and file."

The state cops exchanged glances with Carl. Carl shrugged his shoulders.

Jesse picked up on the gesture. "What did that little shrug mean, Carl?"

"It mean that I personally think filing any stories would be a stupid idea that would only get a bunch of people in here and killed or hurt. And I can tell you that you're leaving yourselves open to getting hurt, or worse, if you try to file them."

"Screw you and your threats. The public has a right to know," Sonya said defensively.

"Enjoy your walk back to town," Daly said with a thin smile. "It's only about fifteen miles . . . through the least-populated area with the heaviest timber in the county."

"You wouldn't!" Sonya yelled at him.

"See you, Carl," Tolson said with a grin. The state cops walked out the front door.

"You son of a bitch!" Sonya shouted at the men.

Tolson turned and gave her the bird.

* * *

The gathering was a silent and sullen lot. But they were doing nothing against the law. None of them were drinking. There was no excessively loud music playing. No one was making any profane gestures or behaving in any lewd or lascivious manner.

They were breaking no laws.

Jim walked up to the owner of a hardware store. "Will. You wanna tell me what you're doin' out here at night?"

"Am I doing something against the law, Deputy Hunt?"

"No."

"Then what business is it of yours?"

Jim arched an eyebrow and moved on to the owner of a drugstore. "Jeff. Ain't it about time to go home?"

"No."

Jim sighed and walked up the crowded sidewalk. He shoved people out of his way; not roughly, but with enough authority that they felt the shove. They offered no comment or resistance as he pushed them aside.

"This is totally ignorant," Mike said to Father Vincent, as they walked behind the chief deputy. "What are these people *doing?*"

"Passive resistance for the moment. Subject to change very abruptly."

"I agree." Jim tossed the words over his shoulder. "To hell with this. It could get dangerous in a hurry. We'll block off the area and watch them; see what they do then. Y'all have noticed that none of the main guns that Crowley woman told Carl about ain't here, haven't you?" When he didn't get a reply, Jim turned around to see if the others were still with him.

They were gone, vanishing without a trace. Jim noticed then that many of the people standing around him sure did need a bath in the worst way. The body odor was tough. Then, from within the close-packed and strange-behaving crowd, a chanting sprang up, and the mass of unwashed bodies began closing in on Jim.

"You won't take us back to town?" Sonya asked Carl.

He shook his head. "I was hired to protect Dee, Sonya. If some of the young people here want to take you back, that's fine with me. Why not ask them?"

She looked at the young people. Jack shrugged his shoulders. "If they want to go back, me and Tommy can drive them in. But personally I think it's a stupid idea. I think the whole town is about to blow up." He looked at Sonya. "I tell you what. I'll drive you as far as the town limits and drop you off. After that, you're on your own."

She grabbed her purse. "Let's go."

But Jesse proved to be more cautious than Sonya. "I don't know about this, Sonya."

She did not attempt to question his courage; she knew better than that. Jesse had undertaken some dangerous assignments in his young career, and had written brilliantly about various violent sub-cultures he had infiltrated. "That's up to you, Jesse."

Jesse turned to Carl. "I'm a good shot with a rifle or pistol. Not an expert, but I grew up on a farm and my father was quite a hunter. I've never shot a man, but I think I could. If you want to go into town, I'll stay out here and get an interview with Miss Conners and the young people about what's going on."

"Go on, Carl," Dee urged. "We'll be all right."

Carl nodded. "All right. I'll drive Sonya in. You

258

young people stay here and keep a sharp eye out."

Dee tossed him car keys. "Take the Jag, Carl. Use the car phone if you need to call."

Later, rolling toward town, Sonya broke the silence. "I saw you slip into that shoulder holster rig, Carl. What kind of gun is that?"

"9-mm."

"You've used it on people?"

"Yes." He did not elaborate. Carl had more than one kill behind him. Many more than one.

He was still mulling over an offer from Edgar Conners. The man had made the offer just before Carl had pulled out with the equipment.

"A hundred and forty-five *thousand* covens in the United States, Carl?" he had asked.

"At least."

"How many of them dangerous to the point of violence toward humans or some sort of dreadful animal sacrifice?"

"Fifteen to twenty percent of them are extremely dangerous. Mostly with animal sacrifices." Conners had then told him that none of his labs were allowed to use animals in experimentation. It cost him only a little more money to go that route, and he'd said he sure as hell slept better at night.

He had then studied Carl's face for several moments. "I sense a lot of . . . well, controlled violence in you, Carl. I also sense that you despise not only Satan but those who profess to serve him."

"That is true."

"On all counts?"

"Yes."

"I have a job offer."

"I thought this might be leading up to that."

"How easy is it to destroy a coven?"

259

"Once you cut the head off, the organization usually falls apart from within."

"By cutting the head off, you mean?"

"Literally. Yes." Verbally dancing around without actually saying the K word.

"I've spoken to your boss. He tells me you are much in demand by . . . certain religious groups."

"Right-wingers. Zealots. I won't work for them. They are as dangerous—in their own way—as many coven members."

Edgar smiled. "That's what your boss said. He said you usually pretty well work as a lone wolf. That you do extensive research on a coven before deciding to take on the job."

"That's correct. I'm not going in to slap around . . . or terminate a bunch of silly kids who aren't really serious about devil-worship. And many covens listed in that huge number are just that. They dabble with it for a few months and then come to their senses and leave it alone, without ever harming anything or anybody except perhaps a wall with a can of spray paint."

"Terminate." Edgar had said the word slowly. "Do you sleep well at night, Carl?"

"Very well, thank you."

"When this . . . situation in Reeves County is over, I want to talk to you again. If you decide to take my offer, only two of us will know of it. You and me. You will be on the payroll as a consultant. And your pay will be more than ample."

Carl had met the older man's eyes. "Be sure you know what you're getting, Mister Conners. When it comes to people who worship the Devil, I play for keeps and never leave any witnesses behind."

"How did you get so hard so young, boy?"

"Watching Satan destroy a town, and many people

in it, and later kill my father brought it all into perspective for me. I realized a few months later that the Dark One is winning. Now, I can't kill Satan; only God can do that. But I can, and do, destroy many of his followers."

"And that's what you plan to do in Butler?"

"Yes. If I conclude that is the only way."

"You went away for a few minutes, Carl," Sonya said.

He smiled. "Sorry."

"Before we left the house, you put several guns in the back seat, under that blanket, didn't you?"

"Yes."

"Do you plan on using them?"

"If I have to."

"If you do, I'll write about it."

He turned his head and for a short moment, their eyes met. Sonya cringed under the icy stare, and a cold sweat broke out on her face at his words.

"No, you won't, Sonya. Because if just one word is written with my name connected with it, I can guarantee that you will never work in journalism again as long as you live."

She found her courage and became angry. "That's the second time you've threatened me this evening, Carl. And I don't like it worth a shit!"

"I don't give a damn what you like, Sonya. Let me tell you something. There is a war going on in this area; not just here—it's international in scope. The battle is between good and evil. And evil is winning. What do you know about devil-worship?"

"I . . . well, not very much. It's a subject that never really interested me. But it sure interests Jesse, I can tell you that. And for some reason, he wants to leave you alone."

Carl filed that away for future reference.

"And I'd like to know how you could keep me out of work."

"Easily. The simplest way would be to put a bullet between your eyes. But I wouldn't want to do that."

"Thanks so very much for that. Are you fucking serious, man?"

The hard look he gave her told her that he was very serious.

"Who do you think you are, Carl—God's warrior?"

"No. That's Michael. Sonya, before the next few days are over, you're going to see things that will haunt you for the rest of your life. And quite possibly change your life. It did mine, back in Ruger County a few years ago."

"What happened back there, Carl?"

"If I answer that, Sonya, and you print one word of it, there are certain agencies within the government that will move very quickly against you. Quickly, and fatally. Believe that, Sonya. I'm telling you the truth."

She was silent for a moment as the road yawned before the headlights of the Jag. The darkness on either side of the blacktop looked menacing. And something else: evil. "I believe it, Carl. Reporters have to make deals and compromises just like anyone else. Any reporter who says he or she doesn't is lying. I don't want to die, Carl. Tell me what happened. What really happened in Ruger County. I won't print it. I've got a funny feeling that a lot of reporters know what happened, and some of those people are dead, right?"

"That is correct, Sonya. Butler is going to blow wide open before too many more hours pass. It's like a pressure cooker with too much steam contained. That's what this particular coven wants—total destruction. Mindless horror and violence. This county and everyone in it destroyed. And no, it doesn't make any sense."

Sonya thought about the micro-cassette unit in her purse. She took it out and showed it to Carl, then placed it on the seat. "It's off. What are we driving into, Carl?"

He told her.

Chapter 26

When Carl concluded his story, Sonya sat in silence during the remainder of the drive into town. Carl didn't know whether she believed any of what he'd told her, or not. But he knew one thing for sure: Before long, she could see much of the same horror for herself.

As he turned onto the main street of the town, the headlights picked up the mob of people and Carl knew the lid had just blown off the bubbling and hate- and horror-filled pot.

He saw Chuck and Mike being dragged off the street, toward a dark alleyway, men and women beating them as they were dragged.

Carl did not hesitate. He accelerated quickly and drove up to the half dozen who were dragging and hammering on Mike. Lowering the window, he shot a man in the head with his 9-mm, then shifted the muzzle and shot another in the chest.

Sonya looked on in numbed and speechless hor- ror—not at the screaming, cursing, howling, and seemingly maddened crowd, who were doing their best to kill the deputy and the priest, but at what Carl had just done. Her mouth was hanging open in shock. She was actually a witness to someone using one of those nasty, terrible, awful handguns.

Carl used it again, this time shooting a club-wielding woman in the belly, knocking her backward and dumping her on the sidewalk, where she lay screaming curses at Carl, the blood leaking from her belly.

Chuck staggered to his feet and stumbled toward the Jag, jerking open the back door and falling onto the seat. He was bleeding from several cuts on his face.

Carl jumped out of the car and jerked out the shotgun from the backseat, shoving the priest to one side as he did. He leveled the shotgun at a screaming mob of people who were running toward him, waving clubs and knives. Some had rifles and shotguns. He started blasting, the double-ought buckshot tearing into bodies and knocking out chunks of flesh, sending those on the receiving end spinning to the street.

The crowd decided that pursuing Carl had been and still was a very bad idea and ran off into the night, leaving the dead and dying on the blood-slick street.

"Carl!" Mike's voice reached him. But it was weak and pain-filled. It came from an alleyway.

Carl tossed the shotgun into the back seat. "Boxes of shells on the floor, Chuck. You know how to use it?"

"Yes," the man gasped, wiping his bloody face with a handkerchief.

Carl nodded and grabbed up his M-16, slinging a bandolier of filled thirty-round clips over his shoulder. He ran toward the sound of Mike's voice.

As before, he did not hesitate when he confronted the mob of coven members who were beating the now-nearly-unconscious deputy. Carl leveled the M-16 and pulled the trigger, holding it back. The M-16 began singing a death song in three-round bursts of .223's.

Those still alive and standing after the thirty rounds of lead ran up the alley. Carl jerked Mike to his feet. "Can you make it to the car?"

"I . . . can damn sure try," the deputy said, pushing the words past bloody lips.

Carl found the deputy's .357 on the littered alley and tossed it to him. "Go. And goddamnit, don't hesitate to use that mag."

"Not after this night," Mike said grimly, and limped out into the street.

Carl heard the sounds of shots and ran up the street, literally knocking men and women to one side. A huge fat man blocked Carl's way, holding his arms out wide while his saliva-slick lips were screaming the most hideous of obscenities at Carl.

Carl shot him in the belly and kept on running. He could hear Jim's voice yelling for assistance. Carl located the man, frantically trying to reload his .357 while attempting to keep at bay a dozen men and women who were circling him, clubs and knives in their hands.

Carl dropped to one knee and began picking his targets, firing select-fire, each shot slamming home into flesh, clearing a hole for the bloodied Jim to limp through.

Then the street emptied as if on silent signal, leaving the chief deputy and the coven-buster standing in the center of the wide main street, amid the bloody dead and moaning dying and wounded.

"I don't know what caused all this," Jim drawled. "But I shore am glad I got you for a friend, boy. You don't mess around, do you?"

"There is no percentage in dying, Jim," Carl re-

266

plied. "Besides, God has other plans for me. I think my work has just begun here on earth."

The look Jim gave him was a strange one. "Yeah," he said softly. "I reckon you're right. Have you knowed that all along?"

"No," Carl said, his voice just as soft. "Something just told me that."

Jim had no intention of asking who, or what had delivered the message, or in what manner it came to the young man.

Tolson and Daly had been on the other side of town, investigating the breakout of the creatures at the clinic and the death of the nurse. By the time they arrived downtown, the melee was all over. Both men could but stand and look with awe in their eyes at the carnage wrought by Carl Garrett.

Carl was leaning up against the Jag, calmly reloading clips with .223 rounds.

"Well, we'd best get ready for a lot of legal action," Tolson remarked.

"I don't think so," Carl said. "We'll just play it by ear, but I doubt that anybody will make any complaints about this night."

"Man, look at the bodies!" Daly waved his hand at the bloody street.

The doctors and the EMTs had arrived, moving among the dead and injured, looking for and giving aid to the wounded.

"If you people don't want to burn these bodies," Carl said, looking at the cops and the priest, "let's get out of here. Their own kind will be along to get them as soon as we leave."

"George MacVeedy," Jim said, squatting down in

the street, looking at the dead body of a man. "Me and George growed up together. Used to fish together on the weekends. All that stopped about . . . oh, two, three years back. I should have known that something was bad wrong back then. I just didn't put it together." He paused as a sheet was spread over the body of a woman lying in a pool of blood on the sidewalk. "Lucy Jordan. She was always a strange one." He pointed. "Over yonder's Ned Carson. He quit the church about the same time George stopped speakin' to me and started actin' funny. It's all beginnin' to add up now. It all started happenin' about the same time, but none of us could see it."

Sonya sat in the Jag, her face pale as she struggled out of a mild case of shock. Carl met her eyes. She just shook her head. He had no idea what that meant. But he did not think the reporter was going to file any stories with her paper. At least not yet. He had gotten his point across to her . . . with technicolor vividness.

Father Vincent was holding a bloody handkerchief to his face. Mike was nearly shirtless—scratched and bruised, but not hurt badly. Jim's nose was bloody and there was a darkening bruise on his cheek. Other than that, he appeared to be all right.

"Don't take the wounded to the hospital," Carl urged. "They'll kill any innocents there."

"Well, what in the goddamn hell do you want us to do with them?" Doctor Loring yelled at him.

"Leave them in the street. I told you, their own kind will come back as soon as we leave. Trust me on this; I know what I'm talking about."

"We're doctors, Carl," Cal Bartlett told him. "We can't just leave these people on the street to die."

"I agree," Doctor Perry said. "These people have to be treated."

268

"Then you're all fools," Carl told him. He turned and walked to the Jag, getting in and closing the door. He cranked the engine just as Jim yelled at him.

"Carl! All right. We'll give it thirty minutes your way. We'll all back off the street and see what happens. We'll get clear away." He looked at the others. "And that's an order. Back off. Do it now."

Doctor Jennings opened his mouth to speak.

"Just shut up and do it," Jim said, closing the man's mouth.

"I'll meet you back at your office, Jim," Carl slipped the Jag in gear and drove off.

They had gone only a block when Sonya said, "You were like a machine." Her voice was emotionless. "A killing machine."

"I did what I knew had to be done, Sonya. There is no hope, no salvation for these people. They are forever lost."

"The last part is highly debatable." He could feel her eyes on him. "You've done this before, Carl." It was not posed as a question.

He hesitated, and knew that hesitation gave it away to her reporter's mind. "Yes. But not on this grand a scale."

"Many times?"

"Two."

"How come the mass killings were not reported?"

"There was no press around. And they weren't that mass. And yes, there were witnesses left. The first time," he added grimly. "But I didn't go in to kill — not the first time or the second time. In the end it wasn't left up to me. They didn't give me any choice."

"Were they in this state?"

"No. A thousand miles away."

"You left witnesses?"

"These people don't call the law, Sonya. They can't afford to draw attention to their activities. In thirty minutes, the main street of this town will be empty and hosed down. There will be no complaints filed with any law-enforcement agency. And I'll bet you a thousand dollars the local funeral home owner and his morticians are part of the coven. Everything has a pattern, Sonya. I've spent hundreds of hours studying these people. I know what they are, and it can be summed up in one word: evil."

"Nothing," Jim said, looking up the main street of town. "This is the damnest thing I've ever seen in my life." Then he remembered the dead fingers of Ermma Barstow goosing him, later grabbing at his privates, and the bodiless head grinning and speaking to him. "Well . . . almost."

In thirty minutes the street had been cleared of the dead and wounded and hosed down clean. The street glistened with wetness.

Max Bancroft turned to Carl, suspicion in his eyes. "How did you know they would do this?"

"Why don't you call it a lucky guess and leave it at that."

Tom Malone had rejoined the group, a bandage on one forearm and his face bruised by the fists and clubs of the coven members.

Pastor Speed had been picked up at his house by a city patrolman and briefed on what had happened. He was silent — for a change — and his face was drawn and pale. He had inquired about Sheriff Rodale and was told that the sheriff was drunk and passed out cold.

"Has anyone filed any complaints or pressed

270

charges?" Sonya asked. "Has anybody done *anything?*"

"Nothing has happened from anyone on the . . . other side," Jim told her.

"What are you going to do from *your* side, Chief Deputy?" she asked.

"Well, ma'am . . . I don't know. Yet. There are lots of things I could do. Like the obvious: arrest those who attacked us." He glanced at Carl. "Those that are still alive, that is. But I'm not going to do that." She opened her mouth to speak and he waved her silent. "I'm not going to do that, lady. And I think you know why."

Sonya's smile was tight and knowing and not a bit friendly. "It never happened, did it, Mister Hunt? If no one on either side presses charges, I can't very well write about something that didn't take place, can I?"

"You catch on real fast, miss," Jim said with a smile.

"I explained to her about the DA being a suspected coven member," Carl said.

Jim nodded. "Most of the town is under suspicion far as I'm concerned."

"I also told her that, as far as I'm concerned, once this is over, if she leaves my name out of it, she and Jesse can have the exclusive story . . . subject to your approval, that is."

Again, Jim nodded his head. "All that's providin', of course, any of us come out of this alive."

Chapter 27

Those known members of the several covens in town and in the county behaved as if nothing had happened. The remainder of the citizens seemed to Jim and Carl and the others who had resisted Satan's call to be in some sort of daze. They functioned, going about their daily business, but their movements were slowed and their speech robotic. Gene Wadell, owner and director of the local funeral home, when questioned by Jim Hunt, shook his head and commented about what a terrible tragedy it had all been.

"What tragedy, Gene?" Jim questioned.

"The outbreak of Legionnaires' disease that killed so many people, of course."

"Right," Jim replied. "Sure."

Jim and the others were curious to see what the local paper would have to say. The editor, Dick Goshen, had been unavailable for comment. When the newspaper came out the day after the shootings on Main Street there was no mention of the violence or any reporting of the dead and wounded.

"So Dick is a part of it," Jim said to Carl, sitting on the front porch of the A-frame.

"Does it surprise you?" Carl asked.

"You've done this before," the chief deputy told

him. "It's my first time. And hopefully, my last." He thought about that remark for a few seconds. "I didn't mean that the way it come out."

"I know. Have you had any word from the governor's office?"

"No. Nothing. Daly said he got word that the governor is walking around with his head stuck up his butt, not wanting to admit that something like this is possible."

"He's not sending more people in?"

"I don't think so. Carl? The other times you done this . . . something like this . . . what was the end result?"

"They forced my hand and I defended myself."

"That don't exactly answer my question."

"A lot of people died, Jim. Like I told Sonya last night, I didn't go in to kill people; not the first time or the second time. But after the last . . . operation, I realized that was the only way to deal with it."

"And there was no press on it? Nothing?"

"No. But entire towns weren't involved. Nothing like the numbers we face now. And speaking of towns, how are things in town?"

"Quiet. No sign of those creatures, the escaped cons, Ralph Geason, Old Lady Barstow—nothing. Rodale sobered up and come to work this morning. He's actin' like he's in charge, but there ain't nobody payin' him no mind."

As if on cue, both men looked toward the timber around the Conners home. Jim said, "Them Old Ones have surfaced, right?"

"I think so. It'll take them two or three days to regain strength and then all hell will break loose. That's the way it was in Ruger."

"That was a good idea your dad had to get rid of

273

them: lurin' them on that metal grid and then shootin' the juice to them."

"Yes. But it won't work again. They wouldn't fall for it twice. You said you talked to the man at the funeral home. Have the dead been buried?"

"Started early this mornin'. I got a man watchin' the cemetery but he can't see much. All the services is bein' held under a tent." He looked at Carl. "Why are you smilin'?"

"They're not being buried."

Jim blinked. "What?"

"I said the bodies are not being buried. I'll bet you they never left the funeral home."

"You mean . . ."

"Yes. They'll walk again."

"I'm a gittin' tarred of sittin' around this damned old motel room," Bullfrog said. "I think I'll take me a run back to the home place now that it's good light out."

"Jim said to stay put," Sonny reminded him.

"We ain't done nothin' wrong," Bubba cried. "Jim Hunt ain't got no right to tell us what we can and can't do."

"I need to get out and fetch me something," Keith said. "I'm a-gettin' jumpy."

All the brothers knew what Keith had to fetch, but said nothing about it. They all knew their brother was a dopehead and would probably die a dopehead.

Bullfrog stood up. "Anybody goin' with me?"

Keith and Bubba rose to their boots.

"Not me," Sonny told them. "I'm some curious to know what all that shootin' was about last night. But I ain't curious enough to venture far from this motel.

274

And that thing that Daddy turned into is probably lurkin' close to the house."

"I'm beginnin' to wonder if that was Daddy a-tall," Bullfrog said as he scratched his head, agitating the various varmints that took up weekly residence there—at least until Saturday night, when he took his bath. "I got to add-mit we was all some skirred that day up on the ridges. I think it was a nut done escaped from the funny farm."

"Yeah! Me too!" Keith agreed. He was in a hurry to get to his stash for a smoke and a snort and a pop. He was so desperate for a fix he would have agreed to kiss a porcupine just to get going.

"Yeah!" Bubba said, tossing in his opinion, along with his bad breath. A passing fly didn't stand a chance when Bubba opened his mouth.

"I think you're all full of shit," Sonny said, and picked up the just-delivered edition of the *Butler Weekly Messenger*. "Ah, crap!" he said, after quickly scanning the front page.

"What's the matter wif you?" Keith said, his eyes watering, his nose running, and his hands shaking. Keith was in dire need of a snort.

"There ain't nothing in the paper about no monsters or ghosts or hobgobblins." He tossed the paper on the bed and stood up, pulling on his boots. "Come on. Hell, there ain't nothing up yonder on the ridges to be scared of!"

The Old Ones were now finally free of the earth. They had crawled slick and slimy and grotesque from the stinking pools of filth. They sat for a time by the pools, regaining their strength. Soon they began howling for something to eat.

The coven members had been busy during the early morning hours, rounding up some tasty morsels for the Old Ones to feast upon.

A deacon and his wife from a local church were tossed screaming to one of the hideous creatures. A teenage boy and girl, both of them drugged to the max, were given to another. A local minister, pastor of a small country church, was tossed to yet another of the ancient ones. A hitchhiker, captured only hours past, was fed kicking and screaming to a creature. A hunter had been taken in the Conners Woods. He was paying for his poaching . . . with his life.

The Old Ones ripped the flesh from living beings and stuffed their mouths full, while coven members sat and watched, satisfaction shining from their eyes as their ears listened to the screaming and begging of those being devoured alive, and the permanently bubbling pools of stale putrid blood gurgled and spewed their noxious stench.

The Old Ones varied in size, from no larger than a child to the size of a great ape. They had arms and legs and a head and were vaguely human-appearing. The hide was a mixture of scales and hair. The head was huge, the mouth wide, with long misshapen teeth. The toes were webbed, as were the hands, the fingers and toes clawed.

They were neither male nor female. They were all things. All things evil.

Maggots began crawling out of the stinking holes of bubbling blood, hundreds of them, identical to the maggot that had attached itself to Carl's ankle. And they were hungry. In the basements around town, the coven members scooped them up with shovels and tossed them outside, to breed and eventually spread all over Butler, Virginia. The maggots were a mottled white-gray, the size of a big man's thumb, with very sharp teeth. They would eat anything living.

"Help me, Bubba." The voice sprang out of a pool that had appeared by the side of the house and it just about scared the shit out of Bubba.

"Whut the hale-fire was that?" Bubba hollered to his brothers.

"Hit sounded lak Daddy's voice!" Keith said. Keith was feeling much better. So much better he felt he could do anything, whip anybody, and maybe even flap his arms and fly — if he took a notion to do that. He had located his stash and toked and popped and snorted. Now he was floating — at least in his mind.

"What the hell would Daddy be doin' down in that there hole?" Sonny questioned. He stepped closer and took a sniff. "Phew!" He stepped back.

"Help me, boys," the voice pleaded. "It's your pa, boys. Get me out of here."

"I tole you that was Daddy!" Keith hollered. He knelt down by the putrid pool. "Daddy, you should have tole us boys about this old cesspool. We could have fallen in there and drowned."

The pool sighed with a parent's patience. "Right," the voice said. "I'm sorry."

"Daddy ain't never said he was sorry about nothin'," Sonny said, suspicion building within him. He backed further away.

Backed right into something cold and grave-smelly just as Keith screamed when a hand came out of the pool and clamped around his ankle.

Sonny turned around and looked into the dead eyes of his mother.

"Come to Momma," she croaked, putting a cold

hand on his shoulder.

Sonny let out a squall that could have easily been heard five miles away and jumped back, slamming into Keith just as Champ was crawling out of the pool, still holding onto his son's ankle.

Bullfrog grabbed up a shovel and gave his father a whack on the back of his head, breaking the handle and doing no damage to his dad's head. But his dad did turn loose of Keith's ankle.

Keith was gone.

He was off and running with a speed that would have put a greyhound to shame. His mother was right behind him, her head lolling from side to side due to her broken neck, her hands outstretched, dead fingers working like hungry spiders.

"Come to Momma!" she croaked, loping along just behind him. "Momma wants her baby boy."

"I ain't meanin' no disrespect, Momma," Keith shouted over his shoulder. "But there ain't no fuckin' way that's gonna happen."

Keith kicked in the afterburners and started putting distance between them.

Back at the house, the other brothers had armed themselves with clubs and were proceeding to defend themselves against Champ.

Keith gave one final whoop and was over the ridge and headed for anywhere that would get him far away from this place.

"You hold him off, Sonny!" Bullfrog yelled. "And me and Bubba'll get the truck."

"Me?" Sonny said. "Hell with you." He ducked a blow from Champ that would have taken off his head.

"I'll get the truck," Bubba said, and took off. He got the truck, all right. He jumped in, cranked up, ground the gears, and took off for town, leaving his

278

brothers behind. He ran into his mother as she was heading back to the house, having given up the chase for Keith. The impact tossed her onto the hood. She grabbed hold of the radio antenna and held on, grinning and slobbering at Bubba through the windshield.

"Oh, Lordy!" Bubba hollered, and mashed the gas pedal to the floor, spinning the wheel back and forth, the truck careening from side to side on the gravel road, trying to dislodge his mother. She held on, grinning and slobbering and howling at him.

Bullfrog and Sonny had run into the house and grabbed up shotguns just as Champ jumped through a side window. The boys let him have it, the buckshot tearing smoking holes in the man and knocking him to the floor. Champ promptly got right back up and charged. The boys fired again, and again the man went down. This time the boys took off out the front door and managed to get to their father's truck and crank it.

Champ ran out of the house and jumped into the back of the truck, holding on with one hand and pounding on the top of the cab with the other as the boys tore down the gravel road, running wide open.

Meanwhile, Keith had cut across country and was now entering the edge of Conners Woods.

Earlier, Pastor Speed had driven to Sheriff Rodale's office and had found him in and sober. Rodale had apologized and both men had bawled and squalled for a couple of minutes. Then they'd decided to take a ride out into the country in the sheriff's county unit. They had turned off the blacktop and onto a gravel road that wound up into the mountains, toward Champ Stinson's place.

Deputy Harry Harrison had slept in his car the previous night, about ten miles from the Stinson place. He was now driving back to town, on a gravel road that would take him past Champ's place and eventually up to Dee Conners's A-frame. This time he was going to kill Carl Garrett and screw Dee Conners and grab all the cash around and get the hell gone.

At the same time, Deputy Mike Randall, still smarting from Harry giving him the slip, was heading out toward the Conners Woods. He had looked all over town for Harry and had not found him. Mike had a hunch Harry was hiding out in the country. He'd find him.

At Dee's house, Jesse and Sonya sat on the front porch, drinking coffee and talking. Carl was in the back, fitting together a flamethrower and checking the refill tanks. Dee was in the kitchen, fixing coffee and wondering how to tell Gary that his girlfriend, Janet, had checked herself out of the clinic and had vanished. Doctor Bartlett had just called, informing her of the girl's decision. The other teenagers were sitting quietly in the den, listening to the conclusion of a statewide news broadcast on the radio.

"There's nothing on the news about what's happening here," Lib said. "If no one is coming in to help us, I want to *leave!*"

"Where would we go?" her boyfriend asked, glancing at her. "We don't have any money. There isn't a quarter of a tank of gas left in the car. And if we did make it out of the county and told people what was happening, who would believe us?"

"I think if we tried to tell anybody about what's happening, the cops would put us all in the nut house," Susie said. "I mean, think about it, people. Things like this just don't happen!"

"But it is happening," her boyfriend said. "And we're caught up in the middle of it. I think we're safer staying right where we are."

Lib raised her head. "What's that sound?"

Dee came out of the kitchen, a cup of coffee in her hand, Dingo by her side. "I heard something too. But I don't know what it is."

"Somebody is honking a horn," Carl said from the back porch door. He pointed up the gravel road. "Hear the car coming?"

They could all hear it now. The vehicle was a long way off, but coming up fast, the engine howling under the strain.

"Somebody's running toward the house, Carl!" Dee said, pointing to the woods.

Dingo started barking angrily and Susie began screaming as a rock came slamming through a window, just missing her head.

The front door burst open, Jesse and a wild-eyed man rolling on the floor, fighting.

"Halp!" Keith hollered from the edge of the woods.

Chapter 28

Becky picked up a heavy ashtray and clobbered the wild-eyed man on the head, shattering the ashtray and stunning the man but not knocking him out. Jesse rolled away from him, got to his knees, and gave him a short right to the side of the jaw just as Peter hit him across the neck with a poker from the fireplace set. The man slumped to the floor, dying before their eyes.

"That's Mister Phillips!" Jack said.

"Halp!" Keith hollered from the edge of the fence. Dingo was out the back door in a blur of snarling and fang-showing.

Harry Harrison slid to a stop and jumped out of the car, a gun in his hand. He left the car in the middle of the road, blocking it.

Shapes began materializing at the edge of the timber, all around the A-frame.

Another rock was hurled at the house, bouncing off the side. Chanting began, a one-word chant, the word becoming louder and louder: "Kill. Kill. *Kill!*"

"Arm yourselves," Carl said in a calm voice. "And shoot to kill." He picked up his M-16 and turned just as Sonya screamed a warning and Harry came charging through the open door. He leveled his pistol at Carl and Carl gave him a three-round burst in the belly. The deputy dropped his .357 and stumbled out onto the porch, falling to the ground, screaming and holding his shattered stomach.

Jesse picked up his pistol from the floor and moved to the open door just as Bubba rounded the curve in the road and slammed on the brakes. His mother was still holding on to the hood. Bubba was sitting in the cab, scared out of his mind and screaming incoherently.

Rodale and Speed rounded the curve from the other direction and slid to a halt in a spray of dust and gravel just as shapes sprang out of the timber, surrounding the car, beating on it with clubs and fists.

Bullfrog and Sonny rounded the curve and hit the brakes. The brakes didn't hold and the truck slewed in the gravel and left the road after slamming into the rear of Bubba's truck. That dislodged the woman from the hood.

It also knocked Champ out of the bed of the truck and he went rolling on the ground, howling and snarling. Sonny and Bullfrog were thrown from the cab and landed hard.

Keith was jumping up and down outside the fence, hollering for somebody to come help him.

"Do you know that nitwit, Dee?" Carl asked, his eyes taking in the hooded shapes growing closer to the house.

"Yes. He's a dopehead. But harmless. I'll let him in."

"Hurry, then. We don't have but a couple of minutes."

Another rock came crashing against the house. Whoever was throwing them had a powerful arm.

Mike Randall came around the curve, saw the traffic pileup just in time, and almost wrecked his unit bringing it to a stop.

A thrown rock spiderwebbed the left side window.

Mike saw the dozen or more shapes—he wasn't exactly sure what they were—surrounding the sheriff's car, pounding on the metal with fists and rocks and clubs. Several more of the things jumped out of the woods and ran to Mike's unit. Mike spun the wheel, floored the gas pedal, and ran over them. He dropped the car into reverse and backed over several more. They screamed as the wheels crushed the evil from them.

Champ Stinson leaped onto the hood of Mike's unit, pressing his grotesque face against the glass. Mike could see the buckshot holes in the man's stomach and chest. A slimy-looking yellow-greenish liquid oozed from the holes.

With a silent scream on his lips, Mike jerked his .357 from leather and emptied it through the windshield and into Champ's belly. The force of the hollow-nose slugs impacting sent Champ rolling off the hood, but he was far from being dead. Mike floored the gas pedal and drove right into those creatures on the driver's side of Rodale's unit. The car, already overheated, stalled. Mike fumbled for his speed-loader, a prayer on his lips as the creatures began surrounding his unit.

Rodale found his courage and began shooting at the hooded shapes just as very accurate gunfire from the house knocked several more spinning to the ground.

"Don't shoot my momma!" Keith yelled at Jesse. "That's my momma out there somewheres!"

Carl had stepped over the unconscious form of Harry and was walking out toward the front fence, the twin-tanks strapped on his back and the nozzle of the flamethrower in his hand. Sonya was in a prone position on the front porch, busy working her 35-mm, the camera humming and clicking.

Carl opened the gate and stepped closer to the mass of howling creatures. He realized that most of them were human, but some of them were grotesque beings from only God and Satan knew where.

Carl hit the trigger and sent a stream of thickened gasoline onto a group of yowling coven members. Their robes ignited with a whoosing sound and they ran screaming in all directions. Carl turned and gave another group a dose of earthly retribution, and that took the fight out of the rest. They scattered, screaming curses and dire threats down on the head of Carl.

Carl hooked the nozzle, pulled out his 9-mm, and calmly shot as many as were in range of the Beretta. The hand-loaded, exploding ammo tore smoking holes in the backs of the coven members and sent them on their way to personally meet their object of worship.

Champ and his wife had vanished into the unfriendly timber.

Then Carl shocked them all by saying, "Get out here, people. We've got to drag these bodies out there in the clearing and burn them."

"That ain't decent!" Rodale said, getting out of his car.

"Do you want to meet them again?" Carl asked him.

Pastor Speed settled the argument. "The young man is right. We'll burn them. Ned, do you have anything to drink in your car?"

Rodale looked shocked. "Yes, Brother Speed. Why?"

" 'Cause I need a good damn slug of it, that's why!"

Rodale looked on, his mouth hanging open, as Brother Speed unscrewed the cap and knocked back a good three ounces of sour-mash booze.

The preacher wiped his mouth with the back of his hand, capped the jug, tossed it on the seat, rolled up his sleeves, and said, "Now let's set about doing God's work, boys."

Carl laughed and said, "Welcome to the human race,

Pastor."

Speed looked startled for a second, and then his lips curved in a wide smile. "Quite right, Young Mister Garrett. And might I add that it's good to be back!"

"Carl!" Dee shouted from the porch. "Harry Harrison is still alive."

Carl walked to the porch and slipped out of the flamethrower harness. "Go on in the house, Dee. You too, Sonya."

As soon as the door closed, a single shot ripped the stillness that had just begun to resettle over the Blue Ridge Mountains.

"The preacher took a drink of hooch?" Jim said, eyes wide. "And said a cuss word too? Lord, have mercy! I always miss the good stuff!"

Mike had called in to Dispatch, and Jim and the two state troopers were at the scene minutes later. Soon the black smoke began spiraling upward into the blue of the Virginia sky.

With everyone working together, a huge pyre had been built and the bodies dragged to it and tossed on. Gasoline was poured over the bodies and Carl ignited the pyre with the flamethrower. The dry wood burst into flames and the smell of burning human and non-human flesh quickly filled the air.

Dee recorded it all on film.

Jim pointed a finger at the Stinson boys. "I oughta put ever'one of you in jail!"

All four of them started whining.

"If those grotesque creatures are really the boys' parents," Speed said, "I should think they've had punishment enough, Jim."

Jim nodded his head in agreement. He had found,

much to his surprise, that he was beginning to like the new Pastor Speed. Sure was a welcome change from the old. "You boys want to stay out at the home place?" he asked them.

"Hell, no!" Bullfrog said. "But after what Carl done tole us what happened in town last night, it don't seem to me there is any safe place in this county."

Before Jim could reply, Daly returned from answering a call on his tach frequency.

"Skyline Drive through the county had been shut down. Orders of the governor. Unsafe driving conditions is the official word. Traffic on the other arteries running through the county has been diverted due to much-needed bridge repairs."

"So he's sealin' us in—is that it?"

"In a nutshell. I've been expecting it, Jim. Hell, it's what I'd do if I was in his shoes."

"Well, it's a pretty damned cold-blooded thing for them to do!" Dee said.

"That's what the Federal Government did in Ruger," Carl said. "Actually, it's the only sensible thing for those in power to do. Five will get you ten the governor has been chatting back and forth with Washington."

"You don't sound like it bothers you much, Carl."

He shrugged. "As a matter of fact, it's a good thing for us. That means we can start terminating the coven members without having to worry about Federal agents looking over our shoulders."

"Terminating them?" Rodale said. "Exactly what does that mean, son?"

"Just think of yourself as working for a pest-control company, Sheriff. The county has been infested with fleas. We've been hired to clean them out."

"Hired by whom?" Daly asked.

Chris Speed walked over to Rodale's unit and took a

riot gun from off the rack mounted on the cage. He answered Daly's question with a firmness to his voice. "God."

Anya and Pet knew the attack against Carl Garrett had failed long before the survivors began trickling back into the safety of the timber. It had been mounted too soon anyway. Really, it made no difference whether they won any battles. If they were all destroyed, the movement would continue to grow. Just as surely as the demon babies were growing in the wombs of dozens of women all over the town. The seeds of Satan had been planted deep.

And Janet was now safe, grabbed almost as soon as she had left the clinic and hidden deep in the timber and closely guarded. Of them all, the girl was the most important, for she, unknowingly, had been impregnated by the Master himself. That was why no real attack could have been launched as long as she was at the Conners home.

Pet purred and Anya smiled. All things considered, matters were progressing quite nicely. Soon the town would be destroyed and the Devil's own would birth. Who could ask for more?

As for those few on the "other side," as they all had begun to think of themselves, it was one thing to talk of terminating the enemy, quite another to put that plan into action.

As Carl had known it would be.

He stood by the house as the funeral pyre burned down and waited for someone in authority to take charge.

No one volunteered.

Carl's smile was both sad and knowing.

"Good Lord!" Pastor Speed said, pointing down the road. "Look at that."

Hundreds of dogs and cats were walking up the road and just beginning to pass the Conners house. It was a strange and silent passing. Max Bancroft's setter, Beau, was pointed out by Jim, as were the mayor's cats.

"That's my dog!" Rodale said. He called for the animal to come to him.

The dog walked on past after only a quick wag of his tail and a turn of his head.

"What the hell's going on?" Daly asked.

"They're getting out of town," Carl said. "They did the same thing in Ruger. They've put aside their natural dislike for each other and have banded together, sensing there is strength in numbers."

"There's my cocker, Jenny," Lib said.

She called to the spaniel. The dog looked at her, wagged its tail in acknowledgment, and kept on walking.

Dingo sat in silence, watching the canine and feline parade.

A big German shepherd left the group and trotted to the fence. He and Dingo stood and looked at each other, messages passing between them that were understood only by the dogs. Then Dingo started barking furiously and the shepherd responded in kind.

The parade stopped. The humans stood in silence, not understanding what was taking place but sensing that a lot of communication between Dingo and the dogs and cats on the road was taking place.

The chilling wavering howl of a wolf cut the warm air as it floated out of the woods.

En masse, both humans and animals turned toward the sound.

Other wolves joined in, filling the air with their calls.

Slowly, the shepherd left the fence and took his place at the head of the column. He turned the column and led it toward the timber, toward the sounds of the calling wolves. Dingo left the fence and walked to Dee's side, plopping down on the ground by her feet.

"Now, what the hell does all this mean?" Tolson asked.

"It might mean we have some allies," Pastor Speed said, as Sonya continued taking pictures of the march of the animals. "I certainly hope so. I don't understand it, but we must all remember that God works in strange and mysterious ways. And these animals are God's children just as surely as we humans are."

Some of the most savage lightning that anyone among them could ever remember seeing began lashing the clear blue sky. There was no accompanying thunder.

"The Dark One is very angry," Carl said. "And he's sending messages."

Sonya was taking pictures of the savage silent storm.

The dogs and cats had disappeared into the timber, oblivious to the lightning. Carl looked at Dingo; he was paying no attention to it.

The Stinson boys were gathered together. To a man they were trembling in fear.

The sounds of a fast-moving vehicle reached the small gathering. The vehicle did not attempt to slow when it reached the still-blocked gravel road. It slammed into the back of Mike's unit with a grinding crunch. Steam began hissing from the overheated radiator. The passenger-side door slowly opened and a man fell out onto the gravel. The driver of the car was crumpled over the steering wheel. From inside the car, a pain-filled and hideous screaming reached the group.

The gathering began running toward the car, Carl

leading the way, Tolson by his side. They both pulled up short at the sight that greeted them and held up their hands, halting the others.

"Holy Mother of God!" Tolson said, struggling to keep the contents of his stomach from spewing past his lips.

Sonya dropped her camera and began screaming.

Rodale threw up on the ground.

The inside of the car was crawling with huge maggots, the thumb-sized creatures working their way through fresh blood that covered the interior of the car.

The left arm of the driver of the car was nothing more than whiteness of bone, all the flesh having been eaten away. Maggots were covering his head, chomping and munching away at the flesh, the hair, and his eyes.

In the back seat, the screaming had stopped as the maggots began eating at the woman from the inside out, having bored deep into her belly.

"Get the flamethrower," Carl told Tommy. "Move, Tommy!"

The boy took off, Susie right with him, glad for any excuse to get away from the terrible sight.

The man who had fallen out of the car stood up and screamed, the yowl chilling them all. He lifted a flesh-eaten hand, the fingers nothing but white bone.

His eyes had been eaten away and huge maggots were dining on his tongue, the blood pouring out of his mouth.

"Forgive me, Lord," Pastor Speed spoke softly. "But as is written, there is a time for all things." He lifted the shotgun he was holding and blew the man's brains out, ending the torment.

Chapter 29

The cars and pickups that could run were quickly moved out of the way, the men being very careful to avoid the maggots that covered the ground around the death car.

Carl stood the maximum distance away and sprayed the ground around the car with napalm, frying Satan's creatures. Then he turned the nozzle on the car, setting it blazing. He ran back to the silent group behind the fence.

"Back up!" Jim ordered. "That thing's gonna blow hard, people."

The gasoline fumes ignited and the car exploded, the ground trembling when it did. When the last piece of hot and smoking debris hit the ground, Carl moved forward and sprayed the area again, making certain all the flesh-eating maggots were destroyed.

"Stretch out some garden hoses," Carl called. "Let's cool down this wreckage so we can shove it out of the way."

While the teenagers sprayed down the smoking wreckage, Carl took Dee to one side. "This might be the last chance for you to get out of this mess, Dee. The governor is keeping people from entering the area, but not preventing anyone from leaving."

Her eyes searched his face for a moment. " I'll make some coffee and sandwiches. I think we'd all better eat while we can. We might not get too many chances over the next couple of days."

She turned and walked into the house.

"That's a brave young lady," Jim remarked. "Was I you, I'd be careful not to let her slip through my fingers."

Carl chose not to respond to that. "How about your wife, Jim? Have you leveled with her about what's going on?"

"All the way. She's a strong-willed and tough woman. Gentle most of the time but tough as wang leather when she has to be. Max Bancroft's wife, Doreen, and Tom and Chuck's wives, Liza and Carol, have moved in with us until this mess is straightened out. They're all country gals and know something about guns. They'll be all right."

Carl nodded in agreement. "I think Sonya and Jesse are going to stay out here along with the kids. With all these dogs and cats surrounding the place, I don't believe there is much chance of any more attacks out here. At least not until those against us begin to sense we're winning."

Jim shook his head. "You got more brass on your ass than Dick Tracy, boy. We must be outnumbered a hundred to one, the governor has sealed us in here, we're human beings"— he glanced at the Stinson brothers—"more or less, up against supernatural powers, and you're as calm and cool as that often-spoke-of cucumber."

Carl smiled and patted the chief deputy's shoulder. "Call it the power of positive thinking, Jim."

"Right," the man replied dryly.

"You've done *what?*" Jim hollered at the sheriff.

Rodale sat behind his desk and grinned at his chief deputy. "I said I have deputized Father Vincent, Brother Speed, Tom Malone, and all those folks out at the Conners place."

"I heard that. I approve. It's that last bit that I hope I misunderstood. You wanna say it again?"

"I said I have deputized the Stinson boys."

"Lord have mercy! That's what I thought you said."

"We need all the help we can get, Jim."

"I understand that and certainly agree."

"For some reason—and I assume God alone knows the answer—the Stinson boys have resisted Satan's call."

"Hell, Rodale, they're so stupid not even the Devil wants them! Those boys are unstable. Ever'one of them is about four bricks shy of a load. Sonny is the smartest one, and his momma had to tie a pork chop around his neck so's the dogs would play games with him. And they outsmarted him ever' time."

Rodale could not hide his smile. Lord knows there was little enough to smile about. He handed Jim a thick file-folder.

"What's this?"

"A hand-wrote confession detailin' everything I've done over the years. All the kickbacks and graft and payoffs I've been involved in. I sat down with Betty May this morning and told her everything. Then we prayed together and then we cried together. Later on, I opened my soul to Brother Speed. I ain't lookin' for no cozy spot in Heaven, Jim. I ain't gonna make it there. But I do feel like a great burden has been lifted from my shoulders. I actually feel like I've been borned again." He pointed to the folder. "In there, I've detailed all the places where I've got money buried around the county. It ain't stole money, but it's still dirty money. When this is over, take that money and use it to help rebuild this town. I spoke to Mayor Purdy just 'fore you come back to the office. He's just as dirty as I am, but he went about it in a different way, is the only thing. He agrees that it's time we bared our souls and set the record straight. I called Brother Speed and he went right over to Wilber's house; he's there right now. Me and Wilber been pals for many, many years. So, he asked me and Betty May to move in with him and Meg so's we'll all go down together. We'll go down fightin' for the Lord. And there ain't no better way to leave this old world." He smiled. "You're a good man, Jim." He stood up and stuck out his hand.

Jim took the hand and gripped it. "Have faith, Ned. It's a long way from bein' over. I believe we can whip this thing."

The sheriff shook his head. "You and that young warrior, Carl Garrett, will whip it, Jim. My string's done run out and I know it. It's past time for it. Wilber feels the same way and for once, our wives agree with us. I may be a crook, but I always feared the Lord and I guess that's why the Devil didn't want me." He squared his shoulders. "All right, Jim. You handle the outside. I'll handle the inside."

"That's ten-four, Sheriff."

Rodale smiled and then laughed out loud. "Them Stinson boys may fool you, Jim. I give 'em all a good talkin' to and I believe I got through to them 'bout the seriousness of this situation. I know there ain't no hope for Keith. There ain't nothin' goin' on between his ears. There ain't nothin' 'cept a pot patch up there. But Sonny said he'd stay with him all the time. One thing 'bout it, Jim: Them boys is all crack shots and they know they got their backs to the wall this time."

"I think I'll assign them to Max Bancroft. Between the four of them and Benny Carter, they might pool their brains and come up with enough sense to do some good."

Rodale laughed. "I thought you and Max was buddies. That's a hell of a thing to do to a friend, Jim."

Jim smiled. "It was just a thought."

Marie Hunt looked out her living room window. "Girls," she said. "Come over here and take a look at this."

The women moved to the window and looked out. The house directly across the street was covered with cats. The cats sat quietly, all of them staring at the Hunt house. The women could feel the evil from the unblinking eyes of the silent cats.

Liza Malone shivered under the malevolent stares.

Carol yelled as something bit savagely at her ankle. Doreen looked down at the floor and screamed.

Ugly mottled maggots, as big as a man's thumb, were slithering and hunching all over the floor. Carol tore the biting maggot from her ankle and stomped the blood-sucking creature into a messy glob. Her own blood left a stain on the carpet.

Marie looked toward the rear of the house, her eyes widening in shock and horror as what appeared to be hundreds of the hideous-looking things were pouring in from the back porch.

Liza took her eyes off the savage advance to glance across the street. If cats could laugh, the felines who were glaring at the Hunt house were laughing, their heads turning from one side to the other, and their mouths opening and closing in silent deadly humor.

"Damn you!" she hissed, then turned to look at the

296

slowly advancing maggots. "Let's go, ladies!" she called. "No way we can stay here and fight all this. Grab what you can and head for the cars."

The women grabbed purses and light jackets and ran out the front door.

"You ride with me, Doreen," Marie said. "Liza can ride with Carol."

"Where are we going?" Liza shouted, over the sudden and very frightening yowling of hundreds of cats.

"I don't know. Just follow me."

The ladies jumped into the cars and took off, just as the cats began leaving the house across the street and running toward the Hunt house.

In that just-abandoned house, what was left of a man and woman lay sprawled in their own blood on the living room floor. They had been clawed to death, their throats torn open from sharp claws and their faces ripped down to the bone by claws and fangs.

The maggots began oozing under the back door of the death house, the blood-scent bringing them to the house. Soon the lifeless bodies of the man and woman were covered with the creatures from Hell. The room filled with the sounds of chomping and sucking as hundreds of maggots moved in waves over the bodies. The mottled white bugs soon became slick and red from the blood, and those who had gorged themselves swollen began falling fat from the bodies, to land on the bloody floor with dull plops.

On the top floor of the high school, what had once been Ralph and Roseanne gnawed on the bones of an unlucky janitor who had ventured into the school building that morning and walked right into the arms of the pair. His fright had been very brief. The pair dined leisurely, cracking open the bones and sucking the marrow from them. After lunch, they mated, and then slept.

"It's time to move," Josh told the other escaped cons.

"Move where?" Mark asked, keeping one eye on the farm couple who had changed before their eyes into horrible creatures.

"And how do you know it's time to leave?" Paul challenged. "I like it here." He looked at the gruesomely grinning man and wife, who were looking at him, evil shining from their eyes. "Sort of."

"I just know." He picked up a riot gun taken from the jail. "Let's go."

"I'm gettin' the hell gone from this crazy place," Mark said. "You guys can do whatever you want to do. Maybe we did make a deal with the Devil. But we been hedgin' out of deals all our lives—all of us. Fuck the Devil!"

He stood up and picked up his rifle, moving toward the door. The others stood or sat quietly, watching to see what, if anything, was about to happen.

Mark put his hand on the doorknob and began screaming and jerking, his body arching and flopping and twisting like a maddened snake. His hair stood up like the hair on an angry dog's back.

Sparks began shooting from the man's mouth as his hair began to smoke. His head erupted in flames. The eyes bubbled and boiled, dissolving into liquid and running down his cheeks. Mark Hay's head exploded, showering those in the room with hot brains and bits of bone.

Mark fell to the floor, on his back, bubbling blood squirting from the stump on his shoulders that had once held his head.

After a long silent moment, broken only by the gasses escaping from Mark's dead body, Josh said, "Anybody else want to try to weasel out of the deal we made?"

The cons looked at one another. Louis Easton sighed and shook his head. "I reckon not."

"Then it's settled," Josh said. "Let's go." He looked at the front door, now spattered and dripping with Mark's blood and brains. "We'll use the back door."

Val Malone, reeking with the odors of sex and sweat and filth, looked at Nick. "Tonight," she said. "It's tonight. Alert the others." She walked toward the door.

"Where are you goin'?" Nick asked.

"I got to go fuck some cons. He just told me so."

Nick did not have to ask who "he" was. "I wanna watch," he said.

"Bring your ass on, then. I got to get it done and get ready for tonight."

"What do we do first off?" Nick asked, as they walked out to the car.

"I don't know. I don't think it really makes any difference anymore. I just get that feeling. You know what I mean?"

"Yeah. I started gettin' the same feelin' early this morning." He looked across the street. An old couple lived in the house with the closed drapes. They had complained to the cops bunches of times about the loud music and had caused Nick some grief with the law. "You go on, Val. I think I'll have me some fun."

She grinned like a poisonous snake about to strike. "I think it's anything-goes time, Nick. Have fun."

He glanced at her. "Anything goes?"

"Whatever you want to do, lover." She looked over at the old couple's house. The drapes parted and the old man stared at them. She gave him the bird and hunched her hips obscenely at him, laughing at the expression on his face.

A deputy chose that time to turn the corner and drive up. He stopped his unit a few feet from the young people and stared at them.

"Cool it," Val said. "We're about to be hassled by the pigs."

The deputy noticed the butt of the pistol sticking out from behind Nick's belt. He started to get out of his unit, and remembered the words from Jim Hunt. The chief deputy had told them that morning: "Let them start it, boys. If any of us get out of this alive, we're gonna have a hard enough time explainin' what went down. What we don't need is charges that we provoked anything. Let them start it."

Nick noticed the deputy's reluctance and laughed at him. "What's the matter, pig? Things getting a little rough around town?"

The deputy sat in his unit and looked at him. Make the first move, shithead, he silently urged the punk.

"Back off, Nick," Val warned him in a whisper. "It's broad daylight and we're out in the open."

"You're the boss since Linda rolled craps. Whatever you say."

The deputy could see their lips moving, but could not hear what was being said. That made him both curious and slightly nervous. He got out of his unit, unsnapping as he did so and keeping his right hand close to the butt of his .357.

"He's gonna push it," Val said.

The deputy stopped at the curb, standing by his rear bumper.

"What's on your mind, Deputy Dawg?" Nick sneered at him.

The deputy opened his mouth to reply, thought better of it, and walked around the car, putting his hand out to open the door.

"Mother-fucker don't have any balls, does he, Val?" Nick grinned. "He probably has to get another pig to screw his wife."

She laughed at the very sudden and ugly expression on the deputy's face.

The deputy walked around the car, this time coming around the front of the unit.

"He's got his pistol unsnapped!" Val yelled. "Look out, Nick!"

Nick grabbed for his pistol and fired, the .38 slug, hitting the deputy in the center of the chest. The man fell back and grabbed for the bumper on his way down. He missed and fell hard, hitting his head on the pavement, cracking his skull wide open.

"The shit's gonna fly now, Nick," Val said, looking up to see the old couple across the street peering at them through the drapes. "And those old fuckers over there seen you kill him."

"Then I guess I got to go over there and deal with them." Nick said it with absolutely no emotion in his voice.

"We'll do it together. I never did like those old creeps."

"I thought you had to hump those cons."

"They can wait. I can get off listening to these creeps scream and it ain't nearly so tiresome."

The young people started across the street.

The drapes were abruptly closed, darkening the room. Soon it would be completely dark for both of them. Forever.

Chapter 30

"Goddamnit, Governor!" Jim lost his temper, hollering at the man over the phone. "I got to have some help in here. And don't *you* tell *me* that a crisis situation don't exist in this county. I'm lookin' at it dead in the face."

"I am quite aware of the problem in Reeves County, Chief Deputy Hunt," the governor replied calmly. "A similar problem existed in Ruger County a few years ago. I have spoken to the man who was governor at that time. He informed me that local elected officials in the county handled it quite well. I am fully confident in your ability to do the same."

Jim held the phone away from his ear and looked at the receiver, disbelief in his eyes. The governor prattled on. "I have been advised by very senior Federal Government people that what I have done thus far meets with their approval."

"Is that a fact?" Jim said sarcastically.

"Yes. I have been advised that the, ah, situation must be contained within a relatively small area. I'm speaking confidentially now, Jim."

"Oh, I can keep a secret, Governor." There was enough sarcasm and contempt in Jim's voice to melt stone.

"A ten-second delay has been placed on all calls

coming out of Ruger County, Jim. That's to prevent any news of your—our—situation from creating panic outside the perimeter of conflict."

"Perimeter of conflict?"

"Yes. A general from the Pentagon is with me now. He has code-named the problem Big Bad Wolf. From now on, if you wish to consult with me, use the code name."

"Big Bad Wolf," Jim said slowly, shaking his head in total disbelief. "What am I, Governor: Little Red Riding Hood?"

"Say, now! That's not bad, Jim. As a matter of fact, I like it! The general has just informed me that the opposition will be code-named Twinkle. You like that one, Jim?"

Jim hung up.

He turned to face Daly and Tolson, Father Vincent and Brother Speed, and several doctors and deputies. He pointed to the phone, and quite uncharacteristically said, "That man is a fuckin' idiot!"

Marie Hunt had led the women across town, taking momentary refuge in the Baptist church parking lot. No maggots could be seen.

"Do we go inside?" Carl asked.

"No. I think we're safer in our cars. At least for the time being. We'll use our CBs to stay in contact. Go to channel . . . oh, 2. We'll probably be picked up on scanners anyway."

A young girl, no more than eight or nine years old, suddenly ran screaming across the parking lot. She was naked from the waist down, with blood on her inner thighs, and being chased by several men, all of them in various stages of undress. Marie did not hesitate. She dropped the car into gear, mashed the pedal to the floor, and pointed the nose of the car toward the men. She slammed into the men, knocking them sprawling to the blacktop parking lot. Doreen opened the door on her side and jumped out, grabbing the hysterical little girl and jerking her inside.

"Go!" she yelled.

Marie grabbed her CB mike. "Head for the clinic, Carol."

Doreen was holding the little girl, trying to calm her. She covered the child's lower body with her jacket and silently, and with much venom in her thoughts, cursed men who would do this to a child

"I wonder if we killed any of those men back there," she said.

"I certainly hope so," Marie replied.

Carl had driven into town in the Jag. The friendly dogs and cats from town had completely circled the house, lying hidden just inside the timber. Carl did not think those in the A-frame were in any immediate danger.

The town lay silent under the hot summer sun. He had not seen one living being since entering the city limits.

Mike rounded a corner, in a new unit, and waved him down.

"We just got a report of a police officer layin' in the street. We can't contact R-8 by radio. You wanna tag along?"

"Right behind you, Mike."

In a few minutes, Mike stood over the body of Deputy McBride and cussed. Then he got a blanket from the trunk of his car and covered the man.

When the young deputy lifted his gaze to Carl, his eyes were filled with hate and fury.

"Take it easy, Mike. It's when you lose control that they nail you. You've got to keep your wits about you all the time. Now grab ahold of yourself and call in."

With an effort that was visible to Carl, Mike calmed himself and walked back to his car to call in. In only a couple of minutes, Jim drove up, Daly in the front seat with him. Jim looked at the blanket-covered body for a moment, his face hard. He knelt down and lifted the blanket and gazed into the dead face of the deputy.

"Me and Mac go back a long ways," Jim finally said. "He'd a had his twenty in next year. He was goin' to pull the pin and do work in his shop. He made little wooden dolls and figures and stuff like that. He give most of his work to needy kids come Christmas time. He was good with his hands." He looked toward the house to his right. "That punk Nick Jamison lives there. You canvassed the neighborhood, Mike?"

"Not yet."

"Get to it. Daly, would you go with Mike? Good. I appreciate it. Me and Carl will work the other side of the street soon as I call in for an ambulance. I want whoever done this and I want him, or her, bad. Mac's gun is still in leather. He was shot down deliberate."

Jim and Carl went from house to house. Those that would respond to the hammering on the doors were hard-eyed, sullen, and uncommunicative. And the stench from inside the homes was an insult to the nostrils of those who were standing outside.

At the fifth house, Jim lost his temper. "Damnit, Johnny! I just lost McBride. Somebody shot him and killed him not two hundred yards from this spot. And you're tellin' me you didn't see or hear anything?"

The man's smile was both ugly and evil. It matched

the stench wafting out from inside his home. "You want me to say I'm sorry about Mac? Fuck you!"

He slammed the door in Jim's face.

Jim walked back to the sidewalk in silence. There, he stopped and looked back at the house. "Johnny Pierson. I always figured him to be one of the most honorable men in the county." He glanced at Carl. "What makes them vulnerable?"

Carl shook his head. "I don't know the answer to that, Jim. I don't guess anyone . . . any mortal being does."

"I had to ask. Come on, let's check the next house."

From inside the house they had just left, deep wild-sounding laughter drifted out to them. Then a woman's laughter joined in, and that was followed by a girl's giggling.

"Does the man have a daughter?" Carl asked.

"Unfortunately, yes. About fifteen years old. Runs with a wild crowd."

"She may have been the key to his going over to the other side."

"Hadn't thought of that," Jim replied, walking up to the old couple's front door and knocking.

He got no response.

Carl tried to see inside, going from window to window on the front porch. The drapes were all pulled. Suddenly the drapes moved, the movement coming from the bottom, near the floor.

"Someone or something is in there, Jim. These drapes just moved from near the floor. Do these folks have a dog or cat?"

"No. They don't have nobody 'cept each other." He tried the front doorknob. It turned under his hand. He pushed the door open and the odor of blood filled his nostrils. "Damn," he whispered, looking into the darkened death house.

Carl looked over his shoulder. Blood splattered the walls and covered the floor with its slickness. His eyes settled on what was left of the old man and his wife. They appeared to have been hacked to death.

"Twinkle has struck again," Jim said.

Carl looked at him. "I beg your pardon?"

"The governor informed me of that this morning. That's the code name for the coven members. I'm Little Red Riding Hood. The, ah, entire problem has been code-named Big Bad Wolf."

"That's an insult to the wolf community. They're on our side."

"I know. I think. But I didn't feel like gettin' into that with the governor. That would have confused him. He's a good man, but kinda slow." Jim waved Carl out of the front door. "Go get Mike and Daly for me, will you? I'll call the coroner from my car."

"There won't be much left for him to look at," Carl said, his eyes catching movement from the rear of the house. He knew what it was and pointed it out.

Maggots. Hundreds of them, moving like one huge mottled wave toward the bloody bodies. The leading edge reached the first body and began feeding on the flesh and sucking up the blood. Carl looked at the bottom of the drapes that had moved. They were covered with maggots.

"People changin' into monsters wasn't enough. Now we got this to put up with."

"You haven't seen anything yet, Jim. Believe me when I say that."

"What do you mean? Jesus God, what else is comin' at us?"

"The Old Ones."

"I can hardly wait."

Once again, from his office, Jim tried to convince the governor to send in some help.

"We can't have press on this, Jim," the governor's aide informed him. The governor was unavailable. He was meeting with the head of the tourism board. "I thought you understood all that."

"I'm not askin' for a platoon of reporters. I'm askin' for some volunteer state troopers to help us on this."

"Sorry, Jim. Your area is in the process of being sealed off. No one is going in there, and no one is coming out."

"The press is damn sure goin' to pick up on that, partner," Jim warned the man.

The aide chuckled. "I don't think so, Jim. Your county is one of the more isolated ones in the state. No industry to speak of. No tourist attractions. It is the governor's belief that we can keep a lid on this for several days—a week even. By then, Big Bad Wolf should be winding down."

"The wolves are on our side."

"I beg your pardon, Jim? Did I hear you correctly? The wolves are on your side?"

"That's what I said."

"Jim, there are no wolves in your area."

"That's what you think, partner."

The aide snorted his disbelief. "Be that as it may, Jim. The governor wishes to commend you and your men for the outstanding work you've done in containing this . . . ah, situation. You'll all receive commendations when the problem has been resolved. And Jim, make certain that it is all cleaned up as quickly as possible. News of this would not be good for the state. Certainly not when the tourist season is getting into full swing. I'm sure you understand that. Now then, the governor further stated that it is fine, brave lawmen such as yourself that makes this state so great, and that he is certain you can handle Twinkle. And furthermore, he—"

Jim hung up.

"No luck?" a deputy asked.

"No. We're all alone in this. There is no help comin'. We've been sealed in. No one comes in, no one goes out." He looked at Carl. "That's what they done in Ruger, ain't it?"

"Yes. But we handled it, Jim. Or rather, my dad and Father Denier did."

"Carl, I can't order my people to go out and just start killin' folks. I can't do that and they wouldn't do it anyways."

Carl took his badge out of his jeans pocket and tossed it on the desk.

"What's that mean?" Jim asked. "And it better not mean what I think it does."

"It means that I'm no longer restricted by the law."

"What are you goin' to do, boy? Just go from house to house killin' people? You try that and I'll put your ass in the bucket. And by God, boy, I mean it!"

Chris Speed had been standing by, listening. The man had strapped on two pistols and had a bandolier of shotgun shells across his chest. He did not look a bit foolish. "I don't think the young man has any intention of doing anything like that, Jim. Wholesale killing is not his plan. Isn't that right, Carl?"

"You know it's right, Pastor. But that isn't to say that there won't be some killing."

"You just make damn sure whatever you do will stand up in a court of law," Jim warned him.

"Jim," Carl said, stepping closer to the man. "Can't

309

you understand there isn't going to be any legal action once this is over? There was nothing done after the smoke cleared in Ruger. Nothing! But we've got to make certain that *we* are the ones still living. Take your legal code books and toss them out the window. We're fighting the *Devil*, Jim. He doesn't play by rules."

Jim walked to the coffeepot and poured a cup. Without turning around, he said, "I don't know you, boy. I never seen you before in my life. And neither has anybody else in this room. You're invisible." He walked into his office.

Carl headed for the front door.

"Go with God," Pastor Speed whispered.

Book Three

Hell's broken loose.
— *Robert Greene*

Chapter 31

Carl flagged down Father Vincent. "You wouldn't by any chance be looking for your wife, would you?"

"Yeah!" The priest almost screamed the word. "She's supposed to be over at Marie's house. But I didn't have to get out of the car to see that maggots were all over the place. I—"

"Relax, Chuck. She's at the clinic with the other women." He explained what had happened. "And I turned in my badge to Jim."

Chuck studied his face for a long moment. "Are you going head-hunting, Carl?"

"I'm not going out to kill indiscriminately, if that's what you mean."

The priest nodded. "Jim has asked for all the . . . untouched, I guess is the way to phrase it, to ride patrol shifts until this is over. Let me check with my wife and get her plans, and I'll meet you . . . where?"

"Chuck, I'd give that some thought. I . . ."

A car pulled up behind Carl, the driver blowing the horn; long, irritating, arrogant blasts. "Get out of the way, you goddamned son of a bitch!" he yelled.

Carl uncoiled his lanky frame from behind the wheel

and walked back to the car. He could smell the man's body odor before he reached the car. Without a second's hesitation, Carl jerked the door open and pulled the man out and to his feet. Carl hit him a vicious blow to the stomach, doubling the man over; then grabbing the man behind his head and bringing his knee up at the same time, he impacted the man's face against his knee, smashing the nose and loosening teeth. The man dropped to the pavement, moaning and blubbering through his busted nose.

Carl knelt down beside the man and reached into his back pocket, coming out with a leather slapper. He laid the leather-covered lead lump against the man's head and the once-belligerent man went to sleep, painfully and totally against his will.

Carl stood up as Chuck walked up to him. "You know this asshole?" he asked the priest.

"Owns and operates a service station. Name's Neuroth, or something like that. Stinks like a cesspool! What are you going to do with him?"

"I'm going to take him out to Conners Woods and ask him a few questions."

"And then?"

"I haven't made up my mind about that."

"I'll help you load him in the car."

Carl handcuffed the odious gentleman and the men tossed him in the back seat of the Jag.

"I'll meet you at the clinic," the priest said. "I'll ride out to the woods with you."

"The interrogation is not going to be pleasant, Chuck."

"Neither is worshipping the devil."

Later, on the way out of town, Chuck pointed to the mobile phone. "I'm told all the calls out are being monitored by some government people, with a ten-second-delay capability to censor anything they might feel would give this situation away."

"That's right. But that's not a standard phone."

"What do you mean?"

"That's actually a shortwave rig. Conners Industries has their own microwave systems and satellite in place. The state and government boys obviously don't know about this phone. I've spoken to Edgar several times during the last couple of days. He has a scrambler on this frequency. It's very high frequency; six- or seven-meter band. Push that button there, and the modular phone takes over. That's the one that's being monitored."

"Well, I'll be. And you didn't tell Jim?"

"No."

"May I ask why?"

"Jim is a good man, Chuck. A fine man. But he's got to be one of the most go-by-the-book lawmen I have ever seen. He just can't seem to get it through his head that the laws he lives by—the ones we all live by—just don't, can't, apply here. But in his own way, he's given me carte blanche."

The man in the back seat moaned and cursed them both until he was breathless.

The men in the front seat ignored him, Chuck saying, "It's going to be a slaughter, isn't it?"

"Not if I can help it. Jim doesn't believe that. But I'll try the course of least resistance first. I have a plan to destroy Anya and Pet; but I haven't got all the details worked out in my mind."

"You're saying that in front of this . . . heathen?" He jerked a thumb toward Neuroth.

"He isn't going to say anything to anybody once I've questioned him."

"You've made up your mind about that." It was not a

315

question.

"Yes."

Neuroth died before any questions could be asked of him. He suddenly moaned, arched his back, and fell over by the side of the road as they were walking toward the timber.

Carl and Chuck knelt down by the body. The flesh that was visible to them was very red, the skin beginning to peel like that of a person with an extremely bad sunburn. Chuck tentatively touched Neuroth's neck with a fingertip, yelped in pain, and jerked his hand back quickly. The tip of his finger was blistered.

"My God!" the priest said. "He's been cooked!"

"Someone didn't want him to talk to me."

Chuck looked long at the coven-buster. "By someone, you're implying . . ."

"Yes," Carl said quickly. "I am." Neither man wanted to speak the word aloud while so close to the dark evil of the timber and what it contained.

"Then . . ." The priest paused in thought. "He has decided to take a direct part in the events . . . is that what you're thinking?"

"Yes. Neither Anya nor Pet has that much power. They didn't have in Ruger, and after what my dad and Father Denier did to them, I'm sure their strength has been severely limited."

"But I thought after what happened that night out at Dee's . . . well, there would be no more interference from . . ." He swallowed hard. "Him?"

"I feel his involvement, his personal involvement, will be minor." Carl shrugged. "But that's only one man's opinion."

The men stood up, the priest looking down at the

cooked body of Neuroth. "What do we do with the body?"

"Nothing. It will probably be taken and given to the Old Ones to feed on."

Chuck shuddered.

"Let's get out of here."

On the short drive to Dee's, Chuck said, "You mentioned that you'd spoken with Mister Conners; could you tell me the gist of the conversation?"

"He's coming in with enough of his security people to secure the A-frame and the property around it."

"How? The roads are blocked."

"Helicopters. And his security people are not taken off the street and paid the minimum wage like so many other companies do. They're all ex-military personnel. Rangers, Marines, Special Forces, SEALs, Air Force SOCOM."

"Air Force what?"

"Special Operations Command."

"Does Jim know?"

"No."

"When are they coming in?"

"Tonight."

"I wish you had told me, Carl," Dee said.

Carl shook his head. "I'm not going to be here to help protect you, Dee. I explained that to your father and he understands. He knows what I have to do — must do. That's why the security people are coming in."

"I know, Carl. And I understand. What's my father's involvement in this?"

"He's also coming in. I don't know whether he's staying. I have a feeling he will. He strikes me as the type of man who enjoys a good fight."

317

"How right you are. And Mother?"

"She's gone out of the country. Your dad sent her to England; something to do with some holdings they have over there. Don't worry about sleeping arrangements, the men will—"

Dee waved him silent. "I know how my father's security people operate, Carl." She smiled to soften her words. "If they come in at first dark, by midnight this place will look like the perimeters around Da Nang." She looked at the forest's edge. "What will happen to the animals who have stationed themselves out there?"

"I don't know. I like to think they'll take the fight to those animals, both four-legged and two-legged, who have aligned with Satan. We'll just have to see."

"And you?"

"You mind if I borrow your car for the duration?"

"Of course not. Take it."

"I'll be back at dark to see the choppers in."

Dee stood up on tiptoe and kissed him, pressing against him. "When this is over, Carl . . ."

"We'll talk of that when it *is* over, Dee. Don't plan on too much of a future for us. I don't know that I have much of a future."

She pulled away from him, an angry look on her face. She walked to the edge of the porch. With her back to him, she said, "Did God talk to you and proclaim you to be His warrior here on earth?"

"In a manner of speaking, yes."

She whirled around. "Why you, Carl?"

"I don't know. Perhaps it's because I'm not a member of the fanatical far religious right. Perhaps it's because I'm young enough to understand that kids are going to experiment and try to buck the establishment, with the majority of them—thus far—returning to God in a few years. Perhaps it's because I'm cold enough to be able to

318

kill and live with it, and compassionate enough to know when to back off. Perhaps—"

"I don't want a damn sermon, Carl!" She tossed the words at him. "Just go on! Put your life on the line for a bunch of people who don't give a damn for you or what you're doing. Just go on!"

She stomped into the house and slammed the door behind her.

Carl began loading equipment into the Jag, Chuck helping him. The priest had said nothing about Dee's tantrum.

Just before they pulled out, Carl stood by the car and watched as Dee came out onto the porch to stand, staring at him.

He lifted his hand to her.

She glared at him and turned, walking back into the house.

"Well, as they say, hell hath no fury . . ." Carl observed, getting into the car.

A dark chuckle rose from the timber as lightning licked at the sky. The chuckling ended with a harsh note as the wolves began howling.

Jim looked at his deputies, minus Carl and Chuck. The priest's wife had called and told him what her husband was going to do. Jim felt the priest was making a big mistake, electing to ride with Carl, but that was his business.

He sighed as he gazed at the Stinson boys. There was a sight that had never been and, hopefully, would never again be equaled in the annals of law enforcement. Jim could but shake his head and hope for the best.

Sonny, Bullfrog, Bubba, and Keith looked like they were preparing to ride out with Quantrill's Raiders to do battle with the Yankees. Each of them carried at least three pistols of various calibers, all of them large magnums and all of them single-action, with bandoliers of cartridges and shotgun shells looped and criss-crossed over their chests. Each of them carried a shotgun and had a lever-action rifle slung by leather over one shoulder.

Brother Speed looked in dress like General George Patton. He wore two pearl-handled .45 pistols. He had looked into the sheriff's department gun room and spotted an old World War II Thompson submachine gun that hadn't — to the best of Jim's knowledge — been fired in more than thirty years. The pastor had requested the SMG and all the ammunition that could be rounded up. Jim had asked him if he'd ever fired one of the old Thompsons. No, the pastor had replied, but he'd seen John Wayne use one in a war movie. Could he please have it?

Jim had said no, and had given him a riot gun instead.

Brother Speed wore bloused riding breeches, polished high boots, and a helmet liner he had picked up — only God knew where.

Tom Malone had picked out a Colt AR-15 from the gun room, and carried a .38 in a holster. Jim wasn't too sure about the Stinson boys and Brother Speed, but he knew that Tom Malone was hell on wheels when somebody was dumb enough to push him.

The women were over at Doctor Bartlett's clinic, the sheriff and his wife over at the mayor's place with Wilber and Meg.

Dee Conners had called and said everything was okay out at her place.

She'd sounded a little bit miffed to Jim, and he figured she didn't like it at all that Carl had taken off

320

head-hunting.

"We got maybe a half hour of daylight left us, people," Jim told his crew. "And I ain't gonna kid you: I don't have no idea what's gonna happen when the sun goes down."

The faint sounds of gunfire silenced him. An M-16 by the sounds of it, and firing on full auto, in three-round bursts. Carl has gone to work, Jim thought.

In a way he envied the young man his cold attitude. But only in a small way.

Jim picked up the ringing phone. Chief Max Bancroft. "Me and my boys are holed up down here at City Hall, Jim. We're bunkered in pretty well with lots of food and water and enough ammo to re-fight Hamburger Hill. I just spoke with Daly and Tolson over at the clinic. He said they were in pretty good shape, all things considered. Those four guys that you and me suspected was some of Edgar Conners's security people just left the motel, all dressed in battle gear. They headed out toward Conners Woods. Is the original plan still in effect?"

"That's ten-four, Max. Me and my people are going to cruise the town until we have to hole up someplace. If that happens, we'll all meet back here at the jail. I'm thinking you're going to have the hot spot, located like you are darn near in the center of town. Keep a sharp eye out, Max."

"I'll do that, Jim. Luck to you, boy."

"Same to you, Max." Jim slowly hung up.

"Chief?" the dispatcher called from the radio room. "The teletype's gone crazy in here. There's some sort of weird picture being printed out. It's . . ."

Jim waited for the rest of it. But the radio room was silent. Eerily so.

Then the dispatcher started screaming as sparks began erupting in multi-colored sheets from the electronic equipment. He was suddenly flung from the radio room as if picked up and tossed by an invisible hand. His clothes were on fire and his hair was a burning torch. Everyone there heard his back crack as he impacted against a door jamb. The dispatcher fell to the tile floor and lay still while the flames began to burn themselves out.

Jim grabbed a fire extinguisher and ran to the man, dousing the flames. He knelt down. The man was dead.

Jim looked into the smoking and ruined radio room. The teletype machine had exploded, as had all the radio equipment and the phone.

Jim had no doubts as to whose picture had been printed out on the fanfold paper of the teletype. The dispatcher had looked at it for too long. He remembered the words back at the Conners place that night: "Anyone who looks upon the face of Satan dies."

He walked into his office, picked up a mobile unit from its charger, and walked back out into the main office and held up the walkie-talkie.

"Everybody take one of these, people. Make sure the units are fully charged before taking them. Tom, try the phones."

The deputy picked up a desk phone and held the receiver to his ear. He met the chief deputy's eyes and shook his head. "Dead, Jim."

"Use your handy-talkie to bump Max down at City Hall. Have him try his office phones."

The phones were out at City Hall, and as far as Max knew, dead all over the town.

"The Devil's doin' this, ain't he?" Keith Stinson asked, literally shaking in his cowboy boots.

"Yes," Pastor Speed told him. "Get ahold of yourself,

boy. God is with us. We have to fight His fight and you can't do that trembling like a leaf in a storm."

"I been a sinner all my life, Preacher!" Keith shouted the words.

"Of course, you have. We all have. But the main thing is to try to obey God's words. All of us have been spared for some reason, and that reason is to fight the evil that has taken this town. You're part of God's army now, boy. Now straighten up and get a grip on yourself."

The sun was sinking fast, the evening shadows casting long over the town.

"The electricity will probably go next," Tom said.

"I ain't lookin' forward to this night," Bullfrog said, his eyes on the dead dispatcher.

"I hope Judy made it over to the clinic." Mike whispered the words.

"I thought she was out at the Conners place," Jim said.

"She come into town to check on her mom and dad. They were drunk and naked and screwin' on the floor. Them and half a dozen neighbors. She decided to stay at the clinic."

"Your wife, Pastor?" Jim asked.

"At the clinic with the other women. She's badly frightened but holding on. She can be a rock when she has to be." He sighed. "And if there ever was a time, this is certainly it."

More gunfire drifted to the men at the jail. This time the automatic weapon's fire was joined by a shotgun's heavy booming.

"Father Vincent is sure lettin' the hammer down," Tom said. "He's giving them hell."

"That is certainly one way of putting it," Pastor Speed agreed.

Night settled swiftly over Butler, Virginia.

The lights suddenly went out, hurling the room into darkness.

"Here we go, boys," Jim said.

Chapter 32

The rapid thock-a-thock of the blades gave the helicopters away. They were flying low and without running lights. Dee turned on the floodlights to aid the choppers in their landing on the clearing. Carl and Chuck had just driven up, and were watching from the road side of the chain-link fence as the security men jumped from the choppers and assembled on the ground. They were dressed in dark clothing and carried bulky bundles in addition to their backpacks.

Someone called out an order and the men ran for preassigned positions. It was obvious to even the most uninitiated that the men had studied maps and probably mock-ups of the area, for they knew right where to go.

Carl pushed open the gate and Chuck followed him up the walkway. The first two helicopters were taking off as two more came thocking in, kicking up dust and pebbles. Carl waited on the porch as Edgar Conners walked around the house.

"Did you bring what I requested?" Carl asked the man.

"It's being off-loaded now. Unusual request. Even for you," he added.

Carl said nothing.

"My kid miffed at you, boy?" Edgar asked.

"Slightly. The important thing is to win this war. Not just a battle, the whole war. End it."

Edgar nodded. "My men picked up a lot of eyes as they looked down coming in."

"Dogs and cats and some wolves have stationed themselves around the house, in the timber."

"They were moving deeper into the timber as we came in. What does that mean?"

"It's started. Your four men from town are out here. I've told them to keep an eye out for maggots. They're all over the place."

The last two choppers had off-loaded and were taking off, making conversation impossible for a moment.

"Dee's angry with me too," the father admitted. "She guessed that I made you a job offer."

"She'll either get over it or she won't. I'll admit this to you: In all honesty, I could easily fall in love with your daughter, Edgar. But I've deliberately forced myself to keep my distance. Mentally and physically. Stay out here, Edgar. The town is blowing wide open. It's a war zone. And to be honest, I don't know if we're going to win it or not."

"The choppers can be in here within thirty minutes to take us out. Governor Willis knows better than to try fucking around with me. I'll step on him like a bug. He doesn't particularly like me, but he knows I could put a hell of a dent in this state's economy if I elected to pull everything out. Willis knows I flew in. And I didn't ask him, I told him."

Carl nodded in the darkness of the porch. "See you around, Ed." He walked to the Jag, Chuck right behind him, and drove off, back to town.

"Impossible, arrogant, insufferable man!" Dee said from the door.

326

Her father chuckled. "Love him, don't you, kid?"

"Don't be ridiculous!" she snapped at him. "I have better tastes than that, I assure you."

Edgar Conners sat down in a chair. "I like him. He's a good, decent, and strong man. It would take a strong man to keep the reins tight on you."

"Nobody keeps the reins on me!" she raged at him.

"I bet Carl could," her father needled her. "And I bet you'd love it."

"Ohhh!" She stamped her foot and almost tore the front door off getting inside.

Edgar laughed softly. The shivering, wavering call of a wolf cut the night. It produced no fear in the man. The call of a wolf produces no fear in the heart of any intelligent person. Edgar Conners was one of the world's richest men, but he was an industrialist with the heart of an environmentalist; he traveled the wilderness with a camera instead of a gun. There were always many of his men around him with guns, but they were not for shooting *four*-legged animals.

"Well, I'll just be damned," Ed said, listening as other wolves joined in the lonesome chorus. "Probably some animal-liberation group cut you free from cages. But I don't know if they did you any favors or not. At least in that cage you were free from stupid assholes with guns and traps and poison."

"My father," Dee spoke from the screen door. "The big, rough, tough chairman of the board and international wheeler-dealer. But a real softy when it comes to animals." All trace of anger was gone from her voice. She pushed open the door and took the chair next to him.

"What was it I taught you, Dee? You and all my kids."

"Animals cannot speak for themselves. And until

327

they can, I will be their voice."

"Good girl."

"You didn't think I'd forgotten it?"

"Oh, no. Dee? Carl has to do what he feels he must. Yes. You're right. I offered him a job when this situation is cleared up."

"Has he taken it?"

"Not yet. I don't know that he will. He isn't sure he'll come out of this alive."

"Will we?"

"Oh, yes. Unless the Devil personally strikes us all dead. And that could certainly happen. Dee, why in God's name didn't you and those kids in there leave with the choppers?"

"Your question contains the answer, Dad."

"God's name, huh? Carl told me you were very sarcastic about him being God's warrior."

"A woman will do or say most anything to keep her man, Father."

"Oh! So now he's your man, huh?"

"You damn well better believe it. And he damn well better believe it too."

"I'm sure he does, Dee," Ed said with a laugh. "I'm sure he does."

Brother Speed pointed out the body sprawled on the sidewalk. "Over there, Jim."

Jim pulled the unit close to the sidewalk and stuck his arm out the window, directing a flashlight's beam on the body. A pistol was lying just inches from the out-flung hand. Somebody had placed a three-round burst of gunfire into the man's chest.

Pain lanced up and down Jim's left arm as cats covered the car, screaming and yowling and making horrible scratching sounds while their claws scraped painted metal. Jim beat his arm against the door and managed to get his arm free of the fangs and claws, then hurriedly raised the window. His arm was covered with blood.

"Get to the clinic, Jim!" Speed said. "Can you drive?"

"I can drive," Jim said through gritted teeth. He floored the gas pedal and ran over those cats milling around on the street. The crunching sounds beneath the tires almost sickened both men. The cats on the car lost their footing in the acceleration and went flying and yowling from the unit.

On the way to the clinic, Jim's headlights showed one street to be moving up and down and back and forth. He slammed on the brakes.

"What the shit is that?" Pastor Speed blurted out.

"Maggots," Jim said, reversing the car and doing a cop turnaround in the street. "Millions of them, looks to me. But probably more like thousands."

He met Carl along the way and flagged him down, telling him about the maggots.

"Have one of your men grab a gas tanker truck," Carl told him.

"Where the hell will they get that?"

"Steal the damned thing!" Carl shouted at him. "Crawl off your precious law books, you hillbilly! You're fighting for your life!"

"He's right, Jim," Pastor Speed said. "Law and order is gone for now."

"Okay, okay!" Jim said. He looked at Carl. "And do what with the truck?"

"Open the valves in the rear of the truck just before he drives through the bugs. When he's clear, I'll toss a grenade in with them. We'll get rid of some of them that way."

"Along with a few houses," Jim muttered, lifting his mic and giving the order.

Carl got out of the Jag and looked at Jim's arm. "Go on to the clinic. I'll take over here. You go with him, Preacher. Make sure he gets there."

Mike was behind the wheel of the gas truck later when it lumbered to a halt beside Carl and Chuck. Carl opened the nozzles and the gas spewed.

"Drive slow through them, Mike. We want to saturate the street."

"Ten-four," Mike said.

"And don't smoke," Chuck called.

Mike looked at him. The priest was grinning. "Hell of a sense of humor," he muttered, dropping the truck into gear, and smiling at his all-too-accurate choice of words.

The crunching of the maggots under the big tires almost made Mike sick to his stomach. The street became so slick with the crushed and slimy creatures he had to drop the transmission into the lowest range to keep going. When he had cleared the last of the flesh-eating worms, he poured on the coals and got gone from that area.

Carl tossed his grenade and floored the Jag, putting as much distance between the gas fumes and the Jag as possible. The gas ignited and the following explosion rocked the car. One house collapsed as the concussion wave struck it and several small fires were started in the area. Chuck watched as residents ran outside, putting out the fires.

"It doesn't bother you that innocent people might have died in that explosion?" Chuck asked.

"If they were innocent, they would be out here fighting with us, instead of against us or sitting on their lazy cowardly asses letting others do their fighting for them."

330

"There are many children in this town, Carl."

"They are no longer children of God, Chuck. That's what's so horrible about it. I've found it to be true in any of these jobs I've worked. I've had four- and five- and six-year-old kids turn on me and try to kill me."

"And could you kill them?"

"No. I couldn't. I bopped them around and left them in the rubble. They'll be adopted and grow up to be teachers and preachers and heads of business and doctors and lawyers and so forth. Leaders of the community and still, unknown to their friends and neighbors, worshipping Satan and silently corrupting everything and everyone they come in contact with. Just like what has happened in this town. That's why the satanic movement has to be crushed, wherever and whenever one finds it."

A firetruck roared around a corner and the cursing, hate-filled driver tried to smash into Carl. Carl spun the wheel, went up onto the sidewalk, and then back onto the darkened street.

The priest was confused and his face mirrored that. "They are rushing to put out a fire when their sole objective is to destroy the town. I don't understand."

"They don't really know what they're doing, Chuck. Part of them is on automatic, so to speak. They're lost souls, just blundering around waiting for the end. They no longer have control of their minds."

"It's a . . . madness."

"No it isn't," Carl corrected. "It was all very carefully planned by the leaders. Months ago. The field troops are expendable. The leaders will escape, go underground for a time, and then emerge somewhere else with a new identity, but still worshipping Satan, setting up new covens and drawing others to them . . . and to the Prince of Darkness."

331

"And then they'll start plans of destruction all over again."

"That is correct." He turned into the parking lot of the clinic.

"Jim's all right," Doctor Jenkins said. "We've checked blood cells. The cats are not infectious . . . in any kind of, well, devilish way. A week ago I'd have felt like an idiot saying that," he muttered. "Anyway, we have started Jim on a series of anti-rabies shots. Just to be on the safe side."

"Did you get all those horrible bugs?" Liza asked.

"No. But we cooked a lot of them. I'd say we put a dent in their population. They normally have a life span of about a week."

Jim looked up. His left arm was bandaged from shoulder to fingertips. "We can't last through a week of this, Carl."

"I know. I spoke with Edgar Conners. You probably heard the helicopters come in at dusk. He told me that he'd evac out any of you who want to go. Just give him the word."

"Is Mister Conners leaving?" Doreen asked.

"No. He's staying to see it through."

"And you, Carl?" Doctor Bartlett asked.

Carl shook his head. "I can't leave. I've got to see this through."

"By whose orders, young man?" Doctor Jenkins asked.

Jim finally got it through his head and answered for Carl. His voice soft, he said, "God."

Chapter 33

With Dee's safety secure, Carl could concentrate on his mission. He slipped out of the clinic, leaving Father Vincent behind. Chuck was a good man, a solid man, but he really had no stomach for what Carl was going to do. Carl drove to the high school, conscious of eyes on him from behind curtains and drapes in the darkened homes he passed. He parked in the high school's parking lot and set the Jag's alarm system. If anyone even touched the car, a sharp, shrill alarm would sound. Carl got out, standing for a moment in the darkness.

He checked the small .380 auto-loader in his back pocket. It was filled up with exploding ammo, the most lethal and expensive handgun ammunition on the market. A good hit anywhere on the upper torso would almost always drop the target. The 9-mm in his shoulder holster was also filled up with exploding slugs. A pouch on his belt was filled with extra clips. He slipped into a light backpack filled with articles he felt he might need, and left the M-16 and other weapons in the car, after clipping a few grenades to his belt. He had a powerful flashlight in his hand and another clipped to his belt. Carl walked toward the dark, silent building that loomed before him, the many windows seeming to glare at him like the huge evil eyes of some monstrous prehistoric being.

This was as good a place to start as any.

Clean out the town, and then he could direct all his energy, mental and physical, toward the destruction of Anya and Pet and the Old Ones in the country.

He checked the basement first and found fresh bones on the floor. The flashlight beam touched briefly on the head of a man, the eyes open in sudden and painful shock before the severed head had realized it was dead.

There was no life in the dusty and blood-spattered basement.

Carl shone the flashlight's beam on the steps leading to the ground floor, committing the way to memory, then clicked off the light, so his eyes would adjust to the darkness.

He climbed the steps and paused for a moment on the landing, his ear to the door leading to the hall. He could detect no sound. He opened the door quickly and rolled out into the hall, coming back to his feet, in a crouch, against the far wall.

The long silent polished floor of the corridor was empty, the lockers standing like rigid sentries in the dark. Any of them, he knew, could contain the dangerous and changed beings who had taken over the high school building.

He walked a few yards, then paused, listening, all senses working hard. He heard a creaking sound inside one of the lockers, up ahead and to his right. He moved slowly toward the locker, the 9-mm in his hand, the hammer back. Reaching the suspect locker, Carl jerked open the door and almost shot a dead body.

The mangled and half-eaten body of a woman dangled from a clothes hook in the locker. The head had been driven onto the hook, hooked just at the base of the skull.

Carl closed the locker door and moved on, willing his heart to cease its pounding and his blood pressure to fall. A roaring from the far end of the corridor rattled the windows and stopped Carl in the center of the corridor.

He had found his prey. Or had they found him?

A foulness drifted to him on the closed air of the school, a stench that wrinkled his nose.

Carl stepped to one side, his boot touching something soft. He glanced down and could make out what was left of the body of a teenage girl. He was standing in her blood. He stepped out of the gore and stayed close to the banks of lockers.

Two creatures rushed him, moving incredibly fast and very silent on their bare feet. As they ran past windows, the faint light seeping in from the outside clearly showed the drastic metamorphosis they had undergone: the apelike jaw and the long hideous fangs, the hairy body and the clawed hands and feet.

Carl assumed a two-handed grip on the 9-mm and pulled the trigger several times. Both creatures went down to the floor, both of them squalling in rage and pain as the slugs exploded on contact with soft flesh. The larger of the pair struggled to its feet, snarling its hate. It stepped forward, directly into a small beam of moonlight coming through the windows.

Carl put two rounds into the beast's chest, the slugs penetrating and exploded the heart. The smaller beast howled its rage and crawled toward Carl, dripping slime and blood from wounds, its claws clicking on the floor as it advanced.

Carl put two rounds into the beast's face, the exploding slugs stopping its crawling and flinging the creature to one side.

The hellish metamorphosis began its reversal as death touched Satan's creations. The shapes became smaller, the yellowish-greenish slime changing to red human blood. The jaws lost their jutting apeness. The hands and feet became human, the hair disappearing.

Ralph Geason and Roseanne lay dead on the floor.

Carl rose to his boots and ejected the clip, fitting a full one into the butt of the 9-mm. He turned and walked slowly toward the door that would lead to the parking lot.

"Score two for God and zero for the Devil," he muttered as his hand touched the bar of the door. His eyes caught the outline of shapes waiting in the outside darkness. Human shapes. Waiting for him in ambush. He smiled and pulled a grenade from his belt. He eased out the pin, holding the spoon down and placing the grenade on the floor, against the door. Releasing the spoon, he darted back and pressed himself into a narrow gap between lockers, a fire-extinguisher station.

The grenade blew, the explosion knocking out the double doors and filling the outside air with hundreds of lethal shards of glass and wood and metal and fragments from the grenade.

Carl walked to the open space where the doors had been, the air thick with dust and the screaming of the wounded. He stayed against a wall, in the shadows, assessing the damage done to those who had been lying in wait for him. A man struggled to his feet on the sidewalk, a pistol in his hand. Carl shot him in the chest. Two others ran and limped off toward the street. Carl let them go. The others lay still on the dewy grass and littered sidewalk.

Linda Crowley had been wrong in her assessment of the numbers of people in the covens of Butler; probably deliberately wrong, Carl thought. The Devil's silent

336

and insidious hand had touched almost all of the population of the small town. It was as Carl had suspected, so he was not surprised by it.

One of the men on the sidewalk moaned in pain and rolled over on his back. He cursed for a moment, his words profaning God and damning any who worshipped Him. He looked up into the eyes of Carl Garrett, the 9-mm pointed at his bloody head. His left arm was broken, shattered at the elbow, dangling useless. "You'll die," he hissed at Carl, the words savage and pain-filled. "You'll all die and you'll die hard. I can promise you that. They'll keep you alive for days, torturing you, you Christian puke. You can't kill us all."

Carl's eyes were as hard as granite in the faint moonlight. "I can damn sure try," Carl told him, his words very soft in the bloody, evil night. Then he shot the man between the eyes.

Carl looked around him. Most of those who had been standing near when the grenade blew were still alive, although peppered with glass and wood and fragments from the grenade itself. They were mangled and bloody but breathing. Carl left them where they lay. Those few who were conscious had quickly guessed from listening to what had just happened, that if they kept their mouths shut and didn't threaten the young man, they would, in all probability, be allowed to live. They kept their mouths closed.

Carl deactivated the Jag's alarm system by pushing a button on a small matchbox-size plastic remote in his pocket, cranked up, and drove off. The night was still very young and the evil he faced was as old as time itself.

He had a lot to do and not much time in which to do it.

Jim had called off the patrolling, deciding it was just too dangerous, and had grouped his people in the jail building. He had left a fully charged handy-talkie with those who stayed in the clinic, warning them to use it as sparingly as possible. All power had been cut off to the town, and once the radios were gone, there was no way to recharge them.

But the Stinson boys had not responded to any of Jim's radio calls. He had no idea were they might be, but guessed rightly that wherever they were, they were probably in trouble.

He was right.

Bubba had gotten separated from his brothers. Rounding a corner, he had suddenly come upon an Old One who had just moments before left the basement of a coven member. The walking ugly evil had grown hungry, and Bubba looked like he would be tasty.

Bubba had other ideas about being a meal for this ugly-looking bastard. He didn't know what it was that was facing him, but whatever it was, he guessed it wasn't nothing of this earth and it sure as hell didn't drop down from Heaven.

He shot it.

The force of the slug pushed the stinking creature backward. A foul-smelling spray of liquid leaked from the bullet hole in the thing's chest.

It snarled and howled and held its clawed hands out in front of its misshapen body. Then it began moving toward Bubba.

Bubba started hollering for his brothers.

The three of them rounded the corner of the downtown building and came up short, shoe leather sliding on concrete at the sight before their eyes.

"What the hell you done got treed, Bubba?" Sonny

asked.

"I ain't got *it* treed! It's got *me* treed! Shoot the son of a bitch, boys!"

Gunfire split the darkness.

The devil's own was knocked sprawling to the sidewalk by the slugs. It promptly jumped to its clawed feet, roaring and howling and moving toward the quartet, the foulness that was its body fluid leaking out of half a dozen holes.

"I think," Keith said, "that we done fucked up again, boys."

Carl rounded the corner, his headlights picking up the bizarre scene. He pulled to the curb, behind the Stinson boys, and reached behind the seat, pulling out several bottles he had rigged earlier in the day.

Bullfrog had served in the army; he knew what Carl was holding. "Molotov cocktail," he said.

"Fire is the only thing that will destroy these creatures," Carl told the brothers. The Old One had stopped his advance, sensing that this was the mortal he had been warned to stay away from. "You can shoot these bastards ten thousand times, blow them to pieces, and the pieces would still be alive. They were born in fire, they have to die by fire." He lit the rag dangling out of the top of the bottle and hurled it against the Old One.

The hellish creature burst into flames and began howling in fear and pain and panic, beating its hands against the flames.

Carl threw another bottle against the creature. Soon the beast was a running, squalling ball of flames and pain.

It took only seconds for the fire to suck the life from the creature of and from the pits. It collapsed in the street and died, howling and beating its fists against the

339

concrete.

"Get back to the sheriff's office," Carl told the brothers. "I've been listening to the scanner in the car. Jim's been trying to reach you for an hour."

"What are you going to do?" Sonny asked him.

"Stay out here."

"Alone?"

Carl smiled at him. "Go on. I know how to fight these creatures and people. You don't." He walked back to the car and drove off.

Bubba watched the taillights until the car was out of sight. "That there is either the bravest man I ever met, or a damn fool."

Shoe leather scraping on concrete brought the Stinson boys to attention. Faint shapes could be seen moving toward them from far back in the alley. They took off running for their trucks and headed for the sheriff's office.

Wilber Purdy and Ned Rodale had beaten back a half a dozen rushes by howling townspeople they had once called friends and neighbors, and had come close to being overpowered during the last charge. The men and women in the house were red-eyed from the acrid gunsmoke that lingered in the rooms

"We can't let them take the women alive, Ned," Wilber said in a whisper. "They'll be used badly."

"For a fact," the sheriff agreed. "But I ain't got the courage to kill my wife. She's been through enough sufferin' at my hands and from the other things I've done over the years."

"Very well. If those outside breech the house—and we both know they will—you buy me enough time to get upstairs. I'll take care of it."

340

"The next charge ought to do it, Wilber. We got more than enough guns, but they's just too many of them. You best move to the stairs now. Leave the ground floor to me."

"Don't let them take you alive, Ned."

"I wouldn't give those godless bastards that satisfaction," the sheriff said grimly. He stuck out his hand and Ned took it.

Footsteps were heard on the front and back porches.

"Good-bye, Wilber."

"Good-bye, old friend." The mayor walked up the stairs to defend the women.

The sheriff laid his shotgun aside and filled both hands with .45-caliber autoloaders. Each semi-automatic held one in the chamber and six in the clip. Ned would do his best to take out thirteen of the coven members. The last round would be for him.

Upstairs Wilber's shotgun boomed, and a man screamed in pain in the back yard.

The front porch filled with stinking men and women, hate shining in their eyes.

"Come on, you filth," Ned muttered. "For the first time in my life I feel like I got the love of God surrounding me. I ain't afraid to die."

The front door crashed open and Ned shot a coven member between the eyes. A woman threw herself through a front window. Ned finished her before she could get up off the carpet.

"Two," Ned muttered.

He picked his targets carefully, making each shot a good one, and counted the rounds expended. The back rooms of the big house filled with shouting and howling and chanting people, and Ned knew he had lost the race with the Reaper. A warm, soothing feeling spread over the man as dirty hands reached for him. And he

341

knew that while he was not going Home, he'd be close enough to count the stars.

"Take him alive!" a woman screamed. "We'll skin him and listen to him scream."

Ned used his thirteenth round to blow a hole in the woman's head. Above him, standing on the landing, Wilber was blasting away, a pistol in each hand.

"Forgive me, Lord," Ned said. He stuck the pistol in his mouth and pulled the trigger just as friends of the Devil rode him to the floor.

Chapter 34

Cats had completely covered the clinic building. They clung to the screens and the outside bricks; they covered the roof, screeching and yowling and scratching, seeking entrance.

Inside the building, the din was enormous and nerve-stretching. But there was nothing those inside could do except try to endure it. They dared not open a window or crack a door. The slightest entry point could spell their doom.

The cats flung themselves against windows, smashing and mangling their bodies, killing themselves attempting to break the glass.

The sounds of glass breaking in a storage room reached the ears of Tolson.

"They've made it in!" he yelled up the corridor. "Watch the storage room on the south side."

A clawed paw rammed its way under the door. Tolson stomped on it with his boot. Another seeking paw got the same treatment. The cats in the room screamed their displeasure at their inability to gain entrance into the main part of the clinic.

"That door will hold," Bartlett said. "It's a metal utility door." He stuck a key into the lock and turned it, the clicking sound seeming to infuriate the cats inside;

the howling and shrieking and scratching intensified in the room. "Dead bolt on both sides. We used to use this room to store drugs. We'll just have to hang on and try some prayer."

"I been doin' that," the state trooper admitted.

Deep in the timber of the Conners Woods, Janet was wide awake. She had managed to loosen the rope that bound her wrists. Her belly had grown enormous and sometimes the pain was so intense she had to scream. Her captors had found that very amusing. The humor of it was lost on Janet.

She knew one thing for a hard fact: There was no way she was going to birth a demon. She was dead either way it went, so why not destroy the monster that was growing within her?

She had a plan. She wasn't looking forward to carrying it out, but she knew she had no choice in the matter. She began working harder at the ropes that bound her wrists.

The street in front of both the city hall and the sheriff's office gave mute and bloody respect to the deadly aim of those trapped inside: Bodies lay sprawled in death all around both buildings.

"Mike?" Jim called. The deputy looked up. "Bump Max on the tach and tell him to get ready to pull out. Sooner or later those heathens outside will try fire. When they do that, we're screwed."

"Yes, sir."

"Any further word from the mayor's house?"

"No, sir. I think they've had it."

"Damn! I sorta liked Ned the past couple of days."

"Chief?" a deputy called. "Here they come with torches."

"That's it, people!" Jim called. He began assigning those who would first make a try for the cars, the others laying down covering gunfire. "We head for the high school building. We can snipe from the rooftop and keep fire danger down to a minimum. Let's go, boys!"

On the front porch of his daughter's home, Edgar sat with Terrell, one of the four original men he'd sent into Butler after meeting with Carl and learning what was really happening. "I sure would like to know what's going on in town," Edgar said.

"You want me to take some of the boys and go in?"

"No. Not yet. We'll go in at first light."

"We?"

"Yeah. We. I've been asked to assess the situation and see just how much cover-up is going to be needed."

Terrell sat quietly, waiting for the boss to drop the other shoe.

"I was asked by certain people placed very highly within the Federal Government to do that little thing."

"So they are aware of what's going on and monitoring things?"

"Yes. They have a man inside the town now."

"What?"

"Certain people within the government realized they had a very serious and rapidly growing problem with this Satan-worship business about eighteen months ago. So they contacted a man who had some expertise in the field and he went to work for them . . . in a manner of speaking."

"You know who he is?"

"I have a very good idea."

"Carl Garrett."

"Right."

"But I thought you said he was interested in the job you offered him."

"I thought he was. Maybe he really is. I haven't spoken much about it since we got here. It isn't the money; I know that much. Carl was checked out very thoroughly by my people. Carl isn't that interested in money. I think what he wants more than anything is insurance . . . if you know what I mean."

"The government doesn't have the greatest track record in the world for staying loyal to people in its employ who are in high-risk security areas. Believe me, I should know."

"Yes. Right on both counts. Carl is a very smart young man. He knows I have many, many government contracts and probably suspects that I do other, shall we say, clandestine work for our government whenever I go overseas. Carl is thinking—and rightly so—that if he ever gets in a jam where Uncle won't back him, I would. And Uncle couldn't say a damn thing about it for fear of what I know. And he's right."

"He's a damn smart man, Mister Conners. And something else: He's driven. He's obsessed with wiping out satanism."

"I know that too. And the government is obviously limiting him as to what he can use. That's why he asked me to get those supplies for him."

"Naturally. This is good ol' America, boss. We can't have hired killers on the government payroll out stalking our streets, blowing away dealers and serial murderers and the like."

Edgar snorted in disgust. "God save us from the government, Terrell."

346

A few attempts were made to breech the high school building. Once again, the marksmanship of the cops kept them at bay. The lawn was wide front and back and the parking lots were vast, offering very little cover for the coven members. After two attempts, the lovers of Satan gave it up.

Carl drove by the sheriff's office and jail shortly after it had been set ablaze. He emptied his 9-mm into the crowd of coven members who had gathered around, chanting and making joyful noises to Satan. At least a half a dozen of them would make no more noises — ever.

Carl drove far out into the county and went to sleep.

He awakened an hour before dawn and took a container of water from the trunk to brush his teeth, rinse out his mouth, and wash his face and hands. He drank a small can of tomato juice and ate a few crackers for breakfast.

He knew, from past experience in dealing with the more violent of coven members (those who had given their hearts and souls to the Devil in return for some odious and oftentimes unhonored deal), that while the previous night had been terrible and bloody in terms of human life, the worst was yet to come. The coven leaders would whip their followers into a wild frenzy and the mindless rampage would begin.

He had seen it before, although not on this grand a scale.

He checked his guns and the gas gauge of the Jag. He would have to gas up somewhere. He drove to within a few miles of the still-dark town and found a farmhouse. There were no candles or lamps burning inside the frame house. Using his headlights and a flashlight, he carefully checked the ground for any sign of the large maggots. None. He got out of the car and walked to the house, knocking on the door. He had not anticipated any response and he received none.

He pushed open the front door and the smell of death assailed his nostrils. He cautiously prowled the small home, the flashlight's beam guiding the way.

Carl found the couple on the kitchen floor. They had been hacked to death. Horribly and mindlessly murdered for no other reason than black evil viciousness. He picked up the receiver of the wall phone. No dial tone. He tried the lights. Flicking the switch produced nothing.

And he didn't think the coven members had a damn thing to do with the power outage. As had happened in Ruger County years back, he could see the not-too-subtle hands of the Federal Government in this: cut them off and seal them in and stonewall the press for as long as possible and hope for the best.

"Bastards!" Carl muttered.

He knew why the government was doing it, but he didn't have to like it.

He filled the Jag's gas tank from the dead farmer's tank, drove to the outskirts of Butler, parked on the road, and got out. The smell of smoke was hanging thick in the air. He guessed the coven members had torched both the jail and City Hall. From listening to the scanner, he knew that the cops had taken refuge in the high school building and were holding.

Carl hated what he had to do next. Hated it but knew it had to be done. And he also suspected that there was only one man who could do the job: Carl Garrett.

He drove to a service station just inside the city limits and parked the Jag behind the building. He slipped into his battle harness, checked to make sure he had everything he would need, picked up his M-16, and silently began his mission, entering the first house he came to.

The rank odor of the house left no doubt that it was the home of those who groveled at the feet of the Prince of Darkness.

That knowledge still didn't make what he had to do any easier.

He silently prowled the house. It was empty except for a man and a woman sprawled naked and filthy on a bed. The sheets were rumpled and stinking. Various signs and symbols praising Satan were on the walls; an upside-down cross hung over the bed.

Carl raised the M-16, leveling the muzzle at the couple on the bed. His finger slid to the trigger. Part of his mind silently screamed for him to pull the trigger.

He couldn't do it. Had it been some hideous creature from the foulest bowels of Hell, he would have killed it with no qualms. Had the couple on the bed awakened and attacked him, he could kill them. But not under these conditions.

Now what, mighty earthbound warrior of God? Carl asked in his mind. Now what do you do?

The heavens did not open and no messages from God reached him.

A noise on the back porch turned him around, the muzzle of the M-16 coming up. He slipped from the stinking bedroom and walked to the porch. Chris Speed and Father Chuck Vincent were standing on the porch, looking at him. Pastor Speed waved him out of the house. Both of the men were heavily armed. Pastor Speed led them some distance from the house and stopped.

"Couldn't do it, could you?" the minister asked.

"No," Carl admitted, knowing instantly what the man meant, and sensing that he and the priest had the same thought in mind. "Could you? Either of you?"

Both men shook their heads.

"We were starting to work the block over from this one," Chuck told him. "That's when we saw Miss Conners's car; we knew you were driving it."

"Does Jim know you're out?"

"We left him a note," Speed said. "Dear God in Heaven, I know what we had in mind, what you had in mind, is what God wants us to do, but we can't do it."

"Well, I couldn't either," Carl said, a sour taste on his tongue. "I thought I'd psyched myself up to where I could. So much for that."

"The leaders," Chuck said.

"What about them?" Speed asked.

"What would happen if the leaders were . . . disposed of?"

"The movement here in town would probably fall apart," Carl said. "But that's just a guess. The real leaders are in the woods out by Dee's house. But there is no way of getting to them. The woods somehow disorient you, confuse you. We'd be dead meat before we got five hundred yards inside the timber. Believe me, I've been in those woods and don't care to go again."

"You have a plan to destroy this Anya and Pet?" Pastor Speed asked.

"Yes. I don't know how good it is, but it's a plan. First we have to neutralize the town, take away the base of support."

"Which brings us back to square one," Chuck said.

"Yes. We can't arrest them all. We don't have the people to do that and no place to keep them even if we could. Whatever we do, we're going to have to make up our minds about it and get going. I—"

"Hey, Preacher!" a woman called from the next house

350

up the line. "You want some pussy?"

Pastor Speed flushed and raised his rifle, the muzzle lifting in her direction.

"You can't kill someone just for asking you a question, Chris," Chuck said.

"She's evil." The pastor pushed the words past tight lips. "She reeks of it."

The woman opened her robe. She was naked under it. "You don't want some ta-ta, Preacher, I got another hole."

Speed turned his eyes from her.

She laughed at him and began making the crudest of suggestions.

"I have to keep believing that she doesn't know what she's saying," Chris whispered.

"She knows," Chuck told him. "She's a lost soul. She's given her heart to Satan. But I still can't shoot her until she makes some hostile move toward us."

"Maybe that's the way to go," Carl suggested. "We ignore them and make them come to us. Time is on our side in this game. They've got to make a move and make it fast. The next twenty-four hours ought to do it. Come on. Let's go check out the clinic."

At the clinic the cats were gone. But the shit they'd left behind them covered the roof and the grounds, the odor lingering in the air.

"Jim and his bunch held last night," Doctor Bartlett told them. "But Mayor Purdy, Rodale, and their wives are dead. The house was torched."

"Man," Daly said. "I thought the night would never end. Those cats just about got the best of me."

The men inspected the clinic. Every piece of wood had savage claw marks deeply imbedded. Shingles had been clawed off the roof in the cats' frenzy for blood.

"Among other things that puzzle me about this entire

351

mess," Tolson said, "I'd like to know where the cats went after they left here."

"Not far," Carl said, his words offering no soothing balm for badly bruised nerves. "You can bet that most of them are watching us right now. So be careful."

"You're just a bundle of joy in the mornings, aren't you?" Daly said, only half kidding.

"Have any of you seen any sign of Janet?" Doctor Bartlett asked.

Carl shook his head. "No. The other side probably has her. Those Devil babies are important to their movement. They're probably keeping her under heavy guard. If I had to guess, I'd say she was in the Conners Woods."

"She told me she would never have that baby," Doctor Jenkins said. "She said that since it meant her death either way, she would not be responsible for birthing a child of the Devil."

"I'm sure she meant it."

A savage yowling and hissing wheeled the men around. Across the street, two very large groups of cats had appeared and were locked in death battles.

More cats and dogs were running up the street, to do battle with those cats that were coming out of hiding from under homes and out of trees.

"Jesus, Mary, and Joseph!" Daly said, awe in his voice as he watched the death struggle.

"What does it mean," Doctor Loring said.

"It means the battle is on," Carl said. "The same thing happened in Ruger. Good versus evil even in the animal kingdom."

The cats and dogs that had returned to town appeared to be winning the savage struggle. Many of the cats that for whatever reason had become pawns of the Devil were lying bloody and dead or dying in the street and on the lawns. Many others were retreating, with the dogs and cats that had just reappeared from out in the country hard after them, catching them and killing swiftly.

"I feel like cheering," Pastor Speed said. "Hooray!" he yelled. Others started applauding the victorious animals locked in deadly combat across the street.

Carl checked his 9-mm and stuck it back in leather. "Cheer later," he said, checking the .380 he carried in his back pocket. "Right now, let's go to work."

Daly checked his .357. "We start eliminating the coven leaders?"

"In a manner of speaking," Carl told him.

"You want to explain that?" Chuck asked.

"We try to take as many people alive as we can. We kill only if attacked." He pointed to the bloody street and yards, littered with the bodies of cats. "That tells me the animals have sensed something that we can't: The end is not far off. We may be wasting our time in trying to help the coven members; we probably are. But something just occurred to me: Where are the young kids? The subteens? Has anyone seen any young kids?"

The men looked at each other. Pastor Speed was the first to speak. "Why . . . no, I haven't seen a one."

"Dear God," Chuck said. "You don't suppose they *killed* them?"

Carl shook his head. "No. But they either hid them or got them out of town. I'll bet they hid them."

"I cannot and will not harm a child," Pastor Speed said flatly.

"Nor can I," Carl agreed. "But we can find them and try to help them. Even though, as I've said, it's usually a waste of them."

"Deprogramming?" Daly asked.

"Yes. Sometimes it works, most times it doesn't. Not when the Devil's had a hand in shaping young minds."

"Reshaping," Pastor Speed corrected. "A child is born without sin."

"If we find the kids, will they attack us?" Tolson asked.

"Yes. With anything they can get their hands on. So be careful with them. Don't trust them. They'll con you every step of the way."

"A part of me doesn't want to see this," Chuck said.

"I do know the feeling," Carl told him. "Let's go."

Chapter 35

Janet had freed her hands and untied the ropes around her ankles before she was spotted by a guard. He screamed a warning as she was getting to her feet. She had made up her mind what she was going to do and had spent the past hour psyching herself up to take her own life.

"I love you, Gary," she said, running across the clearing. "And I love you, Lord."

Hands grabbed for her. She twisted away, running awkwardly because of her rapidly growing Devil's pregnancy.

Pet and Anya had awakened slowly from a deep sleep; they still were far from attaining full strength. They could but watch in dread as the girl ran toward a branch growing straight out from the trunk of a tree. It was almost dead and totally leafless. And waist high.

"Stop her!" Anya screamed, knowing then what Janet had in mind. The charred and blood-leaking devil cat beside her ran awkwardly toward the teenager. But it was no contest.

"Praise God in the highest!" Janet screamed, and leaped for the branch.

The branch struck her in the stomach and the force of her jump rammed the branch deep into her belly and tore its way out her back, the tip of the branch leaking her blood. Janet died with her arms around the small tree. She shivered in death as the legs of the demon child within her sprang out of her torn womb and the hideous head ripped through the flesh of her branch-pierced belly.

The branch had torn through the black heart of the Devil's own child.

It was dead.

Savage, violent, and spiteful lightning lanced across the blue of the sky. But this time, a hard clap of thunder echoed over the mountains.

Pet and Anya and the others, of this earth and the sulfuric world beyond, looked up toward the sky, fear in their eyes. Pet hissed and yowled and arched her back while Anya cursed in a language dead for thousands of years. The Old Ones ran around the clearing, snarling and snapping their great jaws in fear.

The born-of-this-earth coven members, those privileged few from Butler who'd been admitted into the inner circle of the darkest and most evil of Satan's followers, sensed the fear of the others and reacted in kind. They moaned and called out for the Prince of Filth to help them in their fight against the small band of Christians.

Lightning again pockmarked the blue of the sky with streaks of red and orange and yellow. But with each wicked slash of lightning, thunder boomed in a seemingly never-ending barrage, overriding Satan's furious attack with God's invisible artillery barrage.

The lightning ceased, but the thunder continued unabated, rolling and crashing and shaking the timber known as Conners Woods.

The charred and blood-leaking devil child and her shapechanger other-being friend and companion in evil, the cat, Pet, cursed and yowled and hissed and fought to contain their fear.

The thunder abruptly came to a halt. God's message had been heard and understood, as had the wicked words from the dark side. God had overruled the voice from the netherworld.

Pet and Anya and the others were alone in this fight. Sensing another defeat, the king of the burning world of sinners had bowed out.

Pet and Anya locked gazes, messages passing between them. If anything was to be salvaged from this debacle, one thing was certain: Carl Garrett had to be destroyed, and if Anya and Pet had to finally and forever die, condemned to the stinking world of burning darkness and pain in order for that to be accomplished . . . then so be it.

Edgar Conners knew from the outset he would lose the argument, but he gave it his best shot. Now his daughter was riding in the back seat with him, heading toward town, Terrell driving and Gabe riding shotgun. Three other men were in the company's pickup truck that Carl had used to transport material from the city, and four others were in a car borrowed from one of the teenagers. All were heavily armed with automatic weapons and semi-automatic pistols. The small caravan pulled up at the clinic just as Carl and the others were preparing to leave.

Dee ran to Carl and threw her arms around him, kissing him while her father looked on, approval in his eyes.

"You shouldn't have come into town," Carl told her. "It's far too dangerous."

"You mean you're not glad to see me?" There was a

twinkle in the young woman's eyes.

"I didn't say that."

She stepped back and inspected his face. He had not shaved in two days and the stubble of beard made him look ruggedly handsome. She told him so, and laughed when he flushed at the compliment.

"There will be lots of time for smooching later," Edgar said, walking up, smiling at the look his daughter gave him. "Right now, let's talk about some plan of action to wrap up this mess." He looked at Dee. "Now I'm going to give you an order and I expect you to obey it. You stay here at the clinic. I'll go with Carl and the others."

His daughter told him what he could do with his order — very bluntly.

Terrell and Gabe both tried to hide their smiles. Pastor Speed looked shocked at the words coming out of the young woman's mouth.

"Let's clear a two-block area around the high school," Carl suggested. "That'll give Jim and the others some breathing room and we can use the building as a command center and holding facility for the kids."

"Kids?" Edgar said. "What kids are we talking about here?"

"The children of the adult coven members," Carl told him. "And it isn't going to be pleasant."

They found two dozen kids in the basement of a house, being guarded by the obscene and evil shape of an Old One.

The children were pulled and dragged kicking and screaming and cursing from the house while the Old One was literally shot to bloody stinking pulp, which stopped the howling and snarling creature while the kids were being pulled away. Then Carl set the house on fire with Molotov cocktails and watched it burn down around what was left of the ancient evil.

"That thing must have taken a hundred rounds," Terrell said. "And it never went down. Jesus Christ! I've never seen anything like that."

"I have," Carl said grimly. "Come on. We've got a lot of work to do and it's got to be done during the day. Tonight will be the finale. They'll throw everything they've got at us as soon as the sun goes down. We're winning now, and Anya and Pet know it." He looked away, his eyes distant. "Janet is dead. She killed both herself and the demon baby."

"How do you know that?" Dee asked.

Carl just shrugged and walked toward the Jag.

"That young man spooks the hell out of me," Daly admitted.

Pastor Speed smiled. "Good. Let's hope he can do the same for the town."

The teams went from house to house, clearing a two-block area in all directions around the high school. Some of the coven members gave up, surrendering without a fight. But those types were few. Most of them, when the word went out about what was happening, chose to flee into the country, leaving behind them what they had spent a lifetime working for.

"Satan has them in a very powerful grip," Father Vincent said. "Had I not witnessed this with my own eyes, I would never have believed it."

"Nor I," Pastor Speed said. "I can tell you all that from this point on, my sermons will be undergoing a drastic change in content."

"I haven't been inside a church in twenty years,"

Keller, one of the quartet of men Conners first sent in undercover, admitted. "Yet I haven't felt any desire at all to worship the Devil. And I've certainly been in town long enough to get infected, or whatever the hell has happened to these people."

"I don't think it happens overnight," Tolson said. "It's got to be a gradual change in a person. And to tell you the truth, I'm not sure I really want to know how it happens."

Tolson turned just as a rifle cracked. The highway patrolman sat down on the grass, a hole in the center of his forehead.

"Praise Satan!" a young man yelled, appearing on a front porch.

Daly shot him in the belly, knocking him back against the house. As he struggled to lift his rifle, Daly shot him again. He fell off the porch and lay still.

"Then you go praise the son of a bitch," Daly muttered. "And take our damn stupid governor with you."

The lieutenant of Virginia Highway Patrol looked down at the man who had been his partner for years and shook his head.

Pastor Speed knelt down and closed Tolson's eyes as Chuck quietly prayed.

Daly punched out the empty brass and reloaded his .357. "I'm losing patience," he said. "I'm tired of this mess and these godless, murderous bastards and bitches." He looked at Jim Hunt. "No more fucking around, Jim. No more playing patty-cake and giving these people all the breaks the lawyers say the Constitution guarantees them. We don't have any lawyers and judges looking over our shoulders. As far as I'm concerned, it's open season on people who spit in the face of decency and love of God. They want to go to Hell? Fine with me. Let's send them there." He walked to his

360

car, slung a bandolier of shotgun shells over his shoulder, picked up a twelve-gauge riot gun, and began walking toward the next block.

Pastor Speed hesitated for just a second, then started walking after the man. Chuck followed, then Mike, and finally Jim Hunt and Max Bancroft.

Carl turned to Dee. "Go back to the house, Dee. We'll have the town cleaned out by dusk. I'll be out there shortly after dark. Tomorrow we take the woods."

She lifted her eyes and glared at him. "Is that an order?"

"That's an order."

Edgar smiled and waited to see who would blink first in this battle of wills. He had never known his daughter to back down from anybody or anything. And he would have bet a hundred dollars that Dee would tell Carl to go take a flying leap.

Terrell and Gabe were covering Tolson's body with a blanket, pretending to be unaware of the silent battle of wills between the boss's daughter and the young man who appeared to have nerves made of steel cable.

Suddenly, in the midst of death and terror, in the middle of Satan's playing field, love blossomed into a full flower.

"However," Carl said, a smile creasing his lips, "I could make that a suggestion."

"I'm always open to suggestion," Dee replied, then kissed him. "I'll see you at dusk." She turned and walked to a car, three of her father's security men going with her.

Edgar winked at Carl. "You're learning, boy."

Two booming blasts from Daly's shotgun shattered the moment.

Carl clicked off the safety of his M-16 and walked toward the sounds.

361

Chapter 36

Carey Ellis had gotten separated from Josh and the rest of the cons. He had stopped to retie the laces on his tennis shoes and when he looked up, the others had rounded a curve in the gravel road and were out of sight.

A flitting gray shape near the timber's edge caught his eyes and turned his head. "What the hell is that?" he muttered. He caught another glimpse of the shape and relaxed. "Big-assed dog, I reckon," he said. He straightened up and continued his walking. The timber was silent all around him. Carey wanted to cut and run away, maybe head for Richmond, get away from this craziness, but the memory of what had happened to Mark Hay stayed fresh in his mind and kept pushing him on. He hoped to link up with the other cons.

A snarl from the darkness of the timber's edge reached him, stopped him, and turned his eyes to the timber. A low growl from the other side of the road spun him around. He could see brown-yellow eyes glaring at him and the long bared teeth glistening as the sunlight touched them.

"Goddamn wolf!" Carey said. He jerked his rifle to his shoulder and fired.

But the wolf vanished just as he pulled the trigger.

"Impossible!" Carey muttered.

Snarling and growling from the other side of the road spun him around, his heart racing from fear.

A half a dozen large gray wolves were staring at him, fangs bared.

Again he jerked the rifle to his shoulder and fired. And as before, the wolves vanished just as he pulled the trigger.

Ghost wolves! The terrifying thought leaped into his brain. He calmed himself by thinking: But if they're ghosts, they have to be on our side!

A gray hairy shape hit him hard in the back and knocked that thought from the con as it sent him sprawling on the gravel. He lost his rifle and cut his hands on the gravel as the wolves nailed him, great fangs ripping his flesh, tearing the screams from his throat and shredding the life from him.

As his bloody life, past and present, painfully left him, the con could see the marks in the wolves' chests and sides, marks left there by bullets. Some of them had mangled paws and legs where they had been crippled by one of the cruelest of all of man's insults to the animal world: steel traps.

Carey Ellis let life leave him and he drifted into darkness. As he drifted from the light side to the dark side, a hideous shape bounced and pranced and chuckled before him. The face was indescribable but still unmistakably, unspeakably, and horribly evil.

The mouth opened, and the foulest of odors circled him like rotting rats' tails. The creature chuckled darkly and spoke.

"As promised, you shall live forever." He flung his arm and the flames and stinking smoke reached Carey. "In *this!*" Satan roared.

Carey Ellis started screaming as the intense pain

363

began creeping over his body and searing his dead but still-living flesh. He would scream forever.

The Devil had kept his promise. In a manner of speaking.

More children were rounded up, most of them savage-eyed and screaming, kicking, and biting as they were carried off—dragged off in most cases.

Daly was true to his word: If an adult coven member was found and offered the slightest resistance, Daly would put a very final end to the evil life. No prayers from pastor or priest were offered for the dead souls. And Daly finished the walking evils with a look of satisfaction on his face.

"Doesn't make a shit to me," the state trooper said. "I can retire any damn time I please."

One group of men and women stayed at the high school, working from tall ladders, nailing up sheets of plywood over the windows of selected rooms, inside and out, creating makeshift cells for the kids and for those few adults who were brought in alive.

Jim used the phone in the Jaguar to call the governor. He got the governor's aide.

"Jim! How's it going in Butler?" the aide questioned cheerfully.

"Bastard thinks we're having a picnic in here," Jim muttered. "Oh, just wonderful. I don't recall ever havin' such a marvelous time of it. The sheriff's dead. The mayor's dead. Their wives are dead. Trooper Tolson is dead. We got bodies of dead coven members layin' all over the damn streets. Half a dozen downtown buildings have been burned to ground level; at least that many more homes are gone. We got no power, no regular phone service. And you got the nerve to ask me

364

how the fuck it's going?" he screamed at last.

"Now, now, Jim," the aide said, an unctuous earnestness to the words. "Look on the bright side. The governor has the power to appoint you sheriff, you know? As a matter of fact, I'll see that that's done within the hour. Tit for tat, Jim. You've done a good job."

"What's your name, boy?"

"Byron Winston, Sheriff Hunt."

"Well, Byron, do you have any idea what's taken place here?"

"I think so. I was on the investigating team that went into Ruger County after that, ah, incident."

"You have any trouble sleepin' at night?"

"Not a bit. Jim" — the aide's voice hardened — "it has to be this way. You surely must sense, and I certainly know, that the governor's come under terrific pressure from, ah, just north of us."

"Hell, say the word, Byron. Washington, D.C."

"You said it, Jim, not I. These conversations are being monitored by more than one agency and organization, believe me."

"Big deal."

"A bigger deal than you might think, Jim. Jim, a story has already been prepared as to what went on in Butler. We know a dozen or more convicts escaped from your jail, most of them already sentenced to long prison terms. It isn't unheard of for those types of individuals to take over and terrorize an entire town, especially one as isolated as Butler."

"It won't wash, Byron," Jim said flatly.

"We think it will, *Sheriff* Hunt."

"Don't try to buy me, boy."

"Oh, I wouldn't think of doing anything that odious, Sheriff. Oh, my, no." He clucked his tongue at just the thought. "But don't you have a son in the service?

Career man, I believe. We wouldn't want to have anything placed in his jacket that might muck up his career, would we? And you have a daughter who works for the FBI, right? She handles a lot of sensitive material. The temptation must be great. One boy in college, yes? A brilliant lad, I must say. I have his file before me now. Yes. Oh, my. Just look at all the government grants he's receiving. Am I getting through to you, Sheriff Hunt?"

"You stinkin', slimy, son of a bitch!"

Byron laughed at him. "It's the way of the world, Sheriff. But you do get my point, don't you?"

"Yeah. I get it. But someday the truth will out. Bet on it."

"Oh, it always does, Sheriff! Years down the road, of course."

"You got reporters in here, boy."

"And they'll get their story, Sheriff! Oh, my, yes. We believe they'll see the light, so to speak."

"So I go along with you on this. Does that mean the state sends some help in?"

"Help? Why do you need any help? Sheriff Hunt, you're still alive. That alone tells me you and your people have the situation under control and are making marvelous progress toward restoring law and order. Keep up the good work, Sheriff."

The connection was broken.

Daly noted the expression on Jim's face. "We're still alone in this thing, right?"

"You got it." Then he told Daly and the others gathered around what the aide had said—all of it.

"I know Byron," Daly said. "That's just like him. He's the next governor of the state, bet on it. And after that, he'll run for U.S. Senate, and win."

"I get the impression that he actually runs the state

now, not the governor."

"You're right. The governor doesn't make any decisions without consulting Winston."

"Well, to hell with Byron Winston. We come this far on our own. . . ." He looked toward Heaven. "Sort of. We'll go on handlin' it our way."

Daly shoved another round into the tube of his riot gun. "Suits me."

Just before dusk settled over the land, Carl headed back to the A-frame, followed by Edgar and his men. He was using a different route, wanting to check out the only other road to the house.

Most of the town was now secure. As the search-and-destroy had intensified in Butler, more and more of the coven members had begun giving up without a fight. The word had gone out: Daly and the others, including Pastor Speed and Father Vincent, would kill if any type of resistance was offered. The bodies were taken to the city landfill and burned. All the slides and cultures in Bartlett's lab had been destroyed by fire.

Acting out of pure spite, those coven members still active—their hearts too blackened by evil to ever be redeemed—had burned as many churches as they could, before running from the town to take refuge in the woods. They had destroyed the fire-fighting equipment of the town's small department, so Jim and the others could do nothing except use garden hoses to wet down the homes close to the churches in an attempt to save them. The more stupid of the coven members had been ordered by the leaders to stay in town with rifles and snipe at those fighting the fires.

They did not last long, and their sniping hurt no one.

As his headlights picked up the body in the road, Carl slowed and stopped. He carefully checked both sides of the road before getting out of the Jag and walking up to the torn body.

He did not know the man, had no way of knowing he was looking at what was left of Carey Ellis.

"Jesus," Edgar said. "What did this?"

"Probably the wolves that came in here. Look at those fang marks."

"There are no paw prints," the industrialist pointed out.

"I noticed."

"And? So?"

"You want a theory?"

"Beats a knock on the head."

"It's a ghost pack."

Edgar sighed. "I think I'd rather have had a knock on the head."

"It's the best I can do."

"The body looks . . . well, strange."

"The soul is gone. I saw that in Ruger. But not taken by God."

"He made a pact with the Devil and the Devil collected?"

"Yes. I would imagine the Devil always gets what's due him, and probably a bit more."

Carl looked up at the sky. Heavy, dark, fat clouds were moving in. The humidity had gone up fifty percent in the past hour.

"It's going to be a very interesting night," Edgar commented.

"And probably going to swing the pendulum for the last time."

"But swing it where?"

"Only two mighty powers know the answer to that,

Edgar."

"I believe very strongly in one and worship Him. I have absolutely no desire whatsoever to have anything to do with the other."

"You meet him every day, Edgar. We all do. In some form or another. I'd guess that maybe fifty percent of us actually try to resist him, and we're not successful much of the time."

"Only fifty percent?"

"Certainly no more than that. Father Denier said that come Judgment Day, a lot of people were going to be sorely disappointed, for Heaven was going to be a very sparsely populated place."

Edgar smiled in the windy and soon-to-be-stormy night. "Why do I get the feeling that you're exclusively an Old Testament man?"

"Because it's true. That's where it all is as far as I'm concerned. God didn't whimper around and make deals and so forth. He said: This is the way it is, and this is the way it's going to be. Screw up, and I'll send Michael down to kick your ass and then I'll ship it off right straight to Hell."

"Sunday School would have been a lot more interesting studying out of your bible," Edgar said with a laugh.

Chapter 37

The most violent storm any could ever remember seeing tore open the sky that night, forcing Conners's security men out of the field and into the house and the shed, into cars and trucks and, in some cases, under trucks.

Edgar used a secure line to call into his headquarters in Richmond. It was a bright, clear, and starry night everywhere in the state. "Except for Reeves County," Edgar said.

"Nothing on the radar, sir," he was told.

"It's a message," Carl said, standing by a rain-slashed window and looking out at the interplay of the elements. "But from whom?"

The others in the crowded house offered no reply or comment, knowing he was thinking out loud. And even among the tough security men, Carl was viewed with no small degree of awe. Anyone who would openly stand up and confront the Devil was either a nut or a very brave man.

And it did not take the men long to discover that Carl Garrett was no nut.

Carl turned away from the window. "What happened in Ruger was an accident. We know that much for a fact. It became time for Anya and Pet to rest, and their sleep was disturbed by engineers. So they were on a journey. Where? If I've got it all sorted out in my mind, their destination was right here." He stamped one booted foot. "Perhaps in the woods, but I don't think so. I think it's right here on the land this house was built on."

"Why?" Dee asked.

"That I don't know. Edgar, how long has this land been yours?"

"My great-great-grandfather bought it. Each reading of the will after that always contained the stipulation that the land must never be sold or given away to anyone outside the family, and that it must never be cleared."

"Why?"

"I have no idea, Carl. I've tried to find out but the secret obviously died with my great-great-grandfather."

"Yet you allowed Dee to clear the land to build this A-frame?"

"No, he didn't," Dee replied. "This has always been cleared ground. At least as long as I can remember."

"For as long as I can remember too," Edgar said. "Trees just don't grow here."

"Why?" Carl persisted.

"I don't know. Nothing grows on this spot. Never has. A few scrawny bushes and some weeds, and damn little else."

Carl was thoughtful for a moment. "Linda lied to me. Everything she said was a lie. She didn't come here to set up a coven. The coven was already here. It might even be the oldest one in the United States. And it might be something else too." He fell silent as he turned to look out the window.

"What, Carl?" Dee asked.

371

"Something unspeakable. Something so evil it scared the crap out of your ancestors and they bought the land and declared it uninhabitable . . . in the only legal way they could."

"Now you're spooking me, boy!" Edgar told him, standing up and walking to the window. "What sort of evil could it be? And if that's the case, why didn't my ancestors give future generations some sort of warning about it?"

"They probably did. But they probably did it in some cryptic form that would be understood only by a Conners. Perhaps in some old family bible."

"I have the oldest one in our family right here," Dee said. "I'll get it for you."

Lamps were turned up and Carl sat down, the old bible in his hands. He handled it very carefully, for the pages were stiff and broke easily. "What's your great-great-grandfather's name, Edgar?"

"Edgar Edison Conners."

He found the genealogy-records section and noted when Edgar Edison Conners was born and died. In the important-events section, he found E.E.C., and in a fine, bold, beautiful handwritten script: "Read not these passages as they are meant to be. Jeremiah Ch 26, V 23, Genesis Ch 23, V 20."

"Anybody ever read these Biblical passages?" Carl asked.

"I have," Dee said. "It doesn't mean a thing to me."

Carl turned to Jeremiah and read. "And they fetched forth Urijah out of Egypt, and brought him unto Jehoiakim the king; who slew him with the sword, and cast his dead body into the graves of the common people." He turned to Genesis and read, "And the field, and the cave that is therein, were made sure unto Abraham for a possession of a burying place by the sons of Heth."

"Death and burial," Dee said. "Everyone in the family has read those passages a dozen times. No one knows what they mean."

"Are there any caves on this property?" Carl asked.

"Not that I'm aware of," Edgar told him. "And no one has ever reported finding any."

"So that leaves the field. The grounds, in other words." Carl laid the bible aside and stood up, once more walking to the window and looking out. The storm had intensified, the rains almost a solid, blinding sheet of silver gray lashing at the earth.

He thought he saw movement and stared hard. There was something moving around, but he couldn't make out what it was.

The A-frame suddenly shifted, throwing everyone standing toward the left front of the home.

One of the girls screamed in fright.

"A piling has broken off or settled into a hole," Edgar said, bracing himself against a wall.

"It settled into a hole, all right," Carl said, his words tinged with grimness. His eyes did not leave the strange movements on the storm-torn landscape around the A-frame. They were lurching movements, stiff and jerky, like that of a person just trying to walk who had been bedridden for many years.

Or someone who had been confined in a casket for several hundred years.

"We got company outside!" a security man yelled.

A horrible scream reached those inside the awkwardly tilted house.

"What the hell?" Edgar said.

"It's a graveyard," Carl said, his words just audible over the howling of the storm. "The whole damn place is a graveyard. Where devil-worshippers have been buried over several centuries. Probably brought in here from all over the state — maybe several states — over God only knows how many years. God and Satan. Brought in at night and buried —"

Hard gunfire cut off his words as the security people still outside began firing at the lurching, staggering, stumbling shapes of those long dead who now had been summoned from their wormy, rotted caskets to once more walk the land.

A hard hammering began against the floor of the house. Boards began cracking and splitting under the impact. More and more ghostly shapes began appearing on the grounds: some women dressed in gowns that were several hundred years out of fashion, some men in evening clothes that predated the Civil War.

A casket rammed through the floor of the house.

The top of the casket burst open under the impact and a foul, musty odor filled the house just as fists began beating at the windows and outside walls of the A-frame. Faces appeared at the windows, gray, rotted faces, many with bits of flesh clinging to the skull bones, worms and maggots of various sizes slithering in and out of empty eye-sockets and nose cavities and the open, moving, but so-far-silent mouths — silent except for the clacking together of yellow and rotted teeth as the jawbones worked.

A man struggled to free himself from the shattered casket protruding through the hole in the floor.

"Hit the floor!" Carl yelled, and gave him a half a dozen rounds from his 9-mm, the exploding bullets shattering long-dead bones and sending bits and pieces of ash-white slivers bouncing against the walls and floor.

Still the undead fought for freedom from his entombment.

Terrell grabbed a poker from the fireplace set and started smashing the living dead. A howling began outside, the sound rising above the screaming of the storm.

The risen dead had found voice and were thanking the Dark One for their freedom.

A window was smashed by a club-wielding skeletal woman, and the risen began attempting to climb inside the house, moaning and howling, their bones rattling.

"Shotguns!" Edgar shouted, lifting his twelve-gauge and blasting the undead that were clamoring and clanking over each other in their hellish death rush to enter the house.

Lib and Becky gave it up as their stretched-to-the-limit nerves could take no more. The girls collapsed on the floor, both of them in a cold faint.

Buckshot struck the forever-grinning, and damned, mottled skulls were blown apart, the headless corpses running around in the rain, banging into each other, bones falling from inside their tattered and rotted clothing.

Dingo had pushed Dee into a safe corner and was refusing to let her out of his protection, pressing his weight against her legs, holding her in place while he snarled and growled, exposing his terrible fangs, daring anybody or anything to try to harm her.

Outside, it was a massacre as the walking dead tore apart the security men, flinging bloody arms and heads to the howling winds. The cold, bone-shining fingers clamped around ankles, dragged the men from under vehicles, and ripped the legs and arms from them, flinging the bloody limbs high into the stormy night with the strength of the insane.

Another casket rammed through the floor of the

house, breaking open and tumbling a grinning woman to the littered floor.

Slimy fingers clamped around the ankle of Sonya and as she screamed, she beat at the rotted flesh of the head with her camera, breaking the old bone and exposing a skull full of fat worms.

Jesse grabbed a meat cleaver from the kitchen and severed the arm of the woman at the elbow. Sonya pried the dead fingers from her ankles and revulsion filled the reporter at the touch.

The grimacing, bloody, brain-dripping head of a security man came crashing through an already shattered window and smashed face-first into a wall, sliding down, leaving a trail of blood and snot.

So much for this glass being bullet-proof! Edgar thought. I'll find the man who sold me this shit and we'll dance a few rounds.

Carl struggled into his flamethrower harness and fought his way to the back porch door, leaving the front and both sides to the others. He sparked the nozzle into life and sprayed the outside, the napalmlike, sticking, thick fuel igniting the clothing of half a dozen of those who had chosen to give their souls to the Master of Evil.

The night was pocked with running blotches of screaming and howling fireballs. They'd been born in the smoking pits of Hell, and the fire returned them to the sulfuric womb that had puked them out.

"Get into those cases of grenades!" Carl yelled. "Start throwing them."

Gabe and Terrell began ripping open the cases of grenades and tossing them to anyone who wanted them. Pins were pulled and the mini-bombs hurled into the savage and ungodly night outside.

The grenades and Carl's flamethrower turned the

tide of battle, the explosions shattering the old bones of the newly risen and blowing them apart. The shrapnel shredded the walking dead, bringing them down like a house of cards in a stiff breeze.

"Gabe!" Edgar shouted. "You boys grab as much equipment as you can and clear us a path to the vehicles. We can't stay here any—"

The rear of the house collapsed, the pilings sinking into the earth and vomiting out more of those long-buried in the Devil's graveyard.

"Let's go!" Terrell yelled. Those security people who had taken refuge in the house moved at the orders, plunging into the outside darkness and the unknown. They formed lines left and right as the others began running out of the lop-sided A-frame, jumping off the porch and racing to the cars and trucks.

"Carl!" Dee wailed.

"Get out of here!" he shouted. "Somebody get her out of here!"

She was picked up and dumped into the cab of a truck. The truck's engine roared into life and was gone down the road.

"Carl!" Edgar yelled, his eyes not finding the young man. "Come on, boy!"

Carl stepped out of the house to stand on the shattered and body-littered porch, Dingo by his side. Carl was loaded down with equipment. "This is my war, now, Edgar. Head for town. I'll see you at daylight."

"You're crazy, boy!"

Carl laughed and Dingo snarled.

Edgar Conners was picked up bodily by his security men and manhandled into the Jaguar. The Jag roared off.

The rain abruptly stopped. The moon hung like a fat ball of ghostly light in the sky.

The undead had clattered off into the darkness of the timber.

Carl jumped off the porch and began walking toward the woods, Dingo by his side.

Chapter 38

At the high school, Jim and Max and the others were taking it easy, and were startled when Edgar and his crew roared up and explained what had happened near the woods.

"A devils' graveyard." Pastor Speed spoke the words softly. "And young Garrett stayed out there?"

"Said it was his fight now."

"He didn't want us to come out and help?" Daly asked.

"Said he would see us at daylight. I guess that's when he wanted us out there."

"One man and a dog against . . . how many?" Max questioned.

Edgar shrugged, remembering what Carl had said on the road. "Only God and Satan know the answer to that."

A hooded shape reared up in front of Carl.

Dingo leaped without growling or snarling, huge jaws open and teeth glistening. He ripped open the man's throat, the force of the jaws breaking the man's neck and leaving the head dangling by only a thin strip of skin. The man kicked and thrashed on the ground for only a few seconds before death took him.

"Good boy," Carl whispered, patting the dog's big head.

Dingo looked up, blood dripping from his jaws. There was a mean look in his mismatched blue and brown eyes. A look that silently said: Come on, boss, let's go kick some ass!

"Come on."

Man and dog pressed deeper into the woods.

The siren's song began its tantalizing and seductive melody.

"Fuck you!" Carl said.

The singing stopped.

A very soft and dry clattering gave the newly risen's position away. Carl tossed a grenade in that direction and hit the ground, pulling Dingo down with him.

The explosion shattered the dark stillness and brought forth a hideous howl that did not come from the dry throat of one just risen from the Devil's graveyard.

A creature lurched from the shrapnel-shattered timber: an Old One, half of its head blown off. Carl gave it a squirt from his flamethrower and the creature exploded before his eyes, stinking blood flying in all directions, along with various parts of the Hell-born creature.

Dingo whirled around, ran hard for a few yards, and then leaped, his fangs wet and savage in the night. Nick Jamison screamed just once as Dingo's jaws slashed and his paws ripped, coming away with half of the flesh of the young man's face in his jaws and blood on his paws from digging into the punk's throat.

Nick fell back, horrible gurgling sounds coming from his torn-open throat. Val ran screaming out of the timber, a pistol in her hands. Carl gave her a squirt of the fire that she thought so much of. Her reaction gave him the impression that she disliked it intensely as she was engulfed in the flames. The oil in her unwashed and greasy hair exploded, the force of the detonation knocking the eyes out of her head, which probably gave her an even more cockeyed view of life than she'd possessed before . . . at least for a few more very painful moments.

She fell to the wet ground, kicking and screaming and howling, as her miserable and wasted life ebbed from her.

Shapes came at a rush toward Carl and Dingo. Carl held the trigger back on the nozzle of erupting fire and death and sprayed the rushing mob, both human and non-human.

Dingo busied himself mauling the life out of two who made the mistake of thinking the animal would be easier to handle than Carl. They died regretting that decision.

Carl tossed two grenades into a second mob which came screaming out of the darkness at him: Fire-Frags, mini-Claymores, which shredded those closest to the twin explosions, turning them into ripped and torn rags of meat, knocking others down and bleeding and out of it.

"Dingo! Back, boy! Come on!"

Man and dog ran from the scene of carnage, out of the woods and back to the tilted house. If this works, Carl thought, we can end this tonight. If it doesn't, I'm screwed.

He only had a few minutes, and he used them well, ripping open crates with a pry-bar and taking out Claymore mines. He quickly activated the mines and pulled out the hand-held pulse generator — commonly called a clacker because of the sound it made when squeezed. He laid out a double row of Claymores, being careful to make certain the "This Side Toward Enemy" warning was really toward the path he hoped the enemy would take and not facing his own position.

Carl tested the firing device and cap. The light in the test kit flashed. Everything was go!

Each Claymore contained at least 700 steel sphere submissiles which were propelled by a healthy charge of C-4. Some called the Claymore the scythe of the Grim Reaper. If Carl's plan worked, the scythe was going to be turned against the Reaper and his odious followers.

He called Dingo to his side and patted the ground. "Lay down, Dingo. Stay. Stay."

The well-trained dog plopped down and stayed down, close to Carl.

Carl quickly changed to full napalm tanks for his squirter and waited. He soon heard the sounds of the running hate-filled beings who sought his death. When they were close enough to spot him, Carl boldly stood up and began yelling at the mob. They changed course and ran straight for him, straight down the alleyway formed by the deadly Claymores.

Carl smiled a warrior's smile as he spotted Anya and Pet among those chanting for his blood. The earthly and unearthly were carrying clubs and knives and axes as they ran, closer and closer, screaming for his blood.

Carl punched the clacker and the explosions were enormous in the night. Those closest to the Claymores were shredded like bloody cabbage, and the shock waves knocked them sprawling in torn heaps.

Carl began tossing grenades into the mangled mass as fast as he could pull the pins and hurl them. Parts of human and non-human bodies were flung into the air as the powerful grenades exploded. Carl stepped into the shattered alleyway of death and sparked the nozzle of the flamethrower into life. Lifting the nozzle, he began systematically burning the dead and dying and wounded. The nose-wrinkling odor of burning flesh filled the cool and wet night.

Carl exhausted the tanks and switched to fresh ones. He burned every body part he came to under God's full bright moon, reducing the part to char, whether it be a hand, arm, leg, torso, or head.

Some of the bodyless heads cursed him as he worked, the curses soon changing into shrieks of pain as the fire consumed them.

He found pieces of Anya and Pet and lingered long over them, turning what was left of the pair of godless shapechangers into lifeless lumps of smoking, unrecognizable heaps. With his boots, he scattered the ashpiles and burned them again.

Carl worked throughout the night, stopping only occasionally for a break. Dingo followed him, staying well away from the flame-shooting nozzle.

Carl knew there were some beings still in the timber, but without the leadership of Anya and Pet, they could be dealt with easily enough when daylight spread its welcoming brightness over the torn land.

Just as the sky was changing from purple to gray in the east, he heard the sounds of vehicles coming up the road. Carl slipped out of his harness and let the empty tanks fall to the soggy ground.

The men and women who exited the vehicles stood in silence as they looked at the wreckage and the burned and still-smoking carnage.

Pastor Speed stood, the faint light reflecting off his helmet liner, the brass of the shotgun shells in the bandolier crisscrossing his chest, and said, "Dear God in Heaven, is it over?"

"No," Carl told them all, the weariness in his voice very plain. "Not yet."

Chapter 39

Carl had asked for front-loaders to be brought in and the ashes of the godless scooped up, to be trucked away and later sealed in thick concrete tombs.

"Isn't this overkill, boy?" Edgar asked.

"No. If just one spark of life remains in any of this"—he waved his hand toward the charred remains—"they'll rise and return." He looked at the industrialist. "You want to take that chance?"

The man shook his head. "No," he said softly.

"I just spoke with Byron Winston," Daly said, walking up. "He's coming in by helicopter for a personal inspection."

"When?" Jim asked.

"Should be here in a couple of hours."

Carl stretched out in the bed of a truck, his head pillowed on a rolled-up tarp. "The sounds of the chopper will wake me. I got to get some sleep."

He closed his eyes and was asleep in two minutes.

Carl knew a couple of the FBI agents; they were the same ones sent into Ruger after his father died. He did not know the lone CIA agent or any of the

National Security Agency men and women. He pegged the governor's aide, Byron Winston, as a pompous, strutting asshole with a big mouth and a bigger ambition.

Carl stood to one side, sipping coffee out of a paper cup and listening to bits and pieces of various conversations. No one had yet asked him anything and he wasn't going to volunteer a word.

He knew somebody would get around to him; it was just a matter of time.

Finally, the Company man walked up to him. "I got half a dozen men laying back, in town. Anything you want us to do?"

"It isn't going to be legal."

The Agency man smiled. "Now that would be novel."

"The timber around this place still contains some coven members."

"I get the picture."

"The wolves are on our side. Leave them alone."

He nodded his head, adding, "Strangest op I ever been on."

"The President send you people in?"

"We came solely out of the goodness of our hearts, all of us being community-minded and good solid Christians." He said it all without changing expression, then turned and walked to his car, lifting the mike and speaking for a few seconds. He tossed the mike on the seat, picked up a small case, and walked down to the curve in the road, squatting down, waiting.

Carl watched him open the case and fit a long silencer onto the barrel of a pistol. In a few minutes, two cars pulled up and parked, and other operatives joined the Agency man. They talked for a moment and then disappeared into the woods.

Carl looked toward the ravaged town of Butler. Thick black smoke was pouring into the sky, clearly visible even miles from town. It did not surprise him, and he had a hunch what it was.

Daly walked to his unit and called in. He acknowledged the message received and walked over to Carl. "Those escaped cons attacked the high school . . . for some reason. They set it on fire before they could be shot dead by Federal agents."

"Sure they did," Carl said.

"That's the story."

"Any survivors from the fire?"

"Very few."

"The kids?"

"They were moved to a secure location before the cons attacked."

"That certainly was thoughtful on somebody's part, wasn't it?" It would have taken a deaf mute to miss the sarcasm in his words.

"I was just told that it's completely out of our hands, Carl. It's all Federal now."

"They'll fuck it up. They always do. They did in Ruger."

"I have no reason to doubt that." He looked around. "Where did those super-spooks go?"

"In the woods."

"So it's over, or soon will be?"

"The latter. But it's going to be a sight to see. The Devil does not take defeat lightly."

Daly grunted.

"How about those in the town who are just now coming out of their homes, professing to know nothing about what happened?" Carl asked.

"How did you know about them? You've been out

here all night."

"I've done this before."

"And will again?"

"I imagine so."

"Will you do me a favor?"

"If possible."

"Take it out of Virginia the next time, okay?"

Carl managed a small grin. "I'll do my best."

Daly sighed. He was tired and he looked it. "We didn't win the war, did we?"

"Oh, no. Just one small battle. The next battle will be completely different from this one."

"What do you mean and how do you know that?"

Carl waited almost a full minute before replying. "It's a cycle, Lieutenant. If you do this often enough you'll see that it all goes in cycles. The Devil opted for violence in this battle. It backfired on him. The next time will be much more subtle and psychological in nature. A war of nerves, probably. Remember, I've seen it before and studied hundreds of case histories. Satan doesn't like me very much. I've figured out his pattern."

"Better you than me," the state trooper said. "I think I'll request a transfer back to traffic."

"Too late for that, Daly. Satan's got your name written down in his book. From this point on, be very, very careful. Don't get into a routine. Watch your back. And be suspicious of everything and everybody."

"I'm going to have a hell of time explaining that to family and friends."

"You'll find a way. If you want to live."

The governor's aide walked over and stood for a time, eyeballing Carl. Carl returned the stare. Byron blinked first.

"I understand you had a lot to do with bringing this, ah, unfortunate situation to an end, young man."

"It isn't over yet."

"Really?" Byron drawled the word while he arched one eyebrow.

Carl wondered how many hours he'd spent in front of a mirror practicing that move. "That's what I said."

"Well, it certainly looks over to me!"

"Do I have to remind you who we have been dealing with here? *We*, not you."

Byron flushed and his eyes narrowed at the obvious slur. "I don't think I like your attitude very much, young man."

"I know I don't give a damn what you like. You're standing in a danger zone, Mister Governor's Aide Winston. There are dozens of beings, of this earth and not of this earth, that are still unaccounted for. And if you think the Prince of Darkness is going to take defeat gracefully, then that makes you as full of shit as I think you are."

"Trying to milk the tragedy for some publicity, Garrett?"

"You are a damn fool, Winston!" Carl turned his back to the man and walked away, Daly right beside.

The aide looked all around him, spotting Jim. "Sheriff Hunt!" Winston shouted. "I command you to arrest this insolent person!"

"Command me?" Jim stuffed a fresh wad of chewing tobacco into his mouth and said, "On what charge?"

Winston sputtered and stammered and finally shut his mouth.

More people arrived from town, Dee among them.

She walked to Carl's side and put her arms around him. "You shouldn't have come out this soon, Dee." He softened that with a smile. "Not that I'm unhappy to see you."

"You look like you're about ready to drop."

"I'm all right. I got a couple hours' sleep. The town?"

"All the animals have returned to normal. Some dogs chasing cats, some cats just lounging about, sunning themselves. Dogs sleeping on front porches. Is it over, Carl?"

Carl looked up at the sun. About eleven o'clock, he guessed. "The Devil, Dee, is a bastard, but he's a dramatic bastard. If he's going to pull something, he'll do it at high noon."

"Is it safe to go into the house?" She looked at the leaning A-frame. "Or what's left of it."

"No. But I went in anyway. I got the manuscript you were working on from your office and most of your files and research papers. They might be a little worse for wear; I tossed them out the side window. I gave the manuscript to your father."

"So what now, Carl?"

"Let's get something to eat and wait for the Devil to make his move."

"You sound so matter-of-fact about it, Carl."

"I don't mean it to sound like I am. I'm really rather curious as to what the Dark One has in mind for his swan song."

"You aren't afraid that . . . he might try to kill you for what you've done?"

"Oh, yes!" Carl answered that very quickly. "But he could do that anytime he wanted to. In his own perverted and evil way, I imagine he sort of likes me."

"*Likes* you!"

"Sure. He hasn't been able to beat me—yet. He enjoys a good fight. He gets his way so often a good challenge is something he probably relishes."

"You sound as though you're sorry this has ended."

"Not this one," Carl said. "This has been the toughest one so far. For me, that is."

"And there will be more?" she asked, as they walked on toward the road. She got the impression that Carl wanted distance between them and the house. Most of the others had already distanced themselves from the house.

"Yes, Dee. There will be more. If you want me to share any of your life, you're going to have to accept that and live with it."

She kissed him right in front of God and everybody else, including the Devil. "I already have, Carl."

The A-frame exploded, the force of it knocking them all off their feet and to the ground. The roof of the house sailed hundreds of feet into the air, breaking up and coming down, the fragments hitting the earth like bombs. When the explosion came, Carl grabbed Dee and shoved her under a Ford Bronco, then crawled in after her, the heavy four-wheel drive protecting them from the debris. Dingo had beaten them both under the Bronco.

The walls of the house caved inward as the earth opened up and the sky changed colors. A whirlwind sprang out of the hole where the house had stood, the mini-cyclone kicking up dirt and rocks and flinging the rocks like bullets in all directions.

One of the men who had flown in with the governor's aide stood up to watch in fascination at the sight unfolding and spinning before his eyes. A timber from the house roared out of the whirlwind and decapitated the man. The headless man stood for a few seconds before collapsing, the blood gushing out of the nub where his neck had been.

The hole widened and the spinning, howling winds intensified, sucking in anything close to the hole, splintering and mangling it, then spitting it out at super-sonic speeds.

Smoke began pouring out of the widening hole in the earth, and with the smoke, pitiful cries and screaming and whimpering from once-human throats, those damned beings forever trapped in the hellish fires of the Devil's pits. The heat followed the smoke and the cries. It blistered the outside lip of the hole and baked the soggy earth for a hundred feet outside the yawning, shrieking, smoking entrance to Hell.

White-hot rocks, some the size of automobiles, began spewing out of the burning crevice; they flew hundreds of feet into the air and then came crashing down, smashing into cars and trucks, destroying them, the heat exploding the gas tanks and turning the area into a besieged no-man's-land.

Edgar crawled under the Bronco, trying to push Dingo aside. The dog gave him one look and Edgar gave up that idea.

"You said it would be quite a show!" Edgar had to lean close to Carl and shout to make himself heard above the roaring.

Carl nodded his reply.

The winds began to abate. The cyclone began to lose its strength and definition. The screaming of the damned faded and grew silent. The heat cooled and the smoke stopped pouring out of the hole.

A hush fell over the area.

Carl crawled out from under the Bronco and stood up. Soon the others followed his lead, to stand in shocked silence.

A screaming began.

Ermma Barstow's dead, bony, and white hands were locked around Byron Winston's throat. Her head was smashing against his, her long hair flopping from side to side as the mouth opened and closed, laughter and howling pushing past her lips.

Byron's head was bloody from the bashing and his eyes were rolling back into his head from the lack of oxygen. Carl ran to the man and grabbed the hair of the bodyless head. She tried to bite him. Carl began spinning like a shot-putter, swinging the head while Jim and Pastor Speed fought to free Byron's throat from the death-grip of the hands.

Carl released the head and it sailed into the huge hot hole in the middle of the Devil's graveyard.

Byron fell to the ground, the life choked out of him. Still the hands could not be torn from his bruised and mangled throat. The fingers had to be broken, one by one, to finally free the governor's aide.

Carl tossed the misshapen hands into the hole.

Jim stood over the dead aide, looking at him. "Well," he finally drawled. "I don't reckon he'd have made a very good governor, noways."

The hole belched.

Chapter 40

Carl made one visit to the lip of the hole in the earth, a tether rope tied to him. The opening appeared to be bottomless. Carl returned to the safety of the road.

"I'll have a construction crew out here at first light in the morning," Edgar said. "They'll build a covering for that hole, put it in place, and then erect a series of fences with warning signs. I don't know what else I can do."

"That's sufficient," Carl told the man. "If somebody falls in there, that's their problem. I don't have any sympathy for anyone who ignores warning signs." He looked around. The cars of the Agency people were gone. They had done their work and silently left the area.

The woods were clean. In a manner of speaking.

"Thank God it's over," Father Vincent said.

"Not yet," Carl said sternly. "That Stinson fellow and his wife are still out there. And no telling how many others who were changed. They'll all surface, sooner or later. You've got some unpleasant days still facing you."

"Will you stay and help us, Carl?" Jim asked.

"If you want me to, yes."

"I'd appreciate it."

The men and women who had survived the ordeal ate hot meals, took long baths, and rested well for the first time in days.

For the most part, except for supplies and Edgar's construction crews, and a host of state cops, the area remained sealed off while the mop-up continued. The farmer and his wife who had been visited by Josh Taft and his band of escaped cons were found and destroyed . . . by Carl and by fire.

Champ Stinson and his wife were not found, and they did not surface during the search-and-destroy period.

"My daddy knows ten thousand places in these woods to hide," Sonny told Carl. "We might never see him and Momma again."

"That shore wouldn't come as no great disappointment to me," Bullfrog said, looking walleyed at the silent timber around the Stinson home place.

Keith was sitting out in the meadow, plucking petals off wildflowers and making up simple little songs to sing. He had found another stash and was off in sugar-pie land again.

The remains of Janet had been located and laid to rest in a quiet little ceremony.

Gary, overcome with grief, had hanged himself that same afternoon.

The owners of the hardware store, the drugstore, the funeral home, and the newspaper, and others who were known to have been coven members, surfaced and went back to work, each of them loudly and solemnly proclaiming what a terrible tragedy it had all been and offering money and supplies to help rebuild the shattered community.

"They give me just one excuse," Jim said sourly, his words tinged with hate, "they step out of line just one time, and they'll get a bullet in the head. I can promise you that, Carl."

And Carl knew the newly appointed sheriff of Reeves County meant every word of it. More importantly, the former coven members knew it. They would all walk very lightly around Jim Hunt for a long, long time.

Sonya and Jesse wrote and filed their stories about the takeover of the town by escaped convicts and the horrible events that followed. None of it true, but it made for good copy. The newspapers and TV played it up for a few days, and then dropped it. Old news.

Doctor Robert Jenkins returned to Richmond, and became a born-again Christian and a leader in his church.

Lib and Peter, Jack and Becky, and Susie and Tommy refused to return home to their parents. Edgar agreed to foot the bill for them to stay in Richmond and attend a private school.

As Carl and Dee were driving out of the small town, Dingo in the back seat, Dee pointed to a group of teenagers standing by a vacant building. One had a can of spray paint in his hand. He had spray-painted an upside-down cross on the building. He grinned at the young couple, gave them the finger, rubbed his crotch obscenely, and lifted the can, painting the numbers 666.

Dee noticed the tight set of Carl's jaw and the hard look in his eyes as they drove past the group. She shook her head. "I thought it was over," she said as they drove on past and out of sight of the teenagers and the symbols denoting the worship of Satan.

"How can they be so bold so soon after all that's happened?"

"That bunch may just be getting started, Dee. I hope so. If that's the case, Jim can slap some sense into them and end it right now."

"If not?"

He said the words that she knew he would, and that she dreaded to hear.

"Then I'll be back."

<u>BOOK YOUR PLACE ON OUR WEBSITE</u>
<u>AND MAKE THE</u>
<u>READING CONNECTION!</u>

We've created a customized website just for our very special readers, where you can get the inside scoop on everything that's going on with Zebra, Pinnacle and Kensington books.

When you come online, you'll have the exciting opportunity to:

- View covers of upcoming books
- Read sample chapters
- Learn about our future publishing schedule (listed by publication month *and author*)
- Find out when your favorite authors will be visiting a city near you
- Search for and order backlist books from our online catalog
- Check out author bios and background information
- Send e-mail to your favorite authors
- Meet the Kensington staff online
- Join us in weekly chats with authors, readers and other guests
- Get writing guidelines
- AND MUCH MORE!

Visit our website at
http://www.pinnaclebooks.com